BAKING COOKIES WITH WHORES

A Manifesto By

Brett Stout

Baking Cookies With Whores is the culmination of a cornucopia of time and life spent dealing with women and all the insane shit that they can put you through, and let's be honest here, make you do to get into their cooters. This is just one loser's documentation of that in the 21st century.

This novel was written on the night shift while mainly wearing underwear, hung-over, and reeking of body odor inside of my nerd lab/apartment in Myrtle Beach, South Carolina.

Baking Cookies With Whores

Copyright © 2015 Brett Stout

Self-Financed and Published by The Cooterific Publishing Company

Layout and Design by Brett Stout and The Fucking Goddess Jeza

Front Photograph by Brett Stout

Edited by Brett Stout and Ron Wagner

Send Hate Mail To: anticondoart@yahoo.com

Ghetto Official Site: http://www.facebook.com/anticondoart

First Edition 2015

ISBN: 978-0-692-45134-2

Thanks Mom for birthing and unleashing me on society

This book is dedicated to all the women out there that passed through my life at one time or another. Without you, these pages would be blank...

I finally finished pounding on her. I was on top of her with my shriveled limp dick, now being surrounded by my own cum that I'd just deposited inside of her. I was sweating profusely and couldn't move. I'm fat, old, and fucking tired now. She wanted to cuddle with me. I asked her if me being on top of her like a beached dolphin counted? She said no. A few minutes later I said that I had to go take a shit. I lied of course. I closed the door to the bathroom and just sat there on the toilet, alone and in silence; minus the fake flushing I did every few minutes to make the shit seem legitimate.

xoxo

She met me at the beach, 65th Avenue to be precise. I rested my head on her stomach and stared at her pussy when she wasn't looking. She's beautiful, nice, her tits are gigantic, and she eats beef jerky out of a plastic bag. I kissed her in the rocky parking lot right before we left. I think I'm love with her already.

xoxo

Your insanity is my crack pipe. You're the dead animal I observe and poke with a stick. Curiosity killed the cat, but excited me. There's nothing else to do here but observe you and what you do. It entertains me because I'm a loser with no life.

xoxo

"Insert a Plethora of Fuck"

The fuck,

censor my fucking original somewhat nasty but true first line

I don't understand what the fuck your deal and/or problem is?

you make no fucking sense at all

you've fucking changed

how can four fucking months do that?

you need serious fucking counseling

I used to fucking respect and unconditionally love you

now I'm growing to fucking dislike you and what you're about

you fucking avoid me

you can't handle it when someone calls you out on your fucking bullshit

you like fucking docile non-confrontational people you can boss around

that is not fucking me

who the fuck are you now?

and how the fuck are you in my life?

where the fuck did we go wrong?

what happened to my fucking friend that I really liked?

it hurts me fucking writing this

the fucking end,

The fuck.

xoxo

We eat breakfast in the early morning hours of some local shitbox late night omelet house. The name escapes me, but it's not important anyways. There's usually nothing but gay guys in here eating breakfast after the gay bars that are down the street close at 5 a.m. Today, there's no entertainment though, just me and her and a trucker looking guy on the other side of the restaurant. I think we were in the smoking section, but I wasn't sure. I smoked anyways and made an ashtray out of the green carpet underneath the booth we were sitting in. I ordered three eggs, bacon, and toast. I knew I shouldn't have ordered the bacon, but I did. Well, really, the booze from earlier ordered them. We talked about nothing really, chit-chat as you normal fucking people call it. Now and then we talked about something, but you don't get to know what. Mainly, because I can't remember what the fuck we talked about I guess. The redneck waitress, let's call her Doris, she was our shitty waitress and never refilled my sweet tea, not even once. She showed up once and brought me my food. I poured salt all over everything. I couldn't find any pepper though. I put ketchup on my eggs, all over my eggs; in fact there was more ketchup than eggs really now that I think back on it. I scarfed it down like I was from Ethiopia and hadn't eaten in a week. I smoked while I ate and ashed on the crappy green carpet. I put a piece of bacon up my nose, and I don't know why. I might have mental problems I guess, or I just wanted to impress her with my acts of jackass bravado. Oh yes, her. I don't remember her name, but she was there. She was there staring at me and eating tomatoes. She only ordered tomatoes. I thought that was weird, but who am I to judge anyone at that hour? Her loss, well not really, the food was shitty but tolerable because of the volume of booze that I drank. She asked for a cigarette and I gave her one. She didn't smoke, but she did tonight she said.

"Why don't you come over?" I ask her.

"Come over and what?" She says.

"Play Monopoly." I say.

"Monopoly?" She says in confusion.

"Yeah, who doesn't like playing board games drunk and late at night?"

8

"Well, when that's usually said other things are meant."

"Oh, really? Well, I just wanted to play Monopoly with you. If you want to fuck though, we can do that afterwards."

"I'm not that kind of girl. I don't fuck someone just because they take me to breakfast. You got the wrong impression." She says.

She stares at me and puts the cigarette that I gave her out in my ketchup laden eggs.

"I'm just fucking around baby, you know me."

"No, not really, but thanks for breakfast."

She waves at me and gets up and leaves the restaurant. I stare at my empty sweet tea and light another cigarette from an almost empty pack. Fuck, that bitch stuck me with the goddamn check!

xoxo

Dear XXXXX,

Well, you've hit another decade today. Don't have a neurotic "Big B" over it though, because it's just a fucking made-up number. You're full of zest for life, still beautiful as ever, and define, at least for me the epitome of what a great human being resembles. I doubt you will ever be told this enough in your life, but it's the truth. I would never really want to return to the point in my life before knowing you, whether it's always evident or not, you have made me a better person, which I can't say about very many of the people that have passed through my life, and for that I thank you. I doubt I'm the person you want to hear this from at the moment, but I truly do love you, and have, ever since I first laid eyes on you and had to get drunk to even mumble a few words to you, and it even hurts in my stomach sometimes, whatever sign that reflects I don't know. I just want you to know that I will always be there for you whenever you need me. But, in closing, you deserve to get everything that you want out of life and achieve some high level of happiness, and I for one hope that you get it.

Happy Birthday,

No Future FBD

xoxo

"did u see al gore won the fukcing nobel peace prize! I'm the only guy to ever get a blowjob during his documentary!

Really now

well u gave it to me weirdo…

when?

when we were watching an inconvenient truth

oh yeah...that was awhile back

haha, yeah I should have forgotten something crazy like that

No way its great.....I remember it.... you just threw me off there for a minute

oh yeah, you forgot that I snuck that other chick in during the movie and I was getting a blowjob while u got some water.

shut up, whatever..onto other subjects"

xoxo

It's there in my stomach, never quite going away. She is the cause of it all, the acid reflux, the heavy drinking, the chafing from masturbation, and the meals alone at Subway. Yes, she is the cause of it all. The thought of her makes my stomach hurt. I start hacking and feel like I'm gonna puke, but nothing ever comes up and out of me. I slowly try and talk myself into regaining my composure. It's difficult and it usually doesn't work very well. This is all new to me, this feeling of extreme love, loss, and pain. No one had ever gotten to me before. She did though, and took a little of me with her when she left. Yes, she is the cause of it all.

xoxo

She doesn't stop talking. She won't stop. She keeps going on and on and fucking on. Granted, the topics of conversation could be a lot worse, and are with most women. But, at this point I've been up for two days straight, I just came twice, and I'm completely sober now. In my mind, I envision her putting on her fucking clothes and getting out of my fucking apartment so I can get some peace and goddamn sleep. I can feel my eyes burning. I'm out of smokes. I just sit in the bed avoiding her and being as lame as possible in hopes that she will grow bored and get the fuck out of here so I can get some fucking sleep. But, she doesn't. She just keep talking and talking and fucking talking. Someone fucking kill me please!

xoxo

Before the Lord of the Rings:

"Put in the Nuuva ring!"
"Oh shit, yeah remind me."
"We need the Nuuva ring so I can fill you full of hot cum and then suck it out of your pussy and then spit it in your mouth you slut!"
"I just did."
"I'll have a giant load of cum for you after it kicks in. I just RSVP'd your pussy!"

10

After the Lord of the Rings:

"I like cumming inside of you and scoffing in the face of God. I still can right?"
"Let me get my sex drive back. That's why I took the Nuuva ring out...."
"We're fucking tonight if I have to get you drunk first and you have to get an
abortion after, so be it."
"I'm drunk. Yum!"

xoxo

"Cheap Notebooks and Godspeed Suffering"

she doesn't call much anymore,

sometimes

I

feel forgotten and marked deficient

she's disappeared

red and white paper milk cartons

only antique memories remain

inside pulsating cerebral cortexes

and

99 cent notebooks

she's fuckin' gone,

and might as well have moved to North Dakota,

we don't hang out much anymore,

sometimes,

I

feel ignored and I don't like it

she's disappeared

red and white paper milk cartons

only antique memories remain

inside pulsating cerebral cortexes

and
99 cent notebooks
she's fuckin' gone,

and might as well have moved to Montana,

she doesn't come over anymore,
ever,

I
feel the loneliness breathing on my neck
she's disappeared
red and white paper milk cartons
only dead skin cells and DNA remain
on fake wooden floors
and
stained discount sheets
she's fuckin' gone,

and might as well have moved to Oregon,

she doesn't kiss or fuck me anymore,
ever,

I
feel the caress of despair
she's disappeared
red and white paper milk cartons
only dead skin cells and DNA remain
on fake wooden floors
and
stained discount sheets

she's fuckin' gone,

and might as well have moved to Arizona.

xoxo

A girl I don't know and had never spoken to recently sent me a love letter:

"eat shit you cunt looter, you dont deserve to live. or be happy. nevermind. stay on this piece of shit planet. i hope you choke on pollution. I hope you get enslaved by a rumpranger and get tortured before you die. i hope your face hits a bunch of fucking bricks and you swallow your own fucking teeth. no, I dont know you. no, you dont know me. Yes I'm fucking crazy. and I dont need a reason to hate you. I just do. and I hope god rapes you up the ass. I hope you shit your pants in public. I hope your shit comes out of your nose and your piss comes out of your mouth. I wonder what I will say to the next piece of shit page i click on. no need to respond. fucking report me and get me deleted you unworthy piece of shit. ps I hope you get gonorhea and genital warts and pancreatic cancer. i hope the next time you take a shit your testicles fall out of your cornhole!"

I asked her to marry me. She said no.

xoxo

I fingered her in the park tonight on a large wooden swing. People passed us by, dogs barked, and I didn't care. I kissed her and she moaned as my index finger moved in and out of her wet inflamed pussy. Her running shorts were wet, but not because of her run. I smelled and licked my fingers on the large wooden swing after she came all over them.

xoxo

Before we fucked,

"So be naked I don't care. I just want a picture of you sucking my cock sillouete style"

"I want to do a naked photoshoot"

"Why Sunday? We need to do that photoshoot. I wanna cum in your mouth again."

"Remind Saturday and hide all the knives and sharp stuff"

"Ok, I lied I want blood and pussy juice on my face. Nuuvaring!"

"Yeah, let me rephrase that. Immediately, meaning next week"

"I don't see how. I don't like period blood on my dick. I want to eat your pussy after ur period and I wan you to cum pussy juice all over my face!"

"I'm a sick fuck but I can't handle blood on my dick. My few limits. Maybe you will let me eat your pussy? I want you to cum all over my face!"

"I want to do it again immediately"

"The other night was awesome. I like looking at your face when I fill your cunt full of my cum"

"I know. I like you walking around with my cum inside of you oozing down your leg…."

"That's so hot"

"What did you have in mind? You're already kind of crazy so you should get back on birth control so I can cum inside of you all the time"

"Is that possible? How about I dress you up like a Polock and I'll be Germany and blitzkrieg your pussy like WWII!"

"I'm thinkign something sicker."

"Huh? You mean like me dress up like Hitler and rape and beat your starving Jew ass…HAHA"

"That sucks let's roleplay"

"My shit's clean. I'm trying not to be a whore anymore"

"Ha,exactly. What are you trying to say? I'm a whore or soemthing?"

"Ahh, yes you have such an insatiable love for women as your book demonstrates time and time again"

"Sweet, you haven't even let me eat your pussy yet and that's my forte!!"

"Nothing, it's hermit time. You were great as well. I came..a lot"

"What you getting into tonight?"

"Cool, thanks. Incredible? I don't know about that honey buns"

"Stress reliever, you're pretty incredible"

"Ahh nice, I guesss I knocked something loose up in that piece. Or at least relieved a little stresss."

"Oh, no need. To put it lightly. I finally got what I wanted. Terrible cramps and then some"

"Sweet, did you go buyt he morning after pill?"

"Me to"

"I had so much fun last night I had to sleep all day and be a fucking hermit"

"Thanks you're not bad yourself. Can you wear your dressed to fuck boots. I like you in them"

"Ha, you're cute. I totally want you"

"Ok, if you wanna fuck my brains out today that's cool. I meant I would come see you at work."

"I might come hang with you if you will still fuck my brainss out,"

After we fucked

xoxo

After I came inside of her for the second time that night, I didn't want to look at her any longer. I was driving her back to her car in the morning and the site of her repulsed me. I knew I was never going to talk to or see her again after today. The only evidence that we'd ever known each other was that my cum was probably now dripping out of her shaved pussy and running down her leg.

xoxo

"How have you been?"

"Just fucking peachy baby..."

"I'm at work and it's dead in here"

"Well yeah, you work in a shithole bar and there's a tsunami outside. Do you feel like fucking without cuddling sometime this week?"

"No cuddling? I think I'm off Wednesday"

"Hell no, Brett is ANTI cuddling but PRO fucking. You gotta accept me as I am. Wednesday is fine for a fuck session."

"Ok fine, no cuddling you win"

"I'm glad you see it my way. Get an Elmo doll, it will cuddle and love you since I don't...lol"

xoxo

I got the text message around midnight, while drunk:

"Hey, your girl is over at a bar making out with some gross old turd."

What the fuck I thought to myself? This didn't make any sense. This had to be a mistake. Is this fucking April Fool's Day already or something? I thought it was only February 11th. She had to have the wrong person. The person texting me had only met and seen her once, and that was in a dark bar months and months ago. Yeah, she's just fucking around or something. But why would she? Fuck, the Jack Daniel's is hitting me now. Yeah, laugh it off it's nothing. I text her back asking her what the fuck she's talking about? She doesn't respond. My friend who I came out to meet, even though I'm broke just got back into town after disappearing for several months. We went outside with our beers because the music was too loud to talk. He tells me that he has a rare immune system disease and he's gonna die within a year. I leaned against the dirty window and had nothing to reply with other than the usual "fuck, are you serious? I'm sorry man." It was a generic and ridiculous response, but what does one say after someone tells them that they're gonna die in a year? He tells me that he's gonna be in town for a few weeks, then he's gotta head back to Chicago for some experimental treatment that they know will probably not work. I offer to go with him there so he didn't have to be alone, it made sense. I didn't have a real job and I was just bumming around spending my last few dollars until the real shit hit the fan and I was broke. He tells me not to worry about it, he wants to go alone and die alone, but that he might just say fuck it and come back and drink himself to death, which to him was a better alterative than being cooped up in a hospital breathing his last breaths among strangers in a cold town. As he continues telling me all about this immune system disease I text my lady friend, mainly hoping this was all a joke.

"Hey baby, are you out drinking? I thought you had to work?"

Send…wait…

I check my phone's outgoing messages just to be anal retentive and because I was drunk.

Sent…wait…

Fuck, maybe I should go over there and check. Nah, bad idea, it's probably just some made-up shit. I can't leave my friend here alone and dying. I haven't seen him in months and the girl bullshit can wait. The hours go by and there's no response from her. Good, she must be asleep. See, I knew it was fucking bullshit.

xoxo

"They Keep Calling Me"

I don't know if she got abducted by aliens or what?

tan bags of personal items

lie

on dirty linoleum floors

perceived change is often bad

when inspired

by

massive mental breakdowns

as the numbers increase

rotten bananas

pissed off monkeys,

I don't know if she got abducted by aliens or what?

time for
a Jerry Springer break
iota's of common sense
and
verbiage broken
new cold linguistic composition
radar detected unemotional
hand and eye
gestures
pull apart the wishbones
silver streaked rolling wheels
vacations south of heaven taken
ladders of trust
crawl my little king snake
to
windows of psychosis
someone be kind enough to dial
911,

I don't know if she got abducted by aliens or what?

letters written
never delivered
pen and purple ink
life's forever
and
last communications
feel free to take

a parting gift with you

insanity

and dirty bowels

when you leave

bon voyage baby

uttered

in smoke infested breathe.

xoxo

I've been fucking the same girl for a while now. It's nice to fuck a really good looking girl on a regular basis. I'm not really used to it, so it's a little odd to me. I can just call her up out of the clear fucking blue and go have sex. It's so fucking simplistic that it's mind-blowing. I don't have to chase ugly whores around at the moment. I still use my rubber vagina when I need a break though. It's like shaving or putting on deodorant, it's just something that I do on a normal basis regardless of the amount of pussy I get.

xoxo

Her ugly bug-eyed fucking dog kept looking at me as I was trying to fuck her. When she wasn't looking I kicked her dog in the head with my foot. The dog made a little moan and left the room. We were finally alone.

xoxo

"how can you really think I don't give a shit? I'm hurting fucking bad over here babe" "seriously I had no idea"

"you always have on you're i dont give a hist attitude"

"shit"

"well maybe I'm just stupid and don't tell you how much I like you."

"I just dont even know, I mean really I dont talk to you for days on end-and thats fine-but I guess I got the impression that we werent really anything-I have no idea"

"i know, I haven't had as much time to spend with you since school started. I don't know, I've missed hanging out with you, I do know that."

"I mean I know that-and I know you like your anti-social artist alone time-I understand this-and Ive missed us hanging out too.."

"I'm sorry, I've never been good abotu telling people how I feel, it's hard for me, I don't know why. After I talked to you today it felt like someone ripped my guts out and stomped on them. Fuck, I even cried. The threat of losing you made me have panic attacks. But I do love you and I don't really want to be with anyone else."

"Baby Im so sorry-I had no idea. I have to ask are you being serious"

"cause ya know it would be just like you to say all this cause you know me well enough to know it would totally make me feel like shit-I could see that being a fun little manipulative Brett game?????"

"Dont get mad at me for asking"

"I'm not mad at you for asking, I'm not kidding around....I really did cry and all that"

"babe Im sorry... i wish i knew this a long tome ago"

"time"

"It's ok, I should have just told you.......I'm weird and I figured you just knew."

"I mean I knew we had something and now and then I would think that maybe we really could be something...but I thought I was just being silly"

"no, ur not being silly. I don't know anything about all the formalities of it, but you;re what I want. I haven't tried to fuck anyone or even talk to anyone since we've hung out. So that's something"

"and obviously with my emotional breakdown today, you do have a lot of effect on me"

"i am kinda in shock-i really had no idea"

"well it's been that kind of day"

"I was in shock that u were gonna dump me...haha"

"i think i've caught you're panic attacks too"

"oh no"

"yes, I'm fucked!!!"

"nah its ok...i'll have some tea-how cliche-haha"

"haha, good idea........I really want to give you a hug and a kiss right now...make everything ok"

"still in shock..r u now suggtesting cuddling"

"Fuck it, I would cuddle with you"

"we may also need counseling...lol"

"I think we'll be fine.."

"neither of us are fine....u know that"

"yea I know, nothign is perfect"

"no shit"

"can I come over and give you a hug, I really need one here" "well I dont know cause i gotta work in the AM"

"well I gotta do homework and do the same so, but I don't care. I just want to be with you for a few minutes"

"Ok 2 min"

"just give me a hug and say everything is gonna be ok and I'll leave u alone"

"haha"

"haha???"

"i'll be over in 5 minutes…"

xoxo

I usually don't jerk off to people I know but she popped into my head last night when I was drunk and masturbating in my friend's bathroom in Charleston. I was so drunk I couldn't cum. I'm a fucking failure.

xoxo

We were waiting on our food and I was fucking starving:

"I'm so hungry I'd eat your used tampon at this point."

"You're repulsive I swear to fucking God."

"I prefer uncouth darling. Does this mean we're not hanging out now?"

There's no response from her.

xoxo

It's starting to feel like she's trying to have a bad time on vacation with me on purpose. She hates me and I can feel it. I feel it for the first time since I've been with her. I don't know why she hates me though; and I'm almost scared to ask her. The good news is there are only thirteen more days of constant twenty-four hour contact with her to go.

xoxo

"STOP ME: Corporate Town USA"

the black coffee drunken liability,

hungover
with the heat of aortas
I often think into deep fried wonder
but
have no answers

etched into the plastic toilet seat,
whose bed did she sleep in last night?
whose bed did I sleep in last night?

I've not thought about the silent fracture
in
the back of my skull
for quite some time
I'm not fucking it all up again
until
next time,

my fresh scabs turn red
in the oven
the cockroaches on the windows
have read and now demand
universal health care and
domestication,

what bed did she sleep in last night?
what bed did I sleep in last night?

the white cloth on the dirty floor
hides the stained tampons
in late September
the water sits silent and morbid
on a wooden bench
you
don't really like my insanity
or weigh
221 pounds,

Oxycodone laced

Kansas wheat

and

Socialist donut holes

the red octagon near the night sky

reads,

STOP,

vandalizing

signs that aren't yours.

xoxo

She eats beef jerky on the beach. I've never seen a girl do that before. I admit that I was impressed. Any girl who eats dried meat out of a plastic bag has to be pretty interesting.

xoxo

Dear XXXXX,

Fuck you emphatically, that's what I wanna say. I realized tonight that it was absolutely over, and there's nothing saving it. There's nothing but anger and fucked up shit inside my head. But, you know for once I actually fucking feel better about it. I'm not gonna tell her off just to make myself feel better. I'm just gonna speak the fucking truth. Fuck you! You know if you wanna end up some fucking slut hanging around with some douchebags instead of me, well knock yourself out. How fucking dare you treat me that way bitch! A phone call would have been bad enough. But I get nothing, nothing face to face because you have no fucking pussy power. Because, you know what you did was wrong. And, you're only pissed off because I found out, and because you got busted. I can't believe anything you tell me anymore because I don't believe you. Yeah, it's over. You may not wanna be my girlfriend, but I don't even wanna be your friend. But, whatever you cunt. Have a nice life, I guess that will be it. Whatever, who the hell knows? Banky or whatever his fucking name is, yeah he's so fucking cool and important. Why do all the people have the most retarded names? Get the fuck out of here! What the fuck kind of name is that? What, Shooter McGavin was taken, or Ducky from Pretty in Pink, or Urkel? Fucking ridiculous, they never have a normal name like Joe or John, never that. You hear a name like these assholes have and you just know they're fucking douchebags. You know right off the bat. Maybe this is a good thing this is happening. Who knows really? Get her out of my life and move on. I'm not saying I'll find anything better out there, but you know at least I won't be fucking sitting around being hassled watching fucking When Harry Met Sally or putting up fucking Christmas trees. I felt like such a lame ass doing any of that shit. What the fuck was I doing? There will be some sort of satisfaction attained tomorrow. I hope so, because I ain't doing this shit. She has some fucking nerve to treat me like that. I just don't fucking get it. Tomorrow, at least I will have my dignity back in some form or fashion.

xoxo

"i may have to make out with you right there!!-LOL

haha, ok

you will have to be drunk to let me make out with you-haha

haha, not always...but yes beer helps PDA....

i've noticed

I can't help it, I'm anti PDA in all forms

sad

yes PDA is sad!

you're repressed.

oh yea that must be it, I don't mind if people fuck in public, but PDA all over the place would be chaos, although for being so anti PDA, I sure as hell do it with u all the time...so there punk!

the world would be such a happier place

fine, but I don't wanna see people making out and holding hands. Goddamn hippies!"

xoxo

I'm trying to rebuild my confidence, slowly, very slowly. After she kicked me in the balls pretty hard, what little I had disappeared. She burst my bubble and I lost confidence in every area of my life. I've been kicked in the balls before, but never by someone I was completely in love with. I'm wearing a cup from now on, at least until I'm weak and decide to love again. Who am I kidding here really? I'd give her a chance to kick me there again today.

xoxo

"Screaming into the Endless Void"

spread

your fucking legs

for,

the paper mache
antler
fury and
the meaningless regret afterwards
don't fret mutual friends
the pictures are only on
social networking sites,

spread
your fucking legs
for,
stains from Hollywood
on laminated kitchen
countertops
next to
dirty non-stick pans
filled with the remnants
of
Ramen noodles
H20
metallic chicken
powdered packaging
turned to
atomic flavored dust,

spread
your fucking legs
for,

the sharpening of preschool

pencils

dunce caps in the corner

and

the retribution of

nonexistent

charcoal erasers,

spread

your fucking legs

for,

shitty late night movie sequels

airing now on

TNT

USA

TBS

FX

that should've

never been made

I'm

not reading a book right now

but

you should be,

spread

your fucking legs

for,

balance and physics

on a massacred rock

somewhere

off of Interstate

70

where

I ate three oceans

and dumped one

slut named XXXXX.

xoxo

I went insane for a few hours and drove over to her apartment when I was drunk as hell last night. I don't know how I made it over there to be honest. I almost flipped my car going around a goddamn curve. That somewhat sobered me up enough to get over there. I banged on the door several times but no one came to the door. I yelled and then kicked her door, and still no one came to the door. That really fucking pissed me off. I saw a gigantic spider web down the hall from her apartment. I went over to the massive web and grabbed that big fucking spider and then placed it right on her door. That will teach that fucking whore. As I walked back to my car I noticed that her car wasn't even in the parking lot.

xoxo

Her stained orange powdered hands grasp a black steering wheel. Fuck, I swear she's gonna fuckin' kill us! We swerve off the road and hit some speed bumps that litter Interstate 95. Please put down the nacho flavored Goldfish you fuckin' crazy bitch! Please concentrate on driving and stop eating fuckin' Goldfish and changing the stations on the radio with those same stained orange powdered fingers. We're only seven hours from home; somehow I get the feeling it will be a white knuckle ride the whole way. Fuck me!

xoxo

"k-I have like 200 envelopes to stuff-can I talk you into helping me?

haha, why what a nice gestrue

i thought so.

yea I guess I can....then can I talk u into letting me stuff you after?

oh theres the catch-lol

hahaha

no just incentive…

such a salesman

haha, well ur gonna let me one day anyways, might as well get me to stuff envelopes first now instead of nothing later

im starting to feel like an envelope stuffung whore-haha

ur not a whore if u do me

i am if i trade it out for stuffing envelopes

well ur really not, I would help u anyways

i can totally see a short story coming out of this- we stuffed envelopes the n i
stuffed her- i came, i left-ahhhhh

it's possible. there's worse things then being enshrined in the pages of literature

absolutely"

xoxo

While I was drunk on PBR and saw her with another guy at a bar I text her:

"Fuck you. Don't ever speak to me again please. You suck seriously. You and
XXXXX are the biggest liars I've ever met in my fucking life!"

"I hope you get the message on your bullshit Blackberry you fucking poser.
You're so fake you make me want to puke!"

"I'd heard from around that you were a whore. But, I wanted to believe you
were more than that. I had hope for you to be honest. You're awful, enjoy
fucking Paul Bunyan you dumb bitch!"

While she was sitting with another guy at a bar I text her:

"WOW"

While I was drunk on PBR and saw her with another guy at a bar I text her:

"You're hilarious. I have to beg you for 30 minutes of your time like its some
fucking privilege. You lie, at the hospital all week you say. If you're my friend
then who's my fucking enemy exactly?"

While she was sitting with another guy at a bar I text her:

"You need to stop"

While I was drunk on PBR and saw her with another guy at a bar I text her:

"You need to stop being so selfish and bossy. I'm not your bitch you whore of
a spoiled brat. There's a reason why you can't keep a man or friends for longer
than two weeks"

While I was sitting in my chair naked and hungover from the PBR I text her:

"Regardless of how self involved, shady and stupid I think you act a lot of
times. It doesn't sit well that you piss me off to the point that I have to be nasty
towards you. I'm sorry I said those things"

xoxo

She makes me nauseous now. I feel vomit wanting to be released from my body
when I think of her or when I talk to her now. She didn't give a shit about me at
all; she made that obviously clear with her actions. Yeah, she was too busy
getting dressed up like a whore and getting drunk and making out with her dad

in a bar, and then whoring her ass down to that yuppie beach town like someone said the world was going to end in two days to fuck a complete stranger. Oh yeah, her desperate clueless nutty friend knew him supposedly, probably from some pathetic dating site she's on or from some how to become a millionaire in thirty days conference or some shit, so I guess that just made it alright then. What a fucking stupid twat. Damn, she is so fucking selfish and clueless. She means nothing to me, she isn't even a friend. As she said, she is nothing anymore and I've known that this whole time. It's a difficult thing to make sense of, or come to terms with I guess. I've known though. I've just gone against my better judgment over and over again like a damn idiot. Admitting that I obviously had no idea who she was for two years and my radars and all my feelings and perceptions were totally off is so hard to do, but I guess that was the truth. I'm not perfect that's for damn sure, but I was way off on that one. She's either complete bullshit and a total liar and a horrible person, or just a fucking retard whose brain must be on another planet in some fantasyland she has morphed out of the clear fucking blue. With her fucking past and history, I'm not surprised really. But, you would think that someone who has been treated badly and been fucked over plenty of times would have the sense and respect to not do it herself to anyone, well, at least to not anyone she gave a damn about and that didn't treat her like shit or lie to her or beat her or any other horrible shit you can think of that most of these humans do to each other in life and relationships. I guess not though. She has no fucking clue, of just about anything. I think I exist on a different mental plane and really always have, she could never grasp that, and she sure as fuck doesn't now. She's too busy flying around on someone else's dime and getting free drinks and rooms paid for with ginger dollars. Now she can forget whatever decency and common sense she had and concentrate on more important things like buying designer purses. What a fucking joke. Like I said, just like every other fake stupid bitch around here. Hell, in her mind I guess I wasn't even important enough and she didn't even respect me enough to give me a fucking phone call. I will always think of that when I think of her. I suppose that's what I get for two years of our fucking lives spent together in her fucked up oblivious world and mind. Shit like that you never forget. I wish I knew what really happened to her. She's more a curiosity and a lab rat to poke with a stick now than anything. I just want to observe her in her maze now. I laugh at her incompetence. What a fucking sheep. She would've made a great Nazi I think. As long as one of her horrid fake best friends was one, she would be one just to fit in, just to be considered fucking normal.

xoxo

I was on my back naked and sweating like a fat girl in a decathlon on the edge of my bed. She comes back from the bathroom, now fully clothed.

"I'm gonna leave now, I gotta get up early."

"Wow, I deserve a better blow off excuse than that after I fuck someone good in the pooper. At least give me that you gotta do your hair or your Grandma is sick and you gotta visit her in the hospital."

"Whatever."

"Sure, sure, see you around ginger. Thanks for not stealing my fucking soul."

"No problem, you have great stamina for an old man."

"Thanks sugar tits."

"Do you remember my name?"

"I'll admit that I don't ginger."

"Good, I don't remember yours either."

I hear footsteps. The door opens and then it shuts. I manage to stumble towards the door and I turn the lock to the left. She has no way back in, just in case her car doesn't start or some shit. I go back into my bedroom and sit in my fake leather chair, smoke cigarettes and watch the night become day as cum slowly drips out of my dick.

xoxo

"The Strokes of Life"

we argue

when we're drunk

and

on a boat,

she hits me

without

her best shot

I call her a bitch

I grab

her arms

and

kiss her

lip gloss smothered

soft lips

and

light beer stained breath
on top
of her
she gives
in,

black panties
off
face buried in
freshly showered
pussy lips
mons pubis
labia
clitoris
we fuck
on a boat,

the next day
hung-over
I only had sex with you
because
I was drunk
yeah baby
whatever you say,

we argue
when we're drunk
and
on a boat.
xoxo

I watch the world from here in the inside. Only cracks reveal the reality. The
doors are open and the shades are closed. I watch and wait from here on the

inside. I'm not a very patient boy though. Pants are becoming boring so I just sit here naked most of the time. I leave now and then, but only for the essentials, coffee, smokes, water, and food. I don't say anything to anyone when I do leave though. No one notices me leave and no one notices me enter. I wrap myself in plastic and burn the days away. The pain is there, but it's numbed by ice and Neosporin. I watch them having fun out there and I'm still not jealous. I just sit on the couch and watch TV from here on the inside.

xoxo

My phone is alive,

There is no drama you're a nut-job lose my number!!!!!

Why didn't you come up with that earlier?

I don't know about you but I'm hungover as shit

There's a bigger pool of guys out there than my close friends u idiot. I feel bad for XXXX. My cum wasn't even dry.

I don't really care. It's a little odd though. Can I have my Camus book back so I have reading material at the free clinic?

Are you gonna blow all my friends or just XXXX? XXXXXX needs one too can he make an appointment?

If you jerk off to it don't tell me you faggot

Ok, actually I texted you for a blowjob at eleven. But whatever I don't see what the big deal is?

I have no idea why chicks like me actually...if I was a girl I wouldn't

I'm busy, some other time

Can I cum on your freshly operated hand, cast and all?

You can come over later if you want. Just don't get all fucking crazy woman!

You're acting nutty and obsessive. Neither are qualities that I like all that much. You need to relax bitch.

Yeah, I'm a little disturbed. We haven't even had sex yet, so u can't love me yet

I sold one of the pieces I made of you last night. You were worth fifty bucks

Calm down killer, I can eat good pussy. That's about all I can offer you

Did you blow me off because I was fat or because I was adopted?

Free food? That might make up for getting rejected for food stamps..

I just drooled on myself......

Can I rape what's left?

I know, I was just saying that I'm no whore. But you gotta fuck someone until your soul mate arrives you know

I find it funny that even though u won't speak to me you love my art. I miss you sweet tits

Towelhead was on HBO last night. It made me think of you. I had a weird dream about fucking you and eating tacos

I like any pizza minus anchovies and pubic hair.

You're insane, I like that

Drive up here so we can fuck

I'm a wino and I'm pretty fun…

Don't call me names you baby!!!!

So who did you end up fucking last night?

Lay off the crack you fucking hooker!

Delete and block?...me? I don't remember doing that, must have been my alter ego or something, what an asshole!

I give up. I'll ask you out again in a year.

We'll load you up with painkillers so I can fuck you in the butt,

My phone is dead.

xoxo

"Thats bullshit. Im sure for crazy people who have great expectations that could be true. I can tell you what will really spoil your romantic life is writing about strangling me! Now that will put a real damper on things. It amazes me that these thoughts can even enter your head in order for you to put them on paper- thats something I'll never understand. And I dont really care too. No wonder I had bad feelings about this trip..."

xoxo

I stumble around in her kitchen. I'm already drinking her last beer when she tells me to help myself with the last beer. It was a "lite" beer, but at this point it didn't matter. What the fuck did she say her name was? Shit, I can't remember. My mind is blank, though it sounds something like XXXXXX I think. Maybe XXXXX, fuck it, it doesn't matter. I grab her and start kissing her in the kitchen and I drunk mumble something about wanting to fuck her. I grab her pussy through her jeans and pinch it as I kiss her. I push her towards her bedroom. She breaks away from me and sits on her bed. I rip off all my clothes as if they were connected and maneuver myself on top of her and start kissing her again. I pull off her shirt and start sucking on her tits. Tits, which in the light reveal lots of stretch marks. They are big for her size so I guess she had to stretch and grow into those big fuckers. I bite her nipples and she doesn't complain about it. I start kissing her stomach and move closer to her cunt. I pull off her shoes and toss them on the floor and her jeans and panties are next. I lick and kiss around her thigh and then I delve right for her cunt. I lick the alphabet on her pussy lips and intermediately pull her clit into my mouth and nibble on it. I was down there on her cunt for a while. She said she was gonna cum several times. I was so drunk I have no idea if she did, well, that was until she screamed "fuck, I'm cumming" and then she pulled away from my face and I had her cunt juice all over my goddamn face. I moved on top of her and fingered her wet cunt with my fingers. I told her how much I wanted to fuck her. I use no names because I don't remember hers, like I said before. She grabbed my cock and started jacking it off as I kissed her. As I went to put my dick inside of her she said…

"I'm not fucking you without a condom."

"What." I asked her?

"No way, I don't even know you."

"Yeah, and I don't know you either but it didn't stop me from eating your pussy out and having your goddamn cum all over my fucking face!"

"Well, that's not my problem."

"This is fucking bullshit." I tell her.

"Whatever." She replies.

I get up off of her bed and put most of my clothes back on and head towards the front door. I call her a fucking cunt as I slam her front door and stumble down the wooden stairs and into the dark rainy night.

xoxo

"It doesn't go in there."

"Oh sorry, hold on a second. Fuck, you've dried up like an old shoe."

"I've got some lube in the drawer; finger yourself or something while I get it."

The good little boy puts a gob of lube on his dick and inserts a lubed finger into a girl's cooter. A dick is inserted into a cooter. A few pumps later…

"Fuck, this shit doesn't last very long. What was that like seven pumps?"

"Here, you do it."

Lube is handed to a girl. She squirts a gob of lube into her cooter.

"Not tonight baby."

"What are you talking about?"

"You're trying to put it in my ass."

"Oh, my bad."

"Put it in my pussy baby, it's aching for your cock."

"Sorry baby, it doesn't go in there."

xoxo

I pull her pants off in the backseat of my mom's borrowed SUV. I finger her and kiss her glossy lips. Bums and bar patrons walk past us. I pull my pants down to my knees and put my swollen cock inside of her. It doesn't take long before I shoot my cum inside of her. I pant like a dog in the middle of summer and exchange sweat with her. It drips from my brow and chest onto her giant fake tits. I kiss her again for a few minutes. My cock and my cum are still inside of her, just a little softer now than before. I whisper in her ear "I love you." I meant it, at least at that moment.

xoxo

I never responded back to my ricehead stalker and I never saw her again. Maybe she did really move.

"Im sorry I let the baryou were being so mean. Can I come over?"

"Well that was weird…"

I met her for a drink. She was fat and Asian and not really what I would expect from my first stalking. I needed an out, so I insulted her with derogatory Asian names. I asked her if she'd ever fucked a black guy before since most slant-eyed women like black guys. She called me an asshole and left the bar.

"uuhmm I'm here and you'e not"

"Yeah call down ricehead I'm leaving now"

"Alright..are you seriously going?"

"Yeah ok, see you in a few"

"So have a dink with me"

"Ok where??"

"What bar..have a drink with me"

"Leaving the bar, headed home"

"Hey what you doing?"

"Well too bad, I'll miss insulting you with derogatory stereotypical Asian names."

She said she was moving and she wanted to meet me for another drink. I agreed, and again, I don't know why. I think I just needed to meet anyone in person who would actually be whacked out enough to want to stalk me.

"We're moving tomorrow. Just tough you'd like to know that"

"Hey, why aren't you answering me?"

"What's up neighbor? Where are you? Why aren't you answering me?"

"Yeah I know I'm a night owl you crazy slant eyed wokhead...."

"You're lights are on and the blinds are open"

She cancelled meeting me for a drink.

"Sorry gotta do a rain check on the drink a friend called"

She wore me down eventually and I agreed to meet her for a drink, while I was already drunk in a different bar.

"I'm painting an aborted fetus with a clothes hanger going into its head. Calm down Hirohito, you're fucking crazy as shit, don't go all kamikaze on me though for calling you ricehead."

"Why aren't you answering me now? What are you doing?"

"Why can't you answer back?"

"Where are you"

"Stop acting like one and I will"

"Stop calling me retard rice head"

"No I'm moving shit out of my car in the front you retard ricehead!"

"Oh you must be in back"

"Where I don't see you?"

"Yeah, I'm in and out. I'm scraping wax off my surfboard"

"You live on the far side right? You outside yet?"

"Well I can't help it you're Asian and can't see shit. I'm about to change my windshield wipers now. Real exciting shit Bruce Lee..."

"No you're not. Your car isn't there. I looked. And stop calling me horrible names."

"It's none of your business where I'm having an orgy mom. I'm at home you fucking retarded soy head"

"ok where are you? Why aren't you home? Who are you with?"

"Where are you, out collecting dogs for China King?"

"I'm not at home"

"I'm gonna take out the garbage in a second you can spy on me if you want stalker rice head"

"No that's not my thingMy roommate is all into being a stripper"

"I thought you were both psycho strippers or something. Just the other one isn't a fish head?"

"We know which apartment you're in!! But we can't see you unless we walk around"

"Fine we're done playing. You're boring!"

"Where are you?"

"Not taking this too well"

"Hey why aren't you answering me"

"Don't call me a gook!"

"I'm not walking around naked for a neurotic gook and a fucked up stripper."

"Walk around naked for us and put onshow"

"What are you doing?"

"You're a stalker and that's ok by me ricehead.I've never been stalker worthy before. And I didn't think my first one would be a teriyakihead"

"We saw you coming home last night"

Some totally random Asian girl who said she lived in my apartment complex yelled at me at the stop light near my apartment and said I was hot and that she wanted my phone number. For some unknown reason I yelled my phone number out to her and hit the gas. Three minutes later I had a text message from a totally random Asian girl who lived in my apartment complex.

xoxo

"Infatuation is Sometimes a Detestable Quality"

infatuation

is detestable,

but

it can't be corralled

it won't obey

it won't be locked up

or down

and

it can't be killed

I tried

with stolen hollow point bullets

and

sharpened Chinese imported knives
but failed miserably
it's running wild in the weeds
freedom was wanted
and granted
now it
hides
like a perverted idea in the depths
of my brain,

infatuation
is detestable,

but
it infects me
like,

bacteria
yeast
Aids
herpes
kleptomania
insanity
cancer
leukemia
neuroticism
and
syphilis
they sell no
creams
ointments
overpriced prescription drugs

magic beans,

or anything else,

for what infects me.

xoxo

I was sitting on the beach with the girl I have been fucking lately. She stares at a very normal looking guy as he passes us. I ask her if she knows him or something. She says that they used to go out. I asked her how long they went out for. She says about two weeks. I ask her if he got any pussy from her in those two weeks. She said that he did, but that she regrets it now. I say that she's a bit of a fucking whore. She gets mad at me and punches me in the arm. It hurts but I take it. She starts crying there on her beach towel. I didn't say anything, but I really wanted to laugh at her. She wanted me to apologize, but I didn't. She didn't fuck me again after that day, and soon after she quit calling me as well. Now I'm like the guy on the beach, just another passing mistake.

xoxo

"so can I fuck you in the butt this weekend? Like saturday?

what?!?! no saturdays not good...I gotta work Sun

haha, ok...well check ur date book and find a good time to make an ass pounding appointment

maybe next week sometime...I have 4 days off in a row. But it kinda scares me

well just get drunk and it will be fine

we'll see how it goes. Next week Im off Wed-Sat. Beach days??? good for you?

yes, except thursday

whats up thurs?

which day is ass fucking day?....I have class

i dont know yet...which ever day you make me happiest I guess-haha........I have no idea

Being ur first time, I will have to sort of force it in there.....but I will take it slow after it's in.....after that, gape city...haha

ugh..I dont know? i mean your dick is alot bigger than anything else thats ever been up there. God it may damage me?

no, it's not gonna damage anything...thousands of people do it all the time

well homos have all kinds of app trouble

ass

well yeah, because their prostate is there and gets fucked up

women have nothing in there of any omportance

no not prostate problems...ass problems

plus who knows, gay dudes shove all sorts of unsafe shit up their asses u know lamps, silverwear, coke bottles

i may need to talk to my gay friend about it first

haha

he may have something good to say....cause everyone else I know has hated it

u will be fine u puss, just recite over and over while I'm doing it "I'm a dirty whore who likes it in my ass"

haha......but that just doesnt seem like me?

yeah I know

so after that will i be a dirty whore? cause I dont want to be

no, not really…u will just be more sexually exotic…haha"

xoxo

"Blood on My Hands: June 1979"

You're just a human

I'm

the

machine,

I confessed to you

late

in the night

you

didn't save those words

that

I spoke

late

in the night

you

just deleted them

when

you

restarted

and began anew

confessions

never heard

words

never read

ideas

never spoken

you fucking bitch!

it's alright

I

forgive you

for now

it's not your

fault

I'm sorry,

you're just a machine

I'm

the human.

xoxo

I opened the door and helped her in. Soon, we were back at my small apartment in the ghetto. Twenty-four stairs and a whole lot of stumbling around later and we were lying in my bed. I played doctor and made her take her pills and change her bloody gauze pads out for fresh new ones. Soon, she was sleeping. I watched her from the corner of the bed. She was peaceful and beautiful. I noticed blood dripping from the corner of her mouth that was now accumulating on my leopard print pillow. I crawled on top of her and licked the side of her mouth. Now that's love and insanity and I couldn't really tell you why I did it. I guess I just wanted her disease in some way. She didn't move an inch and never noticed me licking the blood off of her face. I got bored of watching her sleep and went into the living room and sat on the couch and got a boner from watching Caligula on DVD.

xoxo

She's such a sheep now, a poser just like them and him. They look silly together.
I feel silly for caring or ever loving her. I still do though, but I can't take this
shit anymore, fuck that. How much torture can one person be expected to
tolerate? I'm starting a new life and she can't be a part of it, a medic and a new
job in two weeks. I wonder if she will come to my art show on Saturday. It
might be weird since I haven't seen her in months. Perhaps, it's even weirder
that I mailed her an invitation and a letter saying that I missed her and how
much I loved her. You stupid pathetic fuck! Maybe this was the answer from
the start, maybe the answer I just didn't want to believe. I can't be just her
friend. I need an anger fuck, and probably even a revenge fuck. I want to pull
her hair and slap her ass and call her a whore. I gotta let some time pass and let
her really miss me, and she will I think. How the hell could she ever really
replace me entirely? I'm no egomaniac, but I just know she couldn't, you can't
replace a fucking original all that easily. I finally feel the edge coming back to
me. I feel somewhat alive again and not in the shitter and the depths of despair
and depression and anger like I was. She's gone now, probably forever, and I
guess I have no choice but to accept it no matter how much I don't want to.
She made her choice, now she has to live with it. She hasn't wanted me for
months now anyways. I'm tired of being fucked up over her while she's
indifferent and doesn't really care all that much, at least according to her
actions. All the times we had flash before my eyes: St. Thomas, Goodwill, sex,
Waffle House, bars, beaches, adult libations, snorkeling, cruises, lighthouses,
concerts, bedrooms, eating her pussy, movies, cats, dogs, holidays, Clash
records, Key Lime Pie, wet spots on couches, books written, punk rock lighters,
flowers, trivia, movies, kisses, happy hours, Bukowski, zoos, blowjobs in cars,
rides from airports, crying on beaches, two-hour phone calls, white uniforms,
beef jerky, teeth removed, broken cars, lip gloss, breakdowns, spider webs on
walls, tacos, Victoria has a secret, chicken quesadillas at work, cumming on large
fake tits, Ft. Lauderdale airport, chicken pasta, mini golf, mangos, pawn shops,
cigarettes, graduations, streaks in hair, free crappy art, notebooks given,
conversations, pack mules, sarcasm, bowling, Trivial Pursuit, pedicures,
laughing, elves, purple bathing suits, Georgia pigs, Columbian sloths, photos,
impersonations, bags, tattoos, raunchy jokes, holding hands, shark teeth,
cramped apartments, skull tops and mix CD's all become distant memories and
cloudier everyday. Another girl told me "fuck that ho," and she was sort of
right, but not very eloquent. We haven't talked in forever, and I mean really talk.
We talk about nothing, very general, never in-depth or real. I try but fail. So
what am I missing out on really? Torture for nothing, and basically that's
retarded, almost as retarded as she's acting. I hope she regrets this soon. All I
can do is hope, perhaps that makes me an asshole, who knows? She's so stupid
and clueless now; it pisses me the fuck off! What happened to her, where did
this whacked out phase she's in or whatever come from? I've grown so tired of

all this stupidity and being the only one who cares. That fucking blows hippopotamus dick!

xoxo

4:27 a.m.

I listened to her ramble on about a bunch of bullshit I didn't care about. What boring generic movies she wanted to see coming up, where her parent's lived, if I liked bacon, why didn't I like sushi, do I like her new fucking bullshit designer purse, and why do always appear like I'm not paying attention to her.

4:29 a.m.

I want to strangle her. No, I changed my mind. I want to stab her in the fucking face with a sharp knife or smash her in the head with a machete or a brick and end her shit. I want to rape her limp body on the floor of my apartment and cum on her face one last time. How would I sneak her body down the stairs and into my car without all the fucking nosy elderly neighbors seeing it? That's a good question. These are the things I think about while she rambles on about how she wants a boyfriend, will I take her to dinner later this week, why don't I like sushi, and about her fucking bullshit new designer purse.

4:33 a.m.

Our food arrives and she'll finally have a reason to shut the fuck up. I'll continue smoking my cigarette that I bummed off of her and forget about how exactly I want to go about killing her and disposing of her limp carcass. My chicken sandwich and double hash browns look pretty fucking good, I gotta admit. Thank you Waffle House. I was fucking starving!

xoxo

"Don't worry, you won't lose me unless you find a way to kill me..ha..

thats refreshing..i guess???

I guess so, but oh wait I'm a dick and only love myself...according to you...haha

i never said such!?!?

it something deroggatory like that...haha

when, where, what the hell r u talking about?????

I made it up….ha

i should say

haha, But I do love you and I care about you, so ur not totally alone u know…"

xoxo

I wake up alone and next to no one every single fucking day. It's all the same now, how fucking depressing. Thoughts of suicide fill my cerebellum before I'm even out of bed at 1:37 p.m. I stare at a screen, nothing is learned and nothing is revealed. I grab a bottled water from the refrigerator, it makes an odd sound and sputters away. The garbage can smells as I pass it by, and the trash has been mounting for some time now. I light a cigarette and stare at the screen again. The news today bores me, so trivial, so boring. I want a coffee, but I know there is none in any cabinet, nor any sugar, nor any cream. I lift my arms and smell my armpits; they stink of last night's nightmares and sweat. The air conditioning is on 76, no wonder. I walk into the bathroom and take a piss. The piss from late last night is still in the toilet. The fresh piss makes last night's piss froth and swirl. I see dry drops of piss near the toilet as I hold my cock and watch the piss splash in the toilet bowl. I contemplate taking a shower, but procrastination gets the best of me and I put it off and live with the stink for now. I wash my hands in the sink and splash warm water on my face. I stare into the mirror at myself. What's the fucking point? What's the fucking point to any of this I think to myself? Should I kill myself today, or wait until tomorrow? Decisions…decisions, maybe I'll do it tomorrow or put it off until next week. Where did this misery inside of me come from? Whose fault is it, and who is to blame? I have no answers to that or anything else. I wipe my hands on a crumpled gray towel that was on the floor and walk back into my room. I open the shades a little, it's dark and raining, just like it has been the last three days. There's nothing for me to do today anyways. I'm going back to bed at 1:54 p.m. I will wake up later, alone and next to no one, just like I do every single fucking day.

xoxo

"South of Cooterific"

I play possum with:

My feelings, emotions, and linguistics,

She plays kickball with:

My guts, head, heart, and dick,

It kills like Ramirez and Dahmer:

Slowly, deeply, stinging, and wretched,

We never insert nouns:

Speak, fuck, confess, kiss, sleep, travel, eat, or lay on burning sand

Anymore.

xoxo

I called her on Monday and left a voicemail message. She was either at work or just didn't want to talk to me.

xoxo

Dear XXX,

Well, I'll try this as one last option before I give up. So even me being a crazy drunk gets no response from you? Damn, you're a tough cookie to impress! I really have no idea why you're avoiding me this time? I haven't done or said anything wrong other than buy you coffee and write you a damn poem. Monday it seemed like everything was fine. It's not cool to avoid and not talk to one of your best friends who you're presently fucking. I can handle your neurosis but I don't like these games and avoidance every other week, they get on my nerves. Anyways, I do really love you and care about you of course, and I really want to be with you so just stop being dumb and talk to me and tell what's wrong before you make me fucking insane! I can't be insane and have blue balls, it's not a good combination...see you later

xoxo

"I bought this angel orchid candle at ac moore today. I swear this fucking candle smells just like you"

"Really? Maybe I need to get one then"

"U should they're on sale. My room smells like u and cigs, a nice combo actually! The aroma of my two favorite vices is quite excellent. How u doing?"

xoxo

Ahh, fuck, why did I do it! A fucking chubby mediocre looking stripper, that's the best you could do? Nice rebound there pal. From fucking a really hot girl to fucking a fat ugly stripper that you couldn't even get off to, that will show her damn it. Your penance is to go to the free clinic and hope all the STD tests come back negative.

xoxo

"That's it; I'm not having sex with you anymore."

"What, the hell are you talking about? What did I do?"

"You're making fucking weird faces and you keep talking and saying stupid shit. Don't you know you can't gab when you're having sex with someone?"

"Well, I guess I didn't know that. I'm just fucking around and acting like a jackass."

"Well, this is it buddy so you better enjoy it."

"Are you fucking serious? I know you don't mean that honey buns. I just gave you an orgasm; throw that on top of making you dinner and buying you presents today. Shit, most women would call that a pretty fucking great day actually."

"Well yeah, but the fucking talking has to stop. I had a long day at work and I just can't take it right now."

"Well, if this really is my last time can I put it in your ass?"

"Uhmm, not a chance in hell buddy."

"Alright, come over this way. I don't feel like taking my pants and shoes off."

She slides towards the edge of the bed. A hard dick is inserted into a semi-wet but stubbly pussy.

"I don't like it this way, it fucking hurts."

"Jeez, c'mon, it's my last time; don't I get a choice of what position I wanna fuck in?"

"You can have any position, just not that one."

"Alright, whatever, I'll just get fucking cat hair all over me, but ok fine."

The man gets in bed and on top of her and his dick slides back in a fully wet stubbly pussy.

"Goddamn, your pussy feels good."

"What did I tell you? I told you not to fucking talk when we have sex!"

"What, I can't even say nasty but true shit now?"

"No, I don't wanna hear shit. Put on your pants it's over."

"What the fuck, this is crazy!"

The man gets off of the girl and is back on the floor, standing and pulling up his underwear and pants. He leaves soon after.

xoxo

"Erode, the Stout Consumer"

Feed me,

your friend's
prying
drama queen eyes
and
corporate sponsored fast food chain restaurant and dating sites
dirty red splotchy hands
web engine "search"

of

web designed paranoia,

you made me a hypochondriac

you made me neurotic

you made me insane,

fucking Wikipedia

fucking Google

fucking Jeeves, you asshole,

you made me think I had genital herpes

you made me order a Periodic Table shower curtain

you made me think I had a foot fungus

you made me sign up for social networking sites

you made me order an overpriced shirt

you made gave me clips of free porn

you gave me online coupons for a new brand of popcorn,

I didn't have genital herpes

I didn't need a new shower curtain

I didn't have a foot fungus

I didn't get laid off of social networking sites

I didn't cum in the thirty second clip

I didn't like that new shitty discounted popcorn,

the solution,

sorry

Dell

bashing metal and plastic

with

stolen job site hammer,

no more Wikipedia

no more Google

no more Jeeves, you fucking asshole.

xoxo

We were at the gas station. We had just fucked for hours. I needed water and another pack of smokes. I went in and got them and checked the newspaper as I waited for my change. She didn't want anything and stayed in the car while I went in. When I got back inside the car after getting my change and not paying for browsing the newspaper she said she was thirsty now, even though she didn't want anything when I went in. She went inside to get something to drink. I opened my pack of new cigarettes and lit one and drank my bland water. Out of nowhere I started getting another boner, even though my cock was rubbed raw from all the previous fucking we'd just done. I pulled my cock out of my pants, and yes, it was hard again. She came back in a few minutes and I said "fuck, can you believe this, I have another boner?" All she said was "wow." Which, I guess could've been worse. I asked her if she would suck my cock again. And, surprisingly she grabbed my cock and started blowing me as I pulled out of the parking lot of the busy gas station and tried to maneuver to the parking lot of the closed Italian restaurant next door. Traffic was getting heavy, as most people were headed to work and somehow no one noticed the girl bobbing up and down on my cock as I was driving. The sun was blinding me as I took a right turn and went down several blocks to the closed Italian restaurant. I parked in the back near the dumpster and weathered brooms. She continued to suck my cock. We were in the back of the closed Italian restaurant and I didn't notice before, but it happened to be directly behind some sort of K-12 school or some shit. All of a sudden a shitload of kids came running out near the chain-linked fence and started screaming and running around like lunatics. She didn't seem to notice since my cock was in her mouth and her vision was distorted. I came in her mouth as some little kid slid down a short plastic yellow slide.

xoxo

I called but there was no one home. Are you down the street or in Germany? I was just wondering cause I swallowed what little pride I had left and called you again. You didn't answer and never called back. I'm sitting here drunk and alone, call me.

xoxo

All I'm left with are memories. I still know what it's like to look into your eyes and feel intimidated. I remember the way you smell, often of patchouli. The way you light up a room. The way you like to hide under a hat so you can move around unnoticed. The way you laugh at a sick joke or hug me as we part ways are constant reminders. Your beauty intoxicated me; it was hard to even form sentences while looking at you. Your personality gave me a giant fucking boner. It was addicting and mysterious. I still can't figure you out to this day, and I like that.

xoxo

"hell I'm lucky to even know u

oh dont be silly

I wasn't, I was being honest.

ok well thats sweet, I like you too, for some reason you're very intriguing to me-Im sure Ive said that before?

jeez, it's hard to convince when I say the occasional sappy compliment. yes indeed, u have said that I was intruiging many times

it kinda catches me off guard-i guess. however you dont strike me as sappy unless you wanting to put the weird tiny clams in my pants counts-lol

oh I think it would..haha

yes haha indeed

but no I really don't say that many sappy things to anyone, but it felt sappy when I said it

it was kinda -so unexpected

good, maybe u will believe me if I don't say it very often

i tend to go with the you want something philosophy-LOL

ha, a good philosophy

confirming reality

in general I mean, but I wouldn't say something sappy to get something...I would just ask you…

yeah you do seem pretty straight forward i have to say

good, maybe I should rephrase the above to, I wouldn't say a bunch of sappy lame or untrue shit to get in ur pants....that's the essence of it I guess

yeah I got what u meant

I might for some people...lol....but not u

hmmm-thx

I wouldn't do that to my "soul mate"…hga

Im your soul mate??????

haha, I don't think I have one.....that I was joking around about yeah now that was sappy

of course, but on purpose as a joke

yeah i gotcha. thats a line you could use to get in a girls pants

maybe, I don't think I could ever say that and not laugh...I'm pretty straight forward with everyone

i know-thats a fairly obvious quality of yours

sweet, and a good one I stand for!"

xoxo

A girl blew me off. That's nothing really all that unusual though. I was at the bar I frequent more than most others. It's a fucking dump and it's always pretty dark in there. The freaks were out last night that's for sure. There are always people with issues in there of one kind or another. I suppose that's why I like it and go there all the fucking time. A random girl asked me my name while I was sitting alone at the bar. I lied and said that it was "Ralph." Later that night I left drunk and broke as usual.

xoxo

I hope for a soft knock every single day. Well, specifically a soft knock from her to be precise. It never comes and I doubt it ever will, but I hope and fantasize about it. It's worse at night, when the world slows down and there's silence in my apartment, minus the sounds of rain pellets and crickets. I'm still waiting for that soft knock sitting here alone watching HBO at 10:46 p.m.

xoxo

You cried on my shoulder the other day. It was the first time I'd seen you show that kind of emotion the entire time I've known you. Color me fucking impressed. It only took three years for you to trust me enough to show me that you're fucking emo.

xoxo

Earlier, while still drinking:

We're sitting across from each other in a ratty faux leather booth in a dingy bar known to stay open later than other dingy and non-dingy bars around town. Other friends of mine are playing darts at a dartboard nearby, but not close enough to hear our conversation. I take a sip of my Budweiser draft and the girl sitting across from me in the ratty faux leather booth tells me that a few months ago when we weren't talking or hanging out that she had my abortion. I blew her statement off like "yeah right I'm sure you did." She clarified that her mom went with her to Charleston and got it done. My delayed response while contemplating her statement was

"Don't you think that was something you should have mentioned to me beforehand?"

"Would you have really cared at all?" She asked.

"No, probably not, I'm glad you killed the fucking thing. I don't wanna have a kid with your crazy ass, you can barely take care of yourself much less another living entity, and I'm probably not much better to be honest."

"I wanna fuck you." She says.

"Ok, I guess we can later."

Later, after drinking:

We're in my bathroom and I'm shaving her pussy with my Gillette Mach 3 razor that I usually only reserve for my own crotch and face. I do a shitty drunken job granted, but it was better than the goddamn stubble that was there when I pulled her jeans and panties off though. After I'm done shaving around her pussy lips and wiping the shaving gel off with my tan hand towel that I usually only reserve for my face and hands after washing them, I jam my cock inside of her right there on the counter of the sink. A few minutes later as I'm about to cum she tells me to cum inside of her again so she can have another of my abortions, and I did, fuck it.

xoxo

"I wanna fuck you in the ass and call you Osama"

"Hope I stayed on my side of the bed. I tried to be quite and I am glad that I didn't wake you up. Stealth tech is something I learned at summer camp"

"You got it you think u get the ass on the first time? Ha we'll see"

"Haha that's funny I'll call you Sunday"

"It was a joke. I am not sassy. Who says I want a relationship? I like to hang out and yes no cuddling."

"Oh shut up I would never tip you. Anti cuddling yes. Don't be sassy. I'm anti relationship but I like hanging out with you"

"My parents are still here. Frodo is still locked in the shire. Just wanted to say hi"

"I know. I possess a sense of humor."

"And then light petting hmm and then what a twenty dollar bill on your dresser"

"Uhh yeah sounds like a devious midget plan to me or just call me next week and come over"

"Thank you midgets for helping a nigger. I didn't hear you leave. Stealth Arab tech?"

"Ok sugar tit terrorist"

"Right sneak out of my own house. they leave on Sunday. Maybe we can hang out on Monday?"

"Frodo needs to sneak out in the middle of the Arabian night and come over"

"Exactly remember your heritage. Eyes are ok. Just cut an asshole and pussy hole into the Arab sheet."

xoxo

Dear XXXXX,

You're so hard to understand or decipher these days. How could you possibly think that I would have somehow sifted happiness out of this mess? Sometimes I wonder if you got abducted by aliens and they made you oblivious and delusional, or if it's just an act. I don't really know anymore. I don't say these things to be mean at all, I just say them. Have I woken up one day and been happy that you're gone, or have I come to some conclusion that I'm somehow better off being amputated from your life? No, that hasn't happened. The opposite is true. Have I moved on or had some fling to try and forget you or mask the way I feel? Nope, can't say that I have. It's harder than you might think to really want anyone else when you have my heart/love/feeling. I've tried baby, but it just made things worse and wasn't fair to me or them. I have nothing at the moment to give to anyone else. I've loved and wanted you from the start. I can't help that, it's just the way it is. I had what I wanted and nothing else will do right now. I don't want you to feel bad, that's just the way it is. It's obviously easier for you to go off with someone else and leave me behind. I really don't think I could have ever done it to you. Why would I? You're great for me; you compliment me well and make up for what I lack. You make me happy. I was comfortable with you, we got along like fat girls and ice cream and I always had fun with you so there was nothing I wanted to leave. I didn't really realize it at the time, but you really did complete me and made me a better human being, or at least inspired me to be one. You were on such a high pedestal, that in truth I felt like I really wasn't good enough to be with you or to occupy space in your life sometimes. You really made me the happiest that I've ever been in my life, and I guess on the flipside of that life coin is that you can and have make me the most miserable and unhappy that I've ever been in my life as well. I confess these things to the notebook that you gave me, but not to you. I wish that I could tell you. I wish I could talk to you like I did before, but now you're hard to talk to. You seem bothered and annoyed when I try. It's hard being cast out of your life like a leper or exiled on some remote island like Napoleon. I miss you every single fucking day, that is no lie. I miss my best friend. I miss my girl so much. I miss going to the beach with you. I miss going to Goodwill and Dollar Tree with you. I miss being stranded on islands in the Caribbean with you. I miss your soft lips and the way your body tastes. I miss early dinners and good conversations with you. I miss being inside of you. I miss making you laugh with my stupid antics. I miss doing crazy and interesting things for you. I miss unstopping the Yeti drain for you. Trust me when I tell you that you are missed in every facet of my life. I have no answers really and I have nothing figured out. I have no idea where to go from here. I'm just "being" for now and surviving every single day. I wish I really knew what drove you away from me. It's like I almost wish that I'd done something shitty, so at least I could point to something and be like "oh, there it is that's what did it." I wish things hadn't of gone down like they did. Definitely not your finest hour, not the classy girl I know that you are. Not the XXXXX I know. You're better than that. I know it in my head and in my heart, which is why I'm still here in your life. People have tried to talk me out of it, to stay away from you, to never have anything to do with you, to never speak to you again, and all that type of shit. So yeah, I do defend you just like you defended me, or well like you used to defend me anyways. I just say to myself that she made a mistake and she's still an amazing person and I can't help it. I love this girl and what can I do about it really? Perhaps I should give up, but it's just not in my nature to do so when I believe in something. Maybe I'm a fool. I don't know. My mind does tell me sometimes "man, she left you pretty easily without much care for you, she didn't call you, she didn't come over and talk to you in person or say she was even sorry. She's different now and wants nothing to do with you. She's off doing something else now and just leave her be." I hope my mind is wrong in those instances. My opinions about you change all the time. Thanks for the neuroticism, it's my first taste of it, but I'd rather it come from you than anyone else I've ever met I guess.

xoxo

You're wearing your panties with the little pink stars on them. They have a light blue background. Your shirt and bra are still on as well. You spit and slobber all over my cock. You grab my balls and squeeze on them. My head rests against a pillow, which rests against the plain white wall behind it. I take pictures of you with my small white Austrian camera that I have sitting next to me on my black nightstand. I grab your hair and say "suck my cock you fucking slut" as I snap away with my little white Austrian camera. You don't seem to mind me saying that to you. I like that about you.

xoxo

"did u read any of the book today...on ur day off?"

"i read the whole thing. it dropped in my bath. not lying i promise! i really read the whole thing, its a easy read"

"damn, u must have been really bored...haha. Did it make your pussy wet? That's how I grade my book!"

"Somewhat, if i would have gotten raped i could have maybe made the next book!"

"ha, nah all you have to do is give me a an HJ, though fucking me would get you better placement in weird perverted stories about fucking girls half my age"

"awesome can't wait to show my mom and high school friends. you make me sound so fucking young"

"well, that would be my literary angle with you...chill...I don't think your mentally19, you have the tits of a 27 year old I swear, they're mature for their age...lol"

xoxo

"The Articles of Lipstick Confusion and Rectangular Lighthouses"

Today

I wanted her

Yesterday

I didn't

Tomorrow,

Who the fuck knows?

Today

She was beautiful

Yesterday

She was ugly

Tomorrow,

Who the fuck knows?

Today

I was comfortable with her

Yesterday

I despised the site of her

Tomorrow,

Who the fuck knows?

Today

I fucked her

Yesterday

I didn't

Tomorrow,

Who the fuck knows?

Today

I left her

Yesterday

I was still there

Tomorrow,

Who the fuck knows?

xoxo

I sent her an e-mail message and she hasn't responded. Perhaps she forgave me for calling her a slutty gold digger, though probably not. I'm glad I stuck it to her and got some of my dignity and respect for myself back. I'd been too nice too long.

xoxo

We appear under lamp post lights with rain falling on our heads.

"What the fuck's happened to us? We've gotten lame in our old age. We're fucking over thirty and doing PDA in the corner of a bar. Not to mention holding hands and walking around and taking pictures of us making out."

"Yeah I don't know either. I've lived with guys and never held their hand."

"Really? Who was that?"

"You know who."

"Well, I'm not gonna apologize, and I'm just going with it and trying not to contemplate it too much you know. Fuck, we used to be so cool and hardcore though."

"I know, I don't know what's going on here, it's strange."

"I think I've only held hands with like three girls in my life, including you now. Everything is falling apart and makes no sense, so why should this be any different really?"

"True enough cowboy, let's go back to your place."

"Sound like a plan baby."

We disappear back into the night with rain still falling on our heads.

xoxo

We were walking along the beach in April. Our feet entered the cool water. I bent down to observe a small clear jellyfish that the tide was washing into shore. I picked up a small broken shell and poked the top of the small clear jellyfish with it; it didn't move or react in any way. I then touched it with my raw hand; it still didn't react and didn't sting me. I lost interest in it after that and threw the broken shell back on the beach. We were walking further away from where our towels were. She grabbed my hand as we were walking and wrapped her fingers into mine. I noticed how her stomach was jiggling with every mutual step that we took. I wondered if I should say anything about it. I contemplated this as her hand and fingers were still intertwined with mine.

"You're getting kind of pudgy." I said to her out of nowhere.

A display of shock came across her face. Her hand released from mine.

"Fuck you; you're fatter than I am." She replied.

She walked away from me back towards where our towels were resting on the sand. I followed closely behind her.

"I'm sorry. I was just kidding around. C'mon don't be mad, it was just a joke baby."

As I pulled my black sunglasses off my face to wipe the sweat that had filled the lens she came running towards me and kicked a puddle of salt water and sand in my face.

"I told you to leave me the fuck alone!"

xoxo

"The Quarantine Zone for Sloths and Gloom"

I sadly attempt to invade her mind,

I sadly attempt to invade her soul,

I sadly attempt to invade her existence,

outside,

inside,

the moving cars
with silent stereo systems
taco lunches in the shade of August
pathetic early morning phone calls
and
empty homeless benches at Dunkin' Donuts
vodka flavored kisses
in bars I never go in
walking alone on black pavement
big box stores are now consummated
drunken late night
e-mails are sent
and now regretted
social networking photos are considered
toxic waste and should be
avoided
watching her sleep on the couch
lace black bra
lace black panties
pet the damn cat
that isn't hers
lay on the floor
and appreciate the golden tinged silence,

inside,
outside,
the only thing left,

snail mail
carrier pigeons
smoke signals
and

goddamn fucking paper airplanes,

I badly attempt to invade her mind,

I badly attempt to invade her soul,

I badly attempt to invade her existence,

there is rarely hope at the end of a sentence.

xoxo

Extreme horniness will make you do some crazy shit. I pulled her pants down as soon as she walked through the door of my apartment. I walked her over to the kitchen sink, bent her over, and pulled down her black panties and pink sweatpants. My cock was already hard as shit. Her pussy was a little dry, but after poking at her pussy a few times with my dick it eased right in. I was pounding away like a madman on her. I grabbed her hair and asked if she like having my big cock inside of her. She didn't reply really. I was lying of course; my cock really isn't that big. Like I said before, extreme horniness will make you say and do some crazy shit. My dick slipped out of her and I noticed something smelled sort of funny. It was a fishy smell, and that can only mean one thing, that fishy smell was radiating from her pussy. Could it be? I'd only heard jokes about fishy pussies. I tried to bend down and smell my cock, but that didn't really work too well. I bent down and spread her ass from behind and sniffed near her pussy. Goddamn, that fucking thing smelled like roadkill I thought to myself for a second. What the fuck should I do here? I stuck my dick back in her and contemplated what the fuck to do. I pounded on her a few time before I couldn't take it any longer.

"Damn, your pussy smells funny." I tell her.

"What does it smell like?" She asks.

"Fucking rotten fish or roadkill or something."

"I don't know. I just douched the other day."

"Damn, I don't know that shit reeks and I'm losing my boner."

Fuck. I need to cum. I don't give a shit, fishy smelly pussy or not, it's still pussy, and it will still get me off. I reached over towards the stove and grabbed a black and white striped kitchen towel. I folded it sideways and wrapped it around my face and tied it in the back, with a bow pussy bandit style. I went back to pounding away on her from behind, she, still bent over near the kitchen sink. Like I said before, extreme horniness will make you do some crazy shit.

xoxo

"uh oh it's the illustrious XXXXX

haha.. you're so funny

funny like a clown or like a retarded midget??

hmmm clowns are scary, midgets-uh well not sure, no cute funny

haha, ur scared of clowns? cool, so when I sneak in ur window I'm dressing up like john wayne gacey. is that kosher

like a hebrew national?

yes, I want a rabbi to bless me before I sneak in ur window dressed as a serial killer

how bout dressed as a clown that would be even scarier

that's what I said, john wayne gacey. I'll put the mix cd for making babies in one of my balloons.

dont know him, dont want to know him-oh i guess id have to pop it or something

you can pop the balloon and then I'll pop one in ur oven...lol

whatever...haha"

xoxo

I've been fucking the same girl for a while now. I like her. It's been a while since I've liked anyone really. We get drunk, we fuck, and she doesn't hassle me too much either. That last part is a major key for me let me tell you. And hell, she's even really good looking to top it all off with. The only problem is that she won't let me fuck her in the butt. I need it bad. It's the only thing I want, and she won't give it to me.

xoxo

Dear XXXXX,

I have no idea why I write and confess to you when you're not even here. It's more like I have conversations with a Dell computer screen. Goddamn, I'm so fucked up over you. Nothing makes sense anymore, well very little anyways. You changed me, seriously. I wish I could go back in time and tap myself on the shoulder and let myself know then what I know now. Fuck, I've had to learn such a painful lesson, but I deserve it I guess, and it probably needed to happen to me. You were right; I will never find anyone better than you. I can't accept mediocrity anymore; I don't want that beast in my life ever again. I now give a shit. I now care, I now love, and I always have when it concerned you. It's like impossible to care or be with anyone else when you have my fucking heart and you happen to be the epitome of everything I ever wanted in someone. I'm glad I was picky about who I gave my heart to, and I'm glad it was you. I'm glad that you were the first for pretty much everything minus taking my virginity or something. That list includes first girl I was ever in love with, first girl I ever introduced to my mom, first girl I ever took a vacation with, you name it baby and you were it. I've seen other people and it just doesn't feel right. No one else makes sense with me. I've never met anyone that was that much like me and that much of a counterpart, and I know you know that. I'm not delusional. I don't know what's happened to me really. I have changed, and that's not bullshit. When most people say it, it probably is though, but not with me. I haven't reverted to my old ways and whored around or tried to replace you. I'd really rather be solitary and alone instead. I told you that you made me a better person; I guess there's some of the proof in action. I refuse to waste my time on anything that isn't fucking amazing to be honest. I don't know what the fuck I'm doing. I don't even know why I'm saying all of this. I hid so much before, but I can't do it anymore. I don't care to mask my fear, my insecurities, how much I really wanted you, and how much I was in love with you. I just can't do it anymore. I apologize that I had to use you as an experiment on love and relationships basically. I didn't know what I was doing, what I wanted for a long time, or how to handle what I felt so I reverted to my defense mechanisms by hiding a lot of this shit or pretending like I didn't care sometimes. It was so stupid of me because I trusted you and I wanted to tell you this shit every single day, yet I didn't really. I was always worried that I couldn't live up to what you wanted or give you everything that I know that you wanted and I thought that you deserved. I'm just filled with perverse self doubt that I need to shed.

xoxo

"Embracing the Erectile Dysfunction of Life"

she asks me on the phone,

how my day was,
I want to kill her,

she asks me in person,

how my day was,
I want to kill her,

she asks me after I fuck her,

how my day was,

I want to kill her,

she asks me after dinner,

how my day was,
I want to kill her,

if she asks me one more time,
how my day was,
I'm going to kill myself instead.

xoxo

Love makes me insane. I'm a train wreck of emotions at times over you. I overreact, I'm jealous, I'm tormented, I feel high around you, I love the sight of you, I would give you my spleen, I act ridiculous, I analyze too much, and ten minutes with you is better than a lifetime with anyone else I have ever met. See what I mean. It's a plethora of contradictions. The best way I can put it is to say "you make me the happiest and the saddest I've ever been." That pretty much sums me and you up in my mind.

xoxo

There's no joy in jerking off anymore. There's no joy in women anymore. There's no joy in me anymore. The only enjoyment is in solitary confinement with only my memories to manipulate and torture me now.

xoxo

"Hey, my little bun-head."

Cough, hack, misery.

"You feelin' any better there sweet nips?"

Roll your eyes, huff, cough, and hack.

"Be quiet…just stop."

"What?"

"You don't like all my little pet names for you?"

"Uhmm, no…I don't."

Snake snake snake snake snake snake snake snake snake snake snake snake.

"What are you doing?"

"I don't know, probably annoying the shit out of you while you're sick."

"Just stop it please."

Cough, hack, and further misery.

"Can you turn that light off, it's way too bright and I can't rest."

"Sure thing honey buns."

Roll your eyes again. Blow your nose and keep the snot rag in the bed. Fucking gross, yet I say nothing. Well, back to doing my crossword puzzle. Yep, nothing else to do in Miami. What the fuck is a five letter word for "signified?" I have no idea and bite the end of my pen.

"Can you turn the TV down a little?"

"You got it sugar tits."

"Just shut the fuck up please!"

"What?"

"I turned the TV down, jeez you're cranky."

"Just do your crossword puzzle and don't call me names."

"I didn't, I just called you sugar tits, that's not mean."

"Whatever."

Cough, hack, and, further misery. It's time for a smoke. It's fucking freezing outside and I have no jacket. Fuck it, go out in the hallway and light one up and sit on the plastic futuristic couch. Yeah, that sounds like a better idea than freezing my ass off. Turn the light off, turn the TV down…yap yap yap…the door slams loudly behind me.

xoxo

"Frustrating the Collective Symmetry"

2:11

2:12

2:13

2:14

2:15

2:16,

my head spins

on delicate

cheap ghetto laundromat

inside my cerebral cortex

pupil's dilate

ears pop like an M-80

nose hair singed

visions

past

visions

present

visions

future

visions

past participle

no idea where they're coming from

molestation

suicide,

hi

welcome to Wendy's

do you want whipped cream on that?

any extra sauce?

that will be eight dollars and nine cents

have a great day,

drive my car into that

big pretty fucking blooming

pine tree

sitting in the dark

middle of the day

get a rope and

hang

from the balcony

the clock strikes

digital numbers on a

blue screen,

2:11

2:12

2:13

2:14

2:15

2:16,

someone

anyone

do it for me

madness

lasts

a lifetime in only six

minutes.

xoxo

Dear XXXXXXXX,

I need to stop being so insane over you. Once in a while I read the shit I write about you and I die laughing and wonder what the fuck was or is wrong with me. It felt genuine at the time, but often after rereading the writing I do about you I feel like a goddamn fool. I like you very much, and even though I might write some fucked up things about you, sometimes it's always because I care in the end; and that scares the living shit out of me. In the end all I want is for you to be happy and have everything that you want out of life. I wouldn't be much of a friend to you if I didn't want that for you. It's hard taking a non judgmental approach to you sometimes. I want to be there for you no matter what the situation. But, I will admit it is hard to do in certain situations involving other guys. It hurts sometimes, but I somewhat get over it. You like who you like and I can't force you to like me, and I know that. It's just a little baffling to me why you wouldn't be into me even just a little. That sounds vain; but oh well, it's not meant to be. For the first time in my life the shoe is on the other foot as they say. It's usually me rejecting some girl that likes me. Maybe I'm just being paid back for my cruel acts of the past, I don't know. The other thing that bothers me is that I don't know exactly what I want from you. Is it just a sex thing, or for once is it more than that? I wish I could answer that question as well. My life here would be very boring without you in it regardless of what I say on occasion. You inspire me to achieve greatness; no one has ever done that for me before. All the writing and the art all started because of you in some way or another. So, to sum all this crap up in the simplest of terms, Brett - you = bad.

xoxo

She's drunk and talking to herself on the couch. She put her water down on the table in front of her and stumbled into my room and disappeared. I continued watching TV and got up off of the couch and went into my room as well. She's was on the bed singing some lyrics to I think "the devil went down to georgia" badly, though it was mostly mumbling. I could make out the Georgia part of the mumbling anyways. I crawled into the bed with her and I was soon on top of her. I started kissing her. Her lips tasted like chocolate flavored lip gloss, cigarettes, and vodka. I sucked on her bottom lip and felt up her B-Cup sized tits. I pulled down the right side of her bra and a round mint popped out of it. I continued kissing her, tasting the remnants of chocolate lip gloss, cigarettes, and vodka.

"I want you to have my fucking abortion." I tell her.

"Not tonight, I'm not in the mood for your abortion." She replies.

xoxo

Brett,

Will you delete the most recent comment I sent you. I sound pretty pathetic. Not to mention, looks like you have quite the following of tramps who will leave you plenty of comments. Anywho, please, delete mine.

xoxo

"You make me wanna be bad."

"Every fucking time I get near you I get hard."

"Do you wanna fuck?"

"No, I don't fuck strangers on the first date."

"I'm not a stranger. We've been friends for like two weeks, well at least online that is."

"Because, I'm not that kind of girl."

"I wish you were that kind of girl. I'm horny as shit."

"Though, I will say I want you so bad right now. I told you, you make me wanna be bad."

"Fuck it, lets have sex."

"I probably need to go home before I do something bad."

"Bad, like what?"

"Fuck it, I don't care." She says.

She proceeds to unzip my pants, pull down my underwear, and suck my cock as I lay back on my ratty brown couch and watch the sun slowly rise.

xoxo

I want to hack your mind, not your e-mail account. I tried both and I failed miserably. There's no way of ever finding out the truth now. I cannot trust you now. I cannot trust your cunt. It smells funny and has now been soiled by another.

xoxo

Before we fucked,

We had sex for a long fucking time!

Ha, u left me with blueballs for so long I'm like a girl. Stop being so insecure. And just be with me and don't be filled with neurosis.

I didn't know I was. Ur so sensitive. Whatever, u don't even like me anyways.

Damn, ur one tough cookie, I never get anywhere with you!!!

If it were me I would want to have drinks and sex before I left the country. Just in case radicals take over Costa Rica and execute hot white women

Yeah, I'm ok just sore, got whiplash and some painkillers

I wish you would meet me somewhere so we could have drink and hang out before you left.

Ok, dollface. Sounds fine. You and ur naps. Are you part nappinho?

Be honest did u kiss her?

I'm a neurotic mess. U know that. We'll hang out soon, I suck

I know, I'm, sorry. Drunk and pissed u were avoiding me again. Fuck, u were in a wreck in didn't even tell me?

We are going to have to rain check it til next Monday. I have to get up early and have a test I forgot about. I'm not being neurotic I swear

Jeez, that's not cool. I was worried about you. For good reason I guess.

Never mind I don't care thanks for nothing!

Are you avoiding me for any reason? I'm not communicating with you anymore if you don't repond!

Baby, why won't you speak to me? I'm sorry...

I want to mount you like a stallion! Giddy up…insert horse noises!

OK, I will check with my personal assistant to see if I'm available to answer the phone. U can call me anytime sweet tits…

Give me a call this week and we'll chat

It's all clear now minus the orange finger stains. The baked Cheetos made it 20 percent more rad!

It was such a long day. Excited to see u tomorrow after work as well

A correction to last night's statement. I heart you when I'm drunk alone and eating baked cheetos. Keep it on the DL!

It's a combo of things, I'm at work call ya when I leave. It's been a horrible week. I was in a car accident as well. You message last night was not cool

This is the first text I got all day from u smart ass

I love you when I'm drunk and alone…

I never wanted to get married, but I've always wanted to spend Saturday mornings reading the NY Times and drinking coffe with someone cool

Do u give massages. I need one so bad

I'm gonna call u in a while and whisper sweet nothings in ur ear

Ok that's fine. Can we have sex before next Monday, I'm about to die

Why are you avoiding me, is it because I'm adopted?

Ahh nice, now they match the poem

Yeah it proves u don't really like me.

U dried up like the Gobi and quit,

After we fucked.

xoxo

I got tired of sitting in the car and waiting for the barge. I got out of the car with my water and my cigarettes. She wouldn't let me smoke in the car. She kept bitching about it all the way down her. Every time I lit one up she said her car smelled like cigarettes, but I couldn't smell it. I bought her a dollar ghetto air freshener at a gas station we stopped at and put it in there so that should've shut her up. But, the fact that she makes out with me all the time and comes to my house all the time where I smoke and doesn't say shit, sort of contradicts that, so who knows. I went out and walked towards the bay. A few guys pulled behind us a few minutes later, and they had a bunch of surf boards in the back of their truck. I guess they were going surfing or coming back from going surfing. I saw a wooden table and sat there drinking my water and smoking my cigarettes. I looked down on the bay, there were all of these big container ships headed off to some fucking foreign place, some place a lot more interesting than where I was going. I sat and smoked and watched a big red boat chug along the bay. A few minutes later it disappeared out of view. There were small red chiggers on the bench; I burnt them with my lighter to keep them away from me. The horn honked a few minutes later, it was time to say goodbye to the bench and the small red chiggers. The barge was here; we paid our five dollars, and pulled the car on the barge. We got on the boat and had to stand outside and it launched off. It was only about a ten minute boat ride. I got about 542 mosquito bites all over me, on pretty much every piece of skin I had showing. I couldn't smoke on the boat so I just stood there and got eaten alive. There weren't many people on the boat, only four or five people paid to get on. Some black guy thought my "special lady friend" was hot. He waved and said "hey baby" as we pulled the car off the boat. We just looked away and sped off.

xoxo

I was rummaging through an old drawer earlier. There's a lifetime in there. I came across an old picture from middle school. Her name was Dawn. Her picture had reddened and was losing its once proud luster. On the back she said that she was glad I was in her class and that she liked my hair. She was the hottest girl I'd ever seen back then. She was also the first hot girl that was ever particularly nice to me in any way. You don't forget shit like that. Just so you know Dawn, I still masturbate to you, even to this day.

xoxo

She was riding me on her crappy white couch. She kept digging her clit into my pubic bone. When she was about to orgasm she grabbed my hair and shoved her hair and tits in face. It was hard to breathe. I must have opened my mouth too much because her hair went down my fucking throat and started making me gag. I tried to get it out of there but it was impossible while she was on top of me. I have a terrible gag reflex. It was pretty hard to relay this to her while she was on top of me though. I felt a rumbling in my stomach, and it was only a few seconds until I vomited chicken fingers and fries all over both of us. She didn't seem to mind though. That was pretty cool of her.

xoxo

"See ya at hot topic ya fucking cuntbag!"

"What did I say?"

"You didn't say anything baby, I'm just saying fucking bye. And I lied; I didn't really like your fucking shoes you fucking generic whore!"

xoxo

"I beleive you, ur mind is set. Good thing ur crushing on me or I might not agree

who says im crushing on you??

uhmm jesus told me actually…

he doesnt talk to you

ok ur right, my vanilla ice doll told me

now that i would believe more

He was like "man, that girl is fresh cold crushing!"

he's old and washed up what does he know?

he's "cool as ice" so shut it and actually the doll doesn't age

ok "ice, ice baby"

he just gets dusty that's all.

he still doesnt know shit"

xoxo

He'll be here in May. Yeah social networking friend, pencil in lunch and going out that weekend I read on her friend's profile. I hope I don't see or run into them. That would make me sick to my stomach and fill me with anger. I would sulk at home while she's giving him a blowjob, what a perfect fucking world.

xoxo

"The Algerian Nausea Hotel Room Blues"

hell is modern society

and

myself

Sartre

you French fucking dead prick,

bright rooms

dimly lit hallways

of neuroticism and

the running of bulls and blood

red

demerits of past juvenile behavior

not much

has changed

pink slips and the occasional

depression of bullets

and your life

let's talk about our feelings

let's not

the masses

only find God while in

the depths of despair

and isolation

praise Jesus

praise Valium

praise 12 steps to nowhere

and Kansas

vintage lighters

of past wars

between lovers and nations

acetaminophen 325 mg

aspirin 500 mg

caffeine 65 mg

all a growing boy needs

survival is

twelve hour shifts in length

facial scars reveal liars

and salesmen

isolations rooms without soft padding

or MTV

birthdays and weddings

sadomasochism and minor flesh wounds,

hell is modern society

and

myself

Sartre

you French fucking dead prick.

xoxo

I drove her home the next day. I came inside of her and I wasn't supposed to. She said something about having to go and buy the morning after pill. I'd never head of it until recently. It's better to kill my unborn fetus now rather than later. I might actual feel bad about it then. After putting in my eight hours at work I got to the bank with ten minutes left to spare. I got forty bucks out of my account and put it in my chain wallet. I decided to walk to her apartment which was close to the bank. She said we could split the cost of the morning after pill. She said earlier that it would probably be around fifty bucks or something. It was about a half mile walk through dirty streets and shitty fast food restaurant parking lots until I got to her apartment, which was inside of a big green house. I climbed the old wooden stairs slowly. I had my work boots on and they weighed a ton. I knocked on the door, and there was no answer. I waited a few seconds and knocked again, but there was still no answer. I reached into my wallet; I held both twenty dollar bills in my right hand. After contemplating the situation, I only slid one of the twenty dollar bills under the door. I put the other back in my wallet and slowly walked down the old wooden stairs.

xoxo

The pain starts to subside now. Still, occasionally it feels like I got punched in the fucking stomach though. There's an image here or an image there that passes through my cerebral cortex. And, also, thoughts of her giving a blowjob to that lame ass fuck! Goddamn it, I need a blowjob right now! I'll get her back though, then I'll have blowjobs for days!

xoxo

Pitch black and late at night.

"Bang my head into the wall." She says.

That's what I hear anyways. Images of Quite Riot fill my cerebrum. Admittedly, my ears were sort of covered by the large pillow beneath my head. And really, when you're fucking who pays that much attention to linguistics anyways? I move closer towards the white shadowed wall behind my bed. I grab her back with my hand and aggressively push her forward. There's a large loud thump a few seconds later. Her head hits the wall pretty hard as she is riding me with my cock inside of her.

"Why did you do that? I told you to move forward so I didn't hit my head on the wall. Fuck, that really hurt! Brett…"

Enter a silent pause…

She still sits on top me with my cock inside of her.

"Sorry, sugar tits. I thought you said you wanted me to slam your fucking head into the wall, so that's what I did. I didn't know. I thought you were a fucking sadomasochist or something?"

"Ouch, just move down some."

I move down and take the large pillow with me; she continues riding me in the late night pitch black.

xoxo

I get a crazy vibe from this one. She told me she was on Adderall and Valium, and in fact she is on both right now. I guess with a combination like that there's an insane middle ground. I hate her after I cum in her mouth or on her face. I sit in my chair with a hand towel on my dick letting the "after cum" leak onto the towel instead of my leg, while she just sits there on my bed staring into space. I should shave her head and shoot her into space; I think she would be a good space monkey. The other night she was moving her head to and fro and moving her shoulders like she was listening to music. The apartment was silent though, so I asked her what the fuck she was doing bobbing her head all around? She said she was listening to music. I mentioned that there wasn't any music playing. She said she knew that, and she was listening to the music in her head. What a fucking nut I tell you! I didn't call or text her anymore for late night blowjobs after that. I don't regret it, even though I admit she could suck a damn good dick. Though a wise man once told me to never put wackos with teeth in charge of your dick.

xoxo

"Contaminated Stories from a Southern Gutter"

life is sometimes more exciting when you have something to lose,

I have
nothing,

I have
no one,

no,

woman
money
life

house

deodorant

water

liberty

food

success

internet connection

toilet paper

pussy

pleasure

electricity

cigarettes

booze

cable

coffee

gas

razor blades

newspapers

blowjobs

interesting books

movies worth seeing

someone worth arguing with

photos to take

decent conversations

pens to write with

paintings to paint

lights on my bicycle

just

something to do,

I'm not that

happy

but

I live with it,

life is sometimes less exciting when you have nothing to lose.

xoxo

A bar with a view and the text messages that remained:

"Was it a full on make out session or just like a kiss?"

"Def full out. I was with 5 people who were like wow look at that shit. They were all over each other"

"What did he look like?"

"Well the guy was older and not cool at all. Looked like one of my dads friends…"

xoxo

It's all hazy now, but I was so fucking drunk that I fell down the goddamn wooden stairs that lead up to my shitty apartment. I cracked my head open and went inside and ate my shitty value sized McDonald's food that I got off of the limited late night menu. I woke up the next day on the couch with my phone in my hand, fries on the floor, and ketchup on my stomach. I saw there was a new text message on my phone so I clicked on it and it was from my ex-lady friend. It said "I don't know what brought this on, don't ever text me again please." I went to my text message outbox and read some messages I guess I sent at 3:34 a.m. last night or today or whatever the fuck. It said "You're such a fuckin' joke. I guess it never worked out between us because I didn't have enough money or houses for you. You can saturate in being a fake ass ignorant bitch." I put the phone down and went to the bathroom to take a shit and contemplate how to get out of this situation.

xoxo

"I have a lot of sick ideas I could use you as a model for. It's so hard to find cool disturbed people who will work for free and do it for the sake of art."

"I guess it depends on your ideas."

"Fair enough, like DP'ing someone with plastic Wal Mart crucifixes. Or, say, have a painting of a girl holding my dick like gun she's using to commit suicide and having cum blowing out the back of her head instead of blood."

"Ha, I like the cum gun idea."

"Indeed, I have a plethora of sick ideas. The cum gun would be great. But better if I have a real person to use as a facial model. I would be abstract enough to not know the person but I would know and that's all that's important."

"Right, you can totally be my cooterific model. Do it for the sake of shock art baby. I also think a picture of you licking cum off a printed picture of yourself would be cool and bizarre."

"I'd like that for me."

"Damn skippy, you're awesome. Where have you been all my life? Is it wrong all this art talk made my pussy wet?"

"Let me lick your clit…"

"Ha, ok, you can lick my leg because I have a tattoo of a clit there, or just insert dick for the word clit and you're in business."

"Well I am bi so I might need both."

"Well, then I got you hooked up sugar tits. I'm not surprised by your bi status. I like it, high five. I was seeing a bi girl like a month ago, she got obsessed and I had to say adios. I'm rolling single and masturbator now. My hand can only do so much."

"True that, but it gets you by during dry spells."

"I'm bored with it now."

"I'd been on one for a year. The guy I'm with now isn't serious and will probably cheat on me while I'm gone."

"Ha, well you better cheat on him first then, just in case. Well I have options, but most girls around here are boring and shallow so I have to be in a certain type of mood to fuck any of them."

"Hmm, who would I fuck? The island is bare of people who fit the bill"

"Right, damn I have no idea who would fit the bill then?...cough…cough."

"Hmm, oh well I can always just bring my rabbit."

"Well, obviously you didn't get the cough cough part. But, I fit the bill and I'll fuck the shit out of you."

"You think you can hit my spots?"

"My Magic 8 Ball says yes. I am an EMT so I know more about vaginas than most average people. And, I'm also certified to make out with you."

"Nice, we'll see Mr."

"Ok, sounds like a cooterawesome plan then. What spots were you referring to anyways? Do you have like secret spots that other girls don't or something? I may be a shitty lay, but I'm great at eating pussy to make up for it."

"We shall see sir. This maybe a test of sexual endurance"

"But with the way you speak you may need a condom or twenty. You're nasty!"

"Being a pervert doesn't mean you're dirty missy. I'm totally clean. I get tested after each partner actually. Condoms fucking suck!!!"

"Sweet, no cunt rot for me then"

"Uhmm no. You're not gonna get anything from me darling. That shit scares me. I'm assuming you're STD free as well? We gotta both pinky swear for this to be official."

"Alright I pinky swear."

"High five for both of us being STD free then! Are you on birth control? I so wanna fill you full of cum."

"No, it causes cancer, which I've been though, and I do want a family eventually."

"Only a tiny increase in cancer risk. I've studied that shit. More like girls sleep around and get HPV. But I understand if you had cancer before. What do you do…pull out or something?"

"Yeah, I don't really sleep around much."

"But I do…lol…kidding. Did you have cervical cancer? Everyone's been exposed to HPV at some point. There's like 200 different strains. You don't have to sleep around, it only takes one dude."

"Yeah, no warts, I just can't carry a pregnancy if it were to happen. Which sucks cause I wanted to be a mom one day."

"Right, that blows. So what do you do instead of birth control?"

"Pull out and condoms, I don't trust guys these days."

"Well, I wouldn't trust many people these days either. The pull out and cum classic. I like it. Condoms are pointless. All the STD's you don't want they don't protect you from like herpes and shit…"

"Yep, true people could have the herp on their crotch or balls anywhere really. I don't even have fever blisters. I always look before I kiss someone. So gross!"

"Nothing wrong with a little paranoia. Which, is why I'm not a man whore. I always make girls pinky swear who would break that sacred trust?…haha"

"Yeah most are deceivers. But I have a big heart unlike most. You know more about me than most"

"I never admit to HPV nor the infertility because I feel bad."

"That's cool, sometimes it's easier to tell a stranger. No reason to feel bad about it. Shit happens, you deal with it and then move on. I wouldn't be talking to you if I didn't think you were decent person."

"It's just hard to deal with"

"Yeah I could understand for sure. Not much of anything I can say will make you feel better about it. There's no way you can have a kid?"

"No, yea god hates women. Hey you can cum inside of me and I can't get pregnant though…"

"True, you gotta look for the positives. And, I would love to shoot a load of hot cum inside of you and have it drip down your thigh…yummy"

"And I'd love to taste you"

"I think we could manage that. I can lick it out of your pussy and spit it in your mouth!"

"Yummy…"

"Ha, you fucking perv! I love it, I totally do. Which picture of you should I print off and cum on tonight? I'll send you the pic of you covered in cum."

"Do it, and make me your art. You have my permission."

"Thank, how kind of you. I like that picture of you in black, you look hot and your tits look gigantic."

"Good, save some fluids for the actual me"

"Right, I don't think I will run out darling. At least I hope not."

"Sad if you did."

"Yeah, I'd be dead without any bodily fluids. So what other kind of perverted shit are you into? What gets you off? I gotta do my research."

"Then drop your pants and cough cause I will be in town on Friday. I'll tell you then.."

xoxo

After going on a date I realize why I never go on them. It's pure fucking hell and so boring. These girls seem somewhat interesting when I'm fucked up drunk, but sober, they're such a bore and so insane.

xoxo

"I've been pissed off all day, fucking cunt of a teacher ruined my day early

sorry…you gotta let it go though, cause if you dont your letting those other idiotic people control how you feel

fuck that

well its true

I want to punch the bitch in her face…

good thing you didnt you're already an "at risk kid"

I know, I'm gonna go bitch the head of the department on monday, I won't be satisfied until then!!

all I can hope for is she gets in a car wreck and dies a horrid death!

you are so vengeful....remind me never to piss you off

I know, just the way I am. I like you I wouldn't be that way to you even if I was mad

no you'd just bitch slap me-HA.

nah I wouldn't do anything to you.

Im just kidding

I noticed

well I feel special then...you wouldnt wish any horrid things on me....thats sweet-haaha

you really do look for the bright side in all situations

yeah I guess I do. Lucky for you

I don't know, I'm just sick of the coastal teachers who are miserable pieces of shit, who seem to get off making everyone else miserable.....It's like hating your job, but I can't quit it you know.........why lucky for me??

I just meant lucky cause if I wasnt that way and seen the best in people and situations....we may not hang out

Jeez thats horrible

no it isnt Im saying its a good thing Im not a shallow bitch!!

oh so now I'm not good looking enough?

OMG! Not even.....you know what Im talking about. For gods sakes the first time I met you you were telling me youliked to have 1 night stands with fat chicks...any other girl would have probably either slapped you or exited in disgust

haha, I was just fucking with u anyways.

Uhhhh..

you can take a joke, I give you that

gee thanks

I don't remember saying any of that stuff. I think the fat chick thing was later on

you were going on about finding random girls in bars to take home and bullshit like that

nah, wasn't me....must have been some otehr guy.

nope def you

ha, jeez...how did that work on you?

you're the only one who's ever taken that approach. I guess ok....I still talk to you

haha, either that or ur easy to impress.....see my pathetic approach works....people feel sorry for you when u fuck fat girls

whatever...I didnt feel sorry for you.....I knew you were full of shit

ahh, good call.......I really have never fucked a fat girl in my life

yeah I know

I really like talking about it and writing about it though.....it's like reverse bragging......oh you fucked a model, well I fucked a nasty fat girl! tkae that

haha..yeah Im not sure that really works..."

xoxo

"It's ok, I just miss you a hell of a lot and I'm pretty lonely with you gone, sad but true"

xoxo

Dear XXXXX,

I really miss having you in my life. Not a day goes by that I don't think about you and pine over you and feel like something just isn't right in my life. I didn't really realize how happy you made me, but you really did. And, to be honest there haven't been too many happy days for me since you left. Being with you and hanging out with you all the time was a lot of fun and sure always felt right to me, and I know you felt that way as well. To say I'm fucked up over you is quite the understatement, and I probably deserve it, since most of this is my own fault. I would do or give just about anything to fix everything and have you back. I have to try though. I can't let my dream girl just slip through my hands and not care, and not at least try everything I can to somehow win you over again. You mean everything to me and I don't really want to live the rest of my life without you or as just a casual friend, that much I do know. Really, other than me just being myself and trying to be there for you, I don't really know what else to do to have you again.

xoxo

She sucks my cock as I take pictures of "the act." She moved her mouth and lips down my cock and then back up to the head as I take pictures of "the act." She takes my cock out of her mouth and licks and sucks one of my testicles as I take a picture of "the act." She then sucks the other one of my testicles as I take pictures of "the act." She goes back to moving up and down on my cock as I take pictures of "the act." A few minutes later I shoot a shitload of cum inside of her mouth as I take pictures of "the act." She sprints into the bathroom gagging and spits my cum into the toilet as I don't take pictures of "the act." I sit on the edge of my bed, sweat dripping down my head and face while cum continues to slowly drip out of the tip of my cock as I take pictures of "the pathetic act."

xoxo

"The Fall of Lethargy and Hate Mail"

I'm original
you
only fucked
an
original,

which
doesn't make you
an
original,

just
the same,

average
boring
normal
drama filled
mentally numb
text message queen
Coach purse toting
light beer drinking
too much makeup wearing
pointy shoe buying
Japanese car driving
stupid cunt
that

you were

before

fucking

an original,

I left my

DNA

in your

vagina

and esophagus,

these are the

past remnants

that you

fucked

an original

once.

xoxo

I went to the urologist and sat there for a while. I looked at some sports magazine, but didn't actually read any of it because I don't even like sports. I forgot to bring a book so there's not much else to do or read other than filling out lots of bullshit paperwork, like six or seven pages worth. No, I don't have diabetes. No, I don't have AIDS. No, I don't have any insurance. Yes, I have allergies. What's your Social Security number? Then I had to sign this, date this, sign and date that. I finally got all it filled out and they called me into the office after about an hour wait. At least I got a pretty nurse though. She weighed me and checked my height when I first got back there. She then led me back to another room and I sat there waiting on the doctor. I waited another thirty minutes with nothing to read or do, and the doc finally knocked on the door and came in. Yeah, my balls were hurting for like two months dude. He heard everything down to the most meticulous and boring detail. My dick hurts when leaning this way, shit came out of my dick this night, and then he had me go piss in a cup. He left the room and I sat there in a chair again. He came back and said he didn't find any bacteria in that sample. He then told me to lean down against the table and drop my pants and bend over on the little table in the room. He lubed up his finger on top of the latex gloves he had on. He had big hands and shoved one of his fingers up my ass. It didn't feel too good obviously. I thought I was gonna puke, shit my pants, or cum when he did it. Or, maybe all of them at the same time. He removed his lubed finger from my ass and I pulled my pants back up. He left the room and told me to go piss again. I went into the bathroom once again and pulled down my pants and dribbled the few drops of piss I had left in me into the cup. I sat there with the cup in my hand and looked at my dick, and then looked at the cup, and nothing really happened. I kept pushing and pushing and finally a few more drops came out. I pulled up my pants and got piss on my hands in the process. I washed my hands and I went back into the room and sat down and tried to forget that I'd just been violated by a guy. He came back in the room after a few minutes and got the cup of piss. I apologized for not producing enough piss, and I don't know why. He left and came back a good while later. He said my prostate was filled with pus and white blood cells; he sat down and wrote me a prescription for three months worth of antibiotics. He shook my hand and left the room. I just hope I never have to see this dude again. I folded up the prescription and put it into my pocket. On the way out, I saw the pretty nurse who weighed and measured me; she was in the hallway alone. I walked up to her and asked her "so I guess I can still have sex right?" She said "I don't think it will harm you." I said thanks, paid the checkout lady with a credit card that I can't really pay on, and I walked out past the old men in the lobby reading other sports magazines like I had done previously. I walked out the door and the sun hit me right in the eyes blinding me. Lucky me, I get to take a bunch of bullshit pills for the next three fucking months. This is definitely not the goddamn fucking summer of Brett!

xoxo

"Permeating with Cockroaches"

the bathtub water runs constantly

but only cold now,

the cockroaches scurry

nationalism pride parade

crossing the Atlantic

in plastic bottles wrapped in corporate ad

slogans

to Morocco

prancing hand to thorax

thorax to hand

anointing themselves in burnt sienna

oil,

suicide seems like an option
but someone keeps hiding the bullets,

the clip is exposed
like my guts
the wood smells of
Pine-Sol
discount store variety
the iron feels smooth
like her legs
freshly shaven
greased and ice cold
like her hands,

red paint is scraped from my door
and I committed deadly sins,

a slight knock at the door
no one is there
though
by the time I put my shorts on and
open the door
a greeting card in ultramarine rests against the
screen
is all that's left for me
it's not a holiday though
and it's not addressed to me
it rests half-sealed
on my bed now
driving me insane with child-like

curiosity.

xoxo

Dear XXXXX,

I will always be at least friends with you, even though I might have said differently several times. You knew that as well as I did. You might of had your doubts, but you knew I would be back, and if you didn't then you don't know me very well. I'm very loyal to people I love and care about, and besides that I can't stay away from you anyways, for what reason I don't know, but it's there. I would never betray anything you confided in me, and I haven't. I didn't say anything bad about you to anyone, anything I had to say I always just said it to you. You know that you can trust me; you've always been able to. I don't know what else to do. When I said many times that you're my best friend, I meant it. I know we're nothing and we never hung out or talked very much, but I'm bored without you, and I miss you a hell of a lot. You're the only person I get excited to see or talk to here.

xoxo

I wish you were gone, away from me and out of my mind. I'm sick of writing about you. I'm sick of thinking about you. It's pointless because you could care less. My already low self esteem doesn't need the constant rejection that occurs from you. I'm sick of the self analyzation that I force on myself because of you. I'm tired of trying to figure out why I'm not good enough or what defining quality I don't posses that you want in someone. I bet if I blew you off and acted like an "I could care less about you asshole" you would suddenly like me and I would magically possess that unknown quality that I lacked previously, but I can't do that. It's not me unfortunately. I wear my heart on my sleeve and throw what I think out there. I can't play games and bullshit you. It would be a bigger crime to be untrue to myself then to never have you.

xoxo

Before I fucked her,

"Fuck off!"

"It's so easy to get a rise out of you. You try but it will never happen with me. We both like Rebel Son and agree that your vagina is magical. That's all that matters…."

"I'm not fragile. I'm one tough bitch. Don't underestimate me! Well the mayo thing er got in common, but that's probably about it. I am far from fagile. You like to think tthat go ahead. You don't know anything!"

"Maybe I gotta work until 10"

"Excellent anylysis freud. I just don't like cuddling, never have never will. I don't like crowds or mayonaaise either. You're fragile. Feel free to blame my parents, I do."

"Whatever"

"You aren't an asshole, brett stout, you're a whole ass. I'll try and make it happen. You have never snuggled with anyone or someone broke your heart. Now you're scared to let yourself think outside of "ill fuck you but I hate you when we're done.""

"No not really I was taking the trash out. Pro fucking, anti cuddling. If it will shut you the hell up you can have two minutes of cuddling, but I'm timing it!"

"Ok, lost you with that one"

"I was cracking up thinkint about that night u were here and I was trying to lay on you. You're a weird fucker"

"Oh god that's just way too late for me."

"Promises promises. What about Wednesday night?"

"I know night owl, I can hang with you. If there is fucking, there might have to be cuddling. Can you handle that?"

"Well that wasn't very helpful. When are you available"

"I don't know crazy ass!!!"

"Soon I will be in touch"

"When do you want to fuck again,"

After I fucked her.

xoxo

I called her about 11:30 this morning from somewhere in the middle of nowhere North Carolina. She didn't answer so I left this message:

"Hey XXXXX this Brett. I'm just getting back into town from my Mom's place and I...uhh...basically wanted to talk to you in person face to face. It's kind of weird that I haven't even seen you since all this shit went down or whatever. Anyways, if I could come over later today and we could talk that would be great. You always said you would be there for me if I needed you, well, I guess I'm calling you out on that one. Alright, I hope to hear from you soon, bye..."

The phone call is ended. I was overly nice, part of me wanted to call her an idiotic worthless cunt. She doesn't call, but texts me back at 12:23 p.m. The Slayer ring tone goes off. I feel vibrations on my leg and the song "reign in blood" continues to play. The phone is opened and scrolls to her message.

"I'm not home-not sure what time I'll get in, but I'll call you when I do."

I respond.

"Ok, that's cool, just let me know."

The words "Message Sent" pops up and the phone is closed. Fuck, so she's already out of town huh? And, I bet a million bucks it was to see that dude she's known for what, four days now? How awesome, from me to another guy and then out of town to see him within like three days. Damn, she works fast ehh? This ride somewhere in the middle of nowhere North Carolina just got a lot longer. Good thing I stopped earlier and bought a carton of smokes. They were made for days like these.

xoxo

You bleed me slowly. It's easy to do me in fast these days. I'm sitting here alone with my cigarettes and a dangerous mind. Clint Eastwood flashes across the screen. I hear a door slam. I read the mail and pretend to forget. I tried to forget you today, but I saw you on 17, but you didn't see me. I wondered what you were thinking about when I passed you. I'm an afterthought these days. Please tell me to fuck off and die, it would be a lot easier if I know where I stood with you. Then I could try and forget you. I can't even lie to myself anymore, that's an impossible idea these days.

xoxo

"Of Recalls and Disposable Gas Station Lighters"

cheap

and

disposable,

people and photographs

on barren pages

inside

lonely scrapbooks

long forgotten on wooden shelves,

wilt and curdle,

placenta filled

fetal positions and hangovers

of death

bleached souls
and luxury automobiles
in bottomless drawers
facilitate
impotence and absolute consumption,

Mr. Potato Head
has erectile dysfunction
and hemorrhoids
but only on
Fridays,

the years of sharks
the weeks on end
my blue collar job
under your house
and
this lighter
gives people cancer,

paper clipped nipples
the masses are
milked
in Defiance, Wisconsin
deformed and suicidal
tendencies
horrify some
but not me,

the visitation rights
of
past aches and archery

wounds.

xoxo

Her mole kept freaking me out all night. I couldn't help but stare at it. It had it's own combover for fuck's sake. I wanted to ask her what it was, or why she didn't at least shave the fucking hair off of the giant mole on her arm. I would've shaved it for her. I didn't reject her because of the hairy mole though. I rejected her because she was fucking insane.

xoxo

Dear XXXXX,

I don't know what's wrong with you, but you know damn well we had a lot of fun and good times together. I had a great time for the most part and I don't regret any of it, to me, we became a hell of a lot better friends for doing it then we would have ever been if we didn't. I'm really sorry the last like month and a half was so horrible for you, but I know at least up until my graduation and my art show you weren't that fucking miserable and so insanely unhappy. Again, I apologize, I know I was to blame for some of your unhappiness, and I take responsibility for it. But, the large majority of it is all on you. I can't help the fact that you're neurotic, and constantly change your mind and never know what the hell you want, when you want it, who you want to be with, where you want go, or what you want to do. You're happy, you're unhappy, you love me, you don't love me, I'm awesome, you can't stand me, I make you happy, I don't make you happy, you want to be with me, you want to date other people. I mean in Miami we're talking about moving away somewhere together, and you say we have to move somewhere close so we can be near my mom. Then, not too long ago you're getting mad at your friends and leaving a party for defending me being the father of your kids and starting a life with me. So, to go from that to somehow now it was nothing but absolute misery and it was all a giant mistake for you to be with me is a great example of the craziness I'm talking about. And, especially since I didn't do anything to cause it, you're the one that went crazy and ran off. Seriously, what level-headed person could ever make sense of all that insanity? I care and I tried to help, but fuckin' ehh I'm not a clinical psychologist, so I could only help out so much. But, we're still friends even after all of this, so I guess let the fucking misery continue…

xoxo

"The Mortification of Plastic and Honor"

A blistering sun

is

scratched and sniffed,

another day
another nightmare,

a quixotic life
some
call it a
death
in my bed
smelling of body odor
perspiration
drooling
into the Black Sea
car crashes of Ukrainian origin
and
domesticated rain
outside my stained
window
anura subarctic
inside my stained window
sarcasm: to tear the flesh
cannibals love gelatin
on
Lake Titicaca
nocturnal and camouflaged
exposed dermis
enriched adipose tissue
feast my friends
for respiration and absorption
my uncle is a perverted and demented
tooth fairy
in my bed
in my dreams

pulling and prodding

my

limp soul

my

molars

my

canines

my

incisors

for structural damage

and loose change

awoken

by my own

Apocalypse Now

no

VHS or DVD

has been inserted

nor played

hard piss

and

thoughts of masturbation

water is a hazardous material

nebulous clouds removed,

a blistering sun

is

scratched and sniffed,

another day

another nightmare.

xoxo

"hey that was cajun chicken pasta you wanted right?

no

uhh ok, what do u want

thai chicken

ahh alright

really you dont have to cook

it's no big deal, I already have the chicken and pasta and shit, I just needed to know what flavor you wanted

ok well I appreciate it...I love when you cook.

yea well u won't let me do manly shit like change a battery or a tire so I guess I might as well be a gay cook...ha

haha...whatever, Im the best girlfriend ever......I didnt call you cuz I didnt want you to miss trivia

you're talking crazy talk! uhhh, I'm scared...where's my blankie

anyways, I'll bring it over about 730

haha....ok thats fine. Sorry for the scare-just kidding

it's ok, I only had a minor stroke, luckily the soft carpet padded my fall

well as long as you're still functional...promise it wont happen again

haha, calm down......I'm just messing around

i am calm.....just wanted to scare you alittle-its funny

it's not nice! my heart is old, blackened and weak

ok well...never another word about bf/gf ever.....honestly its not good for me either

it's ok I need to be scared once in a while

anyways, I know a great thai chicken marinade, so it should be pretty good

yummy sounds good

do u want anything else? like a breadstick or something...

no just the chicken

yes em

haha...thanks

no problem

right...off the subject bring walk the line tommorow

I will, it's in my car still

oh cool

yeah

I also got into the wild, maybe we can watch it

ok, not sure what that is

or just keep it simple, food and fucking!

haha, yeah well…"

xoxo

The bartender of my favorite local drinking hole came out of the back door of the bar and caught us making out on the trunk of her Japanese produced compact car. I looked over at him and gave him a wink. He said something that I couldn't hear and closed the door. We were going at it so hard I hardly noticed the shitload of cops on bicycles that pass us by. They didn't say anything and I was glad they were too lazy to hassle us. My boner kept poking her through my pants. I tried to put my hand down her pants, but they had no buttons and were so goddamn tight that I could only grab a little bit of her blue colored panties. I liked it when pants and shirts and shit used to have buttons. In these modern times it's getting really hard to grab a handful of vagina anymore.

xoxo

Dear XXXXX,

Just because you fuck a 40-year-old lame ass fucking used car salesman behind my back that doesn't make you more mature or promote any sort of personal growth, it just makes you a fucking idiot, a liar, and a total lame ass. If you treat best friends this way you don't deserve many, which is also why you don't have many. Yeah, you have a couple, and they're just as clueless and generic as you are XXXX #2. In fact, I've met bacteria that were smarter and more interesting. You're clueless. It's interesting that you still "don't get" a lot of this and I pretty much have had to beat you over the head repeatedly and talk down to you for you to understand that "oh, maybe pulling the shit like you did was pretty shitty and maybe you don't treat best friends and much less people like that if you want to keep them in your lives, and it might seem a little contradictory to say you love and care about them on top of that." Let me tell you, I agree that you have really grown in the past month or so, from an awesome human being that was really decent and had morals to a nutty new age slutty buffoon who can't even think for herself. Wow, I'm so impressed that I don't even want to know you. Please, as a former friend XXXX II de-evolve! You know even less about relationships than I do, perhaps you maybe need to work on your comprehension skills a little and actually really understand what those relationship books that you read are saying. The problem isn't me, it's you. You're never gonna find a dream guy out there, he doesn't exist, and frankly you don't deserve him even if he did. I may stink in a few areas of when it comes to relationships, but every guy will in one way or another and probably in worse ways than I do, because most would lie to you and cheat on you. Good luck finding someone that doesn't do that shit. What guy is gonna wanna listen to a bunch of wacko weak-minded new age nonsense about spirit guides and how Sedona, Arizona is some cosmic area you need to visit to become one with the universe just to get some pussy? Not many, let me tell you. Perhaps, I could suggest, since you want to be and think so much like her, you and XXXX could become lesbians and that way you could both have someone to be with and listen to each other's stupid wacko bullshit. I don't hate you, because basically you aren't worth the energy that it would take to do it. I just want nothing to do with you. Whatever…

xoxo

The Tecate beer cans were empty. It was time. Time to fuck that is. There was no more delaying it. Our lips met and genitalia was fondled. Wetness and erections occur. Legs are spread. Me on top, her on the bottom. Our lips meet again. Necks are kissed, and breasts are molestered. Wetness on phalanges enter darkened holes. Pants on, both removed now. No, don't eat my pussy; just fuck me now she says. My penis now two inches away. Do you have a condom? No, I don't. Are you fucking serious? Yeah baby, I am. I thought you just went to the clinic? I did, but they didn't give me any this time. Besides, I fucked the same girl for two years why would I need any condoms? Nothing is said after that for a minute. I don't have anything, shit, I've been poked and prodded like cattle and I don't have shit I swear. Besides, you just rubbed my dick all over your pussy, so whatever you have, I have now. Good point she says. She grabs my penis and moves it inside of her. Her hole is finally penetrated after all these years, pitch dark, brown couch, and movie playing. You fucking towelhead!

xoxo

"Where Rough Silicone Meets Smooth Sandpaper"

fucking lost,

in

the basement torture chambers

of

my past conscience,

yet,

no one

is putting my face

on the sides of

milk cartons

and

no one

is pasting flyers

of me

on the exterior

of

wooden telephone poles,

fucking lost,

in

the basement torture chambers

of

my future conscience,

no one

is making phone calls

no one

is going door-to-door

no

past sexual predators are being questioned

and

my face does not appear late at night

on

local shitty television channels,

fucking lost,

in

the basement torture chambers

of

my present conscience.

xoxo

I don't even care about fucking her anymore. I like her, I really do. But, in my mind how many times can I fuck the same goddamn woman over and over until I get bored? Well, I guess the answer is like 138 according to the rings on my dick.

xoxo

I almost asked her to be my girlfriend today. My common sense appeared out of nowhere and I changed my mind on that idiotic idea. Pussy, my friend can make you do some dumb ass shit. You come back from it like you've been in a goddamn war in Iraq, wondering what the hell just happened to you. Post-traumatic stress pussy disorder, that's what they should call it.

xoxo

She won't speak to me. I called her "sugar tits" and deleted her ass. I said it would be harder for her to spy on me now. Though, not really, she just has to type in my name now. I text her sometimes when I'm drunk confessing my love for her, my boredom without her, and that I sold a watercolor painting of her to a random drunk person at my art show. There is never any response. I'm starting to think that she was lying when she said that we'd always be niggers.

xoxo

Status Update:

In the span of day, my entire world (XXX) came crashing down, and now I feel like crawling into a PBR bottle for six months...

xoxo

"I apologize if some the previous letter was a bit harsh here and there. I wasn't trying to make anything worse for you or jab you like Mike Tyson. You sort of caught me off guard with your comments and emotions when I ran home last night half drunk after trivia to take a dump and grab my camera. I still don't know what to make of this or how to react to it. I suppose I should contemplate for a while, and then not have any new answers...haha. I thought you were all happy and everything was going right for you with me being gone and exiled on Corsica?"

"Honestly I dont know what to make of it either. I just freaked out and felt like I may lose you from my life all together. I understand you are free To do what you want. I have decided that I would rather suffer you having a girlfriend, or whatever you may be calling her, than to lose you all together. Im sure she dislikes me greatly. I dislike myself at times. Im the most confused person I know right now, and that says alot seeing that Im friends w/ XXX and XXX-LOL Like I said Im just going to remain drunk for awhile and see what happens-haha. Its really not humorous at all, but I have to deal w/ this somehow. Im sorry you have felt that I didnt care because I do and I think (hope) deep down you know that"

xoxo

"Don't worry, you won't lose me unless you find a way to kill me...ha.......

thats refreshing............ i guess???

I guess so, but oh wait I'm a dick and only love myself...according to you...haha

i never said such!?!?

it was something deroggatory like that...haha

when, where, what the hell r u talking about?????|

I made it up

i should say

haha, sucker!"

xoxo

You can't have absolute love without having absolute hate to go along with it. That's just part of the process I believe, but what do I know right? If someone reads the stuff I write about you they will probably think that you are the biggest cunt that ever lived. But, that's actually not the case. You're amazing, beautiful, talented, weird, sweet, interesting, smart, insane, complex, fun, and a million other great adjectives that I'm too lazy to type. I would kill anyone that ever hurt you. I'm willing to do life in prison for you and probably rarely regret it, now that's true love.

xoxo

"Contemplating my Monotonous Rooster"

I don't want a pretty cock,

I want a cock,

used

scarred

burned

gnawed

chaffed

circumcised

raped

ugly

and obscenely abused,

I don't want to die with a pretty cock,

I want to die with a cock,

used

scarred

burned

gnawed

chaffed

circumcised

raped

ugly

and obscenely abused.

xoxo

Hi XXXXX,

Well, I just called to give you a genuine apology. I didn't think you would read the messages I sent you. You probably thought they were more hate mail. Anyways, not that it means all that much, but I'm really sorry for calling you some mean names and saying a lot of stuff that was out of line, and, well, pretty awful. I shouldn't have said any of that to you and I hope that eventually you can forgive me for doing it. I never was an asshole or treated you like shit, so I didn't want to go out like that. I don't even know why I did it. Anyways, again, I'm really sorry. Alright, I'll see you later.

xoxo

Received:

"Hey I got your email. I really do miss hanging out w/you, just so u know…"

Respond:

"Thanks. I miss u a lot as well. I didn't mean that stuff I said to you. I'm sorry. I do want you in my life though, it doesn't feel right with you gone"

Received:

"I know I understand ur hurt and I'm sorry"

Respond:

"Yeah, I am still hurting, I can't help it, u mean a lot to me. I just need a little time. I do hope we can be friends still and hangout again in a while."

xoxo

"Long Walks on the Beach with the Antichrist"

I molest her dress
with a dead rooster
and
a deader soul,

the bee's knees
have lost
and retreat
while pressing
on demand,

the red drunken pavement
drips
memories and
condensation,

Satan wears
a
blackened dress with matching
heels
and a matching purse,

inhaling Russian vodka
the iceberg melts
Rasputin's gypsy hands
make waves

on

ants and uncut grass,

vomit your soul

Cinderella

on your knees,

bring the garbage in

take the cigarettes out

shut the door

piss in the sink,

forever

now sleep

darling.

xoxo

You said even after all the bullshit that I made you happy. I know that you meant it, well because you said it a lot, so I have to really. What's most baffling is why you keep saying as your reason for all of this is you just had to see what made you happy. That's something I have yet to make any sense of, and perhaps, I wasn't meant to understand it.

xoxo

I pass an underage girl in a gas station. I look at her with lust and an insatiable sexual appetite. I was here for a Big Grab of Doritos but now I want more. I want your tight young fucking snatch! I stare at her ass as I wait behind her. Goddamn, what I would I give to fuck that! It will never happen though. My dream of fucking her dies as she pays for her items and exits the store. My love dies there, in line at the gas station.

xoxo

"so does this mean I can go on some dates with whores...or?.....haha, u tramp!

im not going on any date

u better not! or will have to get crazy..

haha, id like to see that

by crazy, I mean crying alone in my room!

oh well i dont want u to do that

damn right, someone might get hurt. Could you live with yourself knowing you killed all those tissues! I don't know about you, but I couldn;t live with that on conscience!

haha, of course never

I thought so!

haha"

xoxo

I like this girl. She's the first one I've liked in a long time. It's refreshing to discover someone worthy of hanging out with. Most people are a waste of my time and effort. I have yet to feel that way with her. I sound pathetic, and for some reason I alright with it for now.

xoxo

"Aloha there XXXXX. I need not say who this is, since you have caller ID. I was just calling to see how you were in general and see how your tests came out. Hopefully all is good in that department and you don't have "gingervitis." I read online that garlic wards off evil spirits, so perhaps maybe I could go out and panhandle enough change to buy you a bottle. I know my heart is much bigger than my dick. Anyways, I'll see ya later tater…"

xoxo

"Spelling Misogynist Right on Purpose"

you're too normal

too normal

for me to fuck

anyways

I want to slap you

in the face

and

call you a dirty

fucking whore

when I stick my cock

inside

of you

I want to lick your

asshole

and cum

in your face

but

I don't

because you're respectable

and don't like

perverted shit

like that.

xoxo

Breathing…pause…birthdays, breakdowns, and bullshit. I've been there through them all…pause…some of the dumbest fucking shit I've ever seen. And, I was there…pause…comforting, listening, talking, and trying to understand, even though I thought most of it was ridiculous and silly and I wanted say toughen up soldier, but I guess it's hard saying that to a girl. And, when you love someone you try and deal with all their bullshit. I guess that was the evil Brett coming out and trying to be tamed by the good Brett. I sit here alone…cough…alone in front of the TV, a drill in my hand fixing a door. I forgot how much I actually enjoyed working on stuff like I did in my previous other shit construction jobs. That's the stuff I did all day and I got paid very meagerly to do it for complete strangers…but, pause…the door isn't being a bitch like it was last time when I just gave up and said "fuck it" and left. Besides that, everything is alright I guess. Pause…I sent her a text message 57 minutes ago and I said "I hope that you have a fantastic Valentines Day" and that was it. It was so nondescript, that really, did I mean it? I don't know. Was there probably some…pause…pinching sarcasm in it? I would say yes…pause… lighting a cigarette. A spark and inhalation…probably so. But, the beauty of that is that the person on the other end doesn't really know for sure if it is. Within a text message there isn't any emotion. It is what it is. It's like reading words on a computer screen. You don't really know what they mean in tone sometimes. You're like "I don't uhh, yeah, really know." A lot of it is acronyms now, and letters mean this and words mean that…whatever. So it's very interesting I don't know…anyways. Pause…puffing on cigarette and breathing heavily. Who fucking knows! Pause…a long pause…and more smoking…I know I had it rough earlier. I was feeling like shit. I was getting fucking crazy in the head, wanting to do crazy shit. Confessing my problems to no one but myself… pause…to people I don't even know asking them for their advice. Seeing what the deal was, seeing if they knew some shit about life and love that I don't. I'm a novice and a project and I don't know much in this department. Plato once said that he was the smartest man in the world because he knew nothing. I like that. I don't know anything right now. Really if she called me four times in a day, she would get four different personalities, four different sides of me, anger, humiliation, acceptance, hope, vindication, and the fucking abyss. Ok, that's like six, but whatever. I don't know what I feel right now at 5:41 p.m. on 2/14/09. The whole world has come crashing down and I don't know what to do. She hasn't responded yet. I wonder if she will. She didn't respond yesterday. So, who knows? She probably ran off with whom, I don't know, some other fucking dude to some other fucking place to have some carefree great time. I don't really know. That's my worst case scenario. Something tells me in my gut that's the truth in this case. I sit confessing to a box, a silver box of batteries. Recording every stupid tedious thought I have that maybe one day I'll laugh at it or I'll get some stupid story out of it. Or, it'll remind me of the misery that I was in at the time. There are no answers, even though I'm a million miles from where the incident took place. There's no internet, no traffic, nothing familiar, no one familiar; out in the fucking middle of nowhere, and I don't feel any better. But, I didn't know if I would when I came up here. At least I'm not there pining away in my nerd cave feeling shitty and rejected...pause...breathing ...and not knowing what to do. Pause...smoking...if I could have her back, would I even want her? I don't know. A lot of the time I knew her all I wanted was something else, a way out, any excuse I could find to keep domestication at bay. And, now that she isn't here, she's all I want. That doesn't make any sense. So, maybe I've been confused longer that I thought. I don't even know what to do with her. In the span of a day it all came crashing down. And, since then, for the past...pause...four days...pause...I've been insane. I wish there was an ending to it. I would feel better. It would be over, this fucking nightmare. That's what it feels like, that's what it is. If I could pinch myself and I think I would wake up, you know alarm clock beeping and just wake up. This is your wake up call. You got nothing to wake up for, but get up. And, everything would be exactly like it was one week ago. But, I don't think that's the way it's gonna be. Unfortunately, reality is a complete and utter nightmare. Some of the times anyways, other times not so much...pause...so...I'm just sitting here smoking too many cigarettes, drinking sweet tea, and eating a chicken sandwich. There's no remedy to the fucking curse I have. Very few things could make me feel better right now. A detox of the brain, where do they sell that at? I don't think they sell that at CVS, Bi-Lo, Kroger, Walgreens, Target, Sprawlmart, or gas stations. Where is my detox? Where is the pill that you take where you feel like you have a future, something to wake up for? Pause...silence...And, I don't think that's ever a job. I don't know, so what then, some passion, yeah there's some there...but...pause...tomorrow I know that when I wake up completely isolated and alone in the world...long pause...and there's no one to talk to and no one to confess anything to, only a small silver square box with batteries... cough...pause...a horrible time without an antidote. When I go back there to the city I live in, what will it be like? What's it gonna be like? That's the question. Will it be complete misery the second I see Myrtle Beach on the highway? Have a great day; now go directly to the box. Sit there, watch TV, paint, jerk off, listen to music, eat alone, walk on the beach, and drink large amounts of shitty booze. Will there be any happiness? Will there be a giant void inside of me? Yes, you can't fix it with Play-Do either, so I'm probably fucked. I don't know what fixes it. Time and booze maybe. Time and booze, but even that has its limits though. Pause…I don't know. I guess I'll figure it out somehow. I don't hear an alarm clock waking me up from this nightmare anytime soon, that much I do know.

xoxo

"I've been drinking vodka all day. I heart u, lets go on a picnic and listen to Noel's silent morning"

xoxo

Dear XXXXXXXX,

So what fucked up mysterious thing did I do now? I don't understand why you haven't even said hello to me in like three fucking months. I've wanted to give up on you XXXXXXXXX for a very long time, but for some reason I never do. I've called, texted, and e-mailed your ass to no avail! Are you too fucking cool now or something? I know that I'm supposed to be some tattooed bad ass and not care or something, but it still hurts my feelings when someone I care about acts like a complete fucking bitch to me for no reason at all!!!!!!!!!!!!!!!!!!

xoxo

"I wish I had your carefree attitude

Ha, yeah i bet u do

Haha…indeed, ur inspiring

i know.....thats why u keep me around-haha

is that why?

i suppose??

wrong, keen hearing haha…

oh yeah the elf ears...i can warn you when danger is still miles away

I know, it comes in handy at the beach. wouldn't wanna be caught in a storm

ok so now Im your protector?

no, your my elf.

oh cool. there were some really cool elves in Lord of the rings

indeed, I figure one day u might let me in on the cookie and toy fortunes

thats reserved for bf status-LOL

ok, how about just some free samples?

haha

you've actually gotten lots of "samples"...its really not fair.

oh, I forgot to mention that AAA will come out and jump u off if it ever happens again

ok well the problem was I didnt know what was wrong with my car

I had no idea it was the battery

well stinky samples don't count, I don't appreciate being the guinea pig for that new fish flavored elfin cracker! haha, dummy! I can show u how to change the battery out, I can even give you a pair of pliers

i have pliers..but the guy at the auto parts store did it for free, I will just go back ther

no, u will call me!

ok...unless you have something else going on that I know about. I wouldnt feel right taking you away from your plans

get out of here!

what? Im serious, I couldnt call anyone else they were the only people who didnt have plans to do anything

man, u must think I'm a crappy friend......who cares, trivia is just a hobby.....if u need me I'll be there

i know you would!!!

unless it's something to do with emotions, then I might have to make up some fake important plans...haha

haha...well its good you didnt come cause if you aoule've saved me it would have probably made me want you even more.....and thats just not a good thing for me-lol

I put my cape on one leg at a time, just like everyone else

see, no saving the day..that would be to overwhelming for me

haha, jeez I didn't know turning a few bolts was that impressive

well its the idea, and its you...so that makes it different

haha, yes I feel a story coming on....he saved the day, then I went psycho over him

haha..see im good for story ideas too-lol

Yeah, I've gotten a few from u for sure..

i guess thats good...even if they are nuts

ahh yes well, I must take creative leave with it

ok well i gotta go to bed..

alright, I will see u tomorrow...food in hand

you're awesome my little cooterific crime fighter...lol

thanks

talk to ya later"

xoxo

Dear XXXXX,

Thinking about it now I feel like an idiot for actually ever caring about you. Even though you'd fucked me over, I still really thought about being your friend somehow down the line. But, your attitude and stupid fucking hand and eye gestures after everything I said made it real easy for me, so thanks for that you fucking cuntbag.

xoxo

I slept horribly last night. I knew when I woke up that I'd made a mistake. There was no point in even moving. All I did today was lay on the couch, watch TV, burn a frozen pizza, watch more TV, beat off, and then finally go to bed once again. Maybe tomorrow I will have a reason to live.

xoxo

Hey!!!

Good morning!!!

Hey what's up hottie????

Hey!!

Have a great morning!!!!

Hi!

Hi, good morning!!!!

Hi cutie!!!!

What's up baby?????

Hi!!!!

There's no response from me, yet the early morning texts of "hi" followed by an extreme amount of exclamation points followed.

Fuck you asshole!!!!!!

Talk to me!!!

Hey!!!

Good morning!!!

Hey what's up hottie????

Hey!!

Have a great morning!!!!

Hi!

Hi, good morning!!!!

Hi cutie!!!!

What's up baby?????

Hi!!!!

Fuck you!!!!!

No, it's not. The hand spreading that pussy is gigantic. And, for that matter that pussy is bigger than my head, so there's no way that's your pussy unless you gained like 300 pounds since your "modeling pics."

That's me I swear.

No not really that vagina picture you sent me is off of a fat girl. I can see the rolls for fuck's sake. You claimed to be a super model and your pictures online are insanely hot, so something is rotten in Denmark here.

Do you not wanna talk to me anymore?

Hey!!!

Good morning!!!

Hey what's up hottie????

Hey!!

Have a great morning!!!!

Hi!

Hi, good morning!!!!

Hi cutie!!!!

What's up baby?????

Hi!!!!

Hi, sexy this is XXXXXX

Finally, she did while I was at work.

I told her to send me a picture of her goddamn fucking cunt already!

I lied and said "yeah they're nice."

They were alright. I couldn't really see much though. It was sort of fuzzy.

She sent me a picture of her tits first.

I thought she was too hot in her pictures so I convinced her to send me a picture of her pussy.

I was tired of being woken up at seven in the morning by such a fucking retarded person saying nothing more than "hi" followed by an extreme amount of exclamation points.

I wanted to degrade her.

I was bored talking to her after an hour.

I had to turn off my phone late at night when I went to bed.

She was insane and texted me every single fucking day at like seven in the goddamn morning saying "hi" with lots of exclamation points.

Hey!!!

Good morning!!!

Hey what's up hottie????

Hey!!

Have a great morning!!!!

Hi!

Hi, good morning!!!!

Hi cutie!!!!

What's up baby?????

Hi!!!!

Then she wouldn't stop texting me.

We talked for a while about life.

She responded.

I pathetically gave her my phone number.

I pathetically messaged the hottest girl I could find.

I pathetically joined a dating site.

xoxo

I took her jeans and panties off. And, there staring back at me was a giant hairy "yeti pussy." My fucking lord, this girl is her twenties what the fuck is she doing with a "yeti pussy" between her legs I thought to myself while I kissed her? I contemplated the who/what/when/where/why of this "yeti pussy" scenario. Had no one ever told her that a "yeti pussy" was fucking awful and hideous? Had no other guy that she'd ever fucked not complained about the "yeti pussy?" Perhaps, they were bitches or scared to tell her for fear of her getting offended and not fucking them. Had she just been lazy for a quite a while and not felt like shaving the "yeti pussy?" Her legs aren't hairy because I felt them when I took her pants and panties off earlier, so she has access to a goddamn razor, so that can't be the issue. I play with the "yeti pussy" with my index and middle finger, even though it was grossing me out with all those little pubic hairs rubbing and frolicking against my skin. Yak, I can't take this shit. She's pretty goddamn good looking and otherwise seems well maintained. She comes from a decent family as far as I know, so how the fuck could she not know to shave her "yeti pussy?" Has she not discussed this amongst her friends? I don't read goddamn Glamour magazine or any of that shit, but I know there's gotta be articles in some of these girly magazines all these white women read concerning the subject of pussy hair maintenance. Goddamn it, this sucks! I gotta do this girl a favor and mention something about the "yeti pussy." I cannot be those other dickheads that obviously kept their fucking mouths shut about the "yeti pussy." I kiss her and then pull away and say "I hate fucking pussy hair, how about you let me shave that shit for you?"

xoxo

"Can we fuck when you get back?"

"Wow I was a mess. We're boarding now"

"Yeah you were kind of mean. It was tacky but funny. You can't have sex with me anymore cause you wanna get married and I don't want to marry you"

"Oh jeez, I obviously drank myself retarded.."

"That could been fun. Until you got drunk and said you couldn't hang out with me anmore cause I might hurt your feelings…ha"

"Ill miss you, jerk off later and send me a sexy pic please sir"

"Ok, I'll see what magic dick tricks I can pull off for you."

xoxo

"I Framed a Picture of My Cock and Hung it on Her Face"

Her red highlighted hair flashes

like streaks of

fire-laced lightning

her red highlighted hair covered my entire

lap

my chair

my new chair

I bought

for ninety-nine dollars

at Office Depot
three days ago
it
had a little back vibrator
on it
I reached down
between red highlighted hair
dead on my lap
gestures
and movements
the ON
button
was pressed
my ass and back now
slowly vibrated
her soft
pale
hand grabbed
rooster death lock
flashes of red
like streaks of red highlighted
fire-laced lightning
I grab handfuls of that red lightning
and press down
gag
cough
spit
now flowed
rivers
of white
perching comfortable
on that red lightning highlighted

hair

and on my

new

ninety-nine dollar chair

that I bought at

Office Max

just three days

ago.

xoxo

I'm sitting on a weathered bench in old North Florida. The heat is sweltering and salty sweat is running down my face and back soaking both my shirt and my already twice previously worn dirty underwear. A multitude of gnats swarm around my head and feet. The wooden bench I'm sitting on is rotting and broken and is hurting my ass. The sign across the street says "no parking after midnight cars will be towed." The street is quiet other than the occasional car that passes me by. An old lady comes out of her house and pours water on some flowers. She disappears soon after. Something is biting my legs now just above my socks. I light a cigarette and the smell of the tobacco fills the sweet Southern air. Moss is hanging from trees and a hippie is now playing an acoustic guitar at a distance behind me. It feels like the humidity is strangling me with every passing second. Sweat continues to pour down my face. I wipe it off with my Black Flag band shirt, which was already soaked with sweat so it doesn't do much good really. All this does is push the sweat into my eyes even more. I haven't been this hot since New Orleans a while back. Fat tourists pass me as I sit on the bench. They're on their way to the nice tourist restaurants and their fucking air conditioned hotel rooms. All I have is my seven cigarettes, my old wooden weathered bench, and a long wait while my special lady friend shops for clothes that she doesn't really need anyways. It's not much, but it's home, for now anyways.

xoxo

I miss her. It's like it was before. There is no healing me. I'm glad I'm blocked though. I can't see anything and I now live in ignorance. Perhaps it's a little easier on me now. But, she's still there in my head, never leaving. I was in the parking lot of Cracker Barrel the other day and I accidentally dialed her number instead of my mom. It was a Freudian slip or something. I caught myself just as the first ring went through. I don't think it registered or went through though, at least I hope not. I look forward to accidentally calling here again. Maybe I'll see her Saturday. Who knows though, she might avoid it just to not see me. I wonder if she misses me at all. I have no answers to anything and live in ignorance now. I don't like it. I miss watching my favorite fucked up reality show, her life.

xoxo

"Spitting Teeth and Eating Fried Chicken: Part Deux"

Clear your mind of fucking,

pardon
my interruption
of
self inflicted
bruises
and contusions,

clear your mind of fucking,

of
self-inflicted destruction
cheap booze
memories
vandalism
and masturbation,

clear your mind of fucking,

of
french fries
Cheeto's
and
black garbage bags,

clear your mind of fucking,
and

take a shit

read the newspaper

that costs

a

fucking dollar

and

learn nothing

take a walk into

the late night

mist,

and,

clear your mind of fucking.

xoxo

We kiss outside of my apartment complex. I taste the cigarettes on her lips and on her breath. I just quit the other day so I'm finally beginning to notice what all the non-smokers tasted and dealt with when they kissed me. It's Halloween and my face is painted white and has rubbed mostly off of my face and onto hers during our make out session in front my apartment complex. She looks like a goddamn mime now. Her lips are soft though, no doubt about that. I try and grab her tits while we're kissing. I don't really get very far, just a tit brush really. I ask her is she wants to come inside. She says no, that she's a lady or some shit like that. I don't say anything back to her, mainly because I couldn't think of anything to say really. I try and kiss her again, but she moves her head away. I sit there for a minute or two and then I say goodbye and get out of her car. I wave goodbye to her as she and her black car that's cooler than mine leaves my apartment complex. I went upstairs and jerked off to internet porn, ate some Teddy Grahams, and went to bed in no particular order.

xoxo

Dear XXXXX,

This is so fucking stupid. We used to be so close and hangout all the time. It didn't have to be this way, and I wish it wasn't. Bizarro XXXXX, it reminds me of when they had a series of Batman comics called Bizarro Batman. I feel like I hardly know you anymore. It's so fucking dumb. I miss you though, and it all seems so different now. You have to be drunk to admit that you miss me, but

I'm glad that you do. It does make me feel better and less pathetic.

xoxo

Numbers are touched into a phone by a dirty black stained thumb:

"Hey, what's up?"

"Uhmm…nothing really, just baking some gingerbread cookies."

"I see. Are you going to make me another cookie shaped like a cock?"

"No, silly, just regular gingerbread men for work tomorrow."

"Ahh, cool."

"Are you at your grandmother's house already?"

"No, there was a slight problem…"

"I drove up past Florence and my car broke down."

"Oh no…"

"While I was out looking at what was wrong with the engine some fucking asshole drove past me and called me a faggot. It was really weird. I thought people were supposed to be nice at least one time during the year, and that's like Christmas time right?"

"Yea, that's generally the rule."

"Like I said who fucking knows, I was more concerned about why the fuck my engine blew up, but having some redneck asshole call me a faggot didn't really help. I just took it and shook it off. What was I supposed to say back you know? No way, you're the faggot or some shit like that. Anyways, just wanted to let you know I would be around."

"If you want to watch a movie later or tomorrow let me know."

"Alright, how about tomorrow?"

"Yeah that's fine."

"You can finally see They Live, it's a fucking classic! If I do say so myself, it is Roddy Piper's finest cinematic moment!"

"Who's Roddy Piper, I've never heard of him?"

"You don't know who Roddy fucking Piper is?…lame ass…"

"No, I'm so sorry."

"Well I'm not telling you, I wish you to remain ignorant of The Piper!"

"I don't care what we watch, at least I won't have to spend Christmas alone like usual."

"Yeah, I guess so, it's nice out and it's just another day to me, it might as well be

March 25th, I don't give a shit you know."

"Yeah, yeah you're such a tough guy."

"Oh yeah, macho fag, that's me. Even if you hate the movie, you can still give me a blowjob…"

"Oh thanks, what a fucking honor."

"Exactly! If you're nice, I might even let you suckle my balls…"

"Great…"

"What a Christmas it will be, Roddy Piper and dick sucking!"

"Alright, I'll see you tomorrow, bye."

"I love you, bye."

The "I love you" is not responded to on the other end. A dirty black stained hand closes a silver phone.

xoxo

I'd been good too long. Well, I definitely made up for being good so long this past Saturday night. These things could only happen while drunk. I'd never had two women before, that was before this past Saturday night. Well, maybe it wasn't two women at the same time, but it sure felt like an orgy at the time. I pulled two women out of a bar with three minutes left until they kicked us all out after last call. At first, I just said goodbye and walked to the gas station to get some shitty food and a coffee. When I came out of the gas station they yelled at me from their car parked in front of the gas station. They wanted to hang out, but they wanted me to know there was no chance of having sex with either of them. I was so drunk that shitty clause sounded fine to me. I'm sure they knew that I would try either way. I went back into the gas station since I didn't have any booze at home other than a half bottle of Jagermeister. I grabbed a six pack of High Life for me and a six pack of Miller Light for them. I was stumbling as I walked to my car and somehow I didn't get pulled over by the cops on the way home. One of the girls started pouring straight Jager shots not long after we walked into the front door. The other girl scoured my record collection and pulled out a Depeche Mode LP and put it on the record player that sat in the corner of my living room. Two beers and one Jager shot in and I was already making out with the hotter of the two sluts. Ten minutes later I had her red panties off and I was eating her shaved pussy on my couch that was covered in black duct tape. The other girl grabbed my camera that was sitting on the table and started taking pictures of me eating her pussy. Soon after, I had my pants off and I was on top of her. She whispered that she wasn't on birth control and I would have to put on a condom. Only, the problem was, I didn't have any condoms. I ran into my room to make sure that I didn't overlook any in the drawer previously. I was right. I went back and laid on top of her grinding my dick into her and whispering in her ear that we didn't really need a condom and I would pull out. After conferring with her friend, she said alright and I slipped my dick inside of her. Every so often her friend would come over and take pictures of us fucking. It was so fucking cool. I really can't remember ever feeling so fucking cool in fact. When we switched to doggy style her friend pulled off her skirt and started masturbating in front of us. If I wasn't so goddamn drunk, I probably would've been way too nerdy and nervous to even do it. I pounded away on the hotter one for almost an hour. Eventually, she said her pussy really hurt so we had to stop, and of course I hadn't cum yet. She gave me a blowjob for a while after that, but I still couldn't cum. I started fingering the other chick after I got up and took a piss. I sniffed her pussy, and it smelled pretty good. I tried to fuck her as well, but she wasn't having any of it. I guess I'm not quite that lucky yet. A few minutes later the two sluts were out of my house and my life. I was on my couch covered in duct tape basking at what had just taken place, while I jerked off. For once in my life I felt truly fucking cool.

xoxo

Status Update:

Brett is riding around in the rain talking to a tape player, while feeling a million miles away from Say Anything.

xoxo

"you should be doing math trivia, we could have made flash cards-haha

haha, no!!!!.....unless if I pass I get the booty, then I would study hard

you should study hard anyway....besides if i gave it up what would you have to look forward to?

lots of booty action?

oh well I didnt think of that. however even if some far off day I did agree to it...i doubt I'd be up for "lots" everyone I ve talked to said its not very pleasant and suprisingly most of my friends have tried it

well no, not the first time.....u gotta get used to it, it probably didn't feel good the first time u had sex either, but u kept trying that

ewww that means you asshole would get all lax and you'd fart uncontrollably and not be able to control your bm's...it happens to gay guys

most people try new things, minus close minded anal people! like u...haha

whatever...i didnt say I d never try it I just need some time

no, I don't think so....I mean if I had a 10 inch dick i woul dbe different. I wouldn't blame u there, but I'm little so it wouldn't be that bad

not really, what ever gave you that impression? seriously it really does happen to gay guys yeah well those guys also put all kinds of shit up there so who knows, fucking lamps and gigantic dildos and shit........hell, I don't know.....I know I don't have some big dick

well whatever, at least its still up for discussion and I havent said no altogether

this is true, I appreciate it and I will have my small victory eventually! I'm average, am I not...u have had some big ones though so maybe not...haha

yep you're like in the 90th percentile, Ive seen a freak large one and a random tiny one...you're just right

haha, sweet......I like mine and I wouldn't trade it for any other one

i like mine too..haha

ha, only because they haven't come up with a bigger one u could get enlarged yet...haha

funny

sometimes

haha

by that 90th percentile, did that mean that my dick is bigger than 90% or 10% of people...I told u my math is horrid

that means your the same size as 90% of guys-at least the ones Ive seen, which hasnt bee that aweful many

ok…lol"

xoxo

She was nervous about telling me. I don't know why really. She didn't seem shy about anything else for the most part. But, telling me what she liked to do when fucking really made her nervous and shy. She finally had a few more drinks and then told me that she liked to feel pain and be choked while being fucked. She was a pretty cool girl actually and even paid for all my booze. Two hours later I was choking her with my right hand and calling her a "fucking vain stupid cunt" in her hotel room near the beach. I left her hotel room near the beach after I came inside of her. I never talked to her again after that.

xoxo

"Poking Things with Sticks"

I poke delicate ideas

with

a

stick,

dreams
of utopia
slowly disappear
with every fragile day
it probably
isn't coming back
but
I hope it will,

I poke delicate ideas
with
a
stick,
explicate it
blow it up like
Timothy McVeigh
sleeping alone and forsaken in
a queen sized comfortable
kiln,

I poke delicate ideas
with
a
stick,
deceased cats whore
hodgepodge
attention
from
television evangelists
isthmus
preconscious
forfeiture of dignity

domicile

coitus on picket fences,

I poke delicate ideas

with

a

stick.

xoxo

I eat her pussy out for what seems an eternity, well, at least until my mouth and jaw are tingling and numb. I put my dick inside of her and start pounding away on her snatch. She's shaved, but prickly, so after a while my dick starts to hurt from the stubble rubbing against the skin of my dick. I feel like my job hasn't been accomplished because she hasn't cum. No matter the hour of pussy eating I did, or the thirty minutes of pounding on her snatch that I did. She says it takes a lot to make her cum and to not get too bummed out about it. She says the only way to make her come is to put my dick in her ass, it just does something to her and makes her cum really fast. I thought to myself "ok, you fucking freak I'll put it in your ass." I grab the bottle of KY lube from the nightstand drawer and pour it all over my dick. She gets in the doggy style position and I jam, poke, force, and spread until I finally get my dick in her tight asshole. I shoved it in there pretty hard, but I guess since she's a fucking freak she didn't say anything or complain about it. I moved it in and out like twenty times while she rubbed her pussy. Soon after, I felt her body moving and shaking and she finally fucking came. I pounded her asshole for a while and then I pulled my dick out of her ass and went into the bathroom and washed the lube and shit off of my dick with antibacterial soap. It didn't really matter since I wasn't wearing a condom anyways, but hey, it made me feel safer anyways. I toweled off my cock and balls and went back to the bed and climbed back on top of her and put my dick back inside of her pussy. I liked her pussy better than her ass for some reason. I continued to pump away on her. At first she told me not to cum inside of her, but now she told me to cum inside of her, so a few more pumps and I filled her snatch with my cum. I guess making her cum changed her mind, who knows?

xoxo

"finally…my day has ended!"

"how was it?"

"fun actually"

"any severed peepees?"

"ran 3 calls…nothing that fucked up"

"any severed peepees?"

" some crazy swiss lady talking to herself and drunk and her husband was cheating on her with another man…haha"

"haha wonderful. how tired are you? like dead or running on low?"

"any severed peepees?"

"I'm ok now…adrenaline rush all day…plus the coffee and a monster energy drink!"

"Ahh ok"

"I jerked off in your mouth this morning…haha"

"haha whattttt? no that never happened"

"I probably did…hmmm…yeah it was nice"

"a mouth full of metal and cum yuuummm"

"I jilled off in your mouth this morning"

"yeah, I almost swallowed some…I would have to give myself the heimlick!"

"i would have let you die and taken advandage of you"

"so you're only a necro whore ehh? I'm sure you peeked at me in the shower"

"I did not peek!!! ok maybe…a little"

"haha, yeah a sillouette of my balls…great site at 630 am. Better than the grand canyon some say"

"not as much as you peeked at my monster tits all night"

"Well yeah, I never denied it!"

"i tried but the periodic table shower curtain is not see through enough. did the nonchalant look over the shoulder when was being good wife material and making the bed"

"that's cool, I don't mind...ha, it was actually nice to have the bed made when I got home though, I would have been more impressed if you had cleaned my whole apartment"

"not happening, i bought you groceries!"

"I know, nor would I want you too"

"go eat the teddy betty crackers. i got honey flavor because i hate the cinnamon flavor"

"honey is my favorite. I like to lather myself in honey and prance around…haha"

"invite the faggots that live across the courtyard over and you guys have a cuddlefest" "fuck you cuntbag!"

xoxo

"Here's the circumference of it, as easily comprehendible as I can make it for you. It's the principle of how this all went down. I know there's a lot more to the story than what you have told me, I'm not fucking stupid you know, and in fact I doubt you will ever come across someone sharper than I am in your lifetime. But basically, by you liking a guy and then going on a date with him and you not telling me anything about it, when there I was thinking we were still together "like that," as usual, was completely wrong, and some part of you still knows that. To make matters worse, yes making out with some pathetic ass fake tanning used car salesman who looks old enough to be your dad who you had known for only two days in a public bar was extremely wrong, thank God my friends were there to see it and tell me, otherwise I might have never known the real story, and you know that you broke our agreement about not fucking around with other people while we were still together. And yes, doing all of this behind my back while I was at home hand making you a Valentine's Day present made it even worse, and made you look even worse actually. You claimed that you always wanted me in your life even if the relationship side our thing didn't work out. You claimed you loved me and cared about me so much, and "oh" I was just such a huge important part of your life. You know you just said pretty much that entire statement to me right after your birthday, that wasn't six fucking months ago you know, that was only a few weeks ago, so what reason would I have not to believe you. I wanted you in my life forever as well, at the very least as a friend. But, your actions that night (or even before that) said to me "she doesn't even care enough about you or respect you enough to give you at the very least a phone call to tell you that she met another guy that she liked and she wanted to go out with him, and to also let me know that we couldn't be what we were anymore." That was really lame by the way. That's really all it took and everything would have been alright. Would I have still thought you lost your mind by running away for the weekend with some lame ass guy you didn't even know and try and insert some logic and common sense in you? Yes, of course I would have. But, because of your actions, you pretty much made it impossible for us to be even friends. How can I be friends with someone who didn't even have the decency to tell me the truth about all of this and for the most part fucked me over, and then to make things worse wasn't even remotely apologetic or caring, and then for some reason turned into a delusional, sarcastic, pissy, sassy, mean bitch. It's nuts, you basically had the attitude that I should have had, and I had the attitude that you should have had. That's what is so shitty, you painted me into a corner with no other options, and it sucked badly for me. I even tried convincing myself that I could still be your friend even after the shit you did, but my dignity and ego couldn't let that happen. Yes, when I came to your house unannounced, I knew it was all over before I even got there and we couldn't even be friends. I was overly nice, decent, and tried to handle this with some maturity and not be too pissed off at you. Yes, like Jesus I wanted to turn the other cheek and treat you better than you had treated me, because yes, I was a sucker, I really did care about you, and love you, and wanted you to be in my life forever. My words weren't bullshit. But yes, you were gonna have to be a totally indifferent bitch to me in person, to my face, I wanted to see it for myself and you didn't disappoint me, unfortunately."

"Well you make me out to sound like a lying bitch...not sure what happened since the last time we talked? I'll get all your stuff back to you ASAP"

"Well, when I came to your house I was still in shock and confusion mode, and yeah, I felt the same way then that I do now. Granted, when I walked in your door and saw the bag it pretty much fucked up whatever I was going to say originally, and I was in further shock really. Can you blame me for that? Nothing has happened since then, other than me feeling shitty while you're out having the time of your life and not giving one flying fuck about any of this. I wake up every day feeling like something is missing in my life or like something isn't right in thw world. Yeah, it bothers me that we aren't even friends now and not in each others lives. You have been acting sort of like a lying bitch. Well, the old XXXXX wasn't, but whoever this "new version" of you sure sort of gives my gut that vibe. I was just trying to be decent and try and understand all of this, but every single time, well minus once and now, you have been so snippy and bitchy to me for no reason. Basically , like you couldn't even stand me or something, who knows, maybe I was wrong. Throw that on top of running around with some other dude and making out in public and me not know anything about it, like I said, me thinking we were still doing our thing, what does that give the appearance of being? Sort of, shady and not even telling me, what does that equate...possible lying? Or just not being very cool or fair to me at all. I have no idea what you would have told me, when you did tell me you met someone else, but I doubt you would have mentioned the incident. So, really it's sort of like what do I trust? I always trusted you, but this whole thing and me being already cynical has cast a shadow over that. I mean I'm sitting here thinking that maybe you never cared about me at all, and you were just going through the motions, of say like when I say I love you, you say that you love me back. I mean this is just all so crazy, well, how it all went down you know. Fucking ehh, you think I like this or wanted this? Trust me I don't. I feel like my best friend/lover and someone I considered to be part of my family just fucked me over and ran off into the sunset one random day. And really the follow-up after the whole finding out incident took place, was the worst thing. The closest thing to a "my bad or sorry" I got was a "I'm sorry you feel that way" and a forced "I could have possibly handled that better." I felt like I made you say that really. It's just like you don't care one bit, which is sort of odd considering that you had said on many previous occasions that you wanted me in your life forever "as something." I don't claim to know where to go from here XXXXX. But, the stuff I gave you, I want you to keep. I wouldn't have given it you if I didn't. You may not believe me now, but one day that art will be worth something. Perhaps, if you said that you were sorry and weren't bitchy to me when I talk to you, maybe after a break to let me get over this we can be friends again or something. I don't know."

"I am very sorry. I never meant to hurt you. I should have handled it all better. BTW nothing I said was forced, it was all heartfelt. I think you know me well enough to know that if I dont feel it I cant say it? If I came off as indifferent or "bitchy" that certainly wasnt my intent. Other than repeating everything I have already said, I dont know what to say, but I do hope you know I am sorry for hurting you, that was never my intent. I hope we can remain friends, it just doesnt feel right for us to not be speaking at all. It was clear you hated me when you deleted me as your friend on stupid fucking myspace. Yes I noticed, but you know me well enough to know Im not going to start drama or creat confrontation, so I just let it go. But yes I noticed."

"Well thank you so much for saying all of that. It might sound sarcastic (don't mean to), but it does mean so much to me. Well yeah I know you, very well...I thought...haha. It was just hurting me badly thinking that you didn't care about me or love me at all. (And no, I don't mean you have to be in love with me or anything). But I'm not ashamed to say I will always love and care for you, even recently when I tried to dislike you, that wasn't gone. I'm glad that you noticed me being gone as well."

xoxo

"The Precision Aggression of Rejection Art"

I eat my three tacos,

chicken

not beef

she steals

my

cheese and my soul

with a dull metallic plated

fork

and

soft refined

hands

manicured nails

she used to

jack me off

with

naked and crispy

tacos

burned edges

with

no cheese

bare and all

she sips my beer

I say she looks

pretty

expensive

Mexican shit beer

Tecate

or something like that

$2.75 a pop

you

motherfuckers!

I stare at her tits

I miss both

of them

saline and all

she forgot her purse

when

it came time

to

pay the bill

delivered by greasy Mexican

Fingers

$18.65

a civil war in

my pants

and
in my head
yeah, I got this one baby
I got,

no job
no future
no car
no one,

and
$20.00 in my pocket
all in
fives
and change
burning
to be lost forever
in weathered
ancient
Mexican
cash registers,

she leaves with
greasy
fingers
my cheese
and
my soul,

I leave with
greasy fingers
no

prospect of pussy,

an

empty wallet

and no soul.

xoxo

Dear XXXXXXXXX,

Granted, I've fallen far from Lab Rat Manifesto to emo love letter/birthday card. But, for some reason here I sit in my chair in my underwear smoking too many cigarettes and drinking Dunkin' Donuts coffee typing away. So, sell-out or not I still maintain some punk rock aesthetic even in an emo love letter/birthday card greeting. Another year goes by and forever will November 18th be engrained in my long term memory as your birthday. I probably won't live to be that old, but it will always be your day in my head. Unless, of course I meet someone more cooterawesome than you with the same birthday that is, but that would be rationally unlikely at best. Granted, it's just a birthday and a number but I want it to be special for you. Perhaps, my ghetto-ass handmade presents and acts will somewhat help in that aspect, but who knows. You're still absolutely beautiful and stunning as ever. You're also one of the most interesting and fun people I've ever known. When I'm around you I feel like I'm fifteen again and you give me some added pep like a giant concoction of Red Bull and Goody's. And if you were ever wondering, yes, I would probably do anything for you, and would probably even break my EMT code of ethics and help you move a dead body if you needed me to. I would probably also even kill your pimp like in True Romance, but with the nursing career I don't think you will need a pimp to be honest. You have a certain zest for life and Haitian Negro voodoo that surrounds you that I can't fucking stay away from no matter how hard I try. Truthfully, you're also probably one of the reasons I've stayed around here. When I see something I want it's difficult for me to ever give up on it, no matter the odds or how many times I hear the word "no."…haha. I don't know why, but ever since the day you spilt that Sprite in your bag just to talk to me in the hallway at CCU, something has been in my cerebral cortex gnawing away at me telling me there's something/someone special here and to go after it for it might not present itself again in your lifetime. I know you get freaked out easily and that's not what I'm trying to do here. But yes, I get well discouraged and perhaps even sometimes pissy over the fact that we're not as close or as good as friends/more than friends as I think we should be. You may consider yourself "fucked up" or whatever you normally say about yourself, but I disagree with you on that. I personally like you just the way you are, and you being "fucked up" or "neurotic" is part of who you are and I like it and accept you for who you are, so whateva! We're a lot more alike than you will probably ever care to admit or notice. Yes, I don't give up, and yes I would like to be your damn boyfriend! Christ, did I just say that? I'm getting soft, but I don't care. Much like a twelve year old girl I annoy and get emo until I get what I want or someone takes me to the fucking mall! Maybe you're right about me not knowing much about love, but sick love is still love regardless. And frankly, I think I could be the best boyfriend you've ever had. I don't think most guys would even fathom much less do the things I would do for you. Hence, the emo letter…lol. Well alright enough rambling, I guess in closing I just wanted to say in a very long drawn out way that I do really love you and care about you more than you know. Regardless of what I say when I'm pissed off at you when I'm drunk on PBR…haha. Anyways, I hope you have a happy and fantastic birthday XXX…Brett

xoxo

"Where do you hide your dildos?" I ask her.

"I'm not telling you." She says.

"Why not?"

"Just because."

"Are they in the nightstand?"

"No."

"Are they in any drawers in here?"

"No."

"Are they under the mattress?"

"No."

"Are they under the bed?"

"No."

"Are they in your bathroom?"

"No."

"Are they in your closet?"

"Maybe."

"Oh, c'mon just show me sugar tits!"

"No way, I don't even know you."

"Please just show me so I can peruse exactly what kind of fucked up pervert you really are."

"Uhmm no, I gotta go to work. I don't have time for this stupid bullshit."

"Fine, that's a strange answer for someone who blew me last night though, calling me a stranger and shit."

"I gotta get ready. I'm already late for work."

"You wouldn't know anything about that Mr. starving artist."

"You're right about that darling. But I don't claim to be a pervert and then hide my plethora of dildos from people; I'm comfortable enough in my own sexuality to exhibit and not be ashamed of my Japanese rubber vagina."

"Whatever, you gotta leave so I can get dressed."

"That's fine, conversation to be continued though. Next time I'm over here I'm going on a dildo hunt just so you know."

"I'm hiding it in a new spot then."

"That's bullshit. Get your little ass over here and kiss me so I can go home and take a shit and pass out."

xoxo

"My Long Term Relationship with Stains"

My bed
smells not
of,
disinfectant
ocean breeze
fresh linen
potpourri
advertising bears
with no apparent genitalia
or
dryer sheets,

my bed
smells
of,

fucking
pussy
cum

cock

lube

pubic hair

penetration

blowjobs

masturbation

sweat

beer

liquor

and

probable

regret

from the night before,

my bed

smells.

xoxo

"are you fucking anyone else?

yes actually

how'd I guess

there's other girls panties on my floor, but that's beside the point

really, well then we cant be special friends anymore

jesus, calm down

im calm

serenity now!

serene as can be- just an advocate for disease control

haha, I'm not fucking anybody else...I was teasing

yes not yet anyway

jeez ur paranoid skully…

hey u started it-haha

the 2 hole doesn't count anyways!

thats even worse

i dont want strange anal bacteria near my cooter

it would live on your dick for days

don't worry, I have dial anitbacterial soap.

no way

i swear, a whole bottle with aloe

no more cooter for you!!!-HAHA

calm down cooter nazi

i'll just go back to being the hot girl you wish you could fuck again

wouldn't be the same, since I already have many times

ok, well whatever i'll just be the hot friend who hangs out while you have anal sex with nasty fat chicks

well anything after you would be a step down

that sucks for you

ha, same goes for you.

yes, why Im pretty happy the way things are

yes, I agree…"

xoxo

What a difference a year makes. It's all changed. It's all different now. I'm still trying to figure my shit out even now. No answers have been discovered so far, and I doubt any will. Summer, just another day for me, a few months for others. Live another day even though you feel and walk with death on a daily basis. Pretend to be happy, drink it down to avoid it, to feel the pain, find solace in friends, school, art, writing, and that's about it. The passion isn't there right now; I'm just getting by these days.

xoxo

How many more days of this? How many more days of fuckin' self-destruction do I have to partake in before it's done with and I'm in a gutter somewhere? It's there everyday with me like an Atlas inspired weight that I can't remove, like a turd memory that I just can't flush. Late night masturbation and the next morning's coffee and energy drink just to get me to the sofa. It's overcast and dark everyday in my world and outside my window. The weather turns cold and the exercise and the energy are zapped from my body. My mind is filed and my wallet is empty. Self-destruction on a budget fucking sucks. It's downtown tomorrow to get back on the food stamps I sell for more beer, for more cigarettes, for more destruction, and for more annihilation.

xoxo

"Nice. I like your foul fucking Polock mouth!"

"I can't wait until you fuck me again. It's so ridiculous"

"I've told you all that beofre. We have an insane sexual attraction. That's been obvious. Duh. Even for a Polock!"

"You're sweet and make me horny"

"Thanks sugar tits, you're pretty hot your self. I pre-cum everytime I see you"

"OMG you're so hot!!"

xoxo

"Uncouth Answers from the Bottom of the Glass"

Me and the darkness and Merle Haggard,

I,

put my
scars
inside of her
she put her
insanity
inside of me,

I,
drive
by her house
almost
every night these days
always late
in
the a.m.
me and the darkness and Merle Haggard,

I,

have pipe bombs

for emotions

and

they are lit and thrown

ok

they were Black Cats

actually

on sale at the discount

firecracker store

down

near the large blue bridge,

pop, pop, pow,

wake the neighbors

fuck it

speed off and blame it on

Pabst Blue Ribbon

in the can

if I get caught,

me and the darkness and Merle Haggard.

xoxo

She was actually beautiful. That was a nice change. I like watching something beautiful unzip my pants and pull out my cock and just start sucking on it. It's like a fucking magic trick or something. One second I'm changing the channel on the TV and the next second my cock is in her mouth and she's massaging my balls.

"Come here and spit all over my cock." I tell her.

She was lying down on my couch. I maneuvered like fucking Mary Lou Retton in the '84 Olympics so I could put my cock close enough to her mouth so she could spit all over it. She made a weird little spitting/drooling noise while she did. I started jerking my cock off with her spit. That lasted like fifteen seconds and then it was dry again, so I attempted to spit all over my cock from quite a distance away. I'm pretty sure I drooled more on floor and my chin than made it on my cock.

"That was so hot." She says.

Even in her crappy fucking Russian version of English it sounded pretty fucking cool to me. It didn't really look hot to me. I looked more like a kid with down syndrome drooling all over himself, but whatever, who am I to judge what she thinks is hot. I keep jerking off with my own spit. It's a little rough but the vision of me cumming on her face is pretty motivating. Fuck, I keep drying up. I think about going into my room and getting the lube and doing it right, but with my pants and everything around my ankles, the hell with that.

"Come here and suck on my cock again." I tell her.

She makes a little face and tries to get up off the couch. On her way up her she kicks her leg and her foot smashes into my hard cock.

"Fuck, are you trying to break my goddamn cock girl?"

"I am sorry did I break penis?" She says in her crappy fucking Russian version of English.

"No, you fucking goddamn Commie! But it sure as fuck hurts though!"

"I am sorry." She says in her crappy Russian version of English.

"Ok, its fine, perhaps sucking on it again until the swelling goes down would help."

I don't think she got the joke, but she did start sucking on my cock again so it didn't really matter whether she appreciated the joke or not I guess. Where there was once a limp cock, there was now a hard cock again. I grabbed her blonde hair and pushed my cock all the way down her throat. Ahh, that gagging sound of someone sticking their cock down someone's throat was worth it. I guide her up and down and up and then down. Fuck, she was pretty amazing at sucking cock. Any girl with dick sucking lips like that should be I suppose. I released her head after the initial joy of hearing that cock gagging sound wore off.

"Come here sit down." She tells me.

"Nah, I like being above you with you on your knees." I tell her.

"This floor is hurting my damn knees." She says in crappy English.

"Sorry, just sit on the couch like you were before."

Ahh, yes, I like dominating her from above. She grabs my cock with her left hand and starts blowing me again. Her mouth is warm and wet, almost perfect for a goddamn Commie! She holds my cock in her little hand.

"I want you to cum all over my face." She tells me in crappy English.

"Fuck yes, I wanna cum all over your pretty goddamn Russian face." I tell her.

She puts my cock back in her mouth and keeps sucking my very hard cock.

"Spit all over my cock. I wanna jerk off in your face and mouth." I tell her.

I straddle her face on the couch. My cock was like six inches away from her face. The vision of my cum all over her pretty Russian face was all I needed. I could feel the cum churning in my balls. I drooled a big wad of spit on my cock for good measure.

"Where do you want my fucking cum you Commie?"

"In my mouth and on my face."

"Give me your cum now!"

I keep stroking with my own spit. Degrading her face with my cum will be a pleasure. Fuck, keep stroking. I make her spit more on my cock. I feel that strange feeling of cum swirling in my balls again.

"Come here I'm fucking cumming." I tell her.

My dick is pointed right near her mouth and finally I explode. Cum goes fucking everywhere. Some in her mouth, some on her face, some on her chin, some on her cheek, and the rest runs down her face and onto her chin and it drips onto my couch. Like it really needed more stains, but hey I'll just flip it over and no one will be the wiser. That was a giant fucking load. I'm glad I saved up the past few days. She swallows the cum in her mouth and licks the little bit left off the end of my cock. That was pretty fucking hot I admit.

"Thanks, that hit the spot." I tell her.

I don't know why I say that, but I always do. I figure some form of appreciation is warranted anytime someone sucks my cock, who knows, maybe that's just me. I sit down on the couch next to her, my cock is now limp and cum still sort of slowly drips out of it and onto my couch. I was in that state of "post-cum euphoria." I didn't really see her do it, but she grabbed me and gave me a kiss on the lips and put my cum on my lips and on my face. I had slightly tasted my cum before out of curiosity, but I'd never quite had that much cum on me or in my mouth.

"Your cum tastes amazing." She says.

"I don't know. I've never tasted anyone else's so I don't have much to compare it to." I say sarcastically.

I started gagging a little, and I pulled my shorts back up and went and washed the cum off of my goddamn mouth. I replayed the cumming in her face visual in my head again. I didn't have much respect for her before, but I sure as fuck didn't now. It's pretty fun degrading something beautiful I thought to myself. I grabbed her some paper towels to get the rest of the cum off her face. I sat down next to her on the couch. As she wiped the cum off her face all I could think of was how the fuck I was gonna get her out of here so I could watch TV in peace and not hear anymore of her goddamn shitty Russian version of English. My mind is blank, my cock is limp, and she now wants to watch some shitty newly released romantic comedy movie that's HBO, just fucking great!

xoxo

I sat on the edge of my bed. She sat in my lap. Eventually, I laid all the way down on my ten-year-old leopard print sheets. Her hands weren't great, but she did a pretty good job of scratching my belly and chest. I could feel the unevenness of her cuticles where she had been biting them at some point recently. She reached down and kissed me slightly on the lips. When she did, I whispered in her ear "do you wanna put my weiner in your mouth?"

xoxo

My phone is alive,

"Well, I've managed so far - Neosporin would be a good idea though"

"Downstairs now"

"RB? Root beer? Ruphenol Barbituites?"

"Just got in and found what appears to be a purple heart? Anywho thanks I like it, def original"

"I have the flu"

"And I never heard from you all day, even left you a message"

"Thanks, I agree, had a great day too"

"prob about 1130. I'm grocery shopping now."

"I love my CD's so far- thanks you. I'm going to best bvuy in a little bit to look for a car stereo, if u want to come along"

"Ok well I'll come there if you want"

"Maybene tomorrow or Tuesday afternoon u will come by and help me"

"I'm back in town how are you?"

"What happened?"

"Ok sounds good"

"I burnt my goddamn cock…sweet jesus!"

"Yeah I know. Ha. I gave a crying ginger kid a sharks tooth today. Didn't even say thanks fucking soulless. I got a B in anatomy though"

"fuckingg shit!!!"

"Thanks I appreciate it. Ready to be back home.."

"ook then. We are in the martini bar"

"Nothing just wonering. Me and XXX are out"

"Such a good citizen"

"He was probably too busy crying lol A b is good"

"Don't want to know but as I said ready to be back"

"Why are you so damn critical? Damn..."

"I love you when I'm drunk and alone"

"Yeah still alive. Came to NC, heading home tomorrow. Thanks for checking on me"

"Lol talk to you tomorrow. Get off the rag!"

"sorry packing"

"Not sure how long we will be here"

"I would rather be gang banged then pack!"

"I was napping when you called. Thursday may work. Not sure though. I'll give you a rjing tomorrow"

"Sorry hope you feel better. Didn't get any other messages. Had to get anew phone"

"Sometimes you don't have to take a bullet to get a purple heart. That's the name of the piece. It just hit me"

"Ha u will be fine, I hope. Next time Neo on the go, just for you darlin'!"

"I def don't want my artistic gift to hurt you. The razor blade is on top of it. Perhaps I should have left some Neosporin with the card...ha."

"Damn girl you rock it eewarly. Ha, I can make it though. Call me in 30 and make sure. I'm up!"

"Yeah close. Razor blade. No heart of mine can ever be entirely safe when handled...ha."

"Sorry really busy. Tech line and wait is insane and dropped and broke my fucking phone."

"well we are all over. Lol"

"It's subjective. It does resemble a heart though. Could be why you got it? Hope you like it. B careful trhere's an RB in it"

"Awesome! I missed you so much. Glad to be hanging out more now"

"I love you darling' Have a good day at work tomorrow. Day 3 was cootertastic!"

"Ur welcome baby. I told you! What time you doing the BB thing?"

"I like your pics. You look good dirty..."

"haha funny"

"I don't know, potent shit. Chemical crap…"

"This health food shit. No permanent damage though, just pain and scabbing. I'm a naked hermit now, ha"

"U happen to be out?"

"Why are you avoiding me, is it because I'm adopted?"

"Not great but oh well. Hope your trip went well"

"Can't find you at martini bar"

"Ahh I see. Well I guess I could meet you somewhere if you want"

"I'm actually not. Just at home painting like a nerd. What do have on your mind?"

"I guess. The cuddling paramedic student has a big heart this is true. Even called 911 for a bad wreck at DD today. Odd day!"

"She ginger, worst of all ginger species. Crying because it lost her sharks tooth, which why I gave her mine"

"ok be there in fifteen."

"A correction to last night's statement. I heart you when I'm drunk alone and eating baked cheetos. Keep it on the DL!"

"I'm gonna call u in a while and whisper sweet nothings in ur ear"

"Ahh ok gotcha. My gpa always said when traveling leavce the ginger snaps at home"

"Ha what are you doing in NC? Or do I not want to know?"

"Ahh ok, No problem. Got a little worried about you. Thought I would check on you."

"I never heard from you last week. Are you ok? Still alive?"

"Ha ok, well idk. I would be happy to meet up with you. Just give me a place to go to. Let me know…"

"Igot a B in anatomy. I guess I'm only slightly better than average. Though wearing that fuck the fat friend shirt the last day of class in honor of my cunt teacher probably didn't help…"

"Oh geez, I'll try not t o get cut,"

My phone is dead.

xoxo

I never told you. When I ran off with tears in my eyes during breakfast on the boat I went and got a coffee and found a deserted corner and a chair and cried like a fucking pathetic baby. I used to have some dignity, but now you can watch me cry if you want.

xoxo

"The Bagnio Millennium Calculator"

Friday
nights
numb,

alone
no one calls
I call
no one
sounds
of rattling overhead fans
and
doors slamming
below
are friends
on,

Friday
nights
numb,

green
blinking lights
orange
constant lights
on
creeping filthy
mouse

rolling

on plastic balls

towards

something or someone

twelve second

free porn clips

they

are friends

on,

Friday

nights

numb,

nowhere land

where

the nowhere man

belongs

solitary chair

confinement

faux leather Hanoi Hilton

cranberry juice

and

discount smokes

are friends

on,

Friday

nights

numb.

xoxo

"what else did u do besides bathe the cooties off u today and read?"

"laundry and took my sister to swim practice"

"exciting stuff there lil missy"

"now im watching tv…"

"wesome possum…did u tell her how I'm gonna lock u up in my closet and feed u lettuce, cum and Gatorade?"

"eah she wants to know if she can come too?"

"k fine, I have enough free time to degrade two women"

"were in love right? dont you love me? Don't run from out love"

"What love? no I only love myself. But I just want to play scrabble with you and jerk off on your head"

"I don't know. I just felt like annoying u"

"no, if u were I wouldn't like u . then I would really treat u like shit…"

"stop being mushy. what the fuck has gotten into you?"

"nothing, I'm kidding around you fucking cunt"

"haha shut it brett stout!!!!"

"you can be my littel rabbit…you said I needed a pet"

"at least I wouldn't beat u"

"haha i know you fucking cunt x 2"

"oh snap///u cunt squared"

"hahahaha"

"mathematical genius"

"You have small balls…"

"I don't have small balls, u just have a rather large hand!"

"o really?"

"haha yeah really"

"just like I will never have a small penis, bitches just had huge pussies..ha"

xoxo

We walk into one of those crappy women's clothing stores that litter every mall across America. She looks around at endless racks of women's shirts and jeans and just about every other piece of clothing any person could ever want really. They all look like shit to me, but I say nothing. She examines pairs of worn out jeans, digging through plastic racks until her size comes up. The next thing I know she is off towards the women's dressing room. I'm left with nothing to do but stand. I can see the feet of women trying on clothes in the private stalls. The little kid who's sitting in the only chair gets up and leaves with her mom. I look around and sit down and the wait commences. It's an endless wait really, the kind you can only have while sitting in a crappy women's clothing store really. It reminds of when I was a little kid and my mom made me wait just like I am now for her to try on her choice of women's mall clothes. I sit and ponder, like I said, there's nothing to do but that. I wondered if she was wearing panties that day, she usually didn't, but you never know. I was thinking to myself that if she didn't, then I wonder how many other fucking pussies had been in that same pair of worn out and ratty jeans that she was trying on? Ten minutes later she comes out of the dressing room, she said the jeans were too tight for her. I asked her if she was wearing any panties and she says no she wasn't. She tossed the jeans down on the dressing room counter. She said that she was going to find a larger size and try them on. She walked past me and towards the rack again. I picked up the jeans and unzipped the zipper and the metal button that held them together. I pulled them towards my face and sniffed the inside crotch. It didn't smell like pussy after all. Sometimes you gotta find out things like this. I went back to my chair and waited around like a fucking idiot once again.

xoxo

"so "lets smoke crack together" HAHA I swear you are on every dating site imaginable. XXXX found some guy on POF and I went on there to check him out and ohhhhhhh, what????? thats Bretts email address. XXXX never caught it cause you can barely see you in that pic, but of course I had to fill her in. So hows that working for you?? No doubt you will find a plethora of women who put out on the first date........I think its the Greenpeace thing that will definately win them over-haha"

xoxo

Dear XXXXX,

I do really owe you an apology XXXXX. I am really sorry. You didn't do anything this time to deserve my drunken wrath. It's not any excuse, but I don't even really remember doing it to be honest, it's all hazy and filled with PBR and Sun Chips. I wasn't even mad at you so I don't really know where it came from. Usually, I get drunk and send you witty yet probably sappy text messages about how much I miss you, so I don't why last night it was different. I guess in deep dark areas, you going to VI with another dude really bothered me. That's all I can think of really. You know I don't want to act stupid, petty, or childish, but sometimes things you do really hurt and bother me and I guess I try and hide them and I file feelings away in deep areas hoping they won't come out. Do you know how hard it is for me to be just your friend? I can't help it. I care about you and I'm very sensitive when it comes to things about you, and yes I hurt, and I cry, and I'm lonely without you all the time. I'm ok with that stuff, I deserve it. But, once in a while I lash out with emotional mean words, mainly while drunk and I know I shouldn't, but sometimes it just happens. I'm really sorry though for saying that dumb mean shit to you, judging you, starting drama and for the pain it may have caused you. Of course, I didn't really mean it. Hell, you know I love you and I always will. And I will always be your friend, even if you don't wanna be mine. You don't have to keep me in your life or even speak to me, but I hope eventually you change your mind about that. I know being my friend isn't easy baby, I'm a work in progress and sometimes I do dumb shit, but I am a decent person and worth keeping around. I don't want there to be anything weird between us. This is way too small of a town and you know we will run into each other. Damn it, I'm ashamed of myself and feel like a real asshole.

Your BFF,

Brett

xoxo

"how about I just whack off in a ziploc bag and we put it in ur freezer?

i think they would die...otherwise its a good idea. i'm no expert, but i think they would be limp sperm when thawed

limp noodle sperm, just my luck....maybe they would have better luck pumping your stomach...haha

haha...nice. actually they face immediate death that way

haha, that was funny

just dont die for the next couple years, just in case I need inseminated

I'll do my best

thats def our easiest option

good idea just in case the marriage perfect life thing doesn't pan out

i never said anything about marriage...and perfect is subjective

ha, I'm just busting ur cunt

yeah who knows...you could be proposing to me at the flea market by next summer-LOL

perhaps missy....perhaps"

xoxo

I sit here night after night looking for something. I sit here night after night looking for someone. I sit here night after night looking for anything. I have a disease, a disease of loneliness and isolation. The grasp of winter depression and angst is here again. I procrastinate and make excuses. I feel more human than normal. I have their weakness for now, but hopefully not forever. I'm constantly disillusioned and paranoid. I want something but I don't know what. Maybe there is light at the end of a narrow tunnel, but the light has not been shown to me yet. Destroying myself has brought no answers and cured no illness. The hangovers, random numbers in my phone, and empty bank accounts have brought no happiness and only temporary tattooed joy into my life. I don't have any answers and I don't know where to go from here or what to do. I will be sitting here night after night burning cigarettes and light bulbs until I do though.

xoxo

I grab her fat roll and pull on it so I can fuck her harder and my little dick appears to go further inside of her fat cunt. Her prickly pubic hair rubs and scratches dead skin off my pelvis and thighs. Last time, well, half an hour ago technically I asked her if I could cum inside of her. She said that she wasn't on the pill but I could cum inside of her anyways. Fuck that I thought, and pulled out of her cunt and came all over her stomach which proceeded to slowly drip down into her belly button and die a slow death until she washed it out into the sink. This time I asked her if I could cum in her mouth and she said "completely no" to my request. I grabbed one of her fat rolls really hard as I pulled my cock out of her cunt and managed to jump on top of her and cum all over her non-existent tits, chin, and some of her face. She was none too happy about it, but the bitch left me no options. I wasn't planning on ever calling her or fucking her again anyways, but I'm stuck here at her house in the middle of goddamn fucking nowhere with no ride. I smoke her cigarettes and make up some lie about having to be at an important meeting for work tomorrow just to get out of there. I ask her if she can take me home soon, she says she'll do it right after she takes a shower, gets dressed, and picks up one of her fucking friends. Fuck me; this is gonna be one long fucked up rest of the day I can already tell.

xoxo

"Smack: Shooting Playground Insanity"

violated,

empty pot holes

circular in

diameter

solid black

in color

the insides

of me,

located between rib cage and pelvis

on display

for the public to witness,

the lights dim every night

just for

you

the public,

coming

living

breathing

pouring

in constant repetitive motion

out of me

free admission

to view,

tips are appreciated.

xoxo

"you know he has to take viagra. Theres no way he goes out and drinks all night and can still get it up

well of course, I will myself boners when I'm shitfaced, but even I can't get a boner sometimes…

yeah imagine if you were 50?

yea I would just overdose on cobra. viagra is cheating, but all natural herbs....that's not

im not against viagra, or herbs whatever works

well I'll go with herbs, no chemically induced boner for me! I can't take cobra very much, it's like I just got out of jail and haven't seen a woman in 10 years

hmm, have you taken it lately?

no, been a whil, it makes me hump furniture and people's legs....no good

haha..take some id like to see that

ok, get your leg ready because I'm coming over in an hour to fuck the shit out of it...haha"

xoxo

"From 'Nam to This"

the last two lights
remove
themselves from the conversation,

one
by
one,

bare feet walking on stained
dirty wood
lint
and other debris cling
to the soles
of those
drunkards behind the white brick wall,
spermo on the hando,

as ghosts long ago
turn voyeurs overnight
watching
me
masturbate and make coffee,

burning 727 minutes

on

bankrupt airlines,

the first two lights

are flicked on

interfering in new wave conversations.

xoxo

Something is fucking wrong with me. The pain in my balls has been there for weeks with no relief in sight. I'm fucked up and there's nothing I can do about it but take it and down a few orange pills. I tried to do a self diagnosis, which involved an internet search of phrases like "swollen balls" and "pain in balls." Who the fuck knows? I just became even more confused than I already was. Could it be cancer, epididymitis, prostatitis, or a hernia, who the fuck knows? I empty the change of various denominations that fill the glass on my computer desk and place it in a previously used plastic bag. It's time for me to take it to the bank and trade it in for enough cash so I can go to the shitty Doctor's Care walk-in clinic down the street and get someone to fix my fucking aching balls.

xoxo

I went to the beach a few days ago and my face and lips got burned as shit and hurt like hell. I read about the side effects of the antibiotics the doctor gave me on the internet. I now possess "photosensitivity." I went back to my "cowboy" doctor and asked him if he could put me on an antibiotic that didn't fucking make me hurt and swell up like a pregnant woman retaining water every time the fucking sun hits me. He grabbed my balls again to see if I was getting any better. He squeezed the shit out of them and poked them more with his fingers and asked me if this hurt or if that hurt, pretty much every time I said yes that hurt, what did he expect really? He was squeezing my fuckin' balls man. He gave me ten more days of some other antibiotic that doesn't make your skin so sensitive to the sun. It only cost me six bucks so I was happy about that, what a fucking deal!

xoxo

My phone is alive,

"By the way when do you want to hangout again?"

"Are you sleeping? I'm going to take a much needed nap"

"Kismet perhaps?"

"I'm not avoiding you. Ur text was funny though. The moment has passed"

"No what the hell! I just get random ones and not the juicy ones. Maybe u are making those too long to go through"

"good job on the test smarty pants!"

"Call me when you get here"

"Oh yeah…a BBq and jealousy…do tell"

"Ok, I guess you are. I'll call you when I get up."

"Key lime is good as fuck and my personal favorite!"

"It's easy breezy baby"

"Email me those photos when you upload them. I need to peruse the drunken over thirty PDA. Funt times, glad we went down there!"

"So ur not dressing up?"

"We'll just have to hang out after you get off or something! A stopover for beer and pretend to watch a movie?"

"I just woke up from a nap and this is the only text from you. Why am I getting these and no the juicy ones?"

"TMI!...lol"

"Happy birthday baby. Had fun and I hope you did too. Were ur friends ok with me?"

"Well what did I miss? You were def on my mind during the trip. It was fun and I didn't want to leave Honduras. I's the most simple and beautiful place."

"Have fun skydiving. See you at 6"

"Ok Saturday would be good. You can stay over. I'll get your pillow out!"

"Right now on the way"

"Even I remember someontimes darlin'!"

"So I'm being really cautious"

"I got a recipe for key lime pie. That means you're a big deal"

"U accept my vitiligo and nurosis. It's special"

"Sorry I'm in bed…"

"Yeson the drink, u had ur chance on the sex and turned it down. Nite, I have to be up at 5"

"Come over Friday night . We will have the place to ourselves. I'll have a 12 pack of Tecate and Pixies waiting for you. If you're nice you might even get a back massage out of it..lol"

"I was glad she was finally human again and cared. But she made her choice and I'm hanging with you and seeing where it goes."

"U were supposed to let me know. I had a blast!"

"We made out sooo many times tonight!!!"

"No making out for us afterwards. See you at 630 I'll be ready. If u come early you can hang out with my mom.."

"Oh Christ! I should get another chance. I wanted to fuck you in the parking lot, but you said no. My parents are to blame! I want you!"

"U can come at 630 I didn't realize what time it was. Where are your parents staying?"

"Of course my horse. I was tell you so we could make plans. But you didn't take the bait and get me to do something"

"I got my work schedule and I'm off till Thursday"

"I agree, I think we have a lot in common and see things the same way and could inspire each other to travel. You make me happy :)"

"I got all sentimental and you say ok"

"an\d thanks for understanding. My battery is dying on this phone. I'll call you when I get home"

"I do"

"I'm rough around the edges but I have a sensitive heart and if we start hooking up and u go back to her, it would hurt me big time"

"Aww did you tell her that or were you nice"

"yyou're the worst texter ever!"

"Did you say anything to her"

"That's cool, I hope you really thought about it while I was gone"

"What did u say?"

"I just got to Georgia. She sent u a message that she was crying and breaking down? Interesting timing don't you think? Did you have a BBQ?"

"Or else ur fucking with me"

"No, I didn';t get shit"

"You must have had a late night last nigh"

"I think we would have a blast on a cruise together by the way."

"Georgia the greatest state in the uniuon! Yeah it's bizarre. Jealous of the raddest girl in Myrtle Beach. I'll read you the messages when I talk to you. I have missed you though."

"You know how to leave a girl hanging"

"Did I miss anything? Looking forward to seeing you"

"I don't care about that stuff. You're special that's why!"

"I know, I stopped at Dunkin' Donuts. I did to. For some reason being with you just feels right."

"No goodbyes…poo"

"What time? This whole work thing is getting in the way of our fun!"

"My underwear has XXXXXXXX stains on it!"

"Happy birthday love"

"If it helps I'll whisper everything I know about vitiligo in your ear afterwards. Driving and Cryinon Sunday!"

"What does that mean?"

"ha well I can only be a gentle man for so long, especially since now I'm leaking pre-cum when I think about you"

"I can't wait to relax. Getting ready"

"What in the world did u say?"

"You are a trip, see ya around 6 If you play your cards right I'll wear a dress"

"Were you drunk last night when you said you wanted to take it to the next level?"

"I agree fully. You're sweet thanks! I hope I make you happy. I told you, if I'm with yoy, I'm with you. Just remember that"

"That's a good question. I'm working Thursday to Monday…poo"

"Ok sounds good"

"And did u decide where u wanted to to dinner for your birthday?"

"This Against Me! song reminds me of you"

"Aww I like you a lot to. The painting is hung"

"Oh stop. You know you don't have to do anything you don't want to. There's no pressure or expectations. I can't help that I like you though"

"We could go out and peoplele watch then Tecate and the Pixies at my place. Perfect!"

"Nite my punk rock boy"

"I have to up at 630 for school, but I'll call you when I get out"

"See ya soon. I'm all ready. Did you forget the painting!"

"I'm ready if you want to head over. I'm starving like an African orphan!"

"I don't care, hell, we can hang out at my place with a twelve of Tecate cans or whatever"

"Damn it that sucks! Well try not to blow me off Saturday night for a gay guy…ha..just kidding"

"Ha, I don't know. I sent like 22 messages. Are you back home? No juive, just bozzaro. The BBQ was just dudes cooking and drinking Tecate. Though XXXXX is all jealous now andSent me crazy messages."

"It's going to be hot out there. But I love people watching"

"I don't know what the deal is. Nothing all that juicy. Just XXXXX sending messages about crying and having breakdowns. Weird? Are you in Florida or back home?"

"Karma I'm telling you. I like you and I'm hanging out with you. Hell, I'm, lame and I thought about you every day you were gone!"

"Ok, I see you're trying to get romantic with just the two of us"

"uur dressing up. In what? I was going to wear shorts and sandals..but it's cute"

"If you avoid me I'm not sneaking you in past my parents to fuck!"

"I was nice and snotty. She knows we're hanging out and that I like you, yes. You make me happy, let her be fucked up…"

"I'm not trying to be a baby. But I gotta be up at 5 and had a 12 hour clinical and have to be up early. I'm beat"

"They're staying with me"

"Should I wear lipstick again?"

"It's cool. I wa just busting your coooter. All you need is a few Tecates and the moment will return. Ha, My dad can't be in the other room watching Nat Geo the first time we do it!"

"Im heading over there hope you're driving"

"I get out at 7 so I will rush home and shower. If you picked me up it would give me more time to get ready so that would be way cool."

"Ur such a night owl. I miss being one too"

"I'll assume by your silence that Friday is good for you? You're the worst texter ever!"

"Just because she feels all of a sudden doesn't change anything. I really do like you and I think we could be good for each other. I understand you being cautious though"

"Anyways, I hope you're kidding. I just wanted to be alone with you and comfortable. I really didn't know how far you wanted to take it anyways. You do it for me and I want you bad, so don't be stupid"

"What time do you have class on Wednesday?"

148

"You don't like cakes? Key lime is something I don't know how to make"

"I invite you over on Friday night after work. The rents will be gone. We can be alone. Tecate, Pixies, and back massages that lead to fornication!!!"

"I have to admit I'm pretty jazzed up about PF Changs and the painting. What kind of cake do you like?"

"Of course I would say yes"

"Do u remember promising me a painting?"

"I had a great time but I was dizzy as hell and so sick to my stomach yesterday. We were so jazzy."

"You saut it like a bad thing. I made it home!"

"Did you ge the last messages?"

"I know. We're the same like that. I'm not going to leave you for her. I don't know, I guess on some levels you will just have to trust me to do the right thing."

"I was so hungover!!!"

"Cool, well if you want to spend any of that time with me that would be cool. You better give me a call tonight or you're getting spanked"

"You still have soft lips"

"what the hell is this rain storm rolling in. I guess it just adds to the rmance watching a storm. Maybe you will even seduce me with some Friday drinks…lol"

"A beer at bh. I love being outside there. Meet me after class?"

"You're avoiding me now"

"Iwih u were here. Turning my phone off. Be good love you"

"I'm back in the USA,"

My phone is dead.

xoxo

"God, her fucking pussy stinks." I think to myself.

"I wonder what the fuck that smell could be?"

"I don't know."

"I search my brain and I still don't have any answers after five minutes."

"I pull my dick out of her pussy and it's all glistening and wet."

"I bet it smells like shit now."

"Well, not really like shit, more like a dead fish."

"No, wait, it smells like some rotten dead animal on the beach."

"Yep, that's it."

"I finally nailed it, hooray for me!"

"She wants to get on top of me, fuck."

"She has no clue how torturous this is."

"Fuck, I wish it was over already."

"Please dick go ahead and cum."

"Come on, just a few strokes more."

"Fucking little bastard, come on!" I silently tell my dick.

"Fine!"

"She cums from all the grinding." Like I give a shit I think to myself.

"It smells even worse now, somehow."

"Jesus, that's awful."

"It reminds me of that dead possum I smelled the other day when I was walking around."

"Yep."

"Alright, just make up some excuse so it can be over."

"Think man, think of something please!"

"I can't take it anymore." I tell myself

"Hey, I really have to take a dump." I tell her.

"And, I don't care if you're upset or think it's weird."

"Ahh, she bought it, at least I think so anyways."

"I don't even care really. That smell was just getting to be too much."

"I'll go into the bathroom and pretend to take a shit, including two flushes."

"Five minutes should be enough time for her to buy it as a real shit."

"Yea, that will do."

xoxo

Please God allow me to stop caring! I fucking despise and dread it. Nothing I do or try seems to ever work. Her voodoo is on me and I can't shake it. Help me please goddamn it. It makes me fucking miserable and come off as a jaded pathetic person, which I am not. What is it about her that keeps me interested and willing to go through this fucking hell over her? Is it her beauty that does it? Is it her personality? Is it the fact that she wants nothing to do with me really? Is it because she rejects me constantly? Is it the chase? Is it the fact that she's the most neurotic human being I've ever come across in all my years? Fuck, I feel ignorant over this question. I can't figure it out and it bothers me. Is it just another of life's mysteries that there is no answer to or reason for? Why do I even care, that's an even better question. I blow off women all the fucking time, why can't I do it to her? Is there some great ending to this that I don't know about? There must be, that's all that I can figure out. No one should go through this shit and not have something decent happen in the end.

xoxo

Hey XXXXXXXXX,

I was really hoping you would accidentally answer the phone so I wouldn't have to leave one of my stupid messages. You haven't responded to any of my previous messages in a long time, so I figured I would call you in person to see what was up with that. Are you seriously trying to avoid me, your close friend Brett Stout? Well I hope it won't take you three months to miss my crazy ass this time and you will want to talk to me soon. I won't annoy you anymore after this. I hope you are doing well…Later Gator

(I actually sat down and wrote and revised this message on little yellow sheets of paper until I thought that I got it right before I called her. That is what this girl does to me. Am I fucking crazy or what?....FUCK!)

xoxo

"Unsent Letters from the Ledges of the Abyss"

I can't be

my

fucked up

unconventional

irregular

eccentric

individual

self

around her

anymore,

I feel weak

like a child near her
butter knives
and
plastic bed sheet covers
purple Crayola crayons,

she knows
she has
the
advantage now
tables turned
worship the golden brunette calf,

I love
I deteriorate
I care
I annihilate
the penis of give a fucks
cum
only on me,

she doesn't
indifferent
blank
and cold as November
gargantuan soiled teeth exposed
shards of glass
now
surround her beauty,

everything I do is
wrong

detested

elevator music

now,

bring me the liquor store bag

of

distant memories

lay it

against my door

bastard child delivered

in the

night,

push the broken button

say goodbye

to

emptiness

to

no one.

xoxo

"I'm one of the few people u can be wacky and nuerotic with and I won't make
any judgements.

i totally know that- can i be boring and normal too and thats ok?

oh of course. I like boring beleive it or not

k cuz thats how i am most of the time

yep, me to actually

i dont believe that for a minute-your mind seems to have a endless array of
colorful thoughts-its great

haha, well my front has worked then!

well i get your crazy bulletins and check out your page now and then

I just meant like hey I sit around in my underwear in the middle of the night
and paint or read harcore books on siberian gulags for fun...lol

that would be boring my most people's standards I would think, maybe not......do u secretly check my page and then fatasize about me being your ccoterific.F.B.D.?

future baby daddy?

damn ur good with acronyms!

nah not really just catchin on to your humor, no fantasizing about FBD'S of any sort

well I'm glad it wasn't a personal slight against me being your FBM, I would have been crushed

no not personal at all we'd have a great kid smart eccentric and damn sexy!

so u have thought about it then?

hmmm well you had to go and plant the naughty thought

I knew I wasn't the only one! finally u admit it

i admit nothing......ever

haha, well of course lots of practice would be needed first.

oh my you actually have a plan

well of course

thought you didnt make plans? just free as the breeze kinda guy

I was thinking about a lot of practice.......practice makes perfect

oh well we would def want it to be perfect- we could have an Aryan child-haha

haha, it doesn't to be perfect ro anything...I was just trying to sneak a lot fo practice in there

practice is good -dont get me wrong

I wouldn't, I was just admitting that seeing u naked as much as possible would probably be a good thing

oh well im glad we're clear on that now

haha, yes I'm sure you had no idea I felt that way...lol

but yes the shocking truth is out there now, and my therapist will be happy

oh good well im glad you made some progress- they say it better to get it all out in the open

ummm maybe not all????

haha, yes...my therapist is dr.brett stout...he's very good...that medical degree from the univ of peru is doing wonders.......ahh, that's the just the way I am.....I say it all no matter how fucked up

thats ok good way to be-so dr stout i guess next time im not feelin so well I'll just call you for some alternative therapy

sure, I'll tell you how gorgeous you are and how rad you are and your problems will just fade away as a distant memory

the newest latest cure for single women every where-dude you could sell that

haha, well people are only looking for someone they can really talk to and be thrown a compliment here and there

you're right about having someone to have a decent conversation with-few and far between.

lucky for u my fee is miniscule! I listen to ur problems and in return I'm the FBD...haha

what a negotiator!

or I will settle for FBD "in training"...lol

thats quite a deal you've got goin

yea I know, it's pretty sweet. maybe if I made u a mix CD it would be more fair?

throw in a mix cd-is it one to "practice" to?

sure, I'm good with themes

im sure you are-have you heard she wants revenge? you probably think they're lame-be honest

I'm thinking more like Ronnie James Dio...HOLY DIVER!!!...haha"

xoxo

"Why are you being such a goddamn fucking bitch and avoiding me!"

"Whoa!!! Okay so I have been a bad friend and not been emailing or anything-but must you call me a bitch? You didn't do anything wrong Brett. I have been working two jobs, after tonight three, and have lots of homework. Besides that, I got back together with XXXX after Christmas and it has been very tough. We have so many issues anyway and to top it off he is really, really jealous of you. I think I've told you that before. Since things have been crazy between him and I about a whole bunch of shit, I was keeping my distance from you for a little while. This probably pisses you off and I'm sorry. I just made the mistake of telling him that you were hot and that I wanted to hang out with you while him and I were still together the first time, last year. Just so you know-don't ever tell a girl you are dating that you think another girl is hot and that you want to hang out with her. The girl you are dating will be paranoid and never let you forget that you said that-lol. But I'm sorry for being so cold and distant and well... bitchy. Like I said you didn't do anything wrong and yes, it is very fucked up. Sometimes I am one selfish cunt and I'm sorry about that. I still listen to your cd's that you made me all the time and think about going to the army navy store as soon as my ass gets some money. I went really into debt not working for awhile and I have to pull myself out. I hope you don't stay mad at me and I will be a better friend I promise. By the way I do not have your new number for some reason, only your old long distance one. Send it to me if you don't think I am a total bitch!"

xoxo

I thought about her while I was watching Benjamin Button. I cried and I don't know why. She's still there, never far removed from my thoughts. I don't think she ever will be. She doesn't know this, only a computer screen knows this. I still suffer from loss, the loss of her. The more time that goes by, the more I feel it. There are so many regrets and things I would change. She should be here with me, doing the things she now does with someone else. But, she is not, and I'm here alone in my room at three in the morning. I wish she was here with me. I wish things had ended up differently.

xoxo

Dear XXXXX,

Wow, if someone would have asked me what the odds would be of me writing you this letter like two weeks after I wrote the one to you on your birthday, I would have said something preposterous like 1 in a 100 million. But, here I sit writing this in my underwear, and it hurts me very badly to do it. But, it has to be done I guess because I can't have all this shit hanging over me without any sort of ending to it. Now, before we get to the bad stuff, I did mean what I wrote in that other letter, it came directly from whatever heart I have inside of me. Looking back now, I guess it was one last pathetic attempt to somehow win you over finally, and keep you for myself, while also avoiding your occasional threat of seeing other people like you threatened me with on the boat. I have tried to solidify our relationship for like three months now and be your boyfriend, but I guess you weren't sure if that's what you wanted or if it was the right thing to do if your heart wasn't all into it. I gave it my best shot though and I did try, but I fucked it all up earlier in our relationship through my procrastination, worrying about ruining our foundation as best friends and I guess just generally being scared of developing a serious relationship with someone. I have no one to blame for that but myself, and I regret that in hindsight. I guess that's just the way it was supposed to be for some unknown reason, but I'm sorry for that, you did deserve better than that from me.

Basically, as a man with some hint of self respect, dignity, and I guess probably some ego as well, I just don't think that I can live with going from what we were to basically just being a passive friend or something. Fuck that, there's no dignity at all in that option for me. We won't be able to be like we were, you will be off with some other guy somewhere, and you're not gonna wanna run around and do shit and hang out with me probably. Besides, what about my happiness, what would I get out of humiliating myself and just being your casual friend, all the fun stuff would be taken away. I might as well be "he who can't move his arms" or something, and frankly I would rather be nothing to you than that. I also can't live with being thrown away like an old used up roll of toothpaste and basically be replaced by some guy you termed a "crazy drunk" you've known for two days. But, if that's how you feel and that's the road that you feel you need to travel down, I'm sorry, but you will be going down that road without me being there. Unfortunately, I'm not an android or a faucet that you can just turn on and off when you feel like it, there are way too many emotions and feelings there for me to live with that. I guess in theory the idea of us just being friends sounds like it could work, but the way things have gone down and the disrespect and your basic lack of caring about me or my feelings at all has pretty much sealed the deal where now I can't even do that. I don't know, if the events of the last few days had been handled differently, maybe it would have worked. You don't realize how much you coming over IN PERSON and perhaps saying you're sorry or maybe even acting like you cared about how this has hurt me would have meant to me. I would have forgiven you and I wouldn't be writing you this letter now. But, if you want to get really technical, then just a fucking phone call before telling me that you were going out with some other dude and that we were done or whatever would have sufficed. You were always such a great and nice and benevolent person, so it's hard for me to even fathom you pulling this Jerry Springer type dramatic and ridiculous bullshit. There's ways to handle things, and there's ways to handle things, and you pretty much ruined it and showed how you really felt about me, which wasn't very much. Again, I really don't think you could have handled things any fucking worse than you did. I realize there's no manual for these sorts of things, but fuck, use some common sense once in a while you know.

Now I feel fucked over and insulted now and it's not sitting well at all with me. Sitting here alone starring at the walls I have experienced the worst feelings of misery, rejection, confusion, pain and pure loneliness that I have ever felt in my entire life. I cannot eat and I cannot sleep. I'm staring into the abyss over this whole situation, and more specifically over YOU. If that's not love, I don't know what is I guess. I'm not gonna sit here and claim confidently that this is the right thing to do, a giant part of me wants to rip this letter up after I write it and never give it to you. Maybe I'm over-reacting and maybe I should just be your friend. I'm confused and torn, and have very few answers. I want you in my life, I don't want to continue writing this. I love you and don't want to treat you like you treated me. Where is my best friend/quasi-girlfriend/lover/sister/psychologist/priest? Where are you for my breakdown? Where are you when I need you the most? Where's my IN PERSON hug telling me that everything would be alright? It isn't there because you're off planning your next date and having a great time out there somewhere with some other dude while I sit here, pathetic, in the depths of Hades. How ironic, considering that I was there for all of your insanity, big breakdowns, medium breakdowns, little breakdowns and every other emotional dramatic episode that you had.

Who was fucking there IN PERSON every single time you called, ME, that's who, ME! You called me, and not because we were nothing, like you claim now, you called because we were something and you loved me. I cared and loved you, and I dropped whatever I was doing regardless of what it was and came to wherever you were at, and I was fucking there with my arm around you, holding you, telling you that everything would be alright. Where are you now? You dump on me and don't even show up IN PERSON and see how I am, say you're sorry, or say anything really. You treated me like I meant nothing at all to you and I was some lowlife who beat you and called you stupid or something. I don't get it. Especially since now you claim that I was nothing and we were nothing. That killed me and sealed the deal for me. How can I possible be your friend or anything else for that matter now? And, FUCK YOU for that! I can't even believe it. You're just gone and indifferent. This is insane, so unlike you, weird, and not you as far as I know you. And I know you, that's the thing. We were inseparable for two years, you know someone after that much intimate time. I have never seen this side of you. I have never seen you be mean to anyone, never say anything bad about anyone, never treat anyone badly, you care, you donate to causes, you are not this person doing this to me. I hope I find out one day that you got abducted by aliens and they did some experimental personality switch on you or something.

I not only feel shit on by my lover/semi-girlfriend, but also by my best friend in the entire world. So this hits me on two fronts really, and it hurts a million times more on the best friend side. I'm sorry but you don't fuck over something that important, which was the foundation for everything we were. Your pissy attitude and basically almost forced apologies, as well as the "I could have handled that differently" line means nothing to me, because actions always speak louder than words. And, basically it said to me, I don't care enough about you to actually think of how this might affect you. It's basically an issue of respect and decency, which you showed very little to me, with the act of going on a date and me not knowing about it and then being all over this middle aged guy you had known for two days right in the middle of a public bar and worse in front of my friends, then replace me with him, and then not give a fuck after that about how I was feeling or what I was having to go through. I hope that you feel horrible about it one day, that's the actions of a fucking lowlife in my book. And, please don't insult my intelligence by claiming it was just a small kiss or something, I've heard the play-by-play. For future reference, you don't pull shit like that with someone who's your best friend, who really loves you and really cares about you and what happens to you, it will really hurt and crush them. And we both know, if that had been me doing it to you, you would be pissed off and hurt as well. Hell, I might as well have fucked XXX behind your back and I guess just apologize if I happened to get caught by your friends doing it and then be like "oh sorry, I meant to tell you about it but I didn't feel like calling you at the time and telling you about it because I didn't wanna answer to you and I thought we were nothing." Then, tell you that you had been replaced, and then be an asshole and not even really care about how you felt, but as added insult give you the option of being just my friend. That's basically the gist of what's happening to me.

But regardless, like I said earlier, it kills me to do this; I really don't want to do this one bit. But you have given me no other option really, so, basically, as short and to the point as I can make it, GO FUCK YOURSELF! You may not want to be my girlfriend, but I don't even want to know you. Everything we were is completely dead and now I want nothing to do with you. I can never trust you again, and I don't give people a second chance to fuck me over, especially a best friend and someone I let get closer to me than anyone I have ever known, and someone who I thought was the best person I had ever come across. I expected a hell of a lot more from you. It really does hurt me badly to say these things to you and to do this.

To the before XXXXX, wherever you are:

Even though I feel this way right now, I can't pretend that I didn't have an amazing time with you though. Two years of my life flew by, and I know that I'm a better human being for having known you and spent that time with you. I don't regret any of it, minus up until the end. The memories before that will always be special to me though. You were the first person I ever loved, other than my mom of course. You proved to me that it's possible to love someone and let someone special in past my obvious hard-like shell and trust someone enough to give them my heart. You made me question everything I though I knew about myself or what I wanted out of life. You had me wanting a life with you, a kid with you, a fucking generic house with a white picket fence in the suburbs with you, all of it, even though it scared me and I didn't want to admit it. You got to me, no one else ever had, so it was very special for me. I hope that you eventually find what you're looking for out there somewhere. You have my heart and a slice of whatever good is inside of me. Part of me will always love you.

xoxo

"Ok, I came, now get the fuck off me and go sleep on the couch." She tells me. "What the fuck are you talking about? I can cum, just give me a little while longer sugar tits. Sometimes it just takes me a while when I'm fuckin' drunk." "You've been fucking me for two hours. I think you've had enough time Brett." "Yeah, what the fuck ever, get yours and it's over. I see how it is missy." "Go jerk off in the bathroom or something. I'm going to bed." A man sighs and pulls his dick out of a girl's pussy and leaves the room unsatisfied. A man goes through the hallway and towards the bathroom grabbing a cigarette off of a hallway table and lighting an ultra light cigarette on the way. He sits on the toilet and smokes his cigarette. He finishes the smoke and tosses it in the toilet. He grabs his now limp dick and some lotion from a large bottle of Jergen's hand lotion next to the toilet and attempts to jerk off. Nothing much happens. Visions of the fuck session that just conspired flashes in his cerebral cortex. This does no good unfortunately. He searches his short term memory for any woman he's wanted to fuck lately but hasn't, and who also happen to better looking than the girl he just had the fuck session with. Finally, at least a little dick movement happens, but it's only a semi-boner at best. He plays with his mostly limp dick furiously as the time slowly drips by. "Fucking shit, I can't believe that bitch didn't let me cum." He thinks to himself. This is such fucking bullshit! That cuntbag whore can go fuck herself. Nothing is really going right for him. He needs something more fucked up to get off to. He smokes another cigarette on the toilet while contemplating what to do now. Whatever it takes, he will be fucking cumming tonight, no matter who has to suffer. He's got it. He takes his limp dick and the large bottle of Jergen's hand lotion back into the room where the girl he just fucked earlier is now sleeping, at least he thinks she is. He crawls onto the bed. She is laying on her side and doesn't move. He moves in closer and observes her for breathing and movement. She's breathing, but there is no movement, so he's good to go he thinks to himself. He straddles the top of the bed and places his limp dick over the back of her head which was mostly just a shitload of hair, good enough. He takes a gob of Jergen's hand lotion and starts stroking his cock. The deviousness of this act is enough to make his cock start to get hard immediately. The idea of jerking off all over a sleeping woman that wouldn't let him finish is enough of an appealing visual for him. He's jerking off as the late night minutes pass him by, but no cum has been released though. She moves an arm or twitches occasionally. This doesn't help things, yet he continues stroking his cock. He comes close to squirting cum all over her head several times, but still nothing really happens. His dick is raw and red now, yet he continues furiously stroking. Fuck, he thinks to himself and stops stroking his cock. "The bitch will never know how close she came to getting jerked off on in her sleep." He goes back to the bathroom and washes the gob of Jergen's hand lotion off his hand and dick and lights another cigarette. "Fuck, I'm a failure and can't do anything right!" I mean he's a failure and can't do anything right! See, I fucking told you.

xoxo

"The Drunkard Rooster and the Waxing June Moon"

we kiss,

I can see in the reflection

of her glasses

that her glittery lipstick

shit

is all over my face now

bar patrons

let's be honest here

drunks

pass us

me in the passenger side

seat

her in the

driver's side

seat

she massages my erect

rooster

I can feel the cum

aching in the bowels

of my

testicles

release us

they say to me,

fuck,

a cop sits at the nearby

stop sign

he stops

sits

forever

it seems

I see him looking at us

inside the car

he finally pulls

away

her hand is still inside

my green fatigue pants

button-fly

one button

two button

three button

the rooster

is

revealed

she leans over

her tits rest on the middle

console

my rooster

is in her mouth

her glittery lips

now wrap

themselves around

the rooster

I say a bunch of dumb shit

because

it feels good

I moan

I grab her freshly cut hair

with my left

hand

and push her face

further down on

the rooster

I feel it

I don't say anything,

fuck,

I push her face down

as the semen

is released from

my testicles and into her mouth

slurping noises

made

I look down

there's no cum left on

the rooster

it's all now dying

in her glittery coated mouth

she says

it's saltier than usual

I tell her

yeah

I ate a double bacon

cheeseburger

and a large

fry

for lunch

earlier.

xoxo

I'm an asshole, but I loved her. I suppose I didn't really realize how much I did until it was all over. Part of me is gone now, taken away. I'm empty inside and feeling it. There's nothing to do now that she's gone. The only thing to do is think and try figure out what the fuck just happened to me. She went insane and it made no sense. She loved me one day and despised me the next. It will never make sense to me. It will be a riddle to me until the day I die. Fucking women, man, they make no damn sense. I miss her worse now than yesterday, and she doesn't even give a fuck. She's out having some great time, and I'm here alone and in silence, wondering what fucking train just ran me over.

xoxo

I went down on this girl recently. I was drunk and it was pretty fucking dark. Her pussy seemed fine to me. It didn't smell funny or anything like that. After she had two orgasms, my mouth was hurting so I quit eating her pussy. I had to take a piss before we started fucking and I went into her bathroom and saw all this white shit all over my face. What fucking luck! I eat the pussy of a bitch with a fucking yeast infection!

xoxo

"Whatever, ok"

"I'm not really down with the sexual friendship anymore. But I'd love to be friends"

"I'm not mad at you and I have no hard feelings towards you. You're a fun girl and I may change my mind but right now I just need a break"

"Yea, that's prob best. Good luck, no hard feelings"

"Yeah I don't know. Just always seems to happen and it gets fucking irritating. I like you thouhg and I'm not trying to hurt you or anything. I'm just really hungover and I have a headache and I just want to be left alone"

"yah me either. I think our personalities clash too much while drunk"

"Didn't you deleete me as your friend? That's the only reason I untagged myself. I don't know what I said. I just know that I've never hung out with anyone where there was always so much goddamn drama."

"Whatever. Great answer. Don't worry about it. I'd honestly rather not know"

"I don't know. I'm too hungover and trying to do homework to deal with this bullshit right now..."

"What did I do? Can you tell me that? You took all our pictures off ore you telling me you don't want to hangout anymore"

"It's fine it's not like I'm mad at you. Just like half the time we hang out it ends in total disaster"

"sorry for being mean"

"If you could give me back my CD's then we could conclude our relationship. I don't really care. I just want my shit back. For once try and act your age bitch!"

xoxo

Both of them are drunk and joke around about giving me a blowjob. I admit it would be cool, but that sort of shit doesn't happen to me. Hell, it's hard enough for a prick like me to even get one girl to suck my dick most of the time, much less two. The faint taste of some sort of liquor is on her lips as I kiss her. I grab her hair hard and pull her closer to me. Her friend who isn't as good looking as she is, but has bigger boobs unbuttons my black jeans and then unzips my zipper and pulls my cock out from underneath my blue underwear. I admit, for some unknown reason I was a little nervous. This sort of shit happens to better looking people and in porno movies. My dick is mostly limp, but it was improving the more the girl who was less good looking but with the bigger boobs sucked on it.

"Do you like watching your friend suck my cock?" I ask the one with small tits.

"Yes, it's fucking hot."

"I know, you were right she is good at it."

"But, I like you sucking my cock. Sharing is caring you know." I say as I kiss her again.

My cock was hard and probably about as big or as little as it could ever be. The better looking girl with smaller boobs gets on her knees on my hardwood floor and starts licking my balls. Then, the girl with the bigger boobs hands my cock over to her and she starts sucking my cock while the girl with the bigger boobs starts licking and sucking on my balls. I feel like I'm in some parallel dimension. For once, I'm in my own fucking VHS porn tape. I grab big boobs and start kissing her while smaller boobs continues to suck on my cock. I grab her head and push my cock down her throat. Shit, this girl is a fucking professional, someone did bless her with "DSL" no doubt about that. I feel my cum swirling in my balls. I stand up, my black jeans now around my shoes.

"I'm gonna fucking cum soon." I tell them.

They both get on their knees on my hardwood floor. Bigger boobs starts sucking my cock again. Christ, I could feel the cum leaving my balls and traveling up my urethra. My legs got weak and tremored a little bit.

"Fuck, I'm cumming." I tell them, and I unleash probably the biggest load of cum that's ever come out of me all over big boob's mouth and face.

"Lick my cum off her face." I tell smaller boobs.

She leans over and licks a wad of cum resting on her friend's cheek.

"I told you his cum tasted amazing." Smaller boobs tells bigger boobs.

I don't know what the fuck just happened, it was almost like a surreal Dali inspired dream. I waddle with my black jeans still around my feet to the bathroom to wash my dick off while cum is still slowly dripping out of my cock and onto my hardwood floor.

xoxo

"The Suppression of Dopamine Receptors in Compton, California"

I met

and fucked

a fat stripper last Friday night,

why?

not

why did I fuck her?

that is an obvious answer

Miller High Life

and

Jagermeister,

why,

did I give her

my phone number?

did she give me

various STD's?

I'm an idiot!

and

now it's Monday,

Text:

hi

not returned

Call:

how are you?

not returned

Text:

not returned

Text:

are you avoiding me?

not returned

Phone call:

are you avoiding me?

not returned

Text:

I had a really great time the other night

not returned

Text:

I hope your ok

not returned

Text:

how was your Easter?

not returned

Text:

are you avoiding me?

yes…

xoxo

"hey how are you feeling today?

not too horrible I guess. How about u??

i have a horrible headache…..i think its sex withdrawl-haha

haha, well I guess I'll have to pork you soon before you explode

good idea… i think it will cure this headache

ha, it's possible

dont get too excited now

well I'm still waking up, so I'm mundane right now

well get your coffee and perk up

I'm out of sugar and milk so no coffee

well you can pick it up on your way-LOL

oh so u want me to pork you now?

whenever you wake up

well I gotta run a few errands but I suppose I could stop by before I do them.

where r u going?

errands wench!..haha. wal mart, post office

oh ok nothing too exciting…why are you going to wal mart...you hate walmart?

I realize, I gotta drop some film off and it's the cheapest

oh ok

yea so I guess I can run by and knock it out before I do all that if u want

ok but shouldnt you do your errands first?

nah, it shouldn't take me too long to knock it out

oh thats great

ha, and ur the farthest away, so maybe after getting laid I will be less angry when I have to go in wal mart

whatever...maybe I'll just go back to bed

well shit, what do u want me to say...

nothing

uhh I don't know, you asked me to come over and get rid of ur headache, I was just ablidging

i know its cool...I porbably just need to lay down

I don't know, make up ur goddamn mind woman!....lol"

xoxo

Right before I went up and talked to you I told my friend, and I actually remember pointing at you and saying to him "do you see that beautiful girl, the one with the leopard print shoes and the big tits? She will be mine one day!" That's pretty much as word for word as I remember it being. I also remember seeing my friend again in a bar not too long after that while me and you were hanging out together. I think you went to the bathroom or something and he came over and was like "holy shit man, that's the coolest thing ever. You pointed and said that she would be yours and now you're together." That was probably the absolute coolest and most awesome I've ever felt in my entire life. I'd never done that in my entire life. I'd never met you and I knew nothing about you other than that you were way out of my league probably. I fucking suck with women in general, so I felt like I had climbed fucking Mt. Everest, at least for a dork like me anyways.

xoxo

"Of Village Idiot Lanes and 3,653 Clay Ponds"

I hope you're happy

I'm not

I sit here

alone

with nothing

but screaming neighbors for companions

I'm hurting

do you even give a fuck?

insert confusion and a question mark

I doubt it

I'm cynical

but

I want to believe you

and in UFO's and

fucking Bigfoot

I wish I had the allusion

of your happy life

never seeming to find

what you're looking for

maybe

it's right here

across the street

from you

blind as you are

you may never realize it

something special resides

in a corner room

writing about you

you may shun it

you may avoid it

you may even hate it on occasion

I hope you open them

your peepers

before it's too late

you're as scared

as I am

we both know that

admitting it

is

another story in itself.

xoxo

"whatever, we can do something thurs if you wan tto Im off then to"

"cool, I might throw trivial pursuit in the car and use it as an excuse to come over and sniff ur panties when ur not looking!"

xoxo

I saw her new pictures from her excursion with "gingervitis." His friends are middle aged and lame just like he is. One was drinking a Bud Light Lime or some lame bullshit. If you ever catch me with one of those, just go ahead and punch me in the goddamn face please and don't apologize for it afterwards! The "fellas" she called them in the picture, minus her "favorites one" she says. Her stupid fucking friends make stupid fucking comments about how hot they are and how they want a free plane ticket out there as well. Goddamn, they're all as fucking clueless as she is. There are plenty of fat ass middle aged ugly people around here who are pussies and drink light beer, no need to travel if that's all you want bitches.

xoxo

"The Primal Therapy of Snatch and Mad Worlds"

She's driving me insane

she says that she loves me

I like her

but

love is a Stretch Arm Strong

I tell her this

and

it upsets her

Tears For Fears

form in her eyes

I rub her hand

and arm

trying as best I can

to comfort her

a little

I didn't know what to say

I had no response

I just sat there

on the edge of the bed

looking at her pussy

that I just

came inside of.

xoxo

She text messages me randomly: "You're finally free- I'm moving out!"

xoxo

I've either gotten old and lame or I've wised up. I'm not fucking stupid nasty random bitches anymore, that for the most part I can't even stand. From now on I'm only fucking girls I get to know, or have at least known for a while that I'm at least sort of attracted to. People are nasty and have all kinds of shit that I don't want. I'm happy being celibate for a while. I have nothing to give these bitches anyways right now, other than a cock and a wave goodbye. Anything else would be asking too much at the moment.

xoxo

"pouring jim bean on ur crotch will be optional

to be clear it was not on my crotch and the only skin I exposed was the fat around my belly button

Ha, I like it, it made u a horndog

uh yeah....I was crazy

yeah, but it was fun for me anyways

not that I really have a problem in that dept anyways, totally fun...I agree

anytime I can get laid with sleepies in my eyes and a big afro can't be bad!"

xoxo

Riding around late at night getting crazy in the head. The Pixies play loudly in my car. I haven't changed the CD since it happened. The letter is over on the passenger seat next to an unopened pack of cigarettes. Revenge is at hand, and the last word will be mine. I was way too nice and in shock when it all came down, and it was eating me up. Fuck that bitch of a whore; she's getting this nasty letter if nothing else. I don't even really care if she opens it and reads it or just throws it in the trash. I know what I said and I won't regret shit after it's sent to her address. Yeah, after what I said, she'll feel something, some emotion will be there. I won't be the only one anymore. I hope she hates my fucking guts after this. I hope it gets there by Monday. I need some shit to go down.

I've been too tame. That stupid fuckin' whore, just the thought of her makes me angry now. I'm riding around getting crazy in the head while she's probably fucking that ugly pathetic motherfucking salesman that she'd known for two days that she ran off with last week. I have her address written on a small piece of torn paper next to the glorious two page letter/manifesto that I wrote. I even remembered to bring those stamps I had with the nutcrackers on them leftover from Christmas. I didn't have any envelopes though, that was the only problem. The track Gouge Away comes on. I like this song and press a button that displays repeat on the CD player. I'm headed to Walgreen's to get that fucking envelope, and I have ten minutes until they close. Anything is better than sitting in the apartment alone right now with nothing but my mind to keep me company. There's nothing else to do but kill time and ride around late at night getting fucking crazy in the head.

xoxo

I made her a mix CD with a safety pin on the front of the case and a track listing typed in purple ink. I do things like this.

xoxo

"When June Spawned a Monster"

My brittle clay remnants

lie

dormant

in a box shaped like

a heart

hidden in cheap wooden

drawers,

my teeth

rest

in peace

submerged

in

white vinegar

solution

0.5 %

quitter

yes I am
so are you,

my hands
press
red inflamed flesh
apart
insanity
folds and lines
flesh colored bumps
of
neuroticism
exposed
through cheap plastic
rental apartment blinds
the June sun,

my mind
delivers
corporate pizza
past sexual endeavors
never dreams
only
fantasies
confusion and plain chicken tacos
no lettuce please
amigo
bad television shows
empty
queen beds
time to
gargle it all

away

then

spit it back into

city-owned

drains.

xoxo

Dear XXXXX,

I realize I'm breaking your wishes of "discontinued communications," but aren't I just a punk rock deviant who doesn't obey all that many rules, so that's to be expected on some levels. I have no idea if you've gotten what I left for you or not, who knows, it may be in the trashcan as I write this, or if you're out of town or something, perhaps some crackhead will have stolen it by the time you get back. But, I can't live with myself and what I said and how I acted without making at least one valiant attempt to patch things up with you, and if nothing else back up my words with some form of action, which I think always means more. I might die tomorrow or next week and I would never want my last actions and words to you to be what they were. I poured my guts out into the most poignant concise letter I've ever written in my life inside of a handmade card with funny art of me killing myself inside of it as well, along with a dozen roses, and a necklace I made for you. I'm not trying to buy you off, but you may never want anything to do with me again, and I have to assume that. So, I wanna go out with something I can live with, knowing I threw everything I had that was good and decent inside of me into something for you. I realize this is all my own fault and doing, but it really bothers me and doesn't feel right if you're angry at me, aren't in my life at all, and won't speak to me...Brett

xoxo

We went back to her place after they kicked us out of the bar. It was early to me, but late to them I guess. Hell, I think they wanted us out of there so bad that's the reason they didn't even ask me to pay my tab. She started blowing me after I was halfway through drinking one of her beers. I couldn't really get her head positioned so I could see her sucking my dick, but it was good enough I guess. She pumped and sucked and jacked me off for a long time. I was fucked up and probably wasn't gonna cum anyways, but I wasn't telling her ass that. This was way too much fun. After a while she ran out of saliva so I had to help her out so I spit in her hand. Granted, it was probably mostly snot, but it was lubrication regardless. My stomach was killing me, probably from all that cheap beer in the can I was swilling down all night. I didn't have to vomit, I just had to shit. But, who in their somewhat right mind would tell a girl to stop sucking your dick just so you can go take a shit? Well, not this cowboy. I let out several small farts; I didn't smell anything and her nice comfortable couch hid any

174

sounds they made. A few minutes later a big one was coming. I could tell and there wasn't much I could do so I just made a few groaning noises and said "fuck that feels good" really loud. I'm sure she thought it was because she was doing a great job bobbing up and down on my cock, but I didn't want to hurt her feelings and tell her that I had just shit my pants on her nice comfortable expensive couch.

xoxo

"Hi Brett! Happy Birthday!!!!!!"

"Aloha, thanks I appreciate it! How you been doing? Still stalking me? Sweet! Where the hell were you a few months ago when my lady friend ran off?...haha"

"I'm a dedicated stalker, but harmless. Haha! Where was I a few months ago....UMMMM you deleted me as a friend & blocked me. Sorry to hear about your lady friend. Anyway, I've been doing great! What have you been up to?"

"Indeed you are little missy! I'm impressed by your dedication though, I admit! Delete and block?...me? I don't remember doing that, must have been my alter ego or something, what an asshole!"

xoxo

"Acronym BFF Doesn't Always Mean Forever"

Sweetheart,

the morons say

the

deeper the love

the

deeper the pain

the fuckin' bitch

stuck it in me good

a scapel blade

a nurse's white benevolent

glove molested hand,

nice and deep

turn

right to left

and

release

rusted old

safety pin

me

back together again,

Mr. Potato Head,

the kids

keep calling me

and hurling their

insults

and

rocks

as I pass them by.

xoxo

"Im watching a movie and resting. I have clinicals tomorrow. You came through in fantastic fashion as always. Maybe I'll see you around sometime you fucking bitch…"

"Ay yi yi"

"Right, keep your word when you give it. I'm tired of being some last option that's so easily blown off. Not a great feeling. If I'm your friend and if you give a shit you don't act like it. Just saying…"

"I'm sorry. I'm listening to my CD now thank you"

"You're welcome. WTF am I supposed to do with you? I really like you but we never hang out or talk and everytime I try to you're way unreliable or piss me off. It's quite frustrating."

"You know I can't stay peeved at you that long. I still want to get food and go to the mall with you or just basically hang out. If you can do that withouth changing the time to do it like 179 times and keep your word them I'm in"

"Lol…I understand your frustrations with me. I'm a brat. I'm at work tonight. Maybe Sunday?"

"I'm glad you do. Being abrasive with you is the only way you notice that. I'm trying to help you get better for what it's worth. Sunday is fine unless you wanna get drunk tomorrow ngiht"

"No drinking"

"You're so fun. I like your insanity and your neuroticicsm but we need to exocices the fucking brat part of you. Did you show her the most awesome card you will ever get in your entire life"

"What card?"

"Yeah some jackass spent a lot fo time to make you a birthday card and left it on your porch in the middle of the night…jeez, you're not helping yourself here missy."

"Was that a card? I just put it up and didn't look at it"

"Wow, are fucking kidding me? Yes, open it up Sarah Palin's baby. It's a fucking giant birthday card. I didn't jerk off in the inside of it for nothing you know."

"I just read my card and actually got a little tear in my eye from your raw honesty and genuine love"

"That's cool. That's probably the sweetest sentence you have ever said to me. Thanks. I'm glad you finally looked at it. I tried to be as honest as I could be"

"I tried to call you but you didn't answer text message queen. Thanks for earlier, maybe now you understand why I took it as as a bit of rejection"

xoxo

I'd never directly seen a girl spit my cum out of her mouth before. I found it interesting though. The route that my cum traveled to make it into my sink would've made Ponce De Leon proud. I asked her to not run the water after she spit it out in the sink. I wanted to get a look at all my millions of dead sperm sitting helpless in my sink. She gave me a weird look and ran some water and washed her hands anyways, and then used my bubble gum flavored mouth wash to get the taste of my cum out of her mouth.

xoxo

The Night before Text Message:

"Ur such an fucking joke. I guess it enver worked cause I never had enough money for you. U and Gingersnap can saturate in being fake ass ignorant people!"

No Response.

The Day after Text Message:

"I'm so sorry for being mean n hurting you. I was shitfaced and being stupid. I'll always be your friend even if u hate me"

No Response.

The Day after That Text Message:

"Will u please accept my apology. I feel so horrid about this. I'm really sorry, I didn't mean that stuff"

No Response.

xoxo

I don't claim to have anything figured out, but I do know that when women act insane and make no sense read some Bukowski, read a lot of Bukowski in fact.

xoxo

"this semester I had some good excuses....friend died in iraq, grandma was in the hospital, prostate problems...I make up some weird shit

i wouldnt joke about prostate probs they seem to be pretty painful from what ive heard

you could be cursing yourself-you know karma

haha, I've had a prostate exam

lovely

next one, I'm coming to ur place and requesting your finger

lol…uh no

I felt violated by his man hands

im sure you di

at least he used some KY

i would wory only if he broke out the fancy stuff

haha, yea if he dimmed the lights on put on michael bolton I would worry"

xoxo

"I Dextered all the Fish in the Sea"

I stalk myself

no one

else

is worthy,

on the

battlefields

of past blood

spilt from

plastic ketchup bottles

and
femoral arteries
the silent day outside
rots
at night
staples inserted into paper
thin dermis
weathered shoes never
walked in
benevolent compliments received
but
never given,

I stalk myself
no one
else
is worthy,

pockets full of disease
no epidemic change to give
the ashtray is empty and clean
and
is no longer on fire
holidays during winter are detestable
even
more than
my family
even
more than
your family
even
more than

their family.

xoxo

"Put bluntly - i'm interested in your sperm. I don't really know what else to say. If you're amenable, I can come to Myrtle Beach, & we can give it a shot. What do you think?"

xoxo

She's always putting on lip gloss. I asked her if I could have some. She offered me the container, nah; I'll just borrow some off of your lips I say jokingly. She puffs out her lips and I kiss her out of nowhere. Her lips are softer than I remembered. She was drunk and I was sort of sober. Fuck it; I'm glad that I did it though. Hell, I even went dancing with her soon after which only happens once every ten years. I had a boner the whole time. I can't dance and she can't dance much better than I can, but I'll give it to her though, she can goddamn "boner dance" that's for sure. I grab her vodka in a plastic cup with my teeth and pour it into my mouth and onto my face. I kiss her again. I rub on her gargantuan fake tits. My crotch rubs against her ass over and over again. We go to the bar and I kiss her a bunch of times while I ordered another beer. I taste honey buns, and I don't why. Do they even make that flavor of lip gloss? I have no idea. I sip on my beer. Out of nowhere she doesn't feel good. I say let's get the fuck out of this shithole. We go outside and sit on a bench. She texts and feels sick, and I kiss her once again. She's not driving home, hell no. Plans are discussed and I tell her that I'll just drive her home. The Clash plays on the way to her house. She sits on my box of mints, and I ask her if her pussy stinks? She mumbles something and then closes her eyes. I pull up to her house, fuck; they all look the same in this fucking suburban planned neighborhood. She gets out of the car and walks towards the grass in the front yard. She gets on her knees and vomits once. A few seconds later and a few more heaves and she vomits all over the grass again. I ask her if she wants me to hold her hair, and she says no. I light a smoke and search my car for a Dunkin' Donuts napkin. I found one, sort of used under the front seat. I hand it to her. I ask her where her keys are even though I knew they were in her purse. I tell her to stay there and I go and unlock the door. As I try and use the garbage can next to the door that would never hold the door to prop it open with, she stumbles over and goes inside. I go back to the car and grab her shoes and purse and bring them inside. I think about leaving one of her shoes in my car so I can pull some Cinderella type bullshit, but it was too late. In the small time between that and going back to my car, she somehow had removed her dress and was already sort of under a blanket on the couch. She had her black bra on. She mumbles a few things, no she doesn't want any water, and no she doesn't want a bag next to her just in case she vomits again. I sit down next to her and play with her cat. I watch her as she passes out. She didn't brush her teeth but I kiss her goodnight on her vomit laden lips anyways. I close the door silently behind me and wave goodbye to the cat. The Clash are still playing as I speed down silent suburban streets where all the fucking houses look the goddamn same.

xoxo

"Pull your pants down baby! I had a bad day and I just need to fuck something."

"What the hell is wrong with you? Why don't you just go somewhere and just fuck something then?"

"Come on baby. I'm sorry. Like I said, I just had a bad day. My dick is hard and I just need to take it out on someone."

"Well, I'm not your fucking whore. I'm not here to fuck you whenever you feel like it."

"Look baby, I don't have the patience for this shit now. I just want to bust a nut. Then, possibly, I'll be back to normal again."

"Well I'm not in the mood. I'm on my period now anyways, and trust me you don't want any of it now unless you want some bloody pussy."

"I don't give a shit; bloody pussy is still pussy in my book!"

The girl disappears down the hall and into the bathroom. The man pulls down his pants, but doesn't remove his shoes or his shirt. The girl finishes in the bathroom and enters the bedroom naked.

"Are you going to take your shoes off? You're going to mess up my sheets!"

"Who cares, I'll just leave them on. You let your nasty ass dog on the bed so who cares about my shoes?"

The man puts his dick inside the girl's bloody pussy and starts pounding away. After a few minutes the urge to piss hits the man and he pulls his dick out of the girl and runs into the bathroom to take a piss. The man yells to the women from the bathroom.

"Jesus fucking Christ! There's fucking blood all over my dick! I thought there was just going to be a little bit."

"Well that's what you get; I told you that you didn't want any of this pussy tonight."

"Yea, I should've listened to you."

"See, I'm always right."

"Yea, maybe sometimes."

"How about I go wash this blood off my dick and then you can give me a blowjob?"

"Yea, I don't think so."

"There's some Lubriderm under the sink, go jerk off in the bathroom. I'm going to watch TV."

The woman leaves the room and turns on the TV in the other room. The man stumbles into the bathroom soon after to search for the bottle of Lubriderm that she said was under the sink.

xoxo

My fucking head is pulsating. It's all coming down now. I was riding high two days ago, and now it's all fucked up. Nothing makes sense today. My fucking head shoots pain up to my eyeballs. I look in the rear-view mirror and see bloodshot eyeballs staring back at me. I need relief for the hangover, but I'm too lazy to stop at a gas station and buy some pills to kill the pain. I just keep pushing the pedal of the car. Me and Iggy Pop, that's all the company I need right now. The song "nighclubbing" is playing. It's cold outside my window, but streaks of sunlight hit my face and arm occasionally. All I do is think, but there are no solutions. Fuck, what am I gonna do with myself? I don't want to be here. I want to be back in Miami doing something. I don't want a straight job. I know where that road leads to, nothing but a waste of time and unhappiness. I can't make it here. I've pushed it as far as I can go. I take a big sip of coffee and light another duty-free English cigarette. It won't solve anything but when paired with Iggy it ain't bad. I pass the hotels on the beach which are all deserted now. There are no tourists to speak of, other than a few Canucks here and there, at least judging from the license plates that I saw from Ontario. I light another smoke and push the pedal again. I cruise the entire town twice and there are still no answers. What am I gonna do? I'm running out of money and I got no one and nothing. I was saving the beer I bought earlier for tomorrow, but fuck it. I crack one open after I park in an abandoned lot with a view of the beach. I drink my beer and watch the waves through the dirty glass of my windshield.

xoxo

"Licking the Lithium Infused Walls at Wonka's Place"

Zero down

and

four pairs of dull blades

but

there's nothing to cut,

ten dollars won

a state lottery investor

but never collected

dried out Sharpie markers

make

great reminders of

angst and apathy,

the lifeless chrome infused lighter

chemical formulas are needed and desired

faded past images

are made into my personal black Jesus

crown of thorns,

isolated unlisted numbers and

blank generic plastic names

in modern yellow stained books

placed strategically

out of my deformed

reach,

uninhabited hearts shaped as assholes

require Bayer and dynamite,

vintage lint remains

but

my pockets are empty

and

so is my fucking life.

xoxo

Dear XXXXX,

Jesus fucking Christ on a fucking stick! I'm still wondering what happened to you. How can I be the only one with any emotions here? You're like a machine or an android now, C3PO XXXXX to get nerdy with my similes. How can you not feel anything for me now or show anything anymore? Damn, was I that forgettable and had you grown to feel almost nothing over time? You used to open up and let at least some emotions come out. You cried around me all the time and you showed feelings. I held you and told you everything was gonna be alright on various occasions. You made me feel, and I fucking knew without a doubt that you loved me and really cared. Damn, now I can feel the indifference. I sense it when I'm around you. How can you just not give much of a shit, is it that easy? Give me a Freudian slip or something, anything, let it out so I fucking know, so I don't feel like the goddamn girl here. This whole thing has been such a bitter fucking horse pill for me to have to swallow down my throat, administered by my best friend of course. Just thinking about all this shit gives me a headache and is so fucking confusing. I used to have pretty good insight into your head XXXXX, now, not so much. I don't know if my powers of perception need batteries or what? I can't tell what's going on with you. I have a hard time reading you anymore. What the hell really happened? I wish I knew, I want to know actually. No answers ever come though, only my theories and hypotheses which are never proved to be wrong or right really. Feel something goddamn it, show something goddamn it! You don't have to be the old XXXXX, but please fucking at least be human again.

xoxo

I finally stopped being nervous. I think this is day number 31, that's a full month and more most of the time. Nothing has happened. I just freaked myself out, shit bullets, prayed to a God that I don't believe in, smoked a lot of cigarettes, and about gave myself a fucking heart attack/meltdown. I'm definitely gonna be taking it easy for a while. I'm fucking scared straight and I didn't even have to go to prison. Actually, I'm just plain scared of fucking vaginas these days. They're fucking dangerous, no doubt about that.

xoxo

"A Faux Pas of Steel Panthers Available in Parenthesis"

Wiping

etched pewter broken hearts

with discount two-ply

toilet paper

etched pewter broken hearts

are now chaffed,

remove the screws

replace the staples

lighter fluid inflamed

veins and arteries

ultramarine blue

a multitude of cocks

peering

through gas station glory holes

and
rusted playground monkey bars
filling a mouth
with mucus and OPEC imported petroleum
bukakke
swapping
photographic evidence
of
germs and feces
facial protein art
my body is a terrorist act
notes
written in pencil
left to rot and be recycled
decaf
shots
syrup
milk
custom
drink,
wiping
etched pewter broken hearts
with discount two-ply
toilet paper
etched pewter broken hearts
are now chaffed,

turn left for the accident
turn right to look away
McDonald's at 3 a.m.
worn skin
white imported cotton panties

dick sucking lips

spit

swallow

purge

get out of my house

close the door

to any future correspondence

tacos and sloppy burritos not on sale

dirty reddened pimples

Erasure sings

stop!

underwear and black socks

inject Magnesium

and

sodium

laden pre-cum

into the brown eyes

of the demon,

wiping

etched pewter broken hearts

with discount two-ply

toilet paper

etched pewter broken hearts

are now chaffed.

xoxo

"So girls night was ok same as usual.???? anyway i got to hang with the shiny people for awhile. it felt very surreal and unnatural. I just dont feel like myself around so much fakeness. we did very little man bashing, but one of my married friends wants to have an affair so that was our main topic of conversation-we're all f'd up, everyone of us!"

"Who are these shiny people you refer to? Is that a nice way to say yuppie douchebag?...haha. I avoid all those places myself....bad music+inept posers=further angst for Brett. I'm glad that you share my anti social sentimate though, it's refreshing. Do people usually discuss the cheating with friends before they do the actual act? Just further proof of why I have no respect for marriage and relationships and why I avoid them. Might be odd, but hey I blame my parents for fucking me up....haha...I have to admit that I really don't have many married friends or really many people into long term relationships, but the few I do seem to have respect for the actual institution and probably wouldn't do any of that stuff. That's my intuition anyways, I could be off though. I think it also has a lot to do with where we live. People are fucking weirdos around here, after 4 years I still don't comprehend them. Beach towns tend to to attract fucked up people from around the globe really. Sorry if my comments are negative, but I gotta call it like I see it. Well I hope you had fun though. It raining like hell now, I hope it clears up....tomorrow I'm hoping to my first day on the beach in 07....supposed to be a great swell so I'm gonna have to bust out the wetsuit and go surfing as well I guess. I also need to get rid of my pasty winter skin suit...haha. Food for thought: what's a poor college student like myself gotta do to see you in a bikini on the beach? Alright enough rambling......sleep tight my statuesque little vixen!"

"Yes the shiny people are the posers, the ones who blieve they are VIP's for some unknown reason. The whole marriage/relationship thing is definately messy. But you're probably right about your friends they are likely trustworthy and respect their relationships. Some people do. I do for sure. Im not against relationships, but it would have to be a quality person-not so easy to find. Esp. here. This place is full of weirdos, old dudes with 20y/o girlfriends,cokeheads, and dont forget the shiny ones. We ended up in a club b/cuz one of my friends is hanging out with one of the Myrtle Beach VIP's-and thats where they like to gather. Again what makes them VIP's I have no clue, but they seem to think they are rather important. There was also a suprising number of old dudes (over 40-way to old for me) looking to hook up. I only have a few friends that are married also. Anyway enough of all that. Im down with going to the beach and plan to on the next hot day we have. kinda windy today?? but probably good for surfing though-Enjoy"

xoxo

I don't know what to do. I love her, no doubt about that. But, do I want her, that's the question? Am I willing to give up all the other pussies to have just hers? That posed question I just can't answer. The word "boyfriend" scares the living fuck out of me. Hell, romance, relationship, responsibility, children, and a white picket fence all scares the fuck out of me. It never felt right, and never felt like my destiny in any way. But, do I chance it and give it a try or do I think rationally and continue in my solitary refinement? This is the first time I've really ever considered any of this shit. She keeps giving me ultimatums and shit now. She doesn't like being referred to as a "special lady friend" or "best friend/fuck buddy." I guess on some levels I can't blame her for that, clarity can be a good thing. I feel like I'm keeping her from being happy and that she's wasting her time on me. On the other hand though, most people are a waste of time and life as well, so I guess it might as well be wasted on me.

xoxo

"The Mass and Velocity of a Sinking Mind"

A total fucking mass car wreck,

with no witnesses
was it that obvious
I punched them in the face
or
did I agree
self-destruction on a budget
can be a stunning thing
when viewed
as a spectator sport
rarely televised
though
hard lessons learned
when there's no one to blame
but personal
"I"
while
standing on the shoulders
of
styled black haired organic matter
I'm 3.5 miles from somewhere
and
6,276 miles from nowhere
the rats with fleas agree
in
unison

24 Pixie vinyl tracks

will remind me forever

of

solo bloodshot eye road trips

and

the girl who is in a rush,

filling my mind with gasoline

leaded or unleaded

both.

xoxo

My phone is alive,

"Will you have my baby so I can starve it to death in an art gallery?"

"It's official I'm gaining weight. I just got hit on by a black guy"

"Cooterific...fuck, I woke up with my clothes on with a boner grasping a pack of tropical flavored Skittles. My life is weird"

"Do you not wake up until noon still? Because I have to be at work by four"

"Ha, you're damn right I did. Don't ratfuck my stereo. Man, I was totally confessing last night. I meant what I said though..."

"Ha. XXX nature painter esquire. Ok, we'll lather each other up in teriyaki sauce and get buck wild. Will you just bring your own eye crap I don't know exactly what kind or brand to buy"

"If anyone tells you anything you always say stupid things like that. I don't know if it's funny or irritating"

"I will be up at eleven darlin'. I just said call me so I'll be up. Take your lithium now."

"Why don't you come over and paint one night this weekend. Spend the night and then we'll go to the beach the next day. Sounds like a dandy plan to me"

"I don't know...it depends"

"not dumbo. I want to do it in oranges"

"Do you ever get any of my texts? I never know. If you don't answer I'm not buying you any Fiddle Faddle at the Dollar Tree!"

"What's the name of that band that sings beds are burning?"

"I added you to my circle of friends so you can now text me all you want. How gay...I mean cute."

"Ahh damn going into hibernation mode in my treehouse then. You'll do fine and pass." "I don't know. That all depends on if you stay over after painting said Dumbo. I don't paint until late so it logically makes sense."

"I want to do a giant elephant painting. Will you help me?"

"Christ your eye solution is expensive as shit. Does Dollar Tree carry that shit. The things I do to get you to stay over I swear!"

"Ha, glad you made it home. I'm getting those items we talked about"

"Damn right, we're going to get tacos. Cooterrad, definitely wear a dress cause' this is a legitimate date. I'll even wear a shirt with sleeves for you."

"I'm fine with you wearing as little as possible"

"I don't mind. Just say I'm pretty and call me your sugar daddy and we'll be even steven"

"I'm hungover and feel like rhino shit. I also ate at Mcdonalds last night so I feel fat on top of feeling like rhino shit. Lie to me and tell me I'm pretty or something!"

"You're taking me on a date, you should be making those decisions"

"Hell yeah missy, this negro is down like a funcky clown. Tacos cool?"

"Jesus fucking Christ, a couple of adult libations won't kill you. I'll molester the stress right off you baby like you were an alter boy"

"No, I'm a much bigger one. I like you either way and accept your neuroticism"

"I found you a Cure sticker but you ain't getting it until I get my real date or a make out session"

"I'm such a fucking goddamn drunk!!"

"Huh, Hootie? Just accept that someone loves you. We need to go to Huntington State Park. I could take some cool photos of you before I knock you up with my love child."

"You don't know what love is. I probably don't either."

"Well I hope you're serious this time. I can't hae my emotions toyed with. I love you, have my cooter love child damn it!"

"ssure thing chicken wing.."

"You already know this. That's why we're astrological soulmates. Cancer and Scorpio go together like peas and carrots. Tacos and skee-ball next week?"

"Ok, on the trashed part, but I gotta watch my girlish figure. I can't job in a white airbrushed Speedo while being pl;ump you know. I'll have a few of your fries though"

"You are so fucked up"

"Ahh fuck, well next week then? I need some XXX time damn it! I miss you darlin'. I applied for a job as an ER Tech, maybe soon I can support you and my illegitimate baby"

"I have a pharmacology test this Friday sorry"

"Maybe I should have lied and said yes. I like it when you're jealous of my hand dates. Are you gonna wear a dress. I like that black one you have."

"So was that cool? Or are you apathetic towards me now? We're astrological soulmates baby. I need a good bossy woman to banter with.I hope so. Real funny. I'm harmlessly busting your cooterneuroticism. I love you beautiful. Just call me at eleven baby."

"No, I was probably gonna play trivia. I only go on dates with you dummy."

"And you never text me back within a reasonable time"

"Where dd the hesitation come from now? Stay in MB for a while and then we'll move to another beach town in California or Florida. Why don't you come over and have a drink with me?"

"I'm so torn on where to live. It's really wearing on me. I really need to talk about it with you. Maybe we can have a dink tomorrow after work"

"Probably true, don't be scared of my chivalry. I'll win you over after I kick your ass at skee-ball and use the tickets to score you a sweet whistle bracelet!"

"That's cool with me. I'll eat a granola bar to keep me alive. As long as I get to spend some quality time with you I'll be happy. So emo, yet so true."

"Why would I be pissed at you? Thursday is totally fine baby. I guess just let me know what time."

"Don't be pissed, but I just remembered it was my friend's birthday party on Wednesday. WE can go Thursday after work though"

"Is this aa real date??"

"I'm going into hibernation mode and will not be seen until after finals week"

"Are we still hanging out tomorrow?"

"I'm so torn about where to live. Date Wednesday I'm off then?"

"It was probably a good wake up call for you. Listen to Earth Crisis then hold a baby"

"You have a date ro something?"

"kk baby, I had a cooterblast. Looking forward to our real date."

"You have a bad mouth. I'll have a couple of drinks and some fattening food with you don't worry"

"It might be a late dinner, but we'll make it work"

"I think we should be totally trashy and get pizza and fries"

"You are too much"

"Tease you, oh I will with a Cure sticker. I get a make out session with you, and you get a sticker..even steven."

"Why are your friends so fucking boring?"

"No, that's pretty normal. Are you going to make it your status?"

"That's so mean, don't tease me with that stuff. I've only had grilled cheese there"

"Do you want to meet up at 6 so we don't have to be sorushed to eat?"

"Ok, well if you flatter me a little I'll be benevolent and tell you darlin'. Beach on Wednesday? Midnight Oil from Australia"

"Yeah. I'll take you wherevever you want to go. I heart you..you fucking moron"

"I listened to that Earth Crisis song, vegan for live"

"Have you ever had their pizza?"

"Tell that niglet to fuck off. You're my special lady friend,"

My phone is dead.

xoxo

Dear XXX,

Before you go to Costa Rica. Look, I like/love you and I can't help that. I always have had feelings for you, that's just the way it is. But, please contemplate these things while you're on vacation. Do you actually want to be with me and can you ever actually cut me a break and give me a real chance? It bothers me when you avoid me all the time and play stupid fucking games like you used to. I really thought you had changed, and please don't make me regret that. The avoidance and stupid immature shit is so lame. Not everything has to do with "her." It would be nice to just be with you with no sort of bullshit held against me, and we could just have a good time. Even though I might not like your ex, if you ever want to talk to me about him or anyone else, that's fine. I don't automatically assume the worst or hold it against you in any way. I'm not kidding when I say I was contemplating never having anything to do with you other than just friendship the last few days, but that's not what I want. But, like I said just think and let me know what you want while you're away. I'm yours if you want me, but if you don't, just tell me so I can find someone who does appreciate whatever it is that I have to offer. It's not fun feeling like you want nothing to do with me except when it's convenient for you or whatever, or always having past shit thrown in your face. I always want to feel like I can tell you the truth or whatever I'm feeling, but that's impossible with you presently. It will cause nothing but avoidance and bullshit, so really, I should just pretend. Stop with the neurosis and insecurity, and just be with me and things will be fine. I will always try and be there for you. It hurt me that you didn't even call when u were in a car wreck, that's so bizarre. I care about you, I really do, so yeah, I want to be the one you rely on and call to fix whatever is wrong. Anyways, just think about these things while you're there and let me know what you think...Brett"

xoxo

I despise her and I don't even know why. I hate her face that resembles a common mouse. Her idioms and neurotic behavior annoy me like nothing else. When I see her, I see red and unleash war verbiage on her person. I told my friends I wish someone would take her off my hands for me. I didn't mean for one of my close friends to fuck her the next week you fucking scumbag Polock asshole!

xoxo

"well I hit it with a bible really hard

haha...........Im going to watch that old movie The Way we Were, with Barbara Streisand.

I dont suppose you've seen it

no, god no

that jew bitch sucks

so what its a great romantic movie

uhmm, all romatic movies suck!!!!!!!!!!!

shut up

when I get a yeast infection maybe I will appreciate them more

and one day I will make you watch one with me

and maybe one day I will say I'm going to the bathroom and I'll squueze through your bathroom window and make a run for it

uh, no! i dont pressure you to watch anything but just once you could watch a

movie I like

well yea, that's because I know a lot cooler movies

thats very subjective

hey fucko, u just were raving about true romance.....

yes that was good, so now its your turn to watch, say when harry met sally with me

good fucking lord!

its a good movie

seriously you will have my balls in a jar if I watch that with you

what???thats the dumbest thing ive heard..

balls in a jar I tell you!

ya know its ok to do stuff like that with me, and I promise it will not affect your balls in any adverse way.....it may only get them licked more-LOL

the best I could compromise on a crappy romantic movie is say......you've got mail

well yeah that one isnt all that great, when harry met sally!!

ur nuts

i promise your balls will be fine

brett stout does not watch that shit!

fine whatever, Im never doing anything you want to do again!

haha

well ur just gonna miss out on some cool shit!

Nope!

good lord! god, ur busting my balls tonight I;ve seen that movie before anyways, I know why u want me to watch it as well

why?

cause they're like pals then all of a sudden they're all in love with each other

haha, yes but it was much more complicated

I told you I have seen it, the fake orgasm in the rest is the best part of that movie by far

yes thats good

I said it sucks, because I have seen it like 3 times

I'm way more cultured than u think I am

well you were the one raving about you're balls falling off in a jar or some madness, over watching a movie

yea well sepcifically watching it, and catching it because tbs is the only cable channel u get is 2 different things

well u can specifically watch it with me and its convenient cause I own it-imagine that-and havent seen it in awhile

ok fine, but afterwards I'm taking out my pent up aggression over watching that shit by putting a dick in yo ass!

haha.....perhaps, but from what Ive read rough and anal dont go together

well from what I read, you shouldn't believe everything u read.

im just saying it specifically said that gentle is key at least at first

and slow

I know! it was just a joke

oh sorry I forgot your the anal expert

yes, well I;ve done it a bunch, not sure if that makes me an expert

you anal whore u

skilled perhaps

well I can get it in there without u dying so

oh great, I wont die???Im there!!

well I don't know. it's gonna be weird and prob be uncomfortable, but take it like a porn star slut…haha

yeah well Im sure I'll do my best

all u can do really. just clean ur shitter out and I'll bring the lube.....the rest is pretty simple"

xoxo

"Pelting Timeshares of Mortification with Rocks"

alone

all alone

bar stool

Miller High Life sitting

alone

all alone

just like me,

the humans are gathering

festering

my scabs
all around
me
all of sudden
me
the center of
unwanted attention spans
fucking boring small talk
blah, blah, blah
who cares, who care, who cares
I don't,

alone
all alone
bar stool
Miller High Life sitting
alone
all alone
just like me,

being nice
never works
I tell you
never
nice
turns
1
8
0
degrees calculated
to asshole
as the time

slowly burns

I don't care asshole

just leave me alone

peace isn't just for hippies

I liked it better

when I was,

alone

all alone

bar stool

Miller High Life sitting

alone

just like me.

xoxo

I drove out to her house in the middle of fucking bumfuck nowhere. It was dark and my lights on bright didn't even really help me see much of anything. After getting lost several times, I finally saw the blue house off of the main road with the porch lights on, and the trampoline out front. The grass hadn't been mowed in forever and the place was a fucking dump, at least from the outside. What the fuck was I doing there? Oh yeah, I do a lot of stupid shit for pussy, I forgot. Well, you drove all the fucking way out here to bumfuck nowhere USA, there was no going back now. Just go inside, fuck her, and make up a lame yet somewhat original excuse and get the fuck out of there pronto afterwards. Carry on soldier.

xoxo

Fuck, you make my stomach hurt. Most of the time I'm near you this happens. Mike Tyson circa 1989 punches me in the stomach. This only happened once before when I was like fifteen. Mostly, I think that it was just nervousness though. The fact that you don't even know it makes it even better. I am in awe of you. I imagine it's the same feeling walking into the Sistine Chapel for the first time. I have to imagine it since I haven't been there yet. You think I'm meticulous, but the truth is I just like looking at you. I like everything about you. Where most people might find flaw, I find the real you. The bump in your nose, or the little scar on your chin are the things I like the most about you. I like you the best when you're wearing those pink sweatpants, no makeup, nails undone, and hiding under a hat. You think no one notices you like that; but I do. When you're dressed up there's too much competition, and compliments lose their luster after a while. How many times can you hear a drunken idiot say "you're hot." I don't want to be predictable and like other guys. I must do everything a little bit differently, that's just my thing. It would probably make me paranoid and annoyed if I knew someone was looking at me that way. Luckily, with the way I look, I doubt many are. I like you just the way that you are flaws and neurotic activity included. You're like a walking "scream" painting on cardboard with a pulse and I like it.

xoxo

Dear XXXXX,

Sweetheart I know I was mean and hateful, but come on, it was just drunken idiotic bullshit that I'm really sorry for doing to you. The words were completely empty and I obviously didn't mean any of it at all. It's sort of like Dr. Jekyll apologizing for what Mr. Hyde did. I've never really lied to you so you should trust me and believe me when I tell you things (sober), like I am now. I think that I deserve the benefit of the doubt on this. I have been one of the very few people who has always been there for you when you needed me, no questions asked, no I'm too busy or no I have better things to do. And, I know that you know in your heart of hearts that I love and care about you like I do no other, and I know that you love and care about me as well even though you won't admit it verbally anymore.

Even so, I'm a tad little midget worried and scared that you may be gone from my life forever. I don't ever want you gone from my life or for us to not know each other and talk and at least be friends, even though I want a lot more than that with you. I have always loved having you in my life and obviously we are meant to know each other, you were right, it will never truly be over. We are special friends, otherwise why would I be completely fucking in love with you and flip out on you? It's because I want you and I don't like you being with anyone else.

Everything that I've said to you about loving you, missing you, caring about you, being fucked up over you and thinking that I have what it takes now to give you what you want are all fucking true. If I have to suffer for you I will and let me tell you I already have, and most of the time I'm fine with that, but me lashing out shouldn't be that big of a shocker really. It's silly really. I love you, and you love me. I make you happy and you make me happy. I like hanging out with you, and you like hanging out with me, so to not be together is dumb to me. I learned my lesson, and I'm not chicken shit anymore like you once called me. I cannot sit idly by and not do everything I can do to win my goddamn dream girl back. That's what all of this has been about from the start. And, it's also the reason I get upset sometimes.

Granted, I realize calling you names doesn't help my case, but I'm very imperfect and mistakes will be made unfortunately. That said, I will put in overtime maximum cooterific effort for you. I believe in you and I wouldn't have suffered for all this time to remain in your life if I didn't think that you were one amazing special beautiful girl that I can't live without and may never find again. When we hung out that night and fucked around and the two days after that, it was the happiest I have been in forever, and it felt fucking right to me. I looked in your eyes and saw it on your face as well. You were happy (and drunk granted), but you were happy being there with me. I got to save the day and take care of you and it felt good and I had hope, hope for the first time in ages with you.

I'm not pissed at you now. I can't help it that I'm passionate and intense about you, and now and then I go a little crazy over you. Hell, maybe I should have showed more of that to you in the past. If I'm gonna be hurt and fucked up sometimes over knowing someone, I'm glad that it's over you. It's true, it bothers me when you disappear for weeks on end and I get worried about you and I don't know if you are alive and ok or dead or in the torture attic of a serial killer dressed as a clown. Then I have to find out you were on another ginger vacation with that guy and it hurts me. I know I'm not your boyfriend, so maybe it's none of my business, but I care and I love you so much that it's hard for me to take that type of stuff. And, I know that you know how that sort of feels and can in some ways relate. When you saw, read or heard things about me and XXX you got really upset and was fucked up as well. Granted, you didn't lash out at me, but maybe if you had to deal with it for six months, you might have.

I hope deep down that you don't really want me gone from your life, which I don't think you really do. Words, even mean ones are just words darling, feel free to call me some mean names, I would probably laugh if you sent me a mean drunk text to be honest. Here I'll help you out because I know you don't like saying nasty things to anyone. I know sometimes I'm a mean cocksucker of a close minded piece of shit asshole motherfucker lowlife know-it-all son of a bastard platypus…see don't you feel better and "even steven" now?…haha

I realize you are very upset with me and you have every right to be. I take full responsibility for my actions even though I was belligerently drunk and don't even remember doing it or saying what I said. I hope that you can forgive me and forget about what I said and did to you. I mean you did and said some bad and mean things to me and I always accepted your apologies, tried to forgive you and trusted your word that you didn't mean them or didn't mean to handle them the way you did. And I do remember still talking to you and hanging out with you even though you had just about killed my ass and ripped out my heart several weeks before. It seems so stupid for things to end this way after all the shit we've been through. Yes, twice I've said bad things to you that I really regretted the next day after I sobered up. For as long as we've known each other, that isn't so bad. I never want to be mean to you or hurt you ever. I mean have I ever (sober) treated you like shit or said horrible things to you or abused you or lied to you or cheated on you or neglected you or ran off with and knocked up strippers? Nope. This time it was sincerely an accident and just insane drunk type of shit you wish you hadn't of done the next day.

I know there is no way that "ginger ale" or any other guy around here for that matter can make you as happy as I can, nor will few if any do the things that I am willing to do for you and have done for you. If you never speak to me again and we aren't even friends, that sucks gigantic elephant cock and I'm gonna cry like I just watched Old Yeller 1,238 times in a row and be a hermit for a solid year, but just remember that a guy out there thought so much of you that he wrote you letters like this, made you random cool things and left them on your door hoping that it would brighten your day, became a paramedic just to impress your ass, wrote about you, was always there for you and gave a crap, made art inspired by you many times, lives daily in FBD misery without you his FBM and is still willing to rip out his spleen and give it to you if you needed it.

I made you this necklace and I give you these flowers and this passionate letter hoping that you will please forgive and forget what happened and be cool and talk to me again and let me be your FBD again for fuck's sake, otherwise I'm killing myself…haha. I promise sober that this sort of dumb shit has never happened and never will, but you know I always tell the truth, so who knows I might get drunk and lash out at you again. Keep me blocked if you want, it's probably better if you're going to be with someone else that I don't have to see that stuff, but I do want you to talk to me and to not be mad at me. Even though it's all my fault, it affects me and makes me sad. The best way to solve this problem is for us to just be together again, then I would be really happy again and then I would have no reason to be upset over you and bring out the drunken cooterclaws! See, problem solved, it was that easy. Anyways, I live for the moment and I could die tomorrow and I would never want my last words and acts towards you to be drunken stupid yak shit. If you really want me gone I will respect your wishes, but I'm going out "the brett way" with bravado and chivalry damn it!

xoxo

"The Post-Waffle House Contingency Escape Plan"

I like it when she puts my

dick in-between her

gargantuan fake tits.

I can feel the silicone

behind her flesh

rubbing against

my cock

and my ball sack.

I wanted to squirt cum

all over them

but they

were too dry

and instead

just rubbed my dick

raw

like sandpaper.

xoxo

You were parked in front of my building when I left today. The night before I bought you the new Charles Bukowski "born into this" DVD. Whether it was to apologize for my drunken acts the other day or just because I knew you would like it, I don't know. I bought it for you either way. I left it in a Target bag underneath your windshield enclosed with a letter saying "I was sorry for being a mean drunk asshole and how that it was ironic I used Charles Bukowski to apologize with." Putting things under your windshield wipers is my trademark it seems. It can't even be called clever anymore, just Brett. I hope the scumbags in our apartment building don't steal it before you get it.

xoxo

Hello lunacy,

"I like your style. Goodbye Brett!"

"I'm not a god damned stalker!"

"Right, funny I've never seen you there or play triiva there before you went with me. Good, I'll go there twice as much now! I promise, I'll paint a picture of you blowing me…xoxo…bon voyage stalker xoxo"

"We go there after work. Sorry. They aren't fond of you there either. Get over it. Go paint a picture xoxo"

"Ok, that's fine. I was trying to be cool about shit and be nice about things but you're such an obsessivelunatic you don't grasp what anyone tries to tell you. So does this mean no more stalking me at bars or five phone calls never returned per day?"

"Um wow, We were supposed to hangout the other day. You know what? Fuck you! This is ridiculous. You're a joke!"

"Well you are being very annoying and obsessive. You need to stop before I don't even want to be your friend. I asked for some space and you haven't respected that at all."

"lokI'm not trying to be annoying. I just wanna know what's up. You're my friend. I don't want that to change."

"So what's the deal with you? You never call me back,"

Goodbye lunacy.

xoxo

I wrote a story about killing her. She was none too pleased when I told her.

xoxo

It was a normal day, a day like any other. My stomach had been killing me all week, yet I was starving and it was only 3:43 p.m. I only eat once a day so it was a little bit earlier than usual for me to crave food of any kind. Hell, I'd just woken up a little over an hour ago. The girl I'd been seeing lately called me on the phone, in a sense of irony or déjà vu she asked me if I wanted to get something to eat. I figured why not go to a place that could clean me out, and there's no better place than the all you can eat Golden Corral just down the street from my apartment. I agreed to meet her over there in twenty minutes. It was a normal day, a day like any other. I got there before she did. I waited in the car listening to a mix CD I'd made and smoking cigarettes. The Misfits were on when I saw her car pull in. I flicked the cigarette outside of the car window and I turned the ignition off. The sounds of the Misfits faded. I headed towards the front door of the slop house. The white trash hogs of gluttony had beaten us there, yet it was still only 4:24 p.m. I was greeted by multitudes of screaming kids, old people, and the sites of overweight Americans indulging in gluttonous behavior in a distance near the food troughs. We waited in line. I grabbed both of us a tray and a set of silverware. She ordered water with lemon and I got a sweet tea. We paid separately. My all you can eat slop cost $13.27, which seemed a little pricey for all you can eat American slop. We found a small booth in the farthest corner of the slop house and sat down. I threw my tray down and headed for the main slop display that housed the steaks, corn, potatoes, tacos, and pretty much everything else of an odd mixture you could imagine. Soon, my plate was an Everest like mountain of slop. Mashed potatoes flowed into corn, which flowed into green beans, which overwhelmed a fried chicken breast. I could barely fit some hushpuppies and a roll on the side. I returned to my small table in the corner of the slop house and put my slop plate down and dug in with my freshly polished fork. The girl I'd been seeing lately returned soon after I'd dug into my slob. Her plate barely had anything on it, especially when compared to mine. She had a few green beans, a few corndogs, and some sort of rice were all that encompassed her plate. I made it through most of the mashed potatoes and corn. The chicken tasted like shit so I didn't eat much of that or the green beans. I got up and walked around and got another fresh plate and looked for something new to try. Trays of unknown fried shit littered the meat side of the main food display. I saw some popcorn shrimp and used the tongs to get half of every scoop onto my plate and the other half went into the baked fish tray. I walked around towards the vegetable side and got some dressing and a slice of pizza and sat back down. The girl I'd been seeing lately commented on how I was a slobby eater. She was right though. I had corn and mashed potatoes all over the table near my last plate. She got up as soon as I sat down. I grabbed a handful of napkins and picked up as much corn and potatoes as I could. There's nothing worse than looking like the biggest slob in a fucking all you can eat slop house. The popcorn shrimp was the best thing I'd tried since I had been in the slop house. It was obviously straight out of a box, but damn they were tasty with a little ketchup. The Thanksgiving dressing was nice and wet and tasty as well. The girl I'd been seeing lately asked me if I was gonna get some dessert from the dessert bar behind us. I didn't say anything and just shook my head. A minute later though I changed my mind. The brownies were the only thing on the dessert trough that looked decent, so I go a little brownie and then went over to the ice cream machine and pulled the lever down and shot out some vanilla ice cream that resembled an impressive gargantuan turd all over the brownie. I went and sat back down and now used a shiny spoon that I'd unrolled along with my fork earlier. It was laying bare on the table so I grabbed a napkin, wiped it off, and then gave it my "I hope I don't get some parasite" approval. The girl I'd been seeing lately sat down with her plate filled with chocolate cake, cookies, and something that resembled some sort of pudding/vomit. I made light chit-chat with the girl I'd been seeing lately. She said that the chocolate cake was the best she'd ever had and couldn't believe that anything could be that good at an all you can eat buffet slop house. I asked her if it gave her an orgasm, she said no. About halfway through my brownie and vanilla turd ice cream she told me that she'd missed all the normal shit that goes along with having a real boyfriend. The girl I'd been seeing lately then said she'd met someone else and that she just didn't think that she could see me anymore. All I could really say was "ok, that's cool" as I just continued eating my brownie and vanilla turd ice cream. She continued eating her chocolate cake and said nothing after that.

xoxo

She told her friends that I was a "self-proclaimed emotionally unavailable douchebag." Neither one of us were lying for once.

xoxo

"Sick of it all: More than just a Clever Tombstone Epitaph"

I'm tired of her pussy,

I'd never thought
I would say that about pussy

about any pussy
in fact
I'm sick of the line of hair
above her snatch
I'm sick of those
big fucking lips
I'm tired of putting
my face
down there
in that big wad
of
pussy lips
that reminds me of
Arby's
Roast beef sandwiches
squirting liquid
into
my mouth
and on
my face,

I'm tired of cumming
in there
white liquid swimming
watching it drip
onto,

sheets
beds
cars
panties
and floors,

it's time

to find a new pussy

to squirt white liquid

into

and

watch it drip

onto,

sheets

beds

cars

panties

and floors

xoxo

I was sitting on the toilet late last night taking a shit. I thought about this girl that I used to fuck several years ago. She loved it in her ass. I got a giant boner thinking about all the times I fucked her tight ass. I miss her every now and again.

xoxo

"hey does it mean anything if there was a bunch of peanuts in my crap?maybe that you ate p-nuts?

Negative, that's why I was asking. I haven't eaten peanuts in years.

no idea

ahh ok, sorry, just thought I would ask, thought it was weird...more peanuts than crap

i really have no idea"

xoxo

"Formal Poetry and all Ethics Forever Perish"

Atlanta

Year Y2K,

yes,

I need to borrow a telephone book
that's a good reason,

no,

it was a horrible reason
pathetic
lame
and some would say
desperate even
just to see her
maybe
even get laid,

yes,

I crave her fucking
snatch all the time
especially
while I'm at work
under a stranger's house
bored
and most likely covered in
their shit
I will knock
on her large wooden door
and ask
if I can use her telephone book,
no,

I don't have one
sorry

it was a horrible reason

pathetic

lame

and some would say

desperate even

I pulled up

near

her apartment

in East Atlanta

inside the

large green building

compact cars parked

in front

those old wooden

stairs soon approached me

sixteen of them

in fact

standing soon

in front of a large

wooden door

knock

three times

and wait

knock

two more times

and wait

a shallow female voice says,

I have company can you come back another time,

thanks,

from behind that

large wooden door

it was a horrible reason

after all

pathetic

lame

and some would say

even desperate.

xoxo

"haha, well a little wincing is ok I guess......are you watching this republican bullshit?

no im continuing to torture myself with ps i love you....seriously even the notebook isnt this good

well these psychos are entertaining...........why are you watching it, I really wanted to

ive watched it every night since i got it......i will watch it with you for sure

i know its nuts, seriously the closest thing to true love that i've seen...cause its all about letting go

p.s. shut the fuck up I've heard enough!"

xoxo

"Granted, I sent this message to myself. But, I hope you made it inside ok, and I'm really not the worst person in the world, as you already know. I still wanna take you out for tacos and skee-ball and fuck the shit out of you afterwards BTW."

"I love u asshole."

xoxo

Fuck, I don't know if I can fuck her or not. What to do? What to do? I read a message on my phone asking me if we're gonna hang out Friday or Saturday night. I don't answer for several hours. I flipped a coin and it came up heads, which means Friday. She says we can drink beer and paint in the next message I get. Yeah, that's cool I guess. I send her a message back asking if I can get any pussy when she's here. She responds back saying that she's on her period. Fuck me man! Jeez, just my luck. I'm fucking no girl on the rag, that's just gross to me. I've had blood on my dick before, and let me tell you it ain't nothing I wanna do too many times again. Shit, I could still get busted even without getting any ass. It would be just my luck to have the girlfriend stop by at some point. I guess I can shut the shades and keep the TV low just in case she does. What to do about my car? Fuck, just leave it, maybe she will think I got a ride with someone else. Maybe I can get the girl coming over to jerk me off at least. Maybe on one of the paintings we're supposed to do, that would be cool as shit. Friday comes too soon. I wake up Friday afternoon late as usual. It's haunting me, my conscience starts bothering me. Shit man, just call her and make up some shit about being sick, or that you had something come up and you can't do it. Fuck, I'm a horrible liar, it will never work. I wouldn't even buy some lame excuse like that. Just do it, who cares, you don't give a shit about this girl. You just want a strange handjob or a blowjob, and then kick her out. I head to the beer store later that afternoon. As I park the car, I hear a noise coming from my phone. It's a message from her, she says she's sorry but she won't be able to make it tonight, she's gotta get up early for class or some shit. What a relief, now I don't have to make up some bullshit and retarded excuse.

xoxo

"Clean Bugs, Dirty Carpet"

The trending of negative scars,

the warzone isn't out there
it's in here,

queer swans
of
the underground resistance
renting ghetto apartments in the unknown
funerals for class fuehrer
wiretap my docile mannequin body
feed me rusted hypodermic formulas
and
vintage cataract addictions
birthday cards addressed,

to:
lard
pineapples
broken teeth

and war,

the trending of negative scars,

the warzone isn't out there

it's in here.

xoxo

It said in the e-mail that I got that she would love me and show me attention. I needed to search no further than her for every perverted desire I could think of. She wanted me, and she would prove it to me. All I had to do is give her my credit card number and she would be mine forever. Not only that, but she also had some pills to make my cock bigger as well. I think I'm in love already.

xoxo

You never got your period after that night we got fucked up on imported beer and went to my place and had drunken sex for two hours, until you said your pussy hurt. So, I got some lube and continued to fuck you until you said you just couldn't take it any longer. We took a break and smoked cigarettes. I convinced you to give me ten more minutes to cum, and you did. It probably took fifteen minutes really, but who's counting? I came inside of you even though I knew you weren't on birth control. Fuck it; it seemed like a good idea when I was drunk on imported beer. A month later I went alone to a shit bar down the street from my apartment. It was cold out and it was in the middle of the day. You were 87 miles away getting an unborn fetus sucked out of your vagina, thus "disposing" of our little problem for three hundred American dollars paid in cash, well mostly your dollars I mean. You called me on my cell phone and told me "it was done." I could sense you were upset, but I didn't care really. I guess I pretended that I cared a little. I ordered a watered down whiskey shot after I got done talking to you. It was a long cold drunken walk back to my apartment later that night. Well, shit, at least I didn't have to worry about my little fucking "problem" any longer. At least I had that going for me.

xoxo

My phone is alive,

"At times its crotch"

"Yeah and I'm a nun"

"Pretty cool to hang out with and yeah we got drunk and hooked up, but I'm not really like that normally"

"Dud u fuck anyone?"

210

"Nothing personally directed at you"

"Which flag? The Peruvian or Canadian?"

"I can't be rough with my nani."

"Now ur telling me I'm crazy? Look here cancerian soul mate I'm far from crazy"

"I like how u put cunt in country"

"are u with a girl?"

"It's none of my business. I was just telling you how I am"

"Certain things aren't anyones busness. Last night was a complete headache. I guess I made my own bed though"

"Oh now u think my mind is fragile? U don't know me!"

"What's that supposed to mean"

"U are prolly a little disappointed u never had sex with any of us"

"Ur so hott btw"

"Yeah I'm hungover to. how was Mastodon?"

"I was drunk last night"

"Lets fuck hardcore!"

"That is really funny"

"Wanna go to aruba?"

"I do and have no hard feelings. But for now I think it's best to discontinue communications"

"Brett even though you come off as an asshole. I think you're pretty cool But I'm not into the whole fuck as many as you can thing"

"Don't treat me like a whore"

"I want you. I want to fuck hardcore"

"I like a good douche…vagisil?"

"You get a bj but I wanna fuck…"

"Aww thanks but I am really sick"

"That can def be a possibility. Are you actually gonna be nice you're kind of a dick remember"

"Ur so funny u know that. I am jus taking my time. Kinda scared to hangout with anyone new. U know I just broke up with my boyfriend 2 weeks ago"

"Why would I hate you silly?"

"Who is this?"

"Huh?"

"Not sure what brought this on please don't text me again"

"So change of subject what are your thanksgiving plans?"

"Did you accomplish anything productive today or did you sleep until noon and smoke cigs all day with dd coffee,"

My phone is dead.

xoxo

Dear XXXXX,

It's no big deal, but I'd like it if you surprised me and came to this art show that's down the street from you Saturday May 9th. I will be debuting my "XXXXX reflux" painting series there. Granted, you won't like them at all, but I made them in your honor because I love you and they're a great example of what a fucked up emotional wreck you make me, or something like that….ha. Anyways, I miss seeing and hanging out with you a lot so stop by if you're not previously engaged.

xoxo

I can't help but talk shit about you now. You deserve it. People deserve to know what and who you really are. Past your pretty face and thousand dollar tits lurks a disgusting disfigured human being. I feel bad for you and anyone that has the misfortune of calling you a friend.

xoxo

I've been like John Cusack in Say Anything, just a guy riding around late at night in the dark talking to a digital voice recorder. No one is around to listen to me ramble on like a fucking lunatic but a fucking plastic silver machine. Maybe it will make an interesting story one day. Here was misery in its purity.

xoxo

"ok, so now we're tattoo twins

oh yeah how'd it go

easiest tattoo I ever got. except now I'm walking around with a the police sketch of the unabomber...haha

yes how lovely...remind me never to get on your badside

haha, oh come on now........you're one of the coolest people I've ever met, I'm not gonna kill you

awesome...I'll sleep sound tonight, but Im still gonna be weary of any suspicious packages in the mail

haha, I'm a believer that the pen is mightier than the sword, so I would just write something fucked up about you...haha. Frankly I'm not smart enough to make a letter bomb

well Im much at ease now-haha"

xoxo

Dear XXXXX,

Fuckin' giant sloth balls I really miss hanging out with you, and well I just miss you in general. I don't know what to do without you other than to write and paint about shit involving you and moan to friends about you, which I'm sure by the amount of ridicule I have been receiving they're probably tired of hearing about. Now for the most part, they think I'm a whiny sensitive pussy who's changed. I've been really fucked up over you, lifted a lot of weights, and lost weight over you, but that's ok. I've learned a really hard painful lesson, that when something great walks into your life, you better jump all over that shit without fear or hesitation like a fat girl on a bucket of KFC. I'm not afraid to admit that not a day goes by that I don't think about you. I can't believe that the "self servicing machine" is actually admitting this, but I really do fucking need you. I don't really need that many people, but I do really need you, because, well this sounds like some lame line from a romantic comedy, but you pretty much complete me as much as anyone ever will and Batman needs his goddamn Robin! You're gone, and damn it sucks and doesn't make me very happy (insert wide range of emotions here). You make me happier and I have more fun with you than anyone I've ever known. I've met and hung out with thousands of people all over the place, so that's saying something there. I went out on a few dates, but I realized very soon that I had been ruined by you, and basically I'm mentally and emotionally unavailable to anyone else. And, also, I'd pretty much rather be alone if accepting less than absolutely amazing girls are my options. I can't go back to what I was/did before you, which was basically an emotionless sort of slut who hung out with people I just tolerated and pretty much didn't give a shit about. Well, when I said you made me a better person here's your proof I guess. You never have to feel anything for me again, that's ok if you don't. I know you loved me, sort of believed in me, and felt like there was something there at one point not too long ago, and maybe it was just your belief in my potential. I don't really know. I don't really want to be 63 and alone and reeking of Old Spice and cheap frozen pizzas for one.

xoxo

"I don't want any money from u so no need to worry

good cuz I dont have any to give-you'd drop me like a hot potatoe-LOL

I like potatoes, so I'd prob eat you instead..

you'd do that anyway-haha

maybe, only if u were clean and well groomed..

what on earth would give u the idea I wouldnt be???

I'm just fucking with u…

whats new

I would lick ur kitty until u screamed or told me to get the fuck off of you...ha"

xoxo

I think in August you move out. When I see the U-Haul back up into apartment #5 in the building across from me, I will crack open a PBR in the can and have a beer in your honor. The fact that I will never have to lay eyes on you or your hippy sticker laden car again is exciting to me, and I can't wait. Goddamn, you make me fucking sick! Bon voyage you fucking bitch!

xoxo

"Scream You Docile Humans, Scream"

the sand walks on me

I don't

walk on the sand,

1,979 steps

backwards

and

ancient letters

rotting

in a rarely opened drawer

the roses of fall

wither

under suburban car ports

and

dehydration,

vacated,

by the

space

now between us.

xoxo

My phone is fucking alive,

"When can we start being fuck buddies. I can't fuck a stranger right now"

"So Wednesday I'll get a hotel"

"Whoa…I didn't know all that. But anything ending is an sdjustment…u will be ok in a couple o fmonths"

"Do u want me to come up one night next week?"

"No I didn't"

"Did you tell XXXXX that I told on her?"

"Ok it's a plan, I'm so tired of men and dating I just want to hang with my friends"

"Yeah we could do that"

"Ok if you promise. Don't want to be in drama or in the middle of you two. People get crazy. Don't try to entertain urself by telling her that I'm coming over. You would think that was funny."

"You out of town tomorrow night?"

"Can't you call a girl back"

"XXXXX is a fool, had a great night"

"I still want you……"

"What if I come down on Friday and stay the night?"

"I'm bleeding. I switched birth control and it fucked up my whole body"

"Ur amazing and she will never find someone as cool as you,"

My phone is fucking dead.

xoxo

We were somewhere between bumfuck nowhere USA and Miami Beach. She was curled up in a sort of fetal position in the seat next to me fast asleep and snoring slightly. The Pixies were playing loudly and the window was cracked. The coffee I had was cold and nearing empty. All I could think about was doing her in. I saw a sign for a rest area not too long ago. I wonder if I could get away with it, that was my only fear really. She has no family and it would be a long time before she was ever missed. I could pull into a secluded dark parking spot at the edge of the rest area and strangle her in her sleep, that's how it would have to go down. Some trucker getting a blowjob or taking a piss would accidentally find her one day, and by then I would be long gone and having the time of my life fucking some Columbian bitch with big fake tits down in Miami Beach. There's another large green sign advertising for the rest area. I have five short miles to make up my mind.

xoxo

"I'm not drunk and I like being called a bitch"

"Or just drunk text someone else bitch!"

"Then change your obnoxious ringtone"

"I am now. No middle of the night texts on school nights please"

"You awake? Did I wake you??"

xoxo

"The Raw Deal after Pumping Sonja until the End of Days"

Feel the burn,

yeah Arnold

I wish it was my

pecs or glutes

and

not my cock

well

specifically the head

of my cock,

it's a

burning

tingling

rubbing

chaffing

not

normal,

why?
that is the question,

could it be:

herpes
fungus
yeast
just plain raw
from fucking
last night
or this morning
whatever,

feel the burn,

soak it
rub it
touch it
put lotion
on it
naked
no more burning
walk around all day
not leaving
the apartment,

naked,

Doritos on the floor
dishes pile up
piss stains near and on

the toilet

the juice and water supply

are running low

put pants on

equals

bad,

feel the burn

again.

xoxo

Dear XXXXXXXXX,

It's pretty stupid that I'm writing you an e-mail when you're 30 feet away from me, but oh well. XXXXX sent me a stupid message saying that I'm freaking you out and all this shit. If it is true, I don't really know why you would be. I think she's just pissed about a few comments I made about her best friend, which is ridiculous by the way. She said the same things to me that night we went out, her words "he's the most spoiled person I've ever known." So why get mad at me for saying it? I could care less about him. I'm just using the lifestyle in my writings, big whoop. XXXXX, I'm not trying to freak u out, talk shit, hurt you, or any other negative connotations you want to throw in there. This is getting to the point of ridiculous. Who cares if I want write about some crazy shit and put it on a few blogs and writing sites where I can actually get my writing out to the masses. Shit, besides everything I wrote involving you recently is in a good light anyways. Maybe not concerning your new friends so much, but I can't help that. I dislike people like them, that's just me. You're my friend and I care a hell of a lot about you, more than you know. You don't talk to me very much anymore so how can I know what you think or how you feel? If my stupid writing actually really bothers you that much and hurts you, then I will take anything involving you down. This drama is so fucking stupid and childish I swear!
xoxo

Months go by and I miss her the exact same as I did then. Nothing changes that. I tried it all man. I hung out and fucked around with other women even though I only wanted her. I cried, I whined, I was pissed off, I was hurt, I tried to have fun without her, I poured my guts out to her, I pretended that I didn't care, I wanted her back, I tried to avoid her, I missed her, I sent her love letters, I fucked with her, I was pathetic, I tortured her, I pathetically confessed to her, I sent hate letters, apologized afterwards, and yet nothing worked or rid me of that emptiness that I am now consumed by. I don't know what to do. I don't know what to do with her. I can't stay away from her no matter what I do. That's all I know at this point.

xoxo

"Howdy there XXXXX. It was fun bowling and drinking with you. Although, I must admit that talking to you was pretty fun to. Thanks for looking me up, it was a nice self esteem boost while sitting here bloated and hungover...haha. I admit that I attempted to look you up last night when I got home drunk, but of course I couldn't even get an internet connection. Just a word of advice, don't eat at Pizza Shack at 4 in the damn morning!"

"Hey Brett it was really cool talking to you too. When I said original I meant it. You're one of a kind! I really am hoping to try to make the art show, tell me what its beside again and what time. Here's my number..wink wink"

xoxo

I've reached my boiling point. That level where you just don't care anymore. I'm sick of your immature head games and frivolous and pointless neurotic behavior. It gets old. Maybe at one point and time it was interesting, but not anymore. Now it's just stupid and a waste of my fucking time.

xoxo

Peddling across clear blue bays. A large red and yellow kayak. Me and my special lady friend not in sync. My black rubber paddle slaps something in the blue water below. Sorry large turtle that's probably on the endangered species list, my bad dude. I whacked you in the head with my paddle and killed you.

xoxo

"Ha, my cum is supposed to make people smarter, I guess it doesn't always work...lol... We'll def go to the beach though sometime soon or whatever. Just text em Sunday and if I'm not doing shit I'll meet you."

"ur mean"

"I only tease darlin'! I think you're just sensitive!"

"Ha ha, ur still mean. Im gonna be back in town tomorrow night, and ill have a baby sitter all night. I kinda wanna go somewhere and get drunk and ur my only friend there. Let me know if u have some free time."

"That's cool and ironic. I'm actually working tonight instead of tomorrow and I got on Sunday so yes I will have free time tomorrow night like around 930 or so. I really want to fuck the shit out of you BTW. I'll go buy the sponge or whatever tomorrow...lol. Have you checked out Yaz birth control, it's synthetic hormones as opposed to the normal birth control. Text me tomorrow..."

"Lol, sorry but I ain't puttin spongebob in my vagina. I read it only has a seventy percent success rate. Not cool. we don't have to do this. We can just be drinkin buddayys. hope u have a nice weekend, talk to u soon."

"Ha, well the one I researched got good reviews, but whatever. Multiple sites say 91% effective for cumming inside, if we pull out, even greater! Haha, calm your cuntry ass down!...lol."

"That mother fucker is huuuge!!! I dont want that thing gettin all lost inside me. Urghhh"

"It's not that big. Well, take the freaking pill and we won't have to deal with sponges...lol....It blocks cum, it has to be big in my case! You've never fucked with it, nor have I. So, let's see how it goes before we decide!...haha"

xoxo

2:30 a.m. we walk into a dingy and dark strip club. We order two drinks. I pay for them. I'm so drunk the girls look only like silhouettes in motion at this distance from our seats at the bar, which are the furthest you can really get from the stage. I squint my eyes but I can't even make out a tit really, much less a pussy. She looked unhappy as we slowly drank our beers in this dingy and dark strip club. I asked her if she wanted to make out or something? She said no. I just looked down and stared at the floor. I lit another cigarette, right after I'd just put the last one out. I took another sip from my overpriced drink. I then asked her if she wanted to fuck or something? She said yes. I said ok, let's go to my place. We left soon afterwards.

"The Depression of Frigid Dial Tones"

she,

called me on the phone

I was out drinking

it was loud inside

so I went outside

so I could hear,

she,

said that she wanted to suck

my dick

too bad

she was 400 miles away

it gave me a boner

hearing her say that though,

she,

said goodbye

and

I had no one to suck my dick.

xoxo

Dear XXXXX,

     I'm really sorry, but I have to leave you now. But, frankly you left me no other options to be honest. I can't sit here every single day torturing myself over you and feeling that you fucked me over and knowing in my heart that I can't trust you anymore, and there's no way I can be your friend after what you did. I did at least try and be your friend after this and give it a shot, even though it killed me inside, which is more than most would have done. I'm pretty sure 99.9% of guys would have told you to "go fuck yourself" after that shit you pulled, but I didn't. At least now I can leave not hating you, I just find you mostly disgusting now. You're the most disappointed I've ever been in a person in my entire life. Hell, I actually thought you were a lot better person than me until all of this took place, but that's not the case in the end. I know I sucked as a special friend on some levels, but you actually sucked worse than I did, thanks for being a cunt and ruining my graduation vacation, lying, breaking our agreement, being a bitch and running off with a stranger and deciding that going through a slutty gold-digger phase was just what you needed to find out who you were as a person, quite impressive! While, the whole time claiming that "oh, you just had to see what made you happy," who the fuck would believe that bullshit line exactly?

     Granted, some part of me will always love the "old" XXXXX, but I'm no fool, and I don't know why you continue to treat me as such. Enjoy your fake new life as a wannabe yuppie hipster, it's not you at all regardless of how much you try, you're fake and bullshit just like them now, and the antithesis of everything I despise. Get your VIP pass out, because you're one of "them" now, the shiny people. Just because you fuck a middle aged ginger lard ass used car salesman after one date behind my back, that doesn't make you more mature than me or promote any sort of personal growth, it just makes you a fucking idiot and a total lame ass. I didn't quite realize how desperate you were for a boyfriend, but fucking ehh, that's disgusting. I showed your new photos to my mom when I was at her house, she actually said you looked pretty trashy and he resembled my dad (and she said that you now had a nice big belly to rest your fake boobs on), and why exactly would I want to be your friend or want anything to do with you after this, she had a point there (which I already knew), she's knows a lot more about women than I do.

If you treat best friends this way, you don't deserve many, which is also why you don't have many. Yeah, you have a couple, and they're just as clueless and generic as you are XXXX #2, in fact, I've met bacteria that were smarter and more interesting than they are, why do you think I never wanted to be around them? You're clueless and goldigging just like XXX, airheaded and nutty just like XXXX, bitchy like XXXXX and should be on Jerry Springer probably drunk just like XXX. It's true, in the end you are the friends you keep. Well, I actually like XXXXX and XXX for some reason, perhaps they're more genuine nice people than the others. It's interesting that you still "don't get" a lot of this and I pretty much have had to beat you over the head repeatedly and talk down to you for you to understand that "oh, maybe pulling the shit like you did was pretty shitty and maybe you don't treat best friends and much less people in general like that if you want to keep them in your life, and it might seem a little contradictory for you to say that you love and care about me on top of that." Go play house down there in "Chas" (as you constantly misspell and don't know anything about it and pretend like you're some "in the know" local now) with some other guy's money, and that's all it is, money. Ha, you fucked me over for a revolting fat ass, short, meathead, freckle faced ugly yuppie buffoon. Man, you better solve the global warming crisis or something, because you have some bad ass karma coming your way and I doubt you ever find happiness of any kind.

It's sad really; you're and adult and have no idea who you are as a person or what you want out of life. You have done nothing but contradict everything you ever said and/or stood for as a person that I highly respected and it's very highly disappointing to me, and should be to you. Like I said, your actions are constant contradictions to your words. How fucking dare you fuck me over after I pretty much invited you in and made you a part of my family, because I cared and knew that you didn't have one of your own of any kind. It was only a month or so ago that you were over at my apartment opening birthday presents that my mom bought you with her meager money, we made sure you had a nice meal after working hard, you were giddy and kissing me and telling me how much you loved and cared about me and how much you appreciated all the birthday stuff I did for you and talking about the breakdown you had over me the day before. You are so fucking low, and I hope you feel horrid about all of this one day when you're sitting around alone in a silent apartment with no one there to give a shit.

As always, you will see it my way in the end and look back on this period of your life and be like "what the fuck was I thinking." I don't have to be there to see it, but I know it will happen. "I don't want to be some thirty year old bar person Brett," oh wait, now all you do is get drunk, look like shit and have your tits hanging out and complain about your hangovers, a perfect example of your hypocrisy. No, you may not wanna be my girlfriend, but I don't even want to be your friend or even know you for that matter, so there, and I haven't, since all of this went down, that was my gut feeling from the start and I should have listened to it. Yeah, you were right about one thing I'll give you that, I shouldn't have to make you feel like total shit, you already should. I can't trust you anymore and that means everything to me and is the foundation of friendship if you didn't know.

You're a liar, a slut, and an airhead. Congratulations, you've grown and matured so much, wow, I hope I never grow that much myself XXXX #2. Regardless of how much you try to be XXXX or how many new age bullshit palm readers you go to you won't find peace, because frankly the only problem with you is yourself. I don't care anymore; I just want to be rid of you and your idiotic bullshit. So, bon voyage! Feel free to respond and go off on me and call me a fucking asshole or whatever will make you feel better. I'll read it, but I won't respond. I'm very sorry it has to be this way. I really do wish it could have all been different. I don't take any pleasure in saying what I said or doing this, I really don't. But, I gotta call it like I see it, like I always have. Some part of me will always love you for as long as I live and I'll miss you very much. All I can say is "this fucking sucks big time." I truly do wish I had other options. Don't ever say I never had a breakdown over you though, I've had plenty lately to make up for two years, and I'm actually crying as I write this. Take care of yourself...Brett

xoxo

"jeez, u already lost the enthusiasm

oh i forgot to tell u i took a vow of celebacy to cleanse my aura-you inspired me to get back into eastern philosophy.....

u must have had a hard day...it's cool though, I talked to Allah and he assured me that ur down with the baby making

yea right, they fuck like rabbits...why do u think they had to cap how many kids u could have

your good, and at least you responded- iwas expecting you to log out

haha, no.....I can wait if I must.

you might be waiting awhile.....lol

I'll just nag u until u give in....taoist did come up with herbal remedies like yahimbe, horny goat weed and all that shit.....sex is a big thing in eastern philosophy so u didn't get it from them....

maybe u switched to southern baptist

not a chance in hell-and i dont even believe in hell

haha, ok so don't pretend ur a buddhist monk now

im kiddn-wooo now i know how to ruffle your feathers-haha

haha, maybe I'm kidding as well

you better be

eeew, sassy

and saucy...

a sassy celebite"

xoxo

"Craig and the Boredom of Humanism"

left click and a few e-mails later,

furniture for sale

I bought a shitty tan couch from you

for 90 bucks

on craigslist

Monday

there were potato chips

and twelve cents

in spare change

three peanuts

and multiple dried

cum stains

underneath the tan cushions

when I got it home

later that night,

left click and a few e-mails later,

a week after

I bought the tan couch

Wednesday

I fucked someone's
wife
that I met
On craigslist
intimate encounters,

MWF seeking,

there's now one more
dried cum stain
on a shitty tan couch
that I bought
for 90 bucks
on craigslist
Monday.

xoxo

"Baking Cookies with Whores," I think that will be the title of the book that I
write about all of them.

xoxo

I wish that I practiced what I preached. The best advice that I can give is to
make sure that you never develop a crush on a girl with fake boobs who works
at a strip club. She is bound to be tougher than you are and fuck you up on
multiple occasions, and there's nothing you can do about it except take it.

xoxo

I lean against her dirty and dead bug covered Asian manufactured compact car.

"Well, when I take you out on a legitimate date sometime I'll put on my finest
pair of black jeans and we'll fuck this town up!"

"I don't like black jeans though."

"Well, me and Johnny Cash think its just fine baby."

"Why don't you just wear a pair of blue jeans?"

"I don't like blue jeans. They remind me of horrid jobs and manual labor. I'll
bust out a pair now and then, but not very often, as you well know. In fact, I
don't even like wearing pants in general. We live at the fucking beach, with the
humidity; it's like what, 100 fucking degrees today. I'm content wearing shorts

year round."

"Oh, I know that. I've seen your closet."

"I mean, the last thing I'm gonna do is go to the mall and buy a pair of 300 dollar designer jeans at Abercrombie with fucking holes in them. The next thing you know I'd be wearing lame ass shoes and coats made out of the hides of some animal on the endangered species list like fucking gingervitis does."

She laughs a little.

"Well, I'm not getting into all of that again."

"I wasn't trying to. Are we seriously standing in the parking lot of "the big pig" and discussing the pros and cons of me wearing black jeans on a future hypothetical date?"

"Yeah, we are."

"Fuck, you're lame. I mean we're lame. Come here and give me a hug beautiful."

I grab her and pull her close to me. I smell her. I touch her back and I kiss her on the neck. I like it all.

"Fuck, I miss you so much baby, no one else does it for me like you do. You've ruined me."

xoxo

Sitting alone in a giant smelly hotel room, America's Best they say, well, the shitty dirty neon sign in front near the aged railroad tracks says so anyways. I'm chain smoking cigarettes and staring at a blank TV screen. The water I'm drinking is no longer cold and is now around room temperature. The only sounds come from a humming air conditioner set to cool and low. I'm dirty and the sheets are clean, minus a few visible stains. I grab my pen and open a new white 99 cent notebook and start writing about her.

xoxo

"probably, I'm not all that concerned about it..........how many times I gotta tell you!...haha.....I'm not interested in anyone but you

10-4 haha, i dont know where that came from

well, I got a sense that it bothered you

what bothered me? the tramps? no, just dont want you catchin, the aynor herpes

yeah, well...u never know......u get nutty sometimes about that stuff.....haha. I'm yours, until you don't want me anymore..

or until we're together a couple years, and you're "bored" according to you thats bound to happen. And donnt make yourself sound like an old sock, I will always want you, you're not expendable well I don't know, I just threw it out there........I haven't been bored of you yet. Jesus, I love you!

haha, i love you too."

xoxo

I sent her a text message: "I hope you have a fantastic Valentine's Day" a few days after the incident. There is no response back from her.

xoxo

"Huffing Gas near the Big Pig"

The world ended today
but
we were the last to know,

we're all hypocrites
in
one way or another
some people
are worse than others
though
I'll keep quiet
and
save the Salem persecution of speaking
truth and reality
for
another sentence
shunned and avoided like
herpes and ghetto dentists
browse me
but don't join in
internet connections
allow a spray painted window
of thought

and

returnable bottles of emotions

but

I have no ride to

Michigan or Maine

ghosts haunt me

in the daylight

why wait,

neurosis of the worst kind

no cure for it

and without answers

a ski mask over my eyes

yet

no ghetto gas stations were robbed

memories lost and new

opinions are discovered and

formed

in my captivity,

we

finally got what we wanted

the humans have returned to their

laboratories

our leashes bound by a confused society

have been lifted

we truly can run free now

just me and you

my imaginary friend.

xoxo

"You can't have sex against a shower curtain. Not exactly stable"

"I'll rape you wherever I want woman!"

"You're a sex maniac"

"Just wait until I bust out my Periodic Table shower curtain next time!"

"I'll bend you over and make you eat uranium…haha"

xoxo

I'm pumping away on her late at night and fucking drunk. The only light shines from the bathroom. She tells me to fuck her pussy. She keeps telling me to fuck her pussy in fact. I admit she had a great one. I asked her if I could cum inside of her. She told me that she wasn't on birth control, but I could do it anyways. I contemplated it for a drunken second and pulled out and came all over her stomach, though most if it ended up in her belly button. I didn't need any kids running around, hell, in fact I hate fucking kids now that I think about it. She says that I have a great dick and this is the best fuck she's had in years. Even if she was bullshitting me I didn't care, it was nice to hear all my pumping impressed someone. My dick isn't big or anything special, and I knew that. I asked her if I was a better fuck than her husband. She said yes, and that he sucked in bed. I'm sure that was a biased opinion at this point. I got her a towel to wipe the cum off her stomach as I went to the kitchen and grabbed another PBR. I walked back into the bedroom and sat on the edge of the bed. She asked me if I was gonna ever call her again. I said no sugar tits, probably not.

xoxo

"Magic Cooter" is no more. A great nickname that was wasted, but it will be recycled on someone else down the line probably.

xoxo

My phone is dead,

"I do accept you and there is no drama"

"I know you did. You get all pissed over nothing. I just wanna be cool and friend without any drmaa and you just accepting me as I am"

"I thought you were pissed since you stormed out?

"What do you mean? I'm not attempting anything? There's no scheme here I just felt bad"

"Why are you attempting a 180.."

"Ok, that's cool. Well soon then I hope"

"Ha I embrace my new nickname. Nothing really Gonna get some coffee and walk on the beach. I feel fat!"

"Ok, deal consider it done missy"

"tmake me a mix CD and I'll forgive you"

"I'm gonna make you a mix CD. That should make everything better"

"I have no idea. I'll try not to though .I'm an asshole drunk sometimes, but I'm trying to be nicer."

"Idk. Until the next time it happens"

"Yes, I'm somewhat human on occasion. I do like you though and would still like to be ur friend. You have every right to be mad at me. But I hope you can forgive me for being a jerk."

"I actually kind of miss you Polock"

"Hell if I know, I was drunk as hell and in a bad mood. It was stupid I know. You didn't deserve that.. I'm sorry for hurting your feelings.."

"Why did you flip out like that? I don't get it?"

"I'm sorry for dissapointing you. I know I acted like a total asshole. Not much I can do about it except say I'm sorry and I feel slighlty bad about it"

"How could you talk ot me like that? It's so dissapointing"

"I was in the shower saw u called"

"Ok, fine. Thank you for not being a dick"

"Itt doesn't matter. That wasn't mean. That was verbal assault. I don't have anyhting to say to you. I'm giving you ur shit back cause I'm not a dick"

"Ok, I'm sorry I was mean to you. You don't need a metal bat to make me ugly"

"Sams's club. I have to motivate myself to leave my house and to put down the metal bat I was gonna bring with me"

"Ok, what pharmacy?"

"I'm coming down that way to to the the phramacy. If you want your shoes so bad you can meet me there. I'm not going out of my way in the slightest"

"Ok, why you gonna be like that? I like those shoes stop being immature"

"Fuck your shoes"

"Ok, I just want my shoes. Don't be stupid. After your done being mad at me can I get them?"

"It's just something you have to deal with. Leave me alone"

"Ok I will. Just give me my shoes and you can hate me after"

"Civil? Are you that fucking ognorant? I am LOL. Fuck off go paint a picture"

"Ok, well thanks. You didn't have to do that. I was just trying to be civil"

"You need to deal with the fact that your shoes just went byr bye on 17. Goodnight and goodluck you fucking lunatic!!!!"

"Huh, whatever. No I didn't I went after you a little but you just need to deal with it."

"You really hurt me seriously"

"Thnks I appreciate it"

"Okk goodbye"

"What did I do that was stupid? Deny you sex? Goodbye Brett"

"I didn't. You were being stupid. Just giv eme my shoes back and you can move on"

"Yes, of course. I just don't understand why you flipped out. I didn't deserve that at all."

"Ok, that's cool. I still want my shoes back if you don't mind then you can be rid of me.."

"I've ben nothing but kind to you. Go throw up another sculpture. I'm extremely hurt and emberasssed. I wish I never met you"

"Because you were being a bitch. You wanna fuck with me you will be sorry.

"I'm sorry I was mean to you, but oh well"

"Why did you act like that Brett?"

"Cool, can you just dump them like a dead body in front of my door?"

"Of course, I had them in my car for you"

"Bye, can I get my shoes back? I'm not trying to be a dick, but I like them"

"I wish you the best. Thanks for your kisses,"

My phone is alive.

xoxo

She's more confusing than ever now. Oh, now she cares and she's supposedly all distraught, crying, and just having a massive breakdown over me or over me seeing someone else. Really though, who the hell knows what she's upset over. I was always good at giving her breakdowns, that is true. This breakdown occurs while laying in another guy's bed of course, while she's on a long vacation to see him. But, it only happens now when I start seeing someone else, well, not just someone else, the girl who busted her ass that night in February in fact. Perhaps, she was upset because I have the dominant "hand" now and she doesn't have shit. She was already jealous of her before, so my retort I'm sure has confused and bothered her. Yes my dear, you really thought there wouldn't be a massive retort coming your way? Hell, part of me had been planning this from the start. It's really just an added bonus in truth. Ironic and convenient timing for this whole situation don't you think honey buns? I believe her, but I don't. Part of me considers her to be a succubus now, and someone not to be trusted entirely. I don't trust her, and in fact I don't refer to her even as a friend anymore. She has no name now, she is just something, something amazing, my best friend that I loved at one point, but now she is just a disappointment, and a complete sellout to me. Yet, I still love her and care about her and I contemplate all the time what part she should play in my life, if any at all. I still have no answers, nothing has been decided, and the riddle still baffles me. Really, only a fool would trust her at this juncture. Would she trust me again if the roles were reversed? I highly doubt it. All she does is talk, mainly evasively, but there's never any action behind any of it. Who knows what she wants from me. Does she want me back; is there suddenly a future for us now? She made it perfectly clear that she didn't give a shit about anyone but herself and we had no future. Only a retard would think you can do fucked up shit to someone you love and then think months later it could be the same or something. She's a fucking nut, that I'm quite positive about. She can't keep doing this to me. She's glad I'm happy supposedly. Somewhat I guess, but only by default really, and just making the best of a fucked situation thrown my way. Something still isn't right in my life though. Something is still off. I don't really know, but it concerns me and her. I have no words, and no sentences to form to explain it really. All I know is that it wasn't supposed to be this way; maybe she finally realizes that now.

xoxo

"haha, I couldn't handle u telling everyone I'm your boyfriend....I might lose my mind and be commited

yeah... oh god what a nightmare-I cant imagine anything worse

so u see my dilemma..haha

yep...im sure it would be absolute torture to be my boyfriend-

well, I like to make out like it would be…ha. it's more a running joke than anything, which I enjoy

yeah and you just like trying to get under my skin...i've got your number

hehe

oh well its fun...you never bore me and I love that

that's weird, I'm pretty boring to myself..

you're not at all

I'm boring and I have a small weiner, ur too good for me!

haha....well maybe Im just easy to please-haha actually thats hardly the case

yeah pretty much

not so much, there nobody-guys anyway that I can tolerate besides you

---

sweet, that's quite flattering. once I get my germs on you there's no going back

haha...I have the cooterific plague

haha, oh u got something!

u could easily find someone around here better looking, but not as far as nerdiness, talent, and jackass bravado is concerned anyways

not really ive dated guys out there and they're not all that, besides I have this attraction to you thats pretty cool I think

what is this galaga tracker beam attraction ye speak of?

i dont know, but its there.

intersting, it's like "the force" in sw

yeas...the force is strong with this one-haha

haha, who knows. I didn't know I had any force

well maybe its not you per sey, but me when I m with you...i dont know?? you cant relate to any of this???

ahh, yea I think it's called "obsession"...haha

not even

ha, I enjoy hanging out with u indeed...but I'm not obsessed over u I don't think

im not obsessed over you either...thats creepy

I know ur not, we have way too much space for any obsession to be going on

obession doesnt really mean having space...just having sanity

well something to that effect yes."

xoxo

Now and then I don't like her. Now and then I don't understand her disposition. I wonder and want to ask her what planet she now resides on these days, planet breakdown maybe. I ask her to hang out and do shit, probably more than I should to be honest. I don't remember the last time she called and asked me to do anything. I guess March or something like that. Months and months ago, that's all I know. I should probably leave her alone, her and her new life without me in it. I always get the "maybe" these days. From "yes" man to "maybe" man overnight, that's me. What a difference a few months make. It's a fucking bizzaro parallel universe I'm living in these days, well, she's living in, and I'm trying to figure out and understand I guess. She's not going to be here on my 30th birthday. She'll be on vacation with the "gingervitis." That bothers me. I remember her 30th birthday very well. I showed up, even though she was cold and distant towards me all night. I was there with the best presents she got from anyone; I was there with a letter written inside of her card pouring my guts out to her. I knew a breakdown was coming so I told her to read it after

I left that night. She said that she loved me the next day and wanted me in her life forever. Nope, now she won't be there for my breakdown, which I'm hoping won't happen. She could at least do me the favor of not fucking him on my birthday, that would be a decent present in my mind.

xoxo

"Forging 187 Metallic Words in Reykjavik"

Making words in winter
making war against everything else,

mucous membranes
dwarves making snot
evolving into
art
every single day
turn the heat
off
on another calendar year
constant reminders on Post-It Notes
strategically placed pixilated
IED's
tinged zinc white
rectangles breed with abstract ideas
stained and soiled
by
discount lubrication
by
abnormal skin cells
and weak coffee
this penitentiary
has a familiar address
inside my head
inside my mailbox

thanks Ed
I didn't win shit,

making words in winter
making war against everything else,

Chile
not
the country
redirected by dead batteries
the temperature
of my extremities
or
your soul
the cobalt blue hue of
lacerations
and cardiac arrest
dropping English
dropping babies
sharpened dicks
dull pencils
this cum will make your I.Q.
go up
by five NASDAQ points
hey man
did you watch that game?
no I didn't
nor
do I care
as intriguing as I seem online darlin'
I still won't
fuck the leftover brains

out of your goddamn skull

lethargy

is more than a word

it's a lifestyle

rarely understood by

bears and aardvarks,

making words in winter

making war against everything else.

xoxo

I'm trying to figure out how to win her back. I don't quite have a strategy devised, it's under the microscope, it's in my head. Whatever it takes to patch this hole up that's inside of me that's what I'll do. I'll get a bottle of Great Stuff and fill it with yellow foam and wait and hope. Then again, maybe I just need to fuck some whore and get it all out of me.

xoxo

Dear XXXXX,

You've basically given me no other options in anything really. How can I feel too bad about degrading or being mean to you when you degraded and humiliated me by not even having the decency to tell me that we were over. Then putting on a big make out display in front of multiple people I know, and that's how I found out about us being over from them by default. It makes me think that you're shady and not very trustworthy at all. Then you act stupid to me and you run off several days later with a guy you knew for three days, how the hell do you think that made me feel? It must be nice to believe that you didn't do anything wrong. I wish I had your conscience. I thought you were one of the most amazing people I'd ever met. Yeah, I admit I'm scared. Scared of losing someone very close to me, a best friend. I've never lost one and it absolutely destroys me inside to think that I have to do it, especially to you. I mean there are like two damn different XXXX'X here to me, the one before Feb 10th and the one after. The one before I love so much it's ridiculous. I would lay down in traffic for her and rip out my spleen with a pair of pliers if she needed it. The one after, I don't like her very much and insert some of the mean things I've said before here. You want to talk about confusion, well there it is in its prime essence.

xoxo

"I'm gonna wait until you want one really bad then kick u in the ovaries and laugh

you're a moron..

I know

you may not be able to get close enough to kick me if thats your attitude

good comeback, I'm obviously not gonna kick u in the ovaries..ha

i know you wouldn't and if you tried..its my switchblade and mace on your ass-LOL

ohh so scary

you should be...

I fucking gargle with mace

haha...its me you're talking to remember?? I know better

better have something a little stronger that I'm scared of, like saurekraut

i have that too-no problem, no i know your weakness...canned or in a bag??

just the smell of it makes me wanna throw up, that and canned tuna."

xoxo

She called me tonight and told me that her sister shot herself in the face. I'd fucked her a few times before, but why she wanted me to be the shoulder to cry on I don't know. I'd only met her sister once while drunk, so I can't say that I cared about her shooting herself in the face anymore than I cared about any other death I read about in the newspaper or see on TV. I told her that I was sorry, I lied. I told her that everything would be alright, I lied again. I asked her if she wanted to come over and fuck. I finally told the truth.

xoxo

"You should come over and hang out missy!"

"I'm really drunk...Sorry"

"It's alright I wish you would come over"

"I know I'm pretty fucked up though so I'd probably just pass out. Did you leave right after?"

"I know. It's alright. I still want you to come over."

"And I still want to"

"So come over or I'll come and get you"

"I wish"

"Wish nothing, I would"

"I'm with my friend and were leaving tom. She'd really kill me"

"So just come over. I like you"

"There's no way I could drive like this"

"So, I'll come pick you up. Let's have fun. Just come over darling...please"

"I so want to"

"So I didn't realize how much olkder you are than me?"

"Yeah I'm so old. I just age gracefully. I got underwear older than you girl"

"lol…"

"Did I really finger you in the bar last night? That's pretty cooterawesome!"

"Yeah until it hit me that we were in public and made you stop"

"Well, when you come back into town we'll do it in private like classy people!..lol"

"Sounds good"

"Excellent, I'll molester you like an alter boy!..haha"

"uuh oh sounds great"

xoxo

Even though worrying about getting genital herpes or some other type of shit from a fat stripper sucks, I'm almost glad in a way. It at least gives something new to worry and think about as opposed to the other girl.

xoxo

My phone is fucking dead,

"That's what they call me at the free clinic!"

"I'm so exausted, don't think I would be any fun tonight at all.. sorry boo."

"Oh a cup of decaf to unwind after a busy day with a boy who can't stay hard for me"

"Living life in the fast lane…."

"Yeah"

"Ok, just so you're clear."

"We are going to have to rain check it til next Monday. I have to get up early and have a test I forgot about. I'm not being neurotic I swear"

"I gave myself a manicure and feel so much better"

"It's a combo of things, I'm at work call ya when I leave. It's been a horrible week. I was in a car accident as well. You message last night was not cool"

"Whatever, ur delusional...I didn't go out this weekend"

"My balls are now blue and burnt from the nair!"

"You go out every nightblah blah blah"

"It hurts Pedro my mexican inner child when u avoid me!"

"I think I met you for coffee and did homework"

"I'm kidding, I did turn into the sahara didn't I?"

"But I would meet you for a cup of coffee at DD"

"Are you going out? I'm totally zapped from moving stuff today to and from the storage unit and then working all ngiht ugh"

"What are you up to tonight?"

"No ur past"

"Yes but it doesn't work for me…didn't take my hair off"

"Charging my phone then going to treat the vitiligo. Call you in a few"

"There are still people in here argh!"

"I'm got up to pee, now I'm really up"

"Not funny, suckerfish…I'll call u when I leave here"

"Oh I can't wait to collect"

"It was such a long day. Excited to see u tomorrow after work as well"

"I think we had a good talk today"

"n hour and then I can count my drawer. See you around 1130"

"It would be a nice gesture"

"Tecate, are you getting the chips and salsa with it?"

"I have to be up at the crack of dawn. I'll call u tomorrow I promise"

"That's the stuff I want to talk to you about"

"But u talk about her all the time!!!!!!!"

"There are a couple of reasons I backed away. School being the main one and the others I will talk to you about."

"We'll talk about it this weekend ok?"

"I'm a neurotic mess. U know that. We'll hang out soon, I suck"

"I'm under a ton of stress and have no free time. Please don't call me lame."

"Oh hell to the no"

"I just saw another guy with vitiligo"

"Will u be mad if I postpone until tomorrow. I've had a week from hell. And I'm exhausted and have to work till late."

"Probably can'ti'm working"

"Haha yeah I'd like to see that"

"Ok, good I like that answer"

"I already know that. Honestly, if that made it easier for you I would understand. I would hate it but understand"

"Really, disappear forever..interesting"

"Where do u want to go?"

"Ur a cornball, u did not say that!"

"Haha, I'm envious I'm at work"

"Yeah well I'm still the first and original…haha"

"Quit, ur not annoying me!"

"Ur spoiled, I'm being jealous..night"

"Going to bed, long day tomorrow…it must be nice to go out every single night"

"That's cute not nerdy"

"I don't feel good, get out of here at 11 and call u then. Whatcha doing today?"

"Can't wait to see the pics"

"Fuck off…"

"Aww night my little cornball"

"I'm going home and go to bed"

"No, just been laying around all morning, what u doing?"

"Sorry to cut you off, finally on the right road now"

"Ur not going to answer that.."

"Damn I have to work"

"It would be a nice gesture"

"I'm a neurotic mess. U know that. We'll hang out soon, I suck"

"Lucky,"

My phone is fucking alive.

xoxo

She's gone all new age on me. She was yapping over tacos about going to Sedona, Arizona and having some spiritual awakening. I think she's fuckin' lost her mind and needs help. I still care about her, but fuckin' hell. I feel sorry for whatever dude has to listen to this shit just to get some pussy.

xoxo

I went to a movie with her. We went to a matinee at two in the afternoon to see the new Batman movie. For some reason, ten minutes into the movie I had my hand lying on her knee, basically because I didn't have anywhere else to put it really. She grabbed my hand and held it tightly. I felt like an idiot at first, but I admit that I sort of liked it after a while. I held her hand so long my damn arm went to sleep. I'm getting goddamn fucking pathetic!

xoxo

"One Last Night of Consumerism"

the nails are dirty

the walls are dirtier

clean your mind

cash in

your soul at the register,

you

old dirty corporate whore

that

changed the tires of my fear

AAA

no charge

no credit to use

anyways

snuff in the glass

of

black market Honduran juice

cardboard boxes

no will to live

cut your hand

wither

the Utah nightmares

blood cell perverts

x-rays of

distant hope

and

opinions never mattered

saliva permeates

on

antique wooden floors

caricature homicide displays

for

the lackluster masses

to see

witness the red carnage

on a

discount

pawn shop TV,

the nails are dirty

the walls are dirtier

clean your mind

cash in

your soul at the register.

xoxo

She is all that's there. I think and smoke and sit and think about her. I contemplate how it all went wrong, how I fucked it up, and how she fucked it up. I have silent conversations with her. I confess it all, but it does no good. A shell like homo sapien is all that's left. She is five hours away from me now and probably hanging out with her new ginger boy toy. He's in town. I only know that because I saw it on various social media sites a while back. When I got the call to leave for a week I jumped on it. Visions of them fucking, eating, drinking, talking, and laying in her bed fill my mind. She keeps doing it to me, yet she knows nothing about it. She's seeing some other guy now and obviously didn't want me anymore. Yet, here I am five hours away dealing with it. I secretly want it all to blow up in her fucking face, let her see how delusional and bullshit she's been acting for the past few months. Were the signs there before?

I don't know. I guess so. I just chalked it up to normal relationship bullshit at the time. Here I am still thinking about her, still wanting her after all this bullshit, but why? Should I even still care? Should I still love her? I don't trust her like I did before, but for some reason I can't give up on her. I can't give up on someone I love and I thought was my best friend in the world. We did so much cool shit together and had so much fun, yet it's over, and she abandoned me for another, or for herself. Who the fuck knows really. Maybe she doesn't even know. I hope she comes to her senses and comes back at some point. She doesn't even have to comeback to me, just back to her old self, the one that was so awesome. I miss that girl badly, but the more days that pass, the less likely I think that's gonna happen. Things will be different this time baby, I swear. I fucked it up and didn't give you all that you needed. I hate myself for that. I didn't care about anyone else and I don't now. I just want her, what I can't have. I'm tired of being fucked up over her. I'm an emotional and mental wreck on a plethora of levels. Fuck, how do I make it right? I can't live like this. I miss her. I miss my best friend. Conversations lack the flare that they once had, and the fun level is pretty low. Do I even know this person anymore? I have no answers, only theories.

xoxo

Dear XXXXX,

After contemplating this whole situation for a while I've decided to take everything I've written about you off my blogs and shit. Whether it bothered you that bad or not, I don't know, but it's gone and off of there. I left two or three of the funnier ones, I hope you don't mind. It's nothing negative or anything but I did really like that one where you got "fuck off" tattooed on your knuckles, it made me laugh. I'll just keep what I write to myself from now on. I wasn't purposely trying to hurt you or make you feel like a shitty person by the way. Some of the shit you do hurts me badly but writing about it is my release. I can't help it that I like you though XXX. I've tried not to but I can't do anything about it. I fully realize that you don't feel the same way about me and probably never will and that's ok. Really, liking a person brings with it a lot of idiotic activity, like sometimes when I'm pissed off or jealous over you I write and say some fucked up mean shit and I know that, and I'm sorry for that as well. But, I do it because I like you, so it comes from a good place, but comes out and ends up all fucked up and I know that's twisted. Sometimes I wonder why you even put up with me. But, thanks for never telling me to fuck off. I've never seen so much drama come from something so stupid in my life. If this will free me from that yoke, then I probably should have done it sooner. I obviously knew that you didn't trust me very much anymore, but it was a paradox of whether to do what I wanted to do and not censor what I thought, or swallow my pride and take everything down and censor myself because of a few mean words now and again. It took me a long time to even put anything I wrote about you up for the public to see. It scared me that I could feel that way about someone and leave myself open like that. Then when people said "damn, you're not a bad writer" I kept putting more stuff up there and it kept on and on. But, hopefully now the drama and bullshit will end. Hopefully, you can maybe trust me again one day and our friendship can be better than it is presently. I guess we'll just figure it out as we go.

Yours truly,

The Asshole

xoxo

"So I went to dinner tonight with XXXX and XXXXX who I havent seen in ages. Anywho, they were both going on and on about these guys in their lives who don't call them, pay any attention to them or are just completely thoughtless. One didnt even call last night to see if she was ok in the storm- dumbassess. So I had to tell them that I knew a guy who did call, was very thoughtful, who called to check on me last night and offered me a place to stay if I was scared, randomly cooked for me, took care of me after I had my teeth pulled, and just plain suprised me now and then. They were both like "whats the problem?". And I went into the whole we dont see eye to eye on the marriage/kids thing and that domestication just wasn't for you. I explained that all in all I just dont know what to do with you? Be your "friend" for the next 50 years? They had very little helpful input, and went back to complaining. I just wanted you to know that I was bragging on how thoughtful and kind you are. Also if you look at it this way it may help you understand why I get upset sometimes. I see that Ive found a guy that does things most others dont and you make me happy. But at the same time, I know that you dont want more that a "cootership" and those dont last forever(haha)...thus the breakdown ensues. Kinda like dreading having your leg amputated- just the thought of it gets you all upset. I hate loss and how it feels really. The only plus is that heartbreak has always been a great diet plan for me- so I'll get back to being supermodel hot- LOL. The main point (that got lost inall my rambling) of this is that I appreciate you thoughtfulness so much, and Im so glad I that you're in my life. And of course I love you."

xoxo

Silence...

A wet oil painting falls with a thud to the floor.

Then the front door slams shut.

"Fuck you asshole! Sorry to inconvenience you again."

A ringing cell phone is discovered in-between the cushions of my couch.

"Call my phone."

"I don't know where the fuck it is!"

"I left my phone. I need my phone."

A man in a wet towel approaches the front door of an apartment.

Banging and ringing.

Ringing and banging.

The man hears noise while taking a shower.

A man takes a shower.

Silence…

"Sorry to inconvenience you."

A girl gets pissed off.

"Whatever, you fucking liar."

"Well, if I have a choice, then go."

"Well, do you want me to stay or go?"

A girl is lying on a ratty black couch.

"I'm tired and need to go to bed."

A man returns to the living room.

After fucking, a man goes to the bathroom to take a shit while a girl gets dressed and goes into the living room.

xoxo

I was drunk and could hardly walk. Somehow I drove to and stumbled into a shitty strip club near my house. I sat at the bar by myself like I do most of the time. I ordered an overpriced beer and didn't tip. She was on stage. She was a beast of a woman, but she did have the largest tits I think I've ever seen in my life. She was at the bar soon after she stopped dancing and tried to hit up a few old men and Mexicans for money and private dances I guess. She ordered a drink. She kept looking at me from the center of the bar. I just sat there in a drunken daze. The next thing I know she occupied the black bar stool next to mine. She said she knew me. I just went along with it, even though I had no idea who the fuck she was. More overpriced beers were ordered, and again I did not tip. I couldn't drink much more. The clock read 6:12 a.m. on my phone. I dropped the phone on the floor; I couldn't find the backing to it. Soon, after a visit to the ATM machine in the corner I had money again. Sixty bucks out of my checking account, along with a nice shitty strip club charge of five bucks. I soon put dollar bills in the beast of a woman's garter belt while she was on stage. Soon, we were back where we started, her in a stool next to mine. She said we should hang out after this and drink more. I gave her my phone number and said I had to go home and puke. I stumbled to my car and made it home somehow. I chugged an orange flavored Gatorade. Ten minutes after I was in bed my phone rang and I made the mistake of answering it. She would be over in ten minutes. I opened the door in my blue underwear. She drank Miller High Life that'd been in my refrigerator for months. I continued drinking orange Gatorade. The next thing I knew I was eating her fat pussy out. I kissed her once but she had a hint of a mustache so I stopped doing that. She sucked my dick as I stood above her and drank Gatorade. Either, I was so drunk that I couldn't feel anything or she was horrid at it. I resorted to fucking her soon after. I came inside of her fat pussy about twenty minutes later. After, I washed her fat pussy juice and my cum off of my dick I said I had to go to bed. She left without saying a word, thank Allah. I was sleeping soon after.

xoxo

"Where Padded Walls Greet the Periodic Table"

the smell of burning

bodies and

nose hair

cannot be understated,

the stolen bank pen

tells

the truth late at night

while alone,

the rusty scissors

sets

the masses free,

dirt clumped coinage

and

no parking

is allowed here,

angelic women

from the sea carrying

bags

of

cheap Chinese presents,

sugar riddled

serving

suggested

property

of

an unlisted number,

Post-It Note

messages

from the insane

on my refrigerator door

scribbled in dark toned ink,

the berry flavored

isolation

floats

escaping Folsom prison

and further

persecution.

xoxo

She says that if it "ever feels right" she'll consider giving me another shot to be her boyfriend.

xoxo

"there's room in my life for both u and the fries, don't worry

great...Id hate for you to have to choose

don't get mad because u have to share, if I see u on the news hitting fries in burger king I'm not hanging out with u anymore

well ya know I might go ape shit on some french fries...and have to bust a cap in their ass-

leave my babies alone

now you have pet names for them????I am hurt

you dont even have a pet name for me-boo hoo

yea I do, u just don't know it...bazooka

wow thats really endearing-

baby momma that's ur pet name, or FBM if u prefer?

oh yeah..thats right

yea see, u don't even know

i do to know there dorkalicious

ha, yea ok....don't pretend like u do

yeah I know.......more than you think, its not really the coffee shop stalker you should worry about-KIDDING!!!

haha, hey now......I like that

really???

oh yes, you're not crazy enough to be a stalker

jno not really...I guess I have acted a little crazy in the past though

lets get married then!"

xoxo

She misses me, but doesn't want me. Go figure that one out. I wonder how she feels about me now. I hear girls like assholes and the unattainable. I'm probably both of those on some level. I wonder if she still loves me, maybe a little I'd guess. Does she like me like that after I called her an airheaded cunt, I would say probably not. She's all smitten over that fat fuck. I hate that fucking guy. I saw a picture of him wearing an endangered animal fur coat in a picture. He has to be the biggest douchebag on the planet, or at least high on the list anyways. I hope some nutjob member of PETA finds him wearing that coat one day and pours a gallon of red acrylic paint on his fucking fat head. That would be fantastic! She has her freedom and chooses that over me. It still doesn't make any sense. When women flip out, they really go to the extreme. I have to leave her alone for a while. I want her back so bad I can taste it, but it's an impossible task at the moment. She has freedom and I have misery. What a nice fucking trade off...

xoxo

"Ahh fuck, my friend request got rejected! How will my self esteem ever recover?...lol"

"lol (insert a smiley face or some shit that looks like one)"

"Well, that smiley face made the rejection sting a little less. I'm actually ok with getting BJ's from you without being FB friends...lol."

xoxo

"Dinner is Served"

Slaving

over reddened hot steel

sweat is pouring
from face
onto
smooth heat resistant
white lacquer paint,
fifteen minutes later
slightly burned chicken
with
sticky white rice
and
dinner is ready
for two,

a few minutes later
rubber tires breed
with wet black pavement
$3.53
a gallon
Al Gore hates me
seventeen miles per gallon
city
her small
metallic silver
Japanese SUV
pulls
into familiar and typical
suburban driveway,

soon,

slightly burned chicken
with

sticky white rice
and
dinner is served
for two,

an hour later
we're fucking
in the kitchen
where
dinner was served
bent over
near the sink
flesh pounds
away
against flesh,
the only problem is
my
diagnosed STD
earlier
that same day
maybe
if I don't cum inside of her
everything will be
ok
I think to myself
ok
too late
now
it felt too good
clap
clap
clap

morphs

and

fills a wet hole

some regret is

felt afterwards,

sometimes,

more than

dinner is served.

xoxo

"Come here and grab my cock and pretend like you like me." She acts repulsed by my cock and barley touches the head of it. I ask her if she's a lesbian or just a fucking prude? She says nothing, and goes back to watching TV. I get up off the couch and pull my hard cock out of my black shorts and slap her in the right temple with it. She was not very happy about it. I went into my room and jerked off while she continued to watch my small TV in the other room.

xoxo

I pop the now deceased herpes blister on my lower lip with a sewing needle that I borrowed six years ago from my grandmother. I suck the herpes tinged river of fluid from the blister and spit it in her face. Maybe we're not soulmates after all, but now we're bonded forever. How fucking romantic.

xoxo

Dear XXXXX,

I'd respect you a lot more if you had the balls to give me my shit back face to face, but that isn't your style these days. The way you handle things now, you'll probably wait until I'm out of town and leave the stuff on my door and some crackhead will steal it. You've really changed, and it's not been in any sort of good fashion. I don't know this new XXXXX, and really I don't want to anymore. If the old XXXXX ever rears her head around again, look me up, because I do want to know her…Brett

xoxo

"speaking of cobra maybe I should take one

oh goodness

haha, I'm doing it for you!

Whatever…lol…i may not be able to take it

it's pretty small, a midget could take it!

oh great lotts to look forward to then

haha, jeez what do u want a fucking horse??

maybe at least pony??-lol

haha, I might pass for one of those mini ponies. it's not my fault I was given a big cranium and a small wang…

yeah its probably like a foot long and would kill me-haha

yeah if you add 9 inches it is…lol"

xoxo

"Ok, so now I have the freedom to basically go whore around and do whatever I want, yet I don't even want to do that now that I can, which is weird I suppose…what's happened to me/wrong with me? I gotta admit, (even though of course in hindsight I didn't take advantage of it or appreciate it enough), it was really cool and also very comfortable to be able to have sex with a really good friend that I could trust. There's nothing all that appealing to me at the moment about fucking a complete stranger in a bar or something, and really unless they're already a friend, they're all complete strangers, and most of those aren't worth knowing. Things to ponder existentially I guess. It might be uncouth to ask you, but have any advice on this one?"

"Yeah, dont have sex with friends. Thats all I have on that matter"

xoxo

Her car was filled with various trash, which was pretty fucking disgusting. McDonald's wrappers and Pepsi bottles littered her dark floor mats. I pushed them aside with my feet when I got into the passenger side door. Her 1996 shit brown Grand Marquis reeked of pot and stale cigarettes. I left the car door open. We kissed several times. Her tongue explored my mouth and lightly brushed against my teeth. My hand moved from her knees to her pussy. I rubbed against it a few times. She pulled back and said to give her a minute. I lit a cigarette while I waited on her. She moved towards the door of the car and opened it. A few seconds later, she grabbed the door handle and leaned out and vomited on the black concrete, turning it green and white. The fresh aroma of vomit even overwhelmed the scent of pot and stale cigarettes. She tried to kiss me again a few minutes later, but I pulled back and said "you just puked for fuck's sake. I'm not going to kiss you, but you can give me a blowjob if you want baby."

xoxo

You aren't even worth the thought processes it takes to think or write about you so the book will end here, with no great finale, and very little fanfare. It was amazing for a while at the start, but then knowing you became a burden. Your actions spoke volumes to me.

xoxo

My phone is alive,

Are you ignoring me fucker???

Ok do you know where the house is. I'll leave the backdoor open

It's always everybody else. U take zero responsibility. Goodbye

Well he didn't take it as a joke and it's fucking awkward. Thanks. U need to calm down with this fucking act and bullshit. I'm done with it

What is your fucking problem? What did you say to the bartender???? He is being a total dick to me tonight. Seriously, you are out of control!

Lube is made for dude's like that. Ha. I'm actually surprised that you and the dude got along. You damned loud mouth.

What the fuck are you talking about. You're both stupid!

You did and he is raunchy. Don't worry about him.

You didn't have to leave

Well what the fuck, you know where my house is cause I will be in bed. But you can come get in.

Are you gone? Want me to get a pizza?

Love it esp with my ipod

Great you can go live it up and I'll be in the sack

Ok I'll stop driniing in a minute in case you need me. But I'm worthless tonight so just let me pass out and cry.

Well hurry the fuck up and let's go to bed. I'll give you two drinks

ppplease come tomorrow you can stay and even shower in a fancer shower. Come early!

MY best friend is dead and I got blown off on a date. WTF is wrong with me?

No I mean the asshole in the picture is gross and raunchy.

Sorry, just got this come tomorrow afternoon. Please?

Ha I'm a fascist because I asked you to cut out your bad ass act for one night and be cool to nice laid back undeserving people. That's funny, have a good weekend

I'll try but fuck come on

Pplease don't come seriously. If being who you are is rude and offends people;e who don't sereve it. I don't really want to hang

LOL are ya'll out. Is this gonna be one of those nights where u get drunk and call me.

OK then don't come it's not cool to be rude to people especially when they're nice and shy. That's not nazi to ask u to be decent..lol

Yeah XXX friend req me so I tagged that photo for him..

he is gross! That's what I mean by raunchy

I totally understand hun. Been there and stayed there a long time. Persue that, it's where your heart is and it's not fair to anyone else. We'll always be niggers

Ur still attatched to XXXXX and I'm not going there

We are a rad item now!!

Ha. That leads to trouble and you talking about sex all the time

U try so hard to get a rise out of me

I'm not amused with this weather. Especially when I'm ghost white

Whatever it's all good. I've been out of it as well

Crazy wom,an? Not all that. Just saying hi…though you didn't want to answer

Ahh that good

I do and I have no hard feelings. But for now I think it's best to discontinue communications

Not sure what brought this on? Please don't text me again

Not a good place to skimp. Hope you can hear. Shoulda cut out your beer fund for a week and bought a good one

Yeah like an alternate universe..

Leave the shock value at home too, these guys are cool and u were kind of rude to my friend the other night

Hah ok I'll try to prepare myself

Ok, no more texts from me

Ha, thanks I appreciate ethe vote. But I will still be kickboxing some ass tomorrow

I totally understand hun. Been there and stayed there a long time. Persue that, it's where your heart is and it's not fair to anyone else. We'll always be niggers

I guess you'll be breaking the news to me to then

I'm sure it doesn't make her wet. The wallet does. That's the one good thing about me having money. I don't have to settle for sercurity.

How are you doing?

I suppose

Uh ok, we'll have to figure out a day. XXXX will be here some. Maybe I can cook u both dinner.haha. I know, not funny

Come get in bed with me.

Lovely as long as you enjoy it

Answer me fuck face,

My phone is dead.

xoxo

I finally got hired for a job the other day. I'd been looking for work for months with no luck. This fucking economy is goddamn ruining me. Anyways, my second night on the job at this shithole bar checking ID's and throwing drunks out I fucked my hot cougar boss who has two kids. I fucked her real good. She came and even moaned my name once or twice. I remember it went something like "oh brett" and "oh my fucking god Brett, I'm cumming" or something to that extent. Then again, I could be lying, you never know. Hell, I ain't lying to you. I wouldn't do that. I was drunk as hell and it took a couple of hours for me to cum, but I did while I was fucking her doggy style just as the sun was coming up. I bet she thought I was a goddamn fuck champion or something. Little does she know it was just the Pabst Blue Ribbon in the bottle, and not really anything in my fucking repertoire that was good. She tried to cuddle with me after I came inside of her. I didn't mind for a while I guess, but I couldn't fucking sleep with her all wrapped around me. I dozed off a few times. I wasn't really sure if I was ever actually sleeping or I was just in the "after you bust a nut utopia" that you sometimes experience after you cum inside of a girl. Anyways, the next morning I couldn't find my cigarettes or cool new lighter that I'd just bought at the gas station, so I smoked all her cigarettes while she took a two hour shower. When I left her house she told me it was cool if I didn't call her, and it was also cool if I did. I didn't call her for five days after I fucked her. She didn't call me back to work after that either, and now it's back to selling everything I own on Ebay, and borrowing money from all my friends. You fucking idiot!

xoxo

"She broke my heart and gave me staph." I'm selling this song to Merle Haggard.

xoxo

"Blind, Bound, and Fucking Forgotten"

everything and else are us,

organize

secrete

constrict

connect

art and E.Coli,

everything and else are us,

observe

sequence

contrast

consume

literature and Hepatitis B,

everything and else are us.

xoxo

Dear XXX,

You're about the last person I ever expected to hear from. I'm not going to celebrate or claim freedom because you moved out. Since we aren't talking or hanging out it was just a little odd to be living on top of each other. Sometimes I find myself missing you, but other times I'm happy that you're not in my life. It's quite the paradox XXXXX. Although, I will say that my life is not as exciting or fun without you around. I've had plenty of time to think about the past. Looking back on it, you had no respect for me at all. You treated me like shit and gave no thought about how any of your actions might affect me and it pretty much crushed me, your supposed "friend." On top of that, you were a fucking total stranger to me the last six months I knew you. I miss that weird amazing girl that I first knew from CCU, not the person you came to be after last Christmas. I forgive you for that shit. I shouldn't, but I do. I will always care about you, consider you a friend and appreciate that I knew you for as long as I live. You're my Myrtle Beach girl. I can't look at anyone for a very long time the way I look at you. It sounds like a line of bullshit I'm sure, but I do mean it. I realize also, that I did some mean juvenile shit in return to you for breaking my heart and fucking with me. Like I said before, you bring out the best and the worst in me. For what's its worth I'm sorry for that. If you decide to never speak to me again, please don't walk away thinking I'm an asshole for the rest of your life. I don't know where we go from here XXXXXXXXX. I guess the next move is yours darlin…Brett

xoxo

Most of the women throughout my life I never gave a shit about. They came and went without much thought or care from me. That's not the case with her.

xoxo

We were fucking in the back seat of my car. Well, it was more like I was driving her around town in a neighborhood that I'd never been to looking for her friend's house and we couldn't find it. Then, maybe out of boredom or drunkenness I said "get in the backseat I wanna fuck the shit out of you again." And, surprisingly she agreed. Which, is where we presently find ourselves. Technically, I've been here for like two hours in the back seat of my car before I needed a new position because my legs were fucking killing me. So, even though it was in front of some random house in a generic suburban neighborhood, I opened the door, got out, pulled my pants down, pulled her near me, and started fucking the shit out of her again even though my cock hurt and was actually burning now from being rubbed raw for over two hours. I was gonna cum one way or another, that I did know. As the birds starting chirping and the sun was coming up I came inside of her in front of this random house in some generic suburban neighborhood.

xoxo

"The CEO of Disappointment"

sorry,

with 25% authenticity

I'm the CEO

of disappointment,

what I want from you is a distraction

no commitment

I love that broad

your secrets

are

better than mine

is that part of the job?

your lies

are

better than mine
I just moved here
I don't give a damn about the air
my children were my life
until
Susan Smith killed them
when am I gonna meet Tarzan?
in hell and Parisian subway stations
the next page
chicken and 'taters
it's not the food
it's the company
flashing halogen lights
last night
I stared at your breasts
when you weren't looking
a grubby little parasite
invading
homeless American Jesus
he still sleeps on the floor
safety pins and hot glue
get me Bogota
abstract South American maps
and
whores on runways
in alluring white shirts
shooting bullets
shooting semen
I took pictures of the whole thing
my uncle touched me
in my special place
he's a killer

don't worry I'll send you some framed copies

give yourself more time

join the CIA

scotch tape psychology

I got something here for your lady friend

not my rooster

just a bigger gun

a jumper

a suicide

I can't do it while you're watching,

sorry,

with 25% authenticity

I'm the CEO

of disappointment.

xoxo

I slithered like a snake into my own personal version of a walk of shame. It had to be done though. I didn't want this idiot hippy bitch, formerly with a hairy pussy that I shaved for her two days ago having my fucking kid. It would've been nice if she would've mentioned not being on birth control before I came inside of her, but what's done is done. Her pussy wasn't bad, and I'm glad I pissed her off and made her leave my apartment, because I do detest sleeping or sharing a bed with anyone. But, there are few things worse than having to go and see or deal with someone whom you never wanted to see again. I called her when I was outside of the store that she worked at. She came outside and I gave her my half of the morning-after pill consisting of one twenty dollar bill and one five dollar bill. I gave her the money and said goodbye. I slithered like a snake back to my car and sped out of the parking lot.

xoxo

"it's always good to drink and 'get busy" before one leaves town

really and you rationale for this theory would be?

don't really know, other than selfish intentions of drinking and fornicating with you...

hmmm, simplistic and easy to understand-well stated

thanks

well you could come over stuff envelopes and get shitfaced, all the while playing some cheesy 80's movie in the background

ok, u talked me into it. although left out the details of the fornication

conveniantly I'm sure

oh oops, well thats just not something u plan

i know but with a combo of 80's movies, vodka and evelopes how could making baby practice not take place really

I know its like opening Pandoras box

that's how orgies start out, envelopes and pretty in pink

or breakfast club-thats my fav

if you have a movie to bring, bring one or I'll make you watch one of mine-like miss firecracker or empire records

I like empire records. trust me I will bring movies u have never seen

really, cool Im somewhat surprised. no porn-haha

I wasn't, we'll make our own

i knew that was coming as soon as i said that-lol

well quit setting me up

didnt mean too, just not thinking ahead

haha…I'm thinking thrashin and blue velvet

whatever, I open to anything

even the 2 hole?

any MOVIE-

haha, u keep giving me these easy opportunities

Yeah Im falling off my game-its my bed time."

xoxo

"Insert a Cornucopia of Fuck Here"

Fuck,

your tits are as fake and empty as you fucking are

how many fucking mental disorders do you possess?

you make very little fucking sense to me

I'm growing to fucking despise you!

you're like every other fucking girl in this town

actually, you're worse because you think you're fucking not

what the fuck do you want from me?

why the fuck do I still have you in my life?

why the fuck am I so interested in you?

I must enjoy fucking sado-masochism or something

maybe I have just as many mental disorders as you fucking do

probably fucking not

the fucking end,

Fuck!

xoxo

I never replaced her like she replaced me. The whole time I was with her I wanted to fuck other people, hell, I even thought about other people when I was fucking her. But, I never replaced her like she replaced me. Her pussy was alright, nothing great though. I got bored of the vanilla flavored sex and avoided fucking her sometimes, but I still liked fucking her though. She wouldn't do anything nasty like letting me fuck her in the ass or jerk off on her face, but I never replaced her like she replaced me. Her pussy smelled for a few months and I stuck by her even though sometimes my face and dick would smell like rotten fish, but I never replaced her like she replaced me.

xoxo

"it's supposed to be nice tomorrow so keep your phone on you tomorrow as I'll prob be calling....

ok

or I could just be stringing you along and never bring u lunch

could be????

yes, adds a little mystery to it I think

definately

u go to lunch at 1 or so right

yeah

ok, I'll try and make it

ok just call me

or I could just take a dump in a to go box and leave it at the front desk for you...har har

nice....you're so charming

ahh, he thought about me and left me a quesadilla....how nice, then she opens the box to find a shit sandwitch.....oh, that little prankster

hmmm yeah

ha…charming is my middle name, when it's not danger or hey asshole

yep I know...you just swept me right off my feet with your charm

well yea, it was probably more of a trip but hey details aren't important

haha

yak

I guess I need to find you an animal name...I would probably go with armadillo or platapuss.....something lame

llama?

yea ok, copycat

maybe I'll just call you muffin

YAK!

hahahaa

aww muffin....you're so funny!

I have no idea where yak came from, I just saw a Y on the bowling game and it hit me and I can't stop saying it

its ok muffin, thats just your wonderful creative mind at work-LOL

no, call me green bean...all the other bitches do

green bean eh?

no idea, just made it up. I just finished that story about calling u chubby, it's funny…

I thought it was pudgy

yeah ur right, I gotta change it

pudgy sounds better too

YAK

haha

I seen a yak yesterday at the waterpark

awesome...maybe we can hook up

I got my bike seat in, so I'm ready to get some exercise later tonight

oh nice

yea indeed

tomorrow night is gonna suck dick..

why?

Yak yak!!

Hahah...ur crazy!

2 words

kid rock.....all night

oh god....well u can come hang out on my couch if you want

haha,well thanks. I might come watch a movie or something

have u ever seen clockwork orange

no

ahh, what about true romance

who's in that one?

christian slater

i dont think so

goo dlord.....what about heathers

nope

good lord. I'm your personal netflix then cause u would like all those

ok well bring one over

oh, I might bring 5 over

ooooohhh

no need to rent shit if you have never seen those classics

alright

heathers can be our movie

oh lord...cant wait to see it, Im sure its bizarre

it's like a black comedy

winnona ryder?

classic teenage angst movie. yes!

Ive heard of it

Cool. have u ever heard of these nuts, yo mouth?

what?

Haha...don't fret, I'll show it to you tomorrow

haha

just close ur eyes and open wide

ewww

haha, salty balls

oh cant wait

haha

im trying to cut back on my sodium though

yeah well, cum doesn't make u pudgy

I dont know...who knows how many calories may be in it

who knows, u do like candy

ive given up candy.....I have to break the addiction

well substitute cum for it

"feed the yak"

oh funny

haha I thought it was funny

hillarious and charming

it has nothing to do with u looking or resembling a yak in any way

haha ok

though, I could just be yakking with you!...lol"

xoxo

My balls are sore, and on top of that it sort of hurts when I take a piss. I must've pulled down my pants and perused my dick about 275 times today looking for signs of trouble. There were no apparent sign of an STD. Even so, I'm still fucking nervous. Maybe because I drank so much orange juice the past few days is the reason my piss burns. That's what I tell myself anyways. I look in the phone book for the number to the free clinic so I can go get a gigantic Q-tip shoved up my dick again. What a fucking great time that will be! I nervously dial the number, but there's no answer. It's 4:56 so they must be closed. Oh well, there's always tomorrow I guess.

xoxo

"Lucky you, you get one drunk and one hungover message...haha. I love waking up at 8 in the morning with all the lights still on, the tv blasting and still wearing my clothes and shoes from the previous night. Alka Seltzer and double-ply toilet paper were made for days like these! I have no idea why I'm telling you this, it's pathetic.....but I miss the shit out of you and I worry about you! I think I've turned like 0.3 % emo, and if the artistic/writing thing doesn't work out I think I could have a future as an emo songwriter making a few bucks selling Dashboard Confessional songs like: BFF doesn't mean forever.haha. I'd have to do it under an alias though, because I would consider it to be "pussy shit" and I'd never buy the albums..haha. I saw your update are you already running off with "party boy" now? Why weren't you this insane with I was with you? Hell, I would have married you six months ago if you had been! Haha!!! Alright, enough of the ramblings....I Hope you're doing well, over and out"

"Well I appreciate the message...loved the emo shit-haha. No Im not off on vacation with XXXX. XXXX and I were trying to work out going in April but my work schedule wont allow it-bummer! BTW I was always this "insane" so its not like Ive changed in that way."

"No problem, I know you were always insane and emotionally unstable...it was just a little sarcasm baby. I told you before that I had a thing for nuerotic chicks....haha. Damn, that would have been cool. But in a perfect world I would have brought you there to hang out with me for free. Yeah, I'm was just really bored of the same old bars. Not going there means I don't get to see a lot of people I like...so fuck it, everyone gets a second chance...even you...ha. I'm glad about the message, I wish I would have seen it a few weeks ago, it would have helped. It brought tears to my eyes...haha...ok no, but it was really nice. Of course I'm gonna worry about you and miss you, especially since I'm not gonna be able to see you or talk to you as much. You did go a little wild there so I didn't really know, even though I knew it probably wasn't true, since yeah I know how you are......picnics, Cosco and romantic comedies...haha. I am going through some XXXXX withdrawls though, so sorry if some of these messages become a little sappy. Still trying to adjust over here!...haha. I never really loved anyone other than myself and like my Mom and shit, so all this sap and emotional stuff/person withdrawls is all new to me....OJT! Having any hint of "cooterific" withdrawls over there? Uhmm, probably not, but a nigga gotta hope!....haha"

xoxo

We were hungover and naked. I was the first to wake up. I layed there naked in the hotel room bed and cleared the crust from eyes. She was next to me, still sleeping, and her friend was still sleeping as well in the other bed next to ours. I had a boner from a combination of the past night's drunken sex and the buildup of urine in my bladder. I was too drunk to cum then, but my balls were telling me that I needed to now. I got up and tried to piss, but my boner made it difficult. I almost had to do a fucking handstand just to get the stream of piss anywhere near the toilet. Half of my piss made it onto the floor. I took a towel and put it on top of the puddle of urine that was now in the corner beside of the toilet. It was a hotel, so that was the best they were getting for the moment.

I walked back into the room with my boner and tried to lay back down. I moved closer towards the girl next to me. I put my hand near her muff. It didn't do much of anything. She was still sleeping, as was the girl in the bed next to ours. My next plan was to turn on the TV. The remote was bolted down on the nightstand next to us. There must be a lot of hotel remote thieves around here or something. I clicked the "on" button and soon the room was filled with crappy Saturday morning shows, of which I didn't recognize. They'd taken "saved by the bell" off years ago, so I didn't know shit about what was on there now. The TV trick worked, and soon both of the girls had awoken just like I'd planned. The next part of my plan was to get the other girl in the bed next to ours out of the room so I could fuck her friend again. The girl next to me was naked, just like me. So, basically she couldn't even go to the bathroom now that her friend was awake. Perhaps, she wanted to give the illusion that I hadn't fucked her on the balcony and in the bathroom last night after her drunk best friend went to bed. I don't blame her I suppose. Her friend went to the bathroom and then returned into the room and sat back down on her bed.

"So what do you guys want to do? I'm thinking about going out and sitting by the pool. Do you guys want to come?"

"Yeah, that sounds good." The girl next to me replied.

All I could think to myself was, yeah, feel free to go to the pool, but only after I bust a nut. Her friend went out on the balcony.

"Get your friend out of here so we can do it again. I'm getting the feeling she's going to be here forever. Tell her to go ahead and you will be down in a few minutes."

"Ok, I will." She says.

The girl comes back inside a few minutes later. My angst is growing, and so is my dick.

SHE WILL NOT FUCKING LEAVE! After digging through some of her luggage she pours herself a drink.

"Well, I think I'm going to take a shower." Her best friend says.

And, the best friend disappears into the bathroom. I instantly grab her pussy underneath the sheets and put my finger inside of her. Not so fast cowboy! The other girl returns back into the room and digs through some more of her bags. My hand is removed from her pussy, but not by me. SHE WILL NOT FUCKING LEAVE! She makes small chit-chat now and throws her bikini and other clothes on the bed. She moves them around as if deciding what ensemble she can come up with. SHE WILL NOT FUCKING LEAVE! She then returns back into the bathroom. I can hear her still fumbling around in there and the door is still open. I make another hand dash towards her pussy, but she tells me to wait until the door is closed. Her friend returns once again and grabs the drink that she'd poured herself and goes out onto the balcony. SHE WILL

NOT FUCKING LEAVE! I watch as she gazes down at the pool, and then towards the Atlantic Ocean. She rests against the railing and sips on her drink. SHE WILL NOT FUCKING LEAVE! She returns a few minutes later and stands near the edge of our bed and asks the girl naked under the sheets next to me what she wants to do tonight. There is more useless chit-chat coming out of their mouths, and still SHE WILL NOT FUCKING LEAVE! Soon, after a cornucopia of chit-chatting she leaves and I hear the bathroom door close. I hear the shower turn on. I make my move towards her pussy again. It's dry as a pancake once again, so I start rubbing on it with my fingers. I kiss the girl again. Her breath smells like shit, but I don't tell her, and I don't stop kissing her. Her pussy is slowly getting wet now and I crawl on top of her. I try to put my dick inside of her but it just doesn't seem to wanna go in. I pull the sheets back after failing a few times. I get a good look at her hole and grab my dick and lunge it inside of her. She makes a weird noise and has a dumb expression on her face, but damn it felt good. I pulled the sheets back over us and started pounding away on her. I hear the shower turn off. Soon, the bathroom door is open once again. Fuck, and I stop pumping away on her, but I was still laying on top of her and still inside of her. The best friend returns into the room with a towel wrapped around her and messes around with the clothes she'd put on the bed earlier. THIS FUCKING ASIAN BITCH WILL NOT FUCKING LEAVE! She had to know that we were fucking now though. The smell of pussy and sex filled the room. Even through my blackened lungs and nostrils I could smell it, so I knew that she could as well. Hurry up with your fucking outfit and makeup and get the fuck out of here woman! She returns to the bathroom once again. I am still inside of her, but I layed still like a serpent waiting to strike a prey. I could feel my once powerful boner now growing slowly limp as the seconds and minutes passed us by. Finally, the best friend comes back into the room fully dressed, and I hoped ready to leave us alone. She fumbled around with her purse, and then tried to organize her little beach bag with her towel and all that bullshit inside of it. I just layed there on top of her friend and didn't make a sound. She finally seemed to get everything organized and turned towards us and said "I'll see you guys down by the pool in a few minutes." We didn't say a word and we both just nodded at her farewell. I was once again pounding away on her friend as the heavy door shut behind THE FUCKING ASIAN BITCH THAT WOULD NOT FUCKING LEAVE.

xoxo

You're weird, I will leave you alone…

xoxo

You gave my Christmas present away to the rich kid. Actually, you said it was a "gift" to his house. You just saying that sounds absolutely ridiculous. Who the fuck gives a gift to a house anyways? Sounds like shit rich people do for each other. I buy gifts for actual human beings, not their "houses." That was a pretty fucking shitty thing to do considering I bought you a really cool gift for

Christmas, so this one stings a little more than usual. I even went out of my way to deliver it on time before the holidays. Man, do I feel like a pretty fucking stupid jerkoff for that one. It's just another fine example of the type of fantastic human being that you've come to be. Your indifference and stupidity repulses me. Or, was that my stupidity? Either way you could care less anyways.

xoxo

The endless wait, yep, 7 p.m. is only four short hours away. I don't want to do it, but it has to be done. I love her, but there is no going back from this spot, this day. When she calls, I will tell her that it's over.

xoxo

"Insert an Overuse of Cunt Here"

These opaque scars of mine will take years to heal,

you hurt me deeply

you cunt

I can never trust any other

cunt again really

I let you in and you

stomped on my fucking guts

you goddamn cunt,

I gave everything and you gave nothing

you cunt

how convenience store of you

you have gone from a

girl

I respected to

and

evolved into

an absolute cunt

I completely resent

and have

gargantuan fucking disillusion of,

268

yes,
insert your name here,
X_____
you are a fucking cunt,

take refuge in your mental problems
and
lithium lined treehouses
if you see fit
I don't disagree with
your
medical diagnosis
and
childhood memories
are rarely resolved
in Ohio
or anywhere else
cunts reside,
forever
and a week later
bullshit and everything else
taken out on every person
that
has ever cared about you
shunned
like postmodern leprosy
and forsaken
like Jesus,

thoughts of better days
remove themselves
and nails

from

the mahogany cross

dangerous and hypnotic

conversations

are now

all but a distant

and

lasting memory for

me,

you fucking cunt,

these opaque scars of mine will take decades to heal.

xoxo

I miss her even more now than I did before. I didn't really think that was possible, but its happening. Her break from me and this hurt I'm supposed to dispose of isn't really disposing of itself, not that I thought it would. I wonder where she is tonight. Where is my mind? And, better yet where is my body? I walk along the beach alone, thinking, and never having any answers. There is never any knowledge gained, just questions, and insane scenarios are pondered in my cerebral cortex. I'm dying inside but my heart remains hers.

xoxo

"what is going on with you?"

"nothing"

"ok, ur sort of acting strange, did something happen today?"

"no, but your always there and then you werent, and I miss you.....and ok maybe having a breakdown"

"haha..well that's sweet of you to say"

"i guess....I dont feel sweet I feel like a nut job. I even told my friend you must be right about me being neurotic"

"haha, well ur a little nuerotic yes…perhaps also a little deranged, but it's ok...I still love you"

"haha...not deranged, that sounds like I could be dangerous...and you know I certainly couldn't"

"delusional then"

270

"no delusional would be like me making up shit in my head thats not real. holy fuck...I am delusional!!!LOL"

xoxo

Status Update:

Brett is going down the unknown road, alone for a while.

xoxo

I have to stop being so fucking nice. I thought I was being really cool by making you mix CD's and buying you interesting purses and stuff. Little did I know you were so materialistic. You have guys buying you MP3 players, jewelry, and trips to California. I didn't realize how generic I was being.

xoxo

We sat down outside at a table, and it took forever just to get a waiter to pay any attention to us. Ten to twelve minutes after we sat down I finally had a sweet tea. Flies landed on the lip of my plastic cup that held my sweet tea. I tried to swat them away, but it did very little good. I finally put a napkin across the cup where my sweet tea was resting. We talked about taking an exotic vacation somewhere. I mentioned Venezuela or Brazil. She said her parents have a place down in Aruba and we can stay there whenever we wanted to. It sounded good to me as long as it was out of America. She mentioned that we could take a boat to Venezuela from there. I just nodded my head and agreed. The waiter came back out and took our order. I got the pork chops that came with the baked potato, and she only ordered soup. I was fucking drained, and why is she ordering soup in the middle of the fucking summer? I'm going on very little sleep for two fucking days. Pile on top of that two fucking hangovers, and also the fact that we just fucked thirty minutes ago, and I was spent. The sun blinded my eyes and I forgot my sunglasses back at her hotel room. There was nothing to say really, we just fucked, and I was too tired for boring chit-chat. She broke the silence by saying that I have a big cock. She also said that she loves fucking me as well. I mention that she must've had a lot of really small cocks in her life, because mine is nothing to write home about really. In fact, it's average at best. I know what it is, but I tolerate her bullshitting me anyways. She dismissed that statement though. Yeah baby, keep lying to me. Trust me, she says, I've seen a lot of cocks in my life and yours is big. I just nodded my head and agreed with her to get off the subject. She loves how fat it is she says. She continued by saying that it fits in her pussy just right. I just nodded my head once again, but I said nothing. Her foot then rises and presses into my dick and balls. I asked her what the fuck she was doing. She said that she was just trying to get me horny again so we could go back to her hotel and fuck again after we finished eating. The waiter brought me another sweet tea. We continued to wait on the food though. I told her to stop putting her foot in my crotch, but she didn't though. I just drank my sweet tea and smoked while we waited. The food was taking fucking forever! The hostess brought over a pack of about nine fat white tourists and sat them down at the table directly next to ours. We weren't alone any longer. They had three loud kids with them as well, how fucking cooterawesome. Of course, the youngest and loudest kid sat down really close to me. His mom was wearing red sweatpants and a red top, she was quite the disaster, and that comes from a guy who currently looked like a giant pile of llama shit. The fat stupid tourists talked loudly about every asinine aspect of their trip down here. Oh yeah, it was a tough drive. Interstate 95 was packed, and they're really sore from the drive…blah…blah…blah…and even more…blah. Literally, fifteen minutes were spent addressing every single tedious detail of their boring drive down here. I didn't want to hear about it, but I had no choice really, and the chops were on their way supposedly according to our waitress. XXXX blurted out "god you're a great fuck!" The mom with the hacked off red sweatpants turned her head and gave us a fucking death stare. I just smiled back at her while I sipped my sweet tea. She diverted her attention back to her fucking whining kid sitting right on top of me. A few seconds passed, and XXXX then blurted out "I want your cock in my mouth!" This time even more louder than before. XXXX there's fucking kids here I tell her. She just laughed at me and told me to relax. Next, she says "fuck these people," very loudly this time as well. She laughed and then complained about the slow service. XXXX continued to ramble on about her goddamn fucking soup. Out of nowhere, she said "fuck the food, take me back to the room and fuck the shit out of me." I thought to myself, no way, I'm fuckin' starving here you crazy goddamn bitch. I needed those damn pork chops before I fuck anything, that's for sure. I didn't care anything about pissing these idiotic people off at the moment. I just wanted my goddamn pork chops and baked potato. I felt even weaker as the time slowly dripped by. I lowered my head and just stared at the checkered red and white tablecloth that was on the table. The kid sitting on top of me started screaming, and XXXX continued to bitch about her goddamn fucking soup! Fuck me, these pork chops can't come soon enough.

xoxo

"why are gay guys always so cute?

I'll never understand the female fasination with gay guys

its not facinating but they're actually men i would date

those same cute understanding gay guys fuck other dudes in their hairy asses…not so cute anymore is it!!!

i know its totally disturbing- i watched brokeback mtn

haha, never seen it

dont no man should watch it

I like my cowboy movies with clint eastwood only and no dirty denim anal sex!

just a crush on clint???….well i gotta hop in the shower

don't get crazy with the showerhead

no worries it attahced

maybe ur limber. I was a plumber for 4 years I know the game woman!"

xoxo

Every woman in this town is a rotten piece of shit in the end. I wake up today and find out in a social networking bulletin of all idiotic things that she's all into some other guy. It was news to me. I guess I was the last one to find out about it. There's nothing like having your guts stomped on by someone you trust. What a fucking cunt!

xoxo

After thinking about it, maybe you and the spoiled rich kid are a perfect match. You would probably both get sassy and then eventually cry if you didn't get your way all the time. Maybe I should quit being cynical and be happy for you two fucking lovebirds.

xoxo

"can I cum inside of you? I think it would be hot if you gushed as I filled you full of hot cum...yummy...well I can be a good special friend who fucks you..lol...but I don't lie so like I said not really into relationship stuff. I'm a dick I know!!"

"whoooo...back up....i am not looking for a relationship. period."

"just a great sexual outlet. fun in and out of the bed. no strings just no dramam fun"

"haha, I didn't think you were...I wasn't accusing you of anything. I know, I think ur pretty cool and fun so I would def wanna be your friend."

"i have a boy toy here, thats about my extent"

"That's cool, I have a boy toy here...jk"

"fun and free and easy and loving ad silly and just looking for a sexual outlet plus a fun hang out buddy in one"

"I was hanging out with this girl, but she went from being cool and hanging out sometimes to wanting to be my damn girlfriend...I was like oh god..."

"bet everything you are bi"

"ha, how dare you! Hell no, nothing about a dick turns me on!"

"come on brett you can tell me will you let me fuck you up the ass?im profecient with a strap on"

"I'm all man baby!...lol. I am telling you Freud...uhmm no, I let a girl put her finger in my ass once...and it fucking didn't do anything for me"

"well see. just dont be so closed minded. mr. will you do double penetration with me"

"fair is fair"

"Hell no...nothing is going in my ass! I'm ok with being closed minded"

"pussy"

"I am what I fuck!...haha"

"sorry me doubling you is just gonna have to do..."

"butt fuck your other boy toy...lol"

"your making me horny.lol"

"you've been making me horny the whole time we've been talking...haha. I'd love to put my fucking hard cock in you right now and have you gush pussy juice all over it!"

"ouch, easy boy easyy!"

"you didn't answer my question before..cause u got all upset..lol"

"Can I cum inside of you? ha, you can't tame this pony!"

"it would please me very much if you did...especially if you tell me before you come...hot hott hott no chance of babies with me...no chance in hell"

"Nice, I love it and I totally will tell you...do u have a cum fetish or something? We'll make dookie babies!...haha.....just tell me whatever gets you off and I'll totally insert it into my long term memory..I told you I'm a cancer and I like pleasing people..goddamn humanitarian!"

"i am an aquarius sweet love, i think i hold more of the humanatarian cards...but we can share"

"good, cause I was lying...lol...aquarius are strange basket cases..lol...I help people for a living, after I clock out I hate them again...lol"

"did you see my mermaid tattoo?"

"I think so, but I'll look again....yes they are! I'm always right!...lol...I found some more pics...since ur into girls didn't know if you wanted like pics of me fucking or not...lol."

"send away sexy man...but im fixing to go tobed. its been fun its been sexy and sweet, now we need to meet"

"I remember the cat tattoo near ur cooter....ok, I will. As long as u promise to gush while lookig at them"

"feel free to text or call me anytime baby. my pretty lil pussy tat is new...my bday in jan."

"i go the mermaid on my bday last year"

"Yeah, we'll def meet up. and I'm not just saying that silly beans. I'll come down then u come up or whatever"

"tired kitty kat..sweet dreams. i will sleep better if i know your jacking off to my pic before you go to bed…lol"

"ok, I was already going to...lol..take one tom of you masturbating...yummy and I wanna see ur hot pussy!"

"OK"

xoxo

"I Was Once a Minor Threat"

I,

in the second person
inside
my head,

cried
cry
crying,

rivers of
blood
on
posh
leather couches,

I,
in the second person
inside
my head,

type
B

positive

the universal

O

type

A

negative,

repeat the transgression

spoiling the varnish

on

cheap wooden floors,

I,

in the second person

inside

my head,

a dog's gluttony

gorge

spot,

now overfed

tongue depression

and

scooping shit,

evidence

is now

acquired and revealed.

xoxo

Time heals everything. The memories, horrors, and depressions are slowly forgotten. The wish of death has even been tamed and relocated to the back burners of my mind. Perhaps, a certain will to live has been reaffirmed. I find myself not wishing to be involved in head-on collision car accidents, or burning alive in a fire like a protesting Buddhist monk or some shit. I'm now looking forward to future events with a little zest. I'm now weak in a way that I wasn't before. I'm now scared of dying and feel like I have something to live for at least. There's a certain amount of weakness and child like apprehension involved when a person has a future and a will to live. There's something to be said for having no future and no will to live. There's a massive amount of energy and excitement in that philosophy. I wish I still had some of that energy and excitement. Sadly, it's in the distant past, now in the back burners of my mind maybe never to be seen again.

xoxo

I ended it with a text message, how ironic since I despise technology.

xoxo

"u still coming to trivia and then coming over and petting my weiner?

haha.....

I'll take that as a yes

well you're very presumptuous

no, ur the one who said it this weekend....remember?

yes i remember

haha, well so there perv!

im not a perv..thats your thing

yeah I know

ha..so there!

I never said I wasn't. I was just curious if I was gonna get some after trivia poonanny.....

uh..possible I suppose

nice"

xoxo

"I'll assume that since you didn't respond to my message or return my phone call, and now I see as I clicked to send you this message that your emotional icon reads "annoyed" that you're sort of peeved at me. Anyways, I only called to smooth shit over with you and make sure you weren't too annoyed or pissed at me for busting your chops/cooter. Perhaps bad weather and extreme boredom made me paranoid...haha. Anyways, I'm sorry, about...well to put it in childish terms giving you a bunch of verbal titty twisters. It wasn't out of spite or to be mean, you know me and how my mind sort of works. It's like I had to fuck with you for a while, or I couldn't live with myself or something like that. I didn't want you to feel like complete shit or anything, just a tad bit bad, that was all. It's perhaps immature in a sense, but a small price to pay for a best friend type. All that is over now though, and it's nothing but nice and sweet cuddlerific Brett from now on. Basically, now I'm like "the hell with it, let's get back to good interesting conversations and having fun." The pathetic love letters were legitimate though, but those are done as well, at least until I get drunk again...lol. I thought I had hot glued and duct taped all that shit up, but going and playing trivia on Tuesday brought some out of me again when I got home and was drunk and alone at 4 a.m. I couldn't post that personal stuff in a blog or something so I pretty much had to send it to you just to purge it from my mind. Everything is cool between us though, and has been, again, sorry for the verbal sandpapering. I don't want to annoy you or smother you or anything so I'll leave you alone until you contact me or whatever.....later tater"

"I didnt get a VM? Yes I was a tad annoyed, just needed a break. Im out of town though so havent really had time to return messages..ect"

"That's cool, Vixen Monkey? Sometimes I like to be mysterious and not leave a Vulva Monkey, or as they're more commonly known a Voice Mail. Thank Allah you were only a tad annoyed, I was about to have to bust out some charm if it was any more than a tad. I'm glad to be getting the fuck out of here tomorrow, I've had enough of moving heavy ass shit all day in the cold rain. Yesterday I put in applications to be a fire fighter, I need a job mentally challenging and dangerous, I think it would be awesome to do. Anyways, have fun and be careful butter bean!"

xoxo

Dear XXXXX,

Just so you know I didn't send you those messages about wanting to fuck or whatever else it was. I always say "nice shoes" first anyways. I was out of town working and I used my brother's computer on Tuesday and I guess he's been hijacking it and sending messages and posting stupid shit about me...Brett

xoxo

"The Equivocator Personal High Five"

Walking,

half moon

45

degree angle

desolation beach

waves crash

head first

into the black sand

stumbling

into a small hole

paw prints observed,

she and I walking into the constant darkness,

she

grabs my hand

I

accept with apprehension

she

doesn't like the way I do it

I

hesitate

she

meshes our fingers together

I

hesitate

but accept it

she

talks endlessly about

nothing

I listen

but

my mind is a thousand miles

away

she

whines and then starts crying

out of nowhere

I

don't know what to do

so

I put my arm on her shoulder and tell her that

everything

will be alright

and

work itself out

I

lied

and

broke up with her the next day,

just I walking into the constant darkness.

xoxo

I came home drunk and almost deleted her from my life again. I can't take many more of the photos of her hanging out and holding hands with that fucking fat yuppie douchebag. All these new friends of hers, well, friends of his that she's making hers are just as fucking lame. Yeah, had a great weekend ehh? I didn't, and you suck you fucking bitch! They're always drinking in every fucking picture of them, no wonder though; I would think most girls would have to be drunk to fuck that fat idiot as well. I saw that she dyed her hair black. It now matches her fucking soul.

xoxo

"It's ok, I just miss you a hell of a lot and I'm pretty lonely with you gone, sad but true!"

xoxo

You disgust me and make me sick to my stomach with every thought and site of you. Every time I walk outside of my apartment I see you or your fucking silver Nazi Volkswagen. When I no longer see either of you, I shall rejoice.

xoxo

"It sucks that you're sick I think Im going to die of sex withdrawls..I dont know what the hell is wrong with me

haha

seriously.....its bad

well I'll fuck u as soon as I don't feel like dying

great

ha, you should get a dildo for occasions like these.

its just not the same...but Im about there...actually I dont need a dildo nor do I like them

haha, why didn't u tell like monday

I was ok Monday..it was yesterday and today...I dont know what happened. I had sex dreams and everything

have u been eating tangerines?...ha

no....maybe thats the problem. I guess its my age

there's nothing wrong with being horny I like it. Actually, I would totally get off if u called me up and said "brett come over and fuck the shit out of me"

brett come over and fuck the shit out of me....

well I mean normally when I'm not sick as fuck

yeah I know...what horrible timing

sorry, I can't help it

i know...maybe I should put on my naughty nurse outfit and come nurse you back to health-LOL

funny, u would most likely be the death of me!

haha...no way it would take your mind off all the aches

it's possible

of course...haha, well do as u wish. I might catch your cooties

probably, my throat is the worst, sore as shit and I got a nasty white coasting everywhere...that tastes funny. Watch out I'll give u a yeast infection

ewwwww

haha

you ruined my mood....yuck

ha, I ruin everything...

whatever

go take a bath and jill off

haha...I already showered

did u jill off?

Nope, i was in a hury greys anatomy was coming on tv

good lord!!!!"

Dear XXXXX,

Just remember any time you start thinking bad shit about me or being annoyed or freaked out about shit, I was the guy there that hunted you down on the beach when you were having serious mental breakdowns. I was the guy that brought you food to work and after work. The guy who took care of you when you were sick or had oral surgery. I was the guy on his hands and knees on the beach making you a Valentine's Day present, and I was the guy there giving you rides to work for a week straight. Just always keep that fresh in your mind. I was the victim here, the sucker who cares, and still does for some odd fucking reason.

I opened the front door today just to gauge what the weather was like, like I do most every day when I wake up and after I take a piss. I happened to see you and your new boyfriend coming out of your apartment. I quickly closed the door and thought to myself the word "fuck!" I'm now a prisoner in my own damn apartment. Where as before I could come and go freely; now I cannot, without in the back of my mind knowing wherever I go in my own fucking apartment complex that you two might be there. When I take out the trash or go to my car I'm looking around my shoulder now. Paranoid might be the word I'm looking for here. Fuck, this sucks gargantuan anteater dick.

My phone is fucking alive,

"Why did you delete your account?"

"Never use it"

"Fine whatever. Never accused you of being a stalker just for the record"

"Ok sounds good"

"Possible if its hot enough"

"Well I gotta still hit the gym so it will be late. Todays prob not the best…thurs?"

"K thanks"

"Still doesn't make up for what I've been through. Maybe I'm just becoming a pansy."

"Yeah well different rules here. Best I'm gonna get is someone offering me the stale cornbread."

"Haha yeah I've gotten into more bodily fluids today than I thought possible"

"I didn't know I was?"

"Good luck at the finals. I wish I was there work sucks today"

"Haha 24/7"

"Funny no, dropped it while giving myself a pedi"

"What new hair?"

"ooh ok"

"I'll look at it soon, never get on there anymore"

"I can't gotta work tomorrow"

"Ur doing something different with it. Perhaps more poof. That pic of you wearing jeans you look smoking hot. Good masturbation material"

"sdorry"

"Thank, hope I don't keel over. Anywho hope you are doing good.."

"Whatever – semantics and insinuations. Ur acting so bizarre and retarded these days. I like old XXX better when u were cool, down to earth and had a sense of humor. Ur inappropriate now!"

"Ah, what about all the good times. Ha, I guess I'm never getting #4 back."

"Cool. Time to dig the speedo out of the drawer then. I'll call u cooterearly on Thursday then. Pump it hard Arnold. Later honeybuns.."

"It said 74 and sunny on Thursday. My pool is always an option if its windy. We can play it by ear or whatever."

"I suppose I could fit you in my schedule for Thursday. It's supposed to be nice...beach nad mex day?"

"Do u wanna grab Mexican food in a little bit?"

"No problem, I'm always on call for FBM hugs...haha"

"Ha, yeah u sound like me now. Ur sensitive not a pansy. When in doubt always blame the bloody cooter! If you need a hug I'm available"

"Don't sell yourself short. I'm sure a clever man could find a plastic flower and a month old TIME magazine."

"Ha...don't let anyone cum or piss on you without at least making them buy you dinner at golden corral"

"Yep it's nothing bad. I don't mind admitting it. Sorry work sucks, just say serenity now a lot until you explode and kill someone...ha"

"Not that you're smitten. I had to admit that I was still smitten over you when asked by his girlfriend."

"Thanks, we came in 6th. Wish you had been here. U did come up in conversation about being smitten though…ha"

"Sleep soundly tonight knowing the cooter really loves, cares, misses and wants you…"

"ahh well better not drop clash like that black widow. U can't buy him on sale at t-mobile you know!"

"Ha, could be worse baby, better than giving people ED and nausea like my pics do. Why did you drown ur phone, was it crying too much?"

"I don't want to know you anymore, just leave me alone from now on please…thank you."

"Ut new hair style looks cooterluscious. My crush on you just went from giant to gigantic!"

"Go to bed knowing that I do still really love you, care about you, and still have a giant crush on you. Love makes you nust sometimes…haha"

"Acutally it's prob PMS"

"I deleted you. I draw the line at stalker accusations. I've had my fill of being hurt by you. I'm completely gone from your life now, fret no more. I'm done"

"Fabulous"

"Well wish me luck, That new gallery has its opening tonight. Hopefull I sell some art to rich assholes. If not there's always the free booze!"

"I notice all."

"I added you on again, can't do the other quite yet. But now at least u have a reason to live,"

My phone is fucking dead.

xoxo

Dear XXXXX,

How many of these letters or confessionals if you will have I written to you that were never mailed and that you will never read? I don't know, a plethora I will call it. I don't get it. I'm still confused. I'm still baffled. I wish I had done something horrible, that way it might make sense to me. I would have something to connect, but here I sit, still fucked up and confused. You're gone. You're indifferent, cold, and non-emotional as I've ever witnessed. I say these things not to be mean or make you feel bad. I say them only to try and make sense of things. You want to talk about duality, here it is. How am I supposed to be, or feel, or act now? These things I don't know or have an answer to. I woke up one day and it was all different. My heart belongs to you. It always has, since the moment I saw you. I pine over you now, I cry over you, and I'm fucked up over you still months later. I still talk to people about you, hoping maybe answers will be rendered that perhaps I don't see, which is doubtful not to sound like an egomaniac. I sit in my apartment alone and empty. I have no one now. I'm as empty as they come. There is no passion for anything anymore. I wish there was. The paint doesn't go on like it did, the words aren't purged as easily anymore, there is nothing but silence and emptiness and the only pleasure I have anymore is self-destruction. It's the only thing that calms it all down and makes me forget you, if only for a few hours, but it's always worse when I get home drunk and alone. You are what I write about now, you are what fills my brain, you are what makes me insane, you are what makes me feel, feel like I never have before. It's fucking awful. I'm guilty of not treating you like a girlfriend as much as I should have, even though it was always there in side of me dying to come out. I hid it and acted indifferent sometimes and took you for granted, that is true, that I am guilty of. Perhaps, I deserved to get left, I don't know. You didn't have to run off though. It never had to be that way. I wake up on a daily basis and wish for death. I feel like walking death in a way, walking around with a hole inside of me that no one but me can see. I've been amputated now. I still feel something though, something that used to be there, but isn't anymore. Man, fuck, this just doesn't feel right to me. Something is wrong in the world, and just doesn't make sense. Perhaps, I can't put it into words, maybe there is no name for it. You can drive me away, you can say whatever you want but I still feel. I always have. Do you realize how long it took for me to find you? Twenty-seven fucking years, that's a long time, and a lot of people to sift through hoping to strike it rich one day. Well, I did, and I fucked it up, this I know. But, don't think I ever never cared or didn't take you or us seriously, I did. I was so scared by it, I didn't know what to do. Do you realize how many times I almost dropped to my knees and begged you to be my fucking life partner? More than you will ever know. Yeah, on the balcony in St. Thomas I almost broke down and asked you. Yeah, in Walgreen's buying deodorant I almost asked. Yeah, when I was drunk, I almost drove to your house at 4 a.m. and asked you. Fuck, I'm so stupid, so "chickenshit" as you put it. That is true, which is why I had no retort when you said it. I don't know what death feels like, but I think it's something like I've been going through, it feels like it anyways. I miss you every single day. I wake up and I feel and know it. I had someone and I slept well at night knowing that. I had a running mate, a partner, someone to spend my time and life with, and I miss that so much. No one else does it for me, they're all worthless and strangers, and I don't like or care about them. I'm content being alone and unhappy compared to that. Whatever I was before I met you, which probably wasn't good, is gone and only a past memory now. I'm not like that now. I have evolved and been shown something else, whatever I said and whatever opinions I had on relationships and life have probably changed, in fact I know they have. I suck, and didn't unleash this beast on you when we were together. I did somewhat, but not what I really wanted to. I did try, but not as much as I should have or could have. I have only my fear, cockiness, laziness, ignorance, personal hang-ups, and issues to blame. I'm guilty of not telling you. I wanted to open up and let you in all the way and allow myself to love you, but I didn't really know how to tell you or how to confess how I really felt to you. You're an amazing person, the best I've ever met, and the closest thing to myself I've ever come across. Regardless of what you might think now, and I admit I have no idea what you think or feel about me anymore, and I haven't for a long time actually. We were something, there was something there, and you've known it for as long as I have. I know you loved me, I felt it, and it wasn't fake or bullshit. You were the first for me in just about every department, minus taking my virginity. You're the first girl I ever loved, the first girl I ever introduced to my mom, the first girl I ever took a vacation with, it was always you and it wasn't just some random thing, it always had a purpose. Yeah, I want a life with you, yeah I want you, and yeah I love you. I don't know much, but that isn't in doubt. It's ridiculous. I think about and miss the way you look, the way you smell, every inch of your body which I know so well I could pick out of a fucking police body lineup, your voice, your phone calls, your sarcasm, your neuroticism, your opinions, your kisses, your medical advice, your hugs, your decency, your touch, your pointy ears, I miss all of it. The majority of me says to never ever give up on you, that you're special, and may only come around once in my lifetime, but some other part of me says to never speak to you again, hence my duality. I have no idea what I'm supposed to do or feel really. I wish I did. All I know is the present situation doesn't feel right or make me happy at all. You make me happy like no one else does. How the fuck am I supposed to replace that exactly? It's not so easy, let me tell you, nor do I really want to. I'm not like you; I can't just pick someone and run off with them. I'm not built that way. When I feel and I love, it's for life. I'm not trying to make you feel bad. That's just the truth of it. You really think I picked being a paramedic out of a fucking hat? No, a giant chunk of why I'm doing this is because of you, perhaps even for you. I don't know. I know I disappointed you on some levels and I know I didn't come through for you as much as I should have, and I know I always tried to be there for you when you needed me, but not as much as I should have or could have. Fuck, do you realize the depths of despair and misery you sent me into? Passion is missing from everything now. I'm fucked up over you, badly. Yeah, I'm a mess and a disaster, there's no hiding it. I've never let anyone in like I let you. You have free access to reach in and rip out my guts anytime you wish. I want you to know that you can, no one else has ever had that power, but I like that you to have it. It makes me feel alive and human and for the first time I know what the fuck Hank Williams and these old blues guys were really singing about. Yeah, you made me human, for better or worse. I'm not neurotic like you said; I'm just neurotic over you. You gave me their disease, their weakness, their problems, insanity, jealousy, anger, hope, rage, love, despair, caring, destruction, benevolence, vengeance, happiness, confusion, retribution; I have experienced them all baby. I don't know you anymore, at least I feel like I don't. I've been amputated. I'm a past memory for you; yet you're a daily memory for me though. No, I'm not happy. How could I be or what makes you think I could be? Move on, stop caring, avoid her, your heart is too big, she's horrible, she treated you like shit, she didn't care, she changed, she sold out for money, she's gone and indifferent, life sucks, whatever and shit happens. Yeah, that's what they say, and perhaps they're right. I don't want to believe them to be honest. I still have hope, which might be idiotic, but I do. Every single day I hope for a knock on my door, and I hope it's you, but it has yet to happen and probably never will. Who the fuck else would ever say or write these things to you or about you, probably not very many people in this fucking world.

xoxo

"you were right this halloween candy may be a problem....I cant stop eating it. You might have to confiscate it from me.....

control yourself girl!

i know its terrible. Im going to brush my teeth and hide the candy

put it in ur butt, no one can get in there...ha

oh you are soooooo funny

that was pretty good

yea it was"

xoxo

She's in the middle of a sentence. About what she was talking about, the hell if I know, care, or remember. I, in my drunken stupor sort of falling leaf towards her and give her a kiss. It was alright, short, and to the point. Her mouth tasted like cigarettes. It's funny and ironic about how I complain about it now, even though I smoked for half my life, and kissed a plethora of women who didn't smoke. I wonder if they tasted what I do now. Oh well, fuck it all to hell and back. I take a couple of sips from my imported Mexican piss beer that she bought me. I watch her smoke another cigarette. I pretend to stare at the TV. Some sports game was on; I don't even remember what sport it was. Between the drags she takes on her cigarette I kiss her again. I taste the ashtray once again. An old man sitting next to her on the right side of the bar starts talking to her. I just stare at the floor and drink my imported Mexican piss beer that she bought me. They keep talking; and he buys us a round of beers and shots. I do the shot and then I start on the beer that he bought me. A few minutes later she goes to take a piss around the corner and down the stained checkered floor hallway that leads to the bathroom. I chug my imported Mexican piss beer that the other guy bought me. I get up from my chair, walk out the front door of the bar, get into my car, and flee into the night. I woke up the next day still in my clothes, covered in Doritos, and most of the lights in my apartment still on. All chaotic idiocy aside, at least I didn't fuck that fat ashtray slut last night. Maybe that old man got lucky though, good for his geriatric beer and shot buying ass.

xoxo

I was over at your house setting up your computer. You unpacked a box that contained some pictures. You sat two pictures of me and you on your computer desk and bookshelf. That really made me feel special even though I don't want to admit it.

xoxo

"Death Row for Cats and Clean Sheets"

Silence,

the night of long conversations
pumping and slicing freshly scratched
nail polish and
the allure of
self inflicted damage to
aortas and
veins
she in the second person
obsesses over skin conditions
and
vinyl scars,

Elvis
died on the toilet
and never meant shit to
me
but you do
and
I just want to lick
your
rare cancer ridden disease,

the physics mask

and

mass of

neuroticism and hypochondriac

algebraic graffiti equations

cheap paint on my withered

hands

and

the sides of Midwest bound

passing trains

they can't

be solved or

outlined in white chalk

by

Ramone's songs

or

plastic surgery designer

lobotomies,

UVB

USB

foreign ports

of entry

burning for a price

soft tanned epidermis

the doubting self and bytes

of insanity

that doesn't appreciate

Kate Moss inspired heroin chic

the

bruises on your neck

crooked capped teeth

abstract marks

leave Hardy Boy trails

leopard print dead pigment

cells

on cheap Target brand sheets

animalistic genetic code

under

devious microscope,

XXXXXXXXX,

baby

you'll make

one good looking fucking corpse.

xoxo

This woman is like crack. No matter how long I go without seeing or talking to her she's always there in my head. She's like a blackhead that you just can't squeeze out of your skin no matter how hard you try, so you just learn to live with it. I think I'm being paid back for the way I treat women on a regular basis. It's true that what goes around comes around I guess. I've treated them all like shit. They meant nothing to me. I'm nice to them until I get laid, then I throw them out like a pair of shit-stained underwear. This serial killer got turned into slush. All it took was one single conversation, and I was addicted again. I was doing well for a while though. It was out of sight and out of mind. But, it always comes back to her, and as long as I stay in this town it always be that way I

xoxo

"I hope your fucking fake tits burst like a water balloon on hot pavement you cuntbag!!!"

xoxo

Everything I do is a failure when it comes to you. No matter how nice or cool I am to you ever seems to mean anything. It's always about some other person that is either completely lame or totally bullshit. They are half the man that I am; and I'm not shit really, so that doesn't bode or speak well for them. That pisses me off badly. Where is this fantastic person that has a mixture of intelligence, humor, decency, and talent all rolled up into one? Maybe in a real town somewhere, like Miami or San Francisco, but not here in Myrtle Beach, and I dare say nowhere within 300 fucking miles other than that person that lives in the building across from you on Clay Pond Village Lane.

xoxo

"This is such bullshit…what were you thinking….out sneaking around behind my back…we did have an agreement you know"

"We're not bf/gf. I'm sorry your disappointed. Xactly how was I sneaking around. I said if I met someone I liked I'm going to hang out with them. That's pretty clear"

"Fuck, you've changed, I liked it better when you were nice"

"I am and I haven't changed"

"Call me I need to talk to you about this….."

"When I get a minute I will"

"Fine, whatever…"

"Stop,it will all be fine. We will always be friends just the dynamics with change some. I will alywas be here if you need me"

xoxo

I'm like an addict weaning myself off an addiction. I do my best to stay away from you and your voodoo, but relapses are bound to occur. I try and mind my own business but a random phone call or text message always brings me back. Damn, I can't wait until they get those anti-XXX pills made down at the nerd lab.

xoxo

"A Legacy of Petri Dishes and Lemon Flavored Cave Paintings"

We're,

all hypocrites in one way or another

some,

people I know are worse than others though

I won't call you out

you can save face for

now,

I'll,

keep quiet

and

save the persecution of speaking

truth and reality

shunned and avoided like leprosy

and Howard Zinn

browse me

but don't join in

internet connections

allow a spray painted window into my thoughts,

today,

is a new day with a line

drawn in the sand.

xoxo

"You should come over later and watch an elitist indie movie with me"

"Exam in the morning, school has become my life…boo!"

"Yeah I know how you feel. I got a test and a quiz tomorrow. Maybe we can do something this weekend. I miss hanging with you…"

"Want to go with me to Charleston on Saturday or Sunday and play around? I have to pick up a bridesmaid dress…"

"What day would be better?"

"Sat would prob be cooler"

"Ok cool"

"Is there a road blowjob involved in said trip to Charleston?"

"Doubt it"

"Fine, maybe I'll still go…maybe"

xoxo

Now and then I don't like her. Now and then I don't understand her disposition. I wonder, and want to ask her what planet she now resides on these days? Planet breakdown maybe. I ask her to hangout and do shit, probably more than I should to be honest. I don't remember the last time she called and asked me to do anything. I guess March or something like that. Months and months ago, that's all I know. I know that I should probably leave her alone, her, and her new life without me in it. I always get the "maybe" these days. From "yes" to "maybe" man overnight, that's fucking me. What a difference a few months make. It's a fucking bizarro parallel universe I'm living in these days, well, she's living in, and I'm trying to figure it out and understand it I guess. She's not going to be here on my 30th birthday. She'll be with the "gingervitis." That bothers me. The last two years she's been there, there with me. Flashes of flipping a jet ski last year and riding go-karts bring back memories, great memories actually. I doubt this one will be much of any fun to be honest. I remember her last birthday very well. I showed up, even though she was cold and distant towards me all night. I was there with the best presents she got from anyone. I was there with a letter written inside of her card pouring my guts out to her. I knew a breakdown was coming so I told her to read it after I left that night. She said that she loved me the next day, and wanted me in her life forever. Nope, she won't be there for my breakdown, which I'm hoping won't happen. She could at least do me the favor of not fucking him on my birthday, that would be a fine present in my mind.

xoxo

Before the insanity,

"I woke up naked on your couch with Babar on and Skittles everywhere"

"clean pussy to you. Yes he knows to stay off the nasty bitches or I'll bobbit him"

"Ok, why you being stingy with the cooter then? You hate all your men but wanna be good and not do me? A few drinks will change your mind!"

"How's the cock?"

"just got the tests back and I had nothing wrong with my vagina. I should have fucked you damn it"

"No, not married just trying to be good"

"Ha, ok I shall blame you then"

"We've been hanging out a lot and I've completely lied to him about you. I just don't wanna hear shit. If he finds out I've been lying there would be bullshit so ur answer is no!"

"Not much sugar tits. I'm staying if that's cool. Hump a pillow in your own room"

"As long as I get to be your towel boy in the carribean. I'm the cause of all your dude problems and I accept that"

"I'm not gonna rat you out. I'm a better friend than that. On the DL. You're right, I'll go wherever you want you're right"

"And no mention to anyone about us fucking"

"Have your ticket for free so just keep your trap shut"

"What are you married now or something? You owe me from last time!"

"Ha yeah right, I forgot that I know you. You're always in love with some idiot every two weeks. You will fuck, I already know!"

"Oh whatever, us fucking a year before had nothing to do with it. He was a dickhead obviously, but fine blame me"

"Nah I never heard from him again and it's all your fault. It has nothing to do with the crazy you pulled!"

"And no is your answer"

"You ratted me out with the Texas dude"

"ha, too bad it was fun calling you dirty pussy. Congrats, tell your boyfriend to stop fucking whores!"

"And you're not allowed to rat me out about us having sex. I;m going through too much here with these gys thinking I'm a ho and playing all of them"

"I'm in love with no one, I hate them all"

"Ok, I'm not saying anything. Feeling less chaffed now, thanks for the cock concern thoigh. Thanks for letting me come down. Let me know about the vacation dates."

"No cum for me mr stout,"

After the insanity.

xoxo

I picked her out of one my usual dingy houses of adult libation about twenty minutes before they kicked all of us usual drunks out. She wasn't one of the usual drunks though, she was from…well, fuck, I don't remember exactly, but I think it was New York or New Jersey. I'm pretty sure it had a "New" in front of it though. The one thing I do remember was her name. She had the first name of a goddamn whore. In particularly, the first name of a goddamn whore that I used to love, but that's another story in itself, which I won't bore you with here. So, anyways her friend left her in this goddamn dingy bar that I hung out in, and me being the coy gentleman that I am, I of course volunteered to give her a ride home, which ended up being a ride to my cramped apartment. I had a few Miller High Life cans in the fridge, and I cracked a couple of them open for us and turned on the TV. I only had a couple of sips and a cigarette before I grabbed her left tit and started kissing her. I pulled her shirt off first and then her bra. What the fuck was this bullshit I thought to myself? She was false advertising a titty! I felt the padding of her bra, that shit must have been three inches thick I swear to fucking Allah! She basically went from being a C-cup to fucking flat-chested in the blink of an eye. I laughed on the inside, it didn't matter at this point, small tits or not she was getting fucked. I pulled my shirt off and jumped on top of her. I slid a couple of fingers past her panties and into her cunt. I worked them inside of her until she was soaking wet. I don't know what the fuck I was thinking, but next I ripped off her panties and started licking her cunt. Why the hell was I was licking the cunt of a girl I just met an hour ago that had the name of a whore? I had no idea, but I was doing it even though I knew better. I don't even know if she got off or not, nor did I really care all that much at this point anyways. I told her that we should go fuck in my room. She stumbled in there and I helped balance her along the way. As soon as we got on the bed she said that she had to take a piss. Fuck, hurry it up I thought to myself. She was a weird broad for sure. She closed the door as she went to take a piss. It's not like I haven't seen your pussy or something there you fucking whore. A few minutes went by and then I went to check on her and see what the fuck was taking her so long. I cracked the door open and there she was leaning over passed out while sitting on the goddamn toilet. What a fucking amateur idiot. I quickly maneuvered into the living room and grabbed my phone. Why I didn't grab my nice camera sitting on a desk in my room, I don't know. But, I quickly went back into my room and got a great shot of her passed out on the toilet. I put the phone on my bed and went back into the bathroom to wake her ass up so we could fuck. I shook her a few times until she stumbled her way up and off of the toilet and over to my bed. I ripped my pants and underwear off and threw them together as one in a distant corner. I crawled on top of her and kissed her again. I grabbed my hard cock and shoved it inside of her piss stained, yet still wet and hairless cunt. I pounded away on her as she just layed there, docile and drunk. Time went by as I pounded away on her. I noticed only one of her giant nipples were pierced, why not the other one I don't know. Her tiny tits barely moved as I fucked her. Intermediately, I would look down and watch my cock move in out of her piss stained, yet still wet and hairless cunt. I didn't really notice it for a while, but her eyes were shut. I shook her shoulders and asked her if she was alright. There was no response. I pulled my cock out of her piss stained cunt and went into the kitchen to get some apple juice, which was all I had other than a few cans of Miller High Life. I walked back towards my room and stood in the doorway. I watched her sleep. Her pussy was still exposed while she was in some contorted Picasso inspired configuration. I sat on the edge of the bed and sipped my apple juice and smoked a cigarette. I decided that I'm sure she would still want me to cum even though she was passed out and drunk. It probably wasn't my most ethical of moments, but when pussy is available, you better use it, at least until you cum anyways. I put my cigarette out. I was covered in sweat and I was worn fucking out from pounding on her little piss stained cunt, but I was gonna cum one way or the fucking other. Perhaps, the apple juice break had sobered me up enough so I could cum now and go pass out on the couch. I crawled back on top of her. I didn't have much of a boner at this point so I rubbed my cock up against her pussy. I spit all over her pussy and my cock. I fucked around with it enough to get it at least hard enough to put inside of her. I shoved my cock back in her and started banging away once again. Sweat poured down my face as I pumped away on a passed out drunk girl named after a whore. Her pussy kept getting dry no matter how much I spit on it, which, granted, I couldn't muster very much spit being dehydrated and all. I pulled my cock out of her piss and spit stained cunt, and grabbed the lube which I kept in a drawer near her head, as well as my phone again. Yes, this KY warming lube was better than my dehydrated spit for sure. I squirted it all over her cunt and my cock and stuck it back inside of her. I opened my phone and started taking pictures of me fucking her. Yeah, that one might be blurry, it was hard to tell, so better take another one of this pose. I took pictures from all possible angles. I guess I was entertaining myself or some shit. I only hoped she didn't wake up to find me violating her like this, which, I sort of felt bad about, yet I did it anyways of course. I pounded on her as the minutes passed by. Fuck, I can never cum when I'm shitfaced drunk! I pretty much have to fuck myself sober. I wondered to myself what would it take to get her to wake up out of her drunken coma. I stuck my right index finger in her ass. That didn't do it, so I stuck two fingers up her ass, and that still didn't do it either. I gave her a "shocker" next, and still it didn't work. Next, I had the great idea to try and fuck her in the ass, perhaps that would do it, but I couldn't seem to get her in the right position so I could. And, really, with all the lube all over the place it made it slippery as shit. I should've conserved the lube damn it. Then again, it's probably not the smartest move to fuck a stranger named after a whore in the butt, but at this drunken dehydrated point who cares. I was sort of sobering up at this point. I pulled my cock amassed in her piss, my spit, lube, and cunt juice and went and took a piss and smoked another cigarette. I washed my hands off and took another picture of her in an even more Picasso inspired contorted position now. She wasn't all that pretty, but sitting there with her cunt spread open and passed out made her look more beautiful than she really was. I gave it one more fuck session try until I gave up and went to sleep on the couch. My cock was red and sore now, but I didn't care. I had to fucking cum goddamn it! It was a mission now. I crawled back on the bed and stuck my cock back inside of her. This time I actually grabbed her hips and really pounded the living shit out of her. It didn't take long surprisingly. I felt my balls tighten up, and the cum finally wanted to come out of me. I pulled out just in time and unleashed a giant load of cum all over her stomach, which in a few seconds started slowly dripping down inside of her belly button. I sat there panting and watching the cum entertainment show. I grabbed my camera and took a picture of my cum resting in her belly button. I dipped the tip of my finger in some cum and used it to sign my name on the right side of her face. An artist must always sign their work you know. I left the cum on her to dry overnight, and I went into the bathroom and washed my hands and cock off with antibacterial soap. I turned the light off and closed the door behind me. Goodnight stranger named after a fucking whore.

xoxo

"I might have to slip something in ur drink eventually

you better be gone and never come back when I wake up....that would be the perfect opportunity to beat you up

ha, ok, you could probably beat me up so I will have to come up with an alternate plan

ha ok

I will get ur 2 hole virginity eventually...

you wish....but its good to have dreams-LOL

yea, I like unrealstic goals

I probably do too

I'll just have to fnd someone that looks like you and put something in her drink and fuck her in the butt instead!

great...that wouldnt make me happy either, but whatever

stop being such an anal downer!...lol"

xoxo

I called her tonight accidentally. Only this shit could happen to me. I made up an excuse that I meant to call my friend XXXXXXX, when really, I guess subconsciously I had her on my mind and called her accidentally. I noticed that my screen said XXXXX after one ring and I hung up the phone. She called back. I didn't answer, but I contemplated answering it. I called her back nine minutes later. I liked talking to her. She said that I was paranoid and she didn't think I was pathetic, an asshole, or a stalker this time. I asked her near the end of the conversation if she still loved me. There was a pause, then she said "what kind of question is that," so I rephrased the question and still didn't get an answer. This time I got "now isn't the time for this conversation." We both had been drinking, I could tell that. She was actually concerned about me, since I called so late. I reiterated that I wasn't in jail or anything, but that I did miss her though. I don't know what to do with her. I stole her line. And, I don't know, and haven't known for a good while. I told her that I wanted to hang out with her, and if she ever called I would always answer the phone and be there for her if she needed me. I'm not sure if I meant it though.

xoxo

"I really made you mad huh?"

"Are you still done with me?"

"I liked your pic of the dead sea gull"

"I'm not mad at all. Are you drunk or something?"

"Yeah a little. I just don't want you to be mad because I still wanna do it again"

"I'm not mad. Calm your ass down. You're a dramatic drunk. I'll fuck you again just tell me when…"

"No I'm not!!! I'm just a girl!! You like girls don't you??"

"You're a total drama queen and you know it. No I'm a faggot didn't you know.."

"You're drama with a capital D. Takes one to know one. Why do you always say that? Nobody has ever said that but you. I hate that!"

"Yeah ok. Whomever told you that was wrong. You freak out over every little thing. When you wanna hang out and fuck let me know. No drama"

"Whatever Brett!"

xoxo

"The Empty Spaces behind Cracked Walls"

With spoiling sidewalk razor blades

and

narcissistic subjective idealism

I wanted to scar something

pretty

so I came in the world's face,

salted

and cured coronets

the illuminated thigh and buttock

of a castrated hog

on

the river Ganges

ogres in office buildings

dirty white collared shirts

and

rebuffed tailors

an hourglass trickles

the eleventh hour for

cross dressers and black horses

the cat guts play

on the rowdy violins
of Jim Crow
stained fingertips
childbirth stigmata
Lazarus is finally
dead and
sitting comfortably
on the sidelines of a suburban soccer game,

Anytown, USA,

burnt oatmeal for Osiris
a hello and
good morning to
dead salamanders in perpetual
motion
a heretic's toast
to marmots and wandering
Jews
cry wolf
and run Forrest
until reaching metamorphosis,

with spoiling sidewalk razor blades
and
narcissistic subjective idealism
I wanted to scar something
pretty
so I came in the world's face.
xoxo

Fucking love and all the complete misery that goes along with it is something I
wish I could've avoided. I made it many years without it happening to me. My

previous nomadic lifestyle allowed me that luxury. I was never anywhere long enough to inherit this bitch called love. I knew that motherfucker would come for even me one day. I had a feeling my domestication back into a "normal" life would bring it upon me eventually. Love is worse than I imagined or ever heard that it was. Love can be summed up in one word, and that's "pain."

xoxo

"ur good looking and fun, I'm sure anyone with a half a cerebral cortex would like u. I do care about u more than anyone else, but yea I doubt I can be some prototypical boyfriend

i suppose thats part of the problem most guys only haev a 1/4 of a cerebral cortex and I have no tolerance for them.....I know you care. I guess I miss like "coupley shit".........

I try to do shit for you and be there for you as much as I can, but I know I could do much better. I'm fucked up and have always had my freedom and only had myself to depend on. I know u need more coupley shit as u put it, that kind of stuff is dufficult for me no doubt

i realize and I give you total credit for all the efforts you make......perhaps if they were more frequent?? I think i understand you, we're actually similar in alot of ways...dont get me wrong I dont want you to be up my ass, thats one of the things I like about you...you give me space, but maybe too much??

BALANCE is the key…my yin and yang......the solution for my life

Yea I know, u don't hassle me and I appreciate that as well. Haha, too much space! I know, I'm sure it comes off like I don't care all that much and or something like that. It just happens that what I spend a majority of my life doing....painting and wriitng, I must do alone. I'm the absent minded special friend...haha

I know that stuff and I realize that you dont have a clue about relationships ("special friends" included) and I think you just forget how much ,just a call to talk for a minute, makes me happy

I actually hang out with u far more than anyone else actually. I guess I'm just a natural loner...haha. We hang out a fair amount I think for completely opposite schedules...but once again, I can't do anything right....as I hit myself in the eye...haha

I call, I called 2 times tuesday and once wednesday...remember I tried!

this is true and I do appreciate everything you do. Maybe it's the tone of our relationship that bothers me more??

like you're a good friend I fuck on occasion-LOL..doesnt really have the affection I desire-LOL

occasion? more than that I think.....haha. If I get u flowers on VD will that shut u up?...hahahaha

actually cuddle time (that you really mean)or holding my hand more often would please me even more...remember I'm thrilled with seemingly simple things, they just mean more to me

haha, oh jesus h christ...the "C" word...blasphemy! I don't mind holding ur hand. Jeez with what I've done the past few weeks, six months ago u would have been in heaven. Bought u presents on ur birthday, made dinner for you twice, watched movies, fucked, went to cosco, went to the flea market, got u drunk a bunch...whew...ur a tough one to please

yeah it was awsome...I guess thats the problem once you "taste" something good you begin to crave it......haha

haha, I knew I should have held out on cosco!!!"

xoxo

"Midnight Faces Molested by Perverted Plastic Chairs"

Protein

copper

zinc

potassium

cholesterol

fat

carbohydrates

selenium

magnesium,

I came in the heart

of Dixie

camouflage rooster meets

Georgia lips

on a bed of rotting

past tense sweat

fashioned

Art Nouveau ovulation,

UHF,
VHF,

flickering lights
on a soiled patio
filled with empty beer cans
dead moths and even deader
ideas
a conversation deviated
from broken television sets
cigarettes under constant pressure
to conform
into their parents
the images of broken mirrors
of empty drawers
the mistakes made by silhouettes
under the waning mitigation of a
June moon
an aroma
Febreeze laden
and stained panties are trapped
in rented apartments
into
dirty emotionless vents and 2011
nanoparticles
the organic aspects of
a fatal discharge
and
the insemination of disaffected girls,

150mg
7%

3%

11mg

6mg

3mg

4kcal/g.

xoxo

"if u want me to come over and hold u now I will

its ok, Im a disaster you'd probab;y never come back

it's ok, I wouldn't hold it against u. sorry, but I make special friends for life, so I plan on being around a while

well we cant be special friends forever, but i would like you to be around for awhile

thanks, you're right, well have to evolve into "special special friend" at some point...ha ha ha ha ha

oh my goodness.......thats a new one

haha, I know, I just made it up

sounds like something you'd try to convince me of...."oh and this is my special SPECIAL friend Brett"-lord

haha, I totally would and it would be funny..

not so much

u say that now!...ha

whatever

haha, it always fun messign with u

well Im so glad you're amused

nah, it's fun cause u go along with it and can take a joke u know

i suppose I can

u can trust me

i do trust you, which is very bizarre- I dont trust any one...

i meant u can take a joke…haha

as in u can, take a joke trust me

oh well Im half drunk and the other half distraught

ha, it's ok, but thank you....I'm glad u trust me

yes I guess I am too its a very unfamiliar feeling

yes, I trust you

cool, you should

I do, if I was in trouble or needed someone to give a shit about me, you would be at the top of the list.

yeah that would be me I suppose, I care about people I dont even know, so certainly I would take care of you however that may be

haha, nah I meant like I know u give a shit about me...that's conforting

of course I do, dotn you go dying now...Id probably hang myself

really, u would kill urself over me? man, that's love

i have no idea, im just in a really weird place right now. I know if i lost you like that it would be horrible

oh snap...that's nice of you

well what you wouldnt be upset if I died

indeed, I would cry then

hmmm cool

yes I would be very upset though

ok well thats good . we should feel the same about each other, cause if one person loves more than the other that just makes for a great imbalance and

always ends in hurt

how the hell do u measure who cares more anyways? ur nuerotic so my love might not be as nuts as urs...har ha har

im not nuts,oh hell i dont know, you can just tell. Like who would be more hurt if it ended?

well I'm not ending anything, so I guess it would hurt me more since I got dissed

you're so avoidant.

avoident of what

i dont know..

I think u know, tell me

ummm..you're avoidant to how you really feel cause you're scared shitless that you and I might be something awesome, and you have not idea what to do with yourself cause you may actually be happy with me

damn, freud u got me!

shut up, u know Im right

I am happy with you, never said I wasn't......we are awesome

ok wonderful

haha, I have no idea.....who knows, maybe ur right, maybe ur not

i know Im right

u like to think u are, and ur scared shitless if u aren't...haha"

xoxo

I should've sat her down a long time ago and confessed my true feelings and how I felt about her. I should've defined things. I know that was important to her and would've given her less breakdowns and minimized her confusion. Yeah, I'm an idiot, that's for sure. I'm filled with regret now. Maybe one day it will disappear.

xoxo

She went to some fucking metaphysical specialist/snake charmer/palm reader. She told me that her family members are in her stomach or some shit. The palm reader lady also told her that she had other people living in her stomach, and that they direct her and give her gut feelings. I made fun of her and asked her if she had a Swedish bootmaker in there as well? She didn't think it was a funny as I did surprisingly. It was bad enough when her cat always used to watch us fuck, now her whole family, Napoleon, half the passengers on the Titanic, and whoever the fuck else is in her stomach can watch us fuck now. That might be a little weird, but who am I to judge other people's level of sanity?

xoxo

Dear XXXXX,

Well, since you steal all my lines I'll steal one from you "I don't know what to do with you." We talk, but we don't talk. Right now I'm observing you and seeing where things go. To put it bluntly I'm poking you with a stick. I don't know how you can say that you miss hanging out with me, yet not want to be with me. I pine over you every single day. I really don't know what to do. I don't know what to do other than just be myself and give you your space and be there for you when you need me, and I hope that you do, because I need you. I'm in a way lost without you. There's very little enjoyment in my life these days. I'm fucked up, and I'm lonelier than I've ever been before, and yeah, I'm unhappy as hell without you. In a way you're just completely gone and it sucks llama dick. It's not what I want at all. Do I pretend like I don't care and pretend to move on? I'm not an android who can just turn off the way I feel and what I want. I've seen and been with other women and it meant nothing to me and it was completely empty. And, to be honest it actually made me feel worse than before to be honest. So, I guess the options are you or being alone, and I'm ok with that. I don't even really know where I stand with you anymore. Do you still mean everything you said in that letter? I've learned my lesson, I really have. If I ever get another shot, I'm jumping all over it without fear and without procrastination. Something great won't be slipping through my hands again, that's what I've learned. It's been a tough lesson, because I know I'm to blame for some of it. Fuck, I miss you so much it's pathetic. It bothers me that you basically forced me to hurt you and be mean to you. I never wanted to do that, ever, but I did it anyways…Brett

xoxo

She had the biggest pussy lips I'd ever seen. Even though they looked like a wad of honey cured Virginia ham I always went down on her and let her cum all over my fucking face. Goddamn, I'm a sweet fucking individual!

xoxo

"The Brevity of Dangerous Conversations"

three stars awarded

for being dead fucking

last,

nothing new,

hey you,

little bastard

tear stained linoleum

floors

what a fucking asshole,

right,

left,

right,

left,

brain conspiracies

KGB paranoia

perhaps

arms were extended
but
there was nothing
there,

greetings and salutations,
fucko,

dictionaries from
depleted library vaults
at a discount
missing 127 pages
G to the J
glue gun armies
from Belize
invade
mixtapes breathing
last gasps
on cheap tan
carpeted
ghetto apartment floors,

metal detector enemas
violated
the parasitic sweat glands,

AARP approved
hemorrhoids feed
a household of three
tax rebate gulags
whip
stained receipts

gas station hotdogs

vacation under a UV

light

forgotten now

just like you

will be.

xoxo

I sucked on the nipples of her giant fucking natural tits. I pulled the top of her green dress down beneath her giant cans and alternated between the left tit and the right tit. I periodically kissed her face, but her tits were better looking than she was. She was chunky, big boned, husky for her age, ok she was fat, so what, like you've never been here before? If I were sober I probably wouldn't be sitting here on my couch sucking on a fat girl's tits, but I'm not, so I am. I reach down and rub her cunt with my left hand, even though I'm right handed. Her pussy is wet I think, or maybe it was just really sweaty. I don't know. She reached down and moved my hand away from her cunt.

"What the hell?" I ask her.

"I'm not fucking you, I just met you tonight."

"Oh, c'mon you gotta be kidding me right?"

"Nope, sorry not gonna happen." She says.

Get the fuck out of here; I'm getting pussy rejected from a drunk fat girl? It doesn't get more degrading than this really. Should I go ahead and kill myself now, or should I wait until later? I contemplate this as she pulls her top back up and starts smoking a cigarette while we both sit on my couch surrounded by an uncomfortable silence.

xoxo

Fuck, check your cock in the mirror. What the fuck is that small bump? There are no other bumps that look like that. Fuck, get the flashlight out so you can see it better. I move my cock around like a fucking circus freak contortionist, left, right, squeeze it there. Fuck, I don't know. Maybe it's just irritated, then again, maybe I'm just paranoid, and driving myself insane. The appointment at the free clinic is next Tuesday, fuck me! Tuesday is a long damn time away. What the fuck is that tingling near my asshole? Shit, there it is in my leg as well. Is that a symptom of it? Shit, I don't remember. I get the magnifying glasses out of the drawer in my room. I inspect the head of my cock again. I squeeze it, and then spread the head apart. Maybe it's just an irritated gland, fuck, maybe not though. Where's my fucking cigarettes? I almost grab one after handling my possibly herpes laden cock. I remember that fact just as I open the pack, but before I grab a smoke. I go in the bathroom and wash my hands off, wash the herpes of your fucking hands, fuck me! I light a cigarette and look at my cock again; does it look different in this darker light spectrum? Fuck, it's hard to tell. Keep driving yourself insane man, do it like a good boy should.

xoxo

"I really miss you. It would be nice if we could be friends and hang out again. You looked really gorgeous tonight with your windblown hair."

"I miss being friends as well. I really do. But there are several things you said to people about sleeping with me and the correspondence between you and XXXXX on a public forum that included me. That I just can't get over right now. It's not a cycle, you let me down..eyes with a frown."

"I'm sorry I let you down. I have a big mouth sometimes, but I know I didn't say anything bad about you. I took that blog down a while ago. In hidsight I shouldn't have mentioned you. I really love you and wouldn't ever diss you on purpose."

"Did you get the text message I sent you the other day? It's very unlike you to not respond. I hope you understand where I'm coming from."

"I texted you back BFF. I honestly don't remember telling anyone about us having sex. If I did, my bad. I understand the blog. I'm sorry for that, I shouldn't have mentioned you. I love and care about you so try and not avoid me for too long."

"Did you get the text message I sen back to you on Monday? You didn't respond and that was very like you BFF! Oh, the vicious cycles of XXX!"

"Nope never got it. You call it cycles, I call it letting me down. Oh well…"

xoxo

"I wanna jerk off in your face." That's what I tell her, surprisingly sober. I don't even know why I invited her over. I didn't want to see her. I didn't want to look at her. In some respects I detest her, well, her and her fucking mind that is. She's on all kinds of pills. Ambien to sleep, even though she doesn't sleep. Adderall to concentrate, even though she can't concentrate, Xanax to relax, even though she can't relax, and who the fuck knows other than her doctor what else she's on. She was already blowing me when I said that I wanted to jerk off in her face. "Come over here." She says to me. She goes and lays on her back while on my bed. I straddled her chest and she started moving her lips back and forth on my cock. The light from the bathroom covers half of her face. I sat there and just watched as she swallowed my cock over and over again. It didn't take long, she's on pills and is a total wacko, but goddamn this girl was great at sucking cock. I'll give her neurotic ass that. Anyways, like I said before, it wasn't long before I felt the cum starting to swirl in my balls. A few seconds later it happened. "Fuck, I'm cumming. I'm gonna cream your fucking face you goddamn whore!" The first of the cum hit her on the lip and nose, yet it kept cumming, and cumming, and cumming out. I don't know where the fuck all that cum came from exactly. I have no answers. Perhaps, it was only the kind of load that could spring forth from really degrading another human being in this way. The next batch sort of hit her cheek and ran down slowly onto her chest. She licks what's left from the tip of my cock. I just sit there basking in the euphoria of having just blown my load all over another human being. Her gargantuan bulging eyes now stare back at me. I straddle my legs from around her and stumble into the bathroom and wash the rest of the cum and her spit off of my cock with anti-bacterial soap. I grab a small red hand towel from the closet and drape my cock and balls with it as I waddle my way back into the bedroom. I toss her the towel as I pass the bed and head for a glass of sweet tea and a Marlboro cigarette. I light up a cigarette and watch her rub all of my cum from her face and onto my hand towel. I hate her giant eyed drug addict ass even more now than I did before, and I hope she leaves sooner than later.

xoxo

"OK, I'm now trying humor to get into your pants, nothing else has seemed to work"

xoxo

I'm done with her and all that bullshit. That's what it was, never-ending fucking bullshit. I got accused or insinuated of being a stalker and a fucking lunatic. Let's see, I've been pathetic, a loser, the guy who won't get over her, the asshole, and now the stalker. Well, that about covers all the spectrums doesn't it? I found an old e-mail when I was clearing spam off my account last night. It was an old invitation from her to look at her photos. I must've missed it somewhere along the line, so I clicked on it and checked out the albums. There were some great make out session pictures of us on there, and a bunch of pictures from all the vacations we took as well. I saved the ones I wanted and threw them on various social networking sites later in the night, not anything of us, just the ones of me falling down drunk and shaking a pirate's hook hand in St.Thomas. That was about it. Then, the drama came when I woke up, and there was a new e-mail from her calling me a fucking stalker. Maybe she's right, but that picture with the pirate is goddamn fucking worth a little name calling!

xoxo

"well ur FBD plays powerball so don't give up hope yet, I'll take care of u after the impregantion process...

cool, go get those lottery tickets! maybe we should put off the whole

impreganation though so I can keep my hot body and just be your trophy girlfriend

haha, don't worry I'll pay for lipo and a personal trainer

nice

then my seed will live and u can keep ur figure!

cool, dont forget the nanny too i dont think infants are allowed in bars

hell I'll give it to my mom to raise so we don't have to raise shit..

oh nice, we can just play with it for fun from time to time

now ur catching on

good plan

damn skippy, I got it all figured out...just sit back and be hot I have it under control

haha ok"

xoxo

Maybe I should get your name tattooed on me so I could have some physical scars to match the mental and emotional ones left by you. A month or so later the hypothetical turned into reality and I did decide to get that tattoo after all. It hurt like hell and the tattoo artist thought I was fucking crazy and tried to talk me out of it, but that was a futile endeavor at this point. So, now I have your name inside a little red heart tattooed on the inside of my hand. Every time I jerk off I will think of you from now on sugar tits.

xoxo

I liked it better when life was simplistic and there was no drama or major problems. Hell, all I got is problems, drama, and bullshit with women these days. I try to sort through it, but who the fuck knows if anything I do is the right decision. I liked it better when no one gave a shit about what I did. Now, all people want to do is get involved in my business. Interestingly, am I that appealing now or is everyone else just that fucking lame and bored with their own pathetic existence? These are things to be pondered.

xoxo

"I will prob drunk text u later and tell u how much I love you and want to be ur boyfriend ...prob"

xoxo

I sit here talking to myself. I seriously think I must be out of my mind, but I was hoping that you would be my girlfriend at some point. I'll always care about you and be your friend, so it just makes sense to me to fucking go for it I suppose. I didn't say these words to her though, I pussied out as usual.

xoxo

"No, but I'll still fuck you tonight though!"

"Dependds.You gonna be my date on NYE?"

"Ok, that's cool, what about after?"

"I gotta dropa friend off"

"What r you doing?"

"Yes, I'm drinking. Don't fret I can still preform"

"Are you drunk?"

xoxo

It's funny that you always refer to me as an "old friend" when introducing me to other people. Averaging in the time you spent avoiding me and being insane, I would say we've only been friends for like six months.

xoxo

"It was good to see you"

"It was cooterfastic seeing you as well darling. I missed you a lot"

"Me too- frowning face"

"Aww you still like me. You're beautiful and awesome. Hopefully we can hang out a lot more now"

"I want to work on a large painting with you"

"Haha ok, sounds like a plan Stan!"

"A giant peace sign this time though."

"Huh, hell no, no hippie shit is going down in my fucking house!"

xoxo

"The Caress of Chaos and Physics"

the sun sometimes rides

the black horse's deception,

a bee stings my adolescent

dying coffee

grit between

rivers of hearsay and teeth

a phone calls

contagion

fondle a plastic cup

the sugar in the jar

suffers

the muscles

naked

restlessness

equitable skills

we

possess only one

exist

and,

crumple the stained

paper at dawn.

xoxo

Not a day has gone by that I haven't thought about her, haven't missed and craved her, and haven't tried to come up with some sort of fuckin' crazy Say Anything scheme to get her back. I'm a complete car wreck of a human being without her. That much is obvious, just without the people stopping to stare at me. I try and live my life without regret, but yeah I do have regrets when it comes to her. I wish a DeLorean time machine would show up outside my door and I could go back in time and change a few things that I fucked up before. I have my Pepsi Free ready to go, now all I need is a flux capacitor and a Huey Lewis and the News tape.

xoxo

"your such a guy!

yeah u know it

I have a dick, so yea I am such a guy......too bad I wasn't born a hermaphrodite

actually that would have probably caused more problems than not???

I wonder if they can inseminate themselves...like earth worms

im sure you'll find out somehow and let me know

haha, well sometiems it's goos to be ignorant

just look it up online you can find an answer to anything-not always accurate but an answer

haha, I'm saying 99% no, as far as them being able to do that

well it could be possible depending on what their plumbing was made up of

it would be hard to bend ur dick up ur own pussy..

but if they could, they should get their own reality show

yes the world really needs another reality show-I htink they're were only 15 on tonight!

haha, I don't follow them.....but I would if a hermaphrodite could fuck themselves...now that's a show I wanna watch

sounds more like porn

yes, there would have to be some but then follow him/her around in normal everyday things

uh huh-not feeln it"

xoxo

"The General Electric Peepshow"

She,

has my heart

and

my

graphite drawing pencils

level

masking tape

phillips head screwdriver

and

a box of screws,

I need to get those back before I say something to her that I might regret.

xoxo

Her second toe was longer than her big toe and it bothered the shit out of me.

xoxo

Dear XXXXX,

I guess the moral of this story is that you just left me with no fucking viable options to be just your friend. And, I don't hate or dislike you at all, contrary to what you probably believe. I do love you and I always will. But, fucking hell, it just isn't fair to me to be put in this situation where I feel like an idiot for being just your friend, or I feel like a dick if I have nothing to do with you. Neither are what I want you know. I never wanted this to ever have to be this way. It truly does suck for me. I'm not trying to make you feel bad, but the way it ended made it fucking impossible for me. I forgive, but I don't forget, how could I? Yes, I think some horrible things about you, and I have a right to. The appearance of it was horrid for me, and I feel like you're some different person now that I don't know, and to be honest I really don't know what to make of you these days. I have that image constantly battling two great years with you, lots of fantastic things I thought about you, and you're someone I thought I really knew very well. I don't want to be constantly pissed at you, try and control it, and then have it all boil up and go off on you. Then I look and feel like an asshole, or have everything I do appear to annoy or bother you, and be overanalyzed or taken the wrong way. I'm not obsessed or a psycho. I'm not hiding in your bushes, calling you 138 times a day, or riding by your house checking on you. I haven't done anything other than check out your shit when you posted something new. And, if that's crazy, well, I guess I'm just fucking crazy then. I haven't said anything bad about you to anyone actually. If I have something fucked up to say, I keep it personal and say it to you. I would always consider letting you back in my life though, but you have a shitload of fence mending to do with me, that requires more than just apologies. It requires action I guess. Show me that you give a shit, that I had this all wrong, and that you weren't indifferent or contradictory to everything I thought about you. I don't like feeling that I wasn't even worth a phone call, and that you thought I meant nothing after all I did for you and we did together. That shit bothers and hurts me. Being just good friends now or whatever can't be one-sided and have all the rules dictated by one person. Once you love and have sex with someone, there might not be any going back to just friends. I don't know. I'm just a homo sapien baby. I never claimed to have any definitive answers to anything.

xoxo

"did u show her the signed magazine?

no it was at my house-she would have laughed though

haha, of course. Maybe I should give u one that wasn't in the back of my car for months...maybe get a frame at the dollar store even....maybe I will surprise u with it one day

awwww, i'll have to find a place for it

haha, right over the toilet...perfect place. maybe I should sign it with my dick, just in case I get in a car wreck and can't have babies naturally with u, they could get a dna sample of the surge...haha

i guess we should just get to the sperm bank soon if you're really that concerned

haha, nah...I jsut like joking around about it really. It makes me laugh, what can I say

i know, you just like it cuz you're thinking about the practicing part

haha, indeed...I wasn't joking about knocking u up though…

u r craaaazy.....haha thats funny

haha, I don't think leaving my dna inside of you is that crazy really

what the hell for?

so damian can be born. Well maybe, after a lot of practice of leaving my dna inside of you...ha

ok well MAYBE then

Haha, it's a dilemma I won't lie. I hate kids but my seed can't die! I need to find some lesbians that want a sperm donor or something.

how can you hate kids???

well maybe I wouldn't hate my own, I just hate other people's, but I hate most people and I love myself so that makes sense

im sure you wouldnt your own, we would have hot kids

I know right, shit u should feel lucky for me to be ur sperm donor

oh i would, that kid would be awesome

haha, he's pop our of ur cooter with a dictionary in his hand, no wait, a mohawk and a dictionary

or she would come out with a book in one hand and lip gloss in the other

why would u put lip gloss in ur vagina prior?

not any mor than i would shove a dictionary up there retard-

ha…we're talking about u here not me!"

xoxo

I respected her insanity until she asked me to cuddle. I said as much, and walked away and drove home drunk.

xoxo

I slither back to her house now like a fucking biblical serpent from Sodom. It's like revisiting the scene of a car crash you were previously in and are trying to develop amnesia for. Why the hell would I do this you ask? Because of a fucking black size medium Social Distortion shirt, that's why. I searched every fucking where in that damn house after she'd passed out from the booze and exhaustion of having me fuck the shit out of her. I looked under the cushions, under her, under the couch, in the bathroom, in the bedroom, under the bed, in her car, under the car seat in the car, in the trunk, in the bushes, in the sink, in the refrigerator, and I still couldn't find that fucking black size medium Social Distortion shirt. It's one of my fucking favorite shirts, and it's not being lost to a random fuck. I didn't know her name so I just addressed the letter written on the back of her daughter's "color inside the giant dinosaur" coloring book page to "sugar tits." It was written in red Crayola crayon. I left her my number and told her to call me if she ever found my shirt deep within the bowels of her house. She did text me several days later saying that she found my black size medium Social Distortion shirt on top of some bushes in her back yard. This was news to me considering that I didn't even remember ever being in her back yard. Who knows, maybe I went out there to take a piss or something, but it's all speculation at this point. You fucking moron! That's like the one place that you didn't look, and now you're sitting outside of a total stranger's house finishing a cigarette and developing the courage to go and knock on the door of this girl's house just to get a goddamn black size medium Social Distortion shirt. I think of a way to get out of it like asking her to put it in her mailbox, or having her mail the damn thing to me, but I didn't and here I sit. I get out of my car and head towards the scene of the past crime. There's no turning back now, fuck me! Just ring the door bell and get it over with you goddamn idiot!

xoxo

There was no need for sleep. It was already 9:30 in the morning and the sun was out and it was hot as hell. My eyes were about to pop out of my fucking head. They were red and full of pollen. My stomach was full of two free Waffle House chicken biscuits and an order of hash browns. My dick was hurting from the mediocre blowjob and handjob that I got before the free Waffle House food that she bought me. I told her that I would call her again. I was lying though. The cum that I left in her stomach will be all the evidence left behind that I'd ever known her.

xoxo

"Want me to come over and cuddlerific you after I handle my mini golf biznass?"

"I appreciate the offer but probably not a good idea – u know what cuddling leads to…LOL"

"Could lead to deep penetrating spooning? Ur willpower will crumble like the berlin wall soon enough missy! With my miniscule charm and a giant bottle of vodka there's always hope for me. U can always use your celebrity excuse…"

"Whatever haha"

xoxo

"The Postmodern Adventures of the Reflux Machine"

it's interesting

and

totally pathetic,

overnight,

I've gone from fucking you
to
whacking off
to
past images
of me fucking you,

scanning…
long-term memory
short-term memory,

us fucking on,

couches
beds
chairs
toilets
kitchen counters
and living room
floors,

us fucking in,
Miami
hotel rooms
old apartments
new apartments
Japanese cars
and
boats,

scanning…
nearest memory,

eating

your pussy

me

down

you

up

inner orgasm

outer orgasm

penetration soon after

me

cumming

inside of you

bent over a table

doggy style

at your house

a towel exchanged

and

fluids forever washed

down the drain,

yeah,

it's sad,

it's pathetic,

but,

a man

has to get by

somehow

in these turbulent times

June 2009.

xoxo

Her tits were hanging out. They were oddly shaped. They were natural with stretch marks on them, and sagged a little. They were pretty gigantic though, so I guess I don't care. I stop sucking on her saggy but large natural tits, and stumble into the kitchen drunk, and open the fridge and grab a water. I insert one packet of my lemon flavored Propel. I shake it. I see a singular tablet of Indian produced generic Viagra sitting on the kitchen counter next to some unpaid bills and a bottle of Advil. It's been sitting there for forever. I open the packet and down the little blue pill followed by lemon flavored Propel. We go into my room and I pound away on her pussy throughout the night. This Indian produced generic Viagra shit doesn't work, at least I don't think. I feel no different and my dick is no harder than normal. I pound away on her for two hours. I hadn't cum and gave up. I pulled my dick out of her and walked towards the bathroom to piss and call it a night. I hold my dick in my hand. It's raw and red and well used. I forget to brush my teeth or floss, and I walk back to the bed and pass out. At 8:27 a.m. I woke up. Fuck, it was way too early. My cock was swollen and hard. Ok, I guess maybe this generic Indian Viagra shit does sort of work. I woke up saggy tits next to me. I made her look at my swollen cock, and I convinced her to sit on my cock and let me pound on her again. It didn't take too long and I came inside of her. I went to the bathroom and washed the cum and pussy juice off of my already swollen and red cock. We go back to bed soon after. Around two in the afternoon I wake up again, fucked up, hungover, and again with a raging boner. I nudge saggy big tits next to me and ask her if we can fuck again. I pull down the sheets and show her my raging boner. She says she has to go to work in a little bit, and she doesn't have time to fuck. I try and pathetically convince her to fuck, and it doesn't work. She gets out of bed and starts finding her clothes scattered around the floor and putting them back on. She's fully clothed by now and says she has to go. I try one last time to pathetically convince her to stay and let me fuck her again, but again she refuses. I beg her pathetically again as she is opening the front door. She tells me to go jerk off as the front door closes. I watch her while naked from the corner window, and I start jerking off as she pulls out of the parking lot and then disappears out of sight.

xoxo

"did u dream about punching me in the eye last night? my eye is all swollen and fucked up today

no punching you in the eye...

it looks like someone did

maybe??

it's really swollen

pink eye?

No, it's been sore and dry for a few days, yesterday I really rubbed the hell out of it so I guess that's why.

weird

yeah, well with my body, weird is normal

yep"

xoxo

Their company makes me feel a little better, but not much. The beer in the glass just hurts my already fucked up stomach and isn't enjoyable. I think I gave myself an ulcer or something. I've been chewing pink pills for two days now, but it hasn't done much good. I stare at a basketball game on TV and talk to myself, but I didn't realize that I was actually talking out loud. My friend next to me asks me if I'm alright, I just look at him and say "no, not really dude."

xoxo

"so you cant cum on my face while you fuck me in the back of your jeep while the sun comes up?"

"ok, I like the mouth better anyways"

"unsoiled?"

"yeah, less unsoiled than someone 30"

"thats good i guess, i dont have whore lips"

"yeah I know, never got a whore vibe. I like the mouth better anyways. soil the unsoiled lips..haha"

"haha ew"

"eww? nothing wrong with that, it's good for you...protein and shit"

"when its being talked about on chat its seems more dirtier"

"yeah I know...it's nothing abnormal...now cumming in your ass and sucking it out with a straw would be…."

"i guess it would be"

xoxo

I wanted to fuck her in every country we went to. I'd never done it so why not try? There's nothing else to do on this fuckin' geriatric pleasure cruise. I fucked her the first night after a few drinks. The waves of an angry rocking ocean didn't really help all that much. I felt like shit. After I came inside of her, she said that she only fucked me because she was drunk. I called her a fucking bitch while I was still on top of her, and she slapped me in the face hard enough that it made my teeth chatter. I grabbed her and started kissing her again. I could feel her freshly shaved pussy and my cum resting underneath my pelvis. She went and took a shower after that, and I guess cleaned my cum out of her pussy while I watched foreign TV and scratched my balls. She got in bed with me after her shower and then we immediately argued over what I was watching on

TV. She gave up and made me turn the TV to an odd angle so she could sleep. She yelled at me like three minutes later because it was too loud. I was keeping her up again she said…bitch…bitch…bitch…it never fucking stops.

xoxo

Mr. Bukowski was right; love is a dog from hell.

xoxo

"Wow, "XXXXXjudas" it just never seems to end with you does it? You might be wondering what the fuck I'm talking about right now? But, I just wanted to let you know that I know all about your lying and whoring that you did behind my back, well basically as far as I can figure the whole damn time I knew you and we were hanging out for two years. You are so busted and your façade has been annihilated like a gallon of Breyer's at a Jenny Craig meeting. Yes, I'm calling you out on your shit, missy. It wasn't very cool of you to do to someone that you supposedly loved and cared about and considered a "giant part of your life." You sure have a funny way of showing it there darling.

Perhaps the "elf ethics" in Middle Earth are different than here or something? I'm pretty sure this kind of bullshit breaks all the known and accepted international rules and standards of being acronym BFF. Did you ever tell me the real truth about anything? Or was it your usual "it would just hurt you worse to know" type of mentality that you have said/shown previously? Or is the truth only reserved for those you think that you're in a "real" relationship with or whatever? Obviously not, weren't you supposedly in one of those when we made out at the bar that night? Really, who knows the answer to that posed question with your massive amounts of neuroticism. Go ahead and downplay and dissect it so that it makes it morally acceptable to you, but always remember that I know how you think on some levels.

Shit, I'm starting to wonder if you're even capable of being loyal to anything or anyone on this planet other than worthless rag paper. I know you have serious daddy issues, that you're desperate for love and looking to make up for what you didn't receive earlier in your life, but actions like this maybe show why you haven't found your white picket fence life yet. Or perhaps, that's just karma coming back to haunt you. You do realize Myrtle Beach is way too small of a town for me to not hear about things eventually and put this 3-D cheater puzzle that doesn't look anything like a famous building together for you. I admit my initial reaction was to be seriously pissed off and hurt, which then manifested into the most vindictive Machiavellian letter that would be a thrice of punching you in the face, making you cry and giving you an eating disorder all at the same time, but after a while of contemplation I've changed my mind and decided to shelve that one and give you this letter instead.

Jesus Christ on a goddamn popsicle stick, you're one devious and conniving bitch/ probable succubus XXXXX! And for some unknown reason I actually kind of respect that about you. I can't explain it and perhaps I'm a fucking whacked out person, but I now find myself more attracted to and interested in you now than I ever have been previously, and I'm not even being sarcastic here believe it or not. Hell, if I had known that you possessed this much talent, depth and bravado I would have been on my knees "Ring Pop in hand" begging you to be my BFF life partner years ago. Now that some of your dirty little secrets have been aired, doesn't it make you feel somewhat free and better now XXXXXjudas? It must be a full-time job keeping track of all your deceptions and lies really.

Now, I have no problem with you acting slutty at all, hell I've had my slutty moments for sure, but it's pretty lame to find out that you lied to my face every single day about it, as well as what was really going on, all the while living some alternate life I knew nothing about. Perhaps you can get "he who robs the Banana Republic at gun point" to buy you a Webster's Dictionary so you can research the words (ethics, class, and morals) because I do believe you need a massive re-education in their working intent and definition. You cannot claim to uphold these values, yet contradict yourself constantly through your actions. They have a word for that in Grenada, and it's called hypocrisy. Hell, from what I've pieced together, your apartment was used for more than just baking cookies and practicing making cooterific babies, and was basically a fucking elf whorehouse. I was never up your ass all the time because I trusted you, thought you were of high moral fiber and I wanted you to have your own personal space and life outside of me, plus I don't think I really demanded all that much from you, so really why you couldn't ever tell me the truth, even the brutal truth is as fucking retarded as Sarah Palin's baby. I would have been upset for a little while true, but I would have forgiven you of course and it wouldn't have been that big of a deal. I thought our lines of communication were very open and you could tell me anything, but I guess obviously not.

I admit that I expected a bit more than this from you Poison Ivy. It's shit like this that really makes me remember why I'm so fucking cynical about people in general and especially about their supposed relationships. They mean nothing obviously and people have zero respect for one another, just like I told you a long time ago. It's a pretty sad, depressing and pathetic world when you basically cannot trust anyone. I would expect this sort of thing from most people normally and I have fucked plenty of whores in my day I'm sure, but the problem I have is when people like you beguile and try to be and maintain a false image and more accurately a façade of something "lily-white," while also masquerading as something they're not, they have a word for that in Ghana, and it's called poser. Kind of like how you're posing now, a girl from a small town that isn't even on a fucking standard U.S. map, who will never be rich on her own being a nurse, who enjoyed simple things in life like going to Costco for free samples and cooterific mix CD's, now thinking she's hot elitist VIP country club soiree shit because she gives blowjobs to gross rich old men who buy her expensive clothes, vacations and whatever else she could never afford herself in exchange for said blowjobs, and also get her car fixed for her in return for her giving it up on the first date to a total stranger, and then bragging about it to me later on. They have a word for that in Germany, and it's called prostitution.

Remember the first thing you ever personally told me about your "gingerdaddy" when I showed up at your elf whorehouse? It wasn't how cool or interesting or decent he was, it was how "pimp" his house was. If that doesn't just say it all I don't know what does really. I made a mistake when saying and thinking previously that you had really changed as a person when you finally got caught by XXX and ran off with your hair helmeted butterball disgusting "gingerdaddy." In fact and truth, (besides that lube was made for guys like him, whose pussy could naturally get wet to that repulsive thing?) it was just a gross continuation of who you really were as a person and what you were already doing in your alternate life anyways, which was basically, as far as I can logic, was spreading your legs for any nasty moronic guy you could find as long as their bank account was sizeable enough and they had enough possessions for you to be entertained by for a period of time of course.

Here I was thinking you were some great honest down-to-earth person before, and I thought you just flipped out, got abducted by aliens and did shady stupid shit the one time with seven chins. It had crossed my mind before that perhaps that wasn't the first time, because people rarely do shady things only once, but I had no proof so I let that theory lapse. You never had to answer to me and never will, but fucking a bunch of dudes while also fucking and supposedly loving me is pretty nasty and put me at real risk, which I don't really appreciate by the way. They have a word for that in Guatemala , and it's called uncouth. Hell, even though you didn't have the decency to tell me, you could have at least had the decency to go to the free clinic and get tested before I ate a random dick sandwich for fuck's sake (YAK for real)! What's weird to me is that you were always the one harping about us having an agreement about not seeing other people and wanting to get into some long term relationship with me, so it doesn't make any sense really. And I do remember one time you saying that if I ever had sex with anyone else you wouldn't be with me anymore. What happened to your "one dick at a time" rule, another one of your plethora of lies obviously? You should be more careful girl; you might pick up an XXX that makes someone's balls hurt for months on end and your pussy smell like week old Captain D's leftover for months on end…oh wait…hahahaha.

I now have a brand spankin' new and very cute pet nickname for you as well, you're now known as "taste of the town," because everybody obviously had a little sample of you while we were hanging out. Now, I'm not saying I know everything or that all of this is 100% accurate, but it's pretty damn close and I've pieced enough together to make myself nauseous. Just like I knew enough from XXX to piece together that you fucked that sweater vest wearing Chris Farley impersonating faggot you live with on the first date, class as always with you right XXXXXjudas? Yeah, "it was just a kiss, XXX's lying," as you told me the next day, you must really think people are that stupid or something.

The problem is I knew three of those people sitting five feet away from you and asked all of them for the risqué details, they're all conspiring against you I'm sure. And yes, they all agreed that your disaster known as your outfit that night was hilarious, trashy and very slutty, but the black guy there did enjoy seeing your tits and pudge hanging out of your shirt, feel special though, he was on a shitty reality show.

Yes, I am really judging you here, and I have the right to whether you like it or not missy. You were wrong as usual previously though, I didn't hurt or disrespect your family, you did, I just happened to be the messenger boy. If I'm wrong about small portions of this, well then my bad sugar tits, but the only problem with being a professional liar is that no one fucking believes anything you say. I realize there's not much you can do about it now, and I'm no expert on manners, but I would say that an apology might be fitting here, even if it is a fake one and another lie, which I expect from you.

Now it's time for you to say I'm being a mean asshole to you, deny it all, minimize your actions so they're morally acceptable to you, practice evasion, diversion and selective memory and come up with one of your classic yet unoriginal Hollywood "blame the Jews or booze" excuses and shirk any and all personal responsibility for your actions like you always do. It's always someone else's fault right? Practice your role as a thespian victim, and of course produce a few crocodile tears for good measure. These are all classic psychological symptoms of manipulation techniques used by human beings by the way.

But, as always, anything concerning you has the duality of an equal yet potent mixture of love and hate on my end. I had contemplated antagonizing the living shit out of you and make your suffering be a part time job for me, but I will hold back for now so don't push it Elfin Cracker! I'll always have an affinity for you and I don't particularly want to do any long term damage to you, but we both know that I know enough about you and your past as well as being smart, motivated, and crafty enough to wage WWIII if I so desired. But, the only penance for this will be me putting my "convergingersation" back up, calling you on your shit and perhaps saying a few mean things to you in this letter, and I for one think I'm being rather nice and pretty fuckin' benevolent given the situation.

I knew there was a reason I've always liked you though, you're the only person I've ever met that is truly a worthy nemesis, but also a worthy counterpart. Few will ever get anything big like this past me, especially with me consistently in-depth psychologically analyzing them for two plus years, but you did, color me impressed, and for those about to rock I salute you and also give you kudos for it! Always remember Newton's Third Law before doing shady fucked up shit to BFF though, it's fitting in this situation I think. This fucked up game of Tetris we've had going on all this time is way too interesting, entertaining, fun and insane to ever really end, so let it continue..."

"insert a conversation copied and pasted that a girl had with a lawyer in bold print, with threats of a restraining order from said girl that I can't put here."

"Wow, my art/writing truly is dangerous, I love it! You have seriously gone off the deep end, getting all legal and shit now. It's called free speech unfortunately, I believe there is a constitutional amendment regarding that whole entity. I never threatened you, nor would I ever hurt you (like I said before) and being eccentric doesn't mean you're breaking any laws. The truth is on my side and I believe you have no case. Even though a restraining order isn't all that big of a deal, you are right in the fact that I don't really have the resources and time to fight you on it. I wish I did, I think it would be a hilarious case, and who knows maybe it would be my Art School Confidential? Though, I don't think a professional liar is really worth all that anyways. Maybe I can sue you over giving me an XXX? It's better to wait until you marry G-snap, then I can really cash in!..haha. Perhaps, you do have plenty of time, but it's "gingerdaddy's" money that you're calling your resources. I had to spend half my lunch break taking shit down...thanks, but they're down so you can stop calling and consulting lawyers Erin Brockovich, and I will leave you alone, with your lies and past indescretions cheater. You get to live the rest of your life knowing that you're not a very good or nice person. And, as a final insult you're gonna be off my Christmas card list this year! Thanks though, I guess I finally have an end to my book now.

Endings are facetious, and for assholes...

www.ingramcontent.com/pod-product-compliance
Lightning Source LLC
Chambersburg PA
CBHW031155020726
47499CB00002B/378